TOTAL
SILENCE

TOTAL SILENCE

T. J. MacGREGOR

PINNACLE BOOKS
Kensington Publishing Corp.

PINNACLE BOOKS are published by

Kensington Publishing Corp.
850 Third Avenue
New York, NY 10022

This novel is a work of fiction. Names, characters, places, and
incidents are either the product of the author's imagination,
or are used fictitiously. Any resemblance to actual persons,
living or dead, or events is entirely coincidental.

Pinnacle and the P logo Reg. U.S. Pat. & TM Off.

ISBN 0-7394-4770-X

Printed in the United States of America

With love to four terrific people in my life:
Rob, Megan, Dad, and Mary

ACKNOWLEDGMENTS

Writers always have people to thank, and at the top of my list are Al Zuckerman and Kate Duffy. Without them, there wouldn't be a novel.

Thanks also to Hazel West Burley, a longtime resident of Cassadaga. Her quiet patience and dedication to her work as a medium are a real tribute to what Cassadaga is about. As far as I know, however, there is no Book of Voices associated with Cassadaga.

Thanks also to Vivian Ortiz, whose love for Tybee Island is matched by her infinite grace and hospitality whenever we have descended on her with kids and animals in tow.

There is a capacity of virtue in us, and there is a capacity of vice to make your blood creep.

—Ralph Waldo Emerson

Fear is the great barrier to human growth.

—Robert Monroe, *Ultimate Journey*

Saturday
December 27

1

An excessive richness suffused the air, a sensual feast. It was evident in the intoxicating scent of woods and wildlife and winter and weaved through the smoky blueness of the mountains that rose in the distance, their shapes painted by some dyslexic artist on a celestial canvas. Just below the balcony where Mira Morales stood, lengthening dark shadows moved soundlessly down the steep slope of barren trees. A thin horse had been turned out in a denuded pasture near the stable to her left and a pair of little goats bleated pathetically in the cold afternoon shadows. Even the knotted pine railing, which had retained the scent of earth where it once had grown, felt excessive beneath her hands.

People often described Asheville, North Carolina, as God's country, a little Eden. Mira supposed that mountains did that to people, made them speak in terms of divinities, epiphanies. But frankly, she just didn't see it. In all fairness to North Carolina, though, she was a Florida girl, born and bred. Her cells were accustomed to heat and sunshine, the smell of salt and sand. Her body craved greenery, blue water, fruit warmed on trees that never shed their leaves. To her, all of this looked as if Providence hadn't finished the act of creation.

It was barely four in the afternoon and already, darkness encroached with the mythic impunity of a god. On

Tango Key in the winter, it was light until almost six in the evening.

Stop it.

She was visiting, not moving here. She wanted to love Asheville and the farm where they were staying because Wayne Sheppard loved it. Because his friends owned all twenty-five acres of it. Because it was the Christmas holidays and she, Sheppard, and Annie had driven seventeen hours to get here. Yet, she couldn't feel her feet. They were frozen inside her Florida shoes, inside her light cotton Florida socks, inside skin that already had begun to pucker and dry in the mountain chill. Mira zipped her jacket to her throat and blew into her hands to warm them.

The door slammed open and Annie rushed out, gushing, "Wow, you've got to see this, Mom. There's a wood-burning stove and everything. It's fabulous."

Mira glanced around, taking in the sight of her daughter's flushed cheeks, her grin, her shiny black hair, a loose cascade that fell to her shoulders, her shining dark eyes like her father's. Annie, fourteen going on forty, had dressed for the weather—a thick parka, hiking shoes with thick, sturdy soles like Sheppard's, wool socks, even gloves. She stood for a moment in the cold air and breathed in, then out, watching her breath. "This is great, really great. Listen, I'm going down to the barn and then over to the house to meet the girl who lives here. Okay? Is that okay? Shep says that besides the horses and the two goats, they've got dogs, chickens, and some cats."

"Let's help Shep unload the car first, then you're cut loose. We'll eat dinner in an hour or so."

"It's a deal." She thrust her hand into the air for a high five.

Their palms came together and Annie's fingers came

down perfectly between Mira's and they drew close. "You okay?" Annie asked, her perfect brow wrinkling slightly, worried that something would intrude on all that she saw as perfection.

"Just a little tired, that's all." And her throat felt scratchy, as though she were coming down with a cold. "Too much sitting in the car."

"We'll do some yoga stretches later. You and me." She gave a small, girlish giggle. "We'll make Shep do them, too."

Mira laughed. Sheppard and yoga were an imperfect match at best, and whenever Mira and Annie got him to do any of the postures, he ended up twisted like a pretzel and groaning loudly. "Deal."

"How's that ring feel?" Annie asked, admiring her mother's engagement ring, turning her hand this way and that in the winter light.

"Strange, but good."

Christmas Eve, Sheppard had given her an emerald engagement ring. It was a deep green Colombian gem that caught the light perfectly. They hadn't set a date yet, but after more than five years together, a date was beside the point. There were so many details to be worked out, namely who would live where and who would give up which house and how would Nadine, Mira's grandmother, feel about staying if Shep was living there, too?

Nadine was beside herself with delight and offered to move into the apartment above the bookstore she and Mira owned. But Sheppard wouldn't hear of it. Mira's house, he'd said, had plenty of room, and if they needed to add on, they would use the money he earned from the sale of his place. Black and white, that was the world that Sheppard inhabited, she thought, and although Nadine had agreed, Mira still worried. But then, she worried about everything, large things and small alike.

She worried that if she married Sheppard, she would be betraying the memory of her husband, Tom, dead now for eleven years. She worried about the bookstore failing and having to dip into Annie's college fund. Those were the big worry items. At the smaller end of the scale, she worried about rust in the pipes at home, that the battery in her car would fail, that the transmission would blow up, that a tire would flatten as she drove to the bookstore at the other end of Tango Key. It wasn't that she looked for trouble, only that since the events of six months ago, something within her had shifted permanently.

You could not go back thirty-five years in time, she decided, and return looking at the world in quite the same way. And since she didn't know anyone else besides Sheppard and her daughter who had had this experience, her means of comparison were rather limited. They rarely talked about what had happened on that summer beach, when a man with a cast on his arm had nabbed Annie, then taken her through the black water and back in time. They rarely mentioned the framed note to Annie, signed by Janis Joplin, that hung in Annie's room, or talked about the black water mass off the coast of Tango Key that had long since dissipated. They definitely didn't talk about the subtle but profound changes that had occurred in Mira's abilities. They didn't discuss her worries that time travel might have done something to them genetically, something that might not show up for months or years. Some things were better left in the past.

Mira and Annie hurried out to the van, where Sheppard was unloading their belongings. He was a tall man, about six foot four, with hair the color of beach sand and a beard threaded with gray. He didn't look like any concept she had of an FBI agent, which she supposed was one of his professional strengths. She still hadn't reconciled herself to the fact that she was in love with a cop. To her, if you carried a gun, then you attracted the circumstances where you would have to use it.

He wasn't carrying a gun right now, but she knew it was stashed somewhere, his faithful P226 SIG Sauer, with a double-column magazine that held fifteen rounds of 9mm Parabellum ammunition. A premier combat weapon, she thought, better suited to SWAT teams and battles on foreign soil.

"Suitcases," Sheppard said, and handed them each a bag. "And a bag of groceries apiece. We should go up to the farmhouse in a while so Annie can meet Tess and I can introduce you to Jerry and Ramona." His friends, the people who owned the farm. "And tonight or tomorrow we can head into Asheville."

"Getting back down that road in the dark could be a challenge," Mira remarked, hooking her thumb toward the crooked and slippery dirt road they had followed in here.

"Oh, Mom," Annie groaned, rolling her eyes. "You worry about everything."

Mira glanced over at Sheppard to commiserate, but he was staring back down the road, frowning slightly. Mira's psychic antenna twitched. "Something wrong?" she asked.

Sheppard looked back, his face breaking into a smile. "Nope. I just thought I heard a car coming up the drive. Probably Jerry and Ramona. Or one of the two guys who works here." He fell into step beside Mira as Annie vanished around the corner of the cabin with her things. "Did you go into the glove compartment for anything last night?"

Last night they had stayed in a motel in Savannah and

the only time she had gone outside was for dinner. But they had walked to dinner. "No. Why?"

He shrugged. "It's probably nothing. This morning when I opened the glove compartment, all the stuff inside was a mess. I couldn't find the map Jerry had drawn of how to get here. I didn't bother locking the van last night."

Tidy Sheppard, she thought. Everything in his personal world had its place, everything just so. An organized man. "Your gun wasn't in there, was it?"

"Of course not. Annie probably went into it looking for her Sims game or something."

"Yeah, probably."

As they reached the porch, the hoot of an owl preceded its appearance by several seconds. It swept in low through the trees, wings beating, its haunting song echoing through the shadows. It touched down on the corner of the cabin roof at the end of the porch and watched them watching it. A chill shuddered through Mira, and Sheppard looked at her quickly, as though he'd felt her chill.

"It doesn't mean anything," he said.

"They're messengers, Shep. Among indigenous tribes, owls are thought to carry the souls of the recently deceased. Or they portend the death of someone close."

"C'mon, Mira," he said, a trace of impatience in his voice. "We don't live in a tribe." He pushed open the cabin door with his foot and went inside.

Mira stood still, watching the owl until it flew off into the bare and ugly trees.

It was completely dark by five and somehow the darkness seemed deeper and more pervasive because it was cold. But the wood-burning stove kept the cabin toasty and filled the air with the sweet scent of burning wood. Sheppard grilled fresh trout on the porch grill and they ate in the cabin's spacious kitchen. Then Annie raced back outside to visit the horses, the dogs, the cats, the entire wondrous menagerie of animals.

As Mira rinsed off the dishes, she wondered where the water came from that poured out of the faucet. Probably a well. But how deep a well? Was the water pure enough to drink? She leaned forward and sniffed. The water smelled like a mountain stream.

"It's not well water," Sheppard said as he returned to the kitchen.

"So where's it come from then?"

"Probably a reservoir, Mira."

He gave her one of those looks that had become so frequent in the last six months, the look that whispered, *You've changed since you went through the black water mass.*

"I feel like I'm in a foreign country," she said.

He laughed and came up behind her and slid his arms around her waist, then up under her sweatshirt and against her breasts. He nuzzled her neck and whispered, "You think Annie will be back in the next thirty minutes?"

"I doubt it." She turned in his arms and they stood there for long, delicious moments, creating a landscape of such intense desire and need that they finally stumbled down the hall, laughing and tugging at their clothes, and collapsed onto the king-size bed.

Sheppard kicked the door shut, Mira pulled back the comforter, they tore off their clothes and snuggled under the covers. When you shared your living space with a teenager, she thought, sex was, at best, an opportunistic venture, stolen moments sandwiched between one obligation and another.

A knock at the cabin door brought them both upright. "Shit," Sheppard murmured, and they hurriedly got out of bed and pulled on their clothes.

As Mira ducked into the bathroom, she heard laughter

and squeals of excitement when Sheppard opened the door. Ramona and Jerry Stevens, she guessed, and wished she felt more sociable. She sneezed and felt that terrible scratching in her throat again. She quickly uncapped her bottle of chewable vitamin C and gobbled down four.

Then she went out into the living room to meet Sheppard's former college roommate and his wife.

Ramona Stevens was tall and wiry, with long, curly red hair which she wore swept up in a ponytail, and a bubbling exuberance that could make anyone feel welcome. She hugged Mira hello as though they had known each other for years and went on at great length about what a nice kid Annie was and how she and Tess, her daughter, were already thick as thieves, down there in the barn, tending to the horses. Her husband, Jerry, was as tall as Sheppard, and had to duck just like Sheppard did when he came through the doorway. His energy felt more Greek to Ramona's Irish, but as it turned out, both were originally from Brooklyn.

The odd thing, the thing that ultimately would become disturbing, was that she didn't pick up anything on these people other than the fact that she liked them. No flashing images, no impressions, not a single psychic detail. Mira blamed her scratchy throat and the congestion that, even now, was creeping up on her.

She and Ramona walked down to the barn to check on Annie and Tess. Ramona had a flashlight with her and kept shining the beam around until the light found a pair of red eyes, watching them from the edge of the woods.

"A raccoon, see him?" she whispered. "We have a lot of them. Jerry hates them because they're such scavengers, but I think they're the cutest little things."

"I saw an owl earlier," Mira said suddenly.

"Really? What kind of owl?"

"Large. Maybe a barn owl."

"How strange. I haven't seen a barn owl here in the winter for I don't know how long."

Mira tried not to dwell on this, on what it might mean. She sneezed and blew her nose and suddenly the owl was the only thing she could think about. "Shep has talked about you for years," Ramona was saying. "Ever since that homicide in Lauderdale where you gave him psychic leads."

"That's how we met."

"So what's it like being psychic?"

Mira laughed. It was the equivalent of asking someone what it felt like to be Asian or black. "I don't know. It's been a part of me for so long that I would feel like half a person without it."

"Shep says you pick up information when you touch people?"

"Or objects that they've touched. It depends." Mira knew where this was going. *What do you pick up on me? On my husband? My daughter?* And pretty soon she would be reading for the family, neighbors, friends, and friends of friends.

"So when we hugged hello, did you pick up anything on me? Does it work that fast, that spontaneously?"

Frequently. "Sometimes. It depends on what's going on in the person's life, on how I'm feeling, on a lot of different things. I'm kind of under the weather tonight, but I'd be glad to read for you all tomorrow."

"Really? How great. Thanks. Jerry's skeptical about this kind of stuff, but Tess and I are fascinated."

They stepped into the barn, where bright overhead lights revealed a four-stall barn and two very happy teens, laughing and chatting like old friends as they brushed down a miniature horse no larger than a large dog. "Mom, isn't this just the coolest and most gorgeous horse?" Annie called.

"That's Beauty," Ramona explained. "She's our newest addition. We bought her to keep Coal company. She's the black horse in the next stall. If you sit in the stall with Beauty, she lays on her side and puts her head in your lap. Like she's a dog or something. Tess, honey, this is Annie's mom, Mira."

"Hi, Mira," called the pretty young girl who was the spitting image of her mother. "Nice to meet you. Can Annie spend the night with us tonight?"

"Can I, Mom? Can I?" Annie asked.

Ramona laughed. "It's fine with me."

"I think Shep wants to take you all into Asheville," Mira said.

"Cool," Tess said. "Let's hurry up and finish the stalls. We'll meet you at the cabin."

Thirty minutes later, Mira was huddled in front of the wood-burning stove, sipping hot tea and waiting for the aspirin she'd taken to kick in. She felt like shit, had a low-grade fever, could barely breathe through the congestion in her sinuses. She begged off on Asheville, and since Ramona and Jerry had to get up early, it would be just Sheppard and the teens and one of the dogs, a gorgeous golden retriever named Ricki.

"If you see a health-food store, can you pick up some zinc and green tea?" Mira asked Sheppard. "That way I'll be fine by morning."

"I thought vitamin C did the trick," Sheppard said.

"If Mom says that's what she needs, then that's what she needs," Annie told him, and gave Mira a hug. "We'll bring you back something special, too."

"Bundle up," Mira called after them.

Sheppard bussed her good-bye on the top of her head, Ricki the dog licked her face, and then they were gone, leaving her to the heat from the stove and the blissful silence.

Mira moved into the huge recliner, turned on the TV, and curled up. With the blanket around her shoulders and a pair of Shep's heavy socks on her feet, she finally understood the phrase, "snug as a bug."

When she woke, it was to wood crackling in the stove and the wind whistling through the trees. It wasn't something she heard very often on Tango Key and the sound spooked her. She threw off the blanket and padded into the kitchen for a bottle of water. It was now nine, but felt like four in the morning. Her fever had broken, but her body ached all over, and when she coughed, her chest hurt.

Flu? Bronchitis? Or hell, why not imagine the worst? SARS.

She tried Sheppard's cell number, but her cell didn't get a signal up here, and when she picked up the cabin phone, she got a busy signal. What'd that mean? Was the cabin on a party line? Did such things even exist anymore? Annie had left her cell phone on the kitchen table, so she tried Sheppard's number on the small, much more powerful Motorola. But it didn't pick up a signal, either.

A knock at the front door. Probably Ramona, she thought, bringing her homemade chicken noodle soup or something. Mira set Annie's phone down on the newspaper Sheppard had left on the table, and went over to the door and turned on the outside light. As she opened the door, a chill wind blew inside, wrapping itself around her stocking feet. A pretty woman about Mira's age, in her early forties, stood there. She was maybe five foot eight, with long, thick black hair, and was bundled up in a parka, jeans, boots. Snowflakes glistened in her hair.

"Hi, is Mr. Sheppard here?" she asked.

"No, he's not. He went into town. You can try his cell phone, if you can get a signal up here."

"You're Mira, right? Mira Morales?"

"Uh, yes. And you are . . . ?"

"Allie," she said, with a pleasant smile, and slid her right hand out of her parka pocket and pointed a gun at Mira's chest. "Don't make me use this, Mira. Just step back inside the cabin."

Mira looked at the gun, at the woman, and all her usual worries about car transmissions and the bookstore failing suddenly shrank in importance. The sight of the gun terrified her, paralyzed her, and her sluggish mind pushed up against the wall of that terror and refused to move beyond it.

"I said, *move,*" the woman barked, and stepped forward, forcing Mira back into the cabin.

Without taking her eyes off Mira, the woman kicked the door shut. "My God, it's like a furnace in here." She unzipped her parka. "Toss me that cell phone in the chair, put on some shoes, a jacket, and put some clothes in a bag. Where's your suitcase?"

"What . . . what the hell do you want?"

Allie's smile snapped like a brittle twig and settled into a thin, hard line. "I ask the questions. Now give me that phone and move down the goddamn hall."

Mira picked up the phone, tossed it to her. She started down the hall, struggling desperately to pick up something on this woman. But her head throbbed from sinus congestion, her body ached, and the only thing she picked up was the obvious—she was in very deep shit.

In the bedroom she put on her shoes and the woman stood in the doorway, watching her.

"Where's your suitcase?"

"Under the bed."

"Get it."

As Mira knelt down and slid the suitcase out, the woman opened the drawers to the dresser and scooped out clothes that she dropped on the bed. "No wonder you're congested. These aren't mountain clothes. And those shoes . . ." She clicked her tongue against her teeth. "They're Florida shoes. Do you have a fever?"

Florida shoes. "How do you know where I'm from?"

"I know quite a bit about you. They say you're psychic, but if that's true, you should have known I was going to be at the door and therefore wouldn't have opened it. So much for the psychic part. You've got a teenage daughter and a handsome FBI agent boyfriend. You were born on October twenty-seventh. That makes you . . . hmmm . . . I'm not really up on my astrology, but I bought a couple of books on the subject at your store. You have a collection of weird books. Anyway, that makes you a Scorpio, right?

"I know that your ancient grandmother lives with you, your bookstore is flourishing, and you have quite a number of clients who come to you for predictions about their lives. Poor suckers. Six months ago, something happened to you or to your daughter, I'm still not real clear on that part. And, oh, I know that your husband, Tom, was gunned down in a convenience-store robbery when your daughter was three or so. Tragic. Really. It's the sort of thing that taints your whole life."

Jesus. Mira just stared at her, unable to understand how she never had picked up any indication that she was being watched, stalked, investigated, researched.

"I know that Sheppard was married years ago to an attorney, during his first stint with the bureau. No kids. He spends a lot of time with your daughter and they seem to be quite close. You help him out on cases from time to time, supposedly using your abilities, like with that case in Lauderdale, where you met him. I figure you just got lucky with that one. You do have some repeat clients, so they must be getting something out of the readings you do for them. Maybe you're just a good listener, huh? More of a counselor, an inexpensive therapist, that's how I see it." She paused. "A few months back, I almost had a reading with you. I'd made the appointment—under a phony name, of course—then I canceled. I figured I didn't really need to talk to you at all. I already knew so much about you. It's amazing what you can learn about a person just by observing, talking to other people, and from the Internet." Another pause. "So, do you have a fever?" she asked again.

"What difference does it make to you?"

"If you've got a fever, then you've got an infection. If you've got an infection, then you need an antibiotic. But if it's viral, then the most that will work is something for the fever and some vitamin C."

She talked like a doctor. And as soon as Mira thought this, she got the only psychic impression she'd had all day, of this woman shouting, *Clear,* and applying cardiac paddles to a patient's chest. "You're a doctor."

The woman frowned, then gestured impatiently with the gun. "Just hurry up, c'mon, we don't have all night."

Keep her talking, stall for time. "Where're we going?"

"Move," she snapped.

Mira zipped her bag shut. "My jacket's in the closet."

"Get it."

She retrieved her jacket from the closet, zipped it up, grabbed her bag off the bed—and sneezed. "I need some Kleenex."

"I've got plenty of Kleenex in the car."

"I need to blow my nose *now,* not ten minutes from now."

The woman slipped a travel pack of Kleenex out of her jacket pocket and tossed it to Mira.

She held it tightly for a moment, struggling to pick up something from the packet of Kleenex, but nothing surfaced, not a single image or impression, not even a tiny inner nudge.

"C'mon, let's move." She gestured impatiently with the gun.

Mira went through the bedroom doorway—and whirled suddenly, swung the bag, and it slammed into the side of Allie's head, knocking her back and the gun from her hand. Mira raced down the hall, threw open the cabin door, and ran outside, shouting for Ramona, Jerry, screaming for them to call the police, to hide, there was a crazy out here with a gun. Her voice echoed in the eerie stillness. Where was everyone? Why weren't the dogs barking?

She headed into the barn, her chest heaving for air, her head in an uproar. A horse. She would ride out of here on the big black horse. But midway into the barn, she tripped, fell, and found herself lying on top of something warm. A body, Christ, it was a body, a man, and he wasn't moving. She leaped up, wild with panic, the horses whinnying, braying, and Allie crashed into the barn, her powerful flashlight stripping away the darkness, Mira's protection.

"Hey, I don't want to hurt you!" she shouted. *"Don't make me hurt you!"*

Mira flew straight for the door on the opposite side of the barn, arms tucked in at her sides, her body moving as fast as a bullet, straight on target. Then those doors flew open, an explosion rocked through the barn, and pain burst in Mira's right thigh. The bitch had shot her. She gasped and tried to keep moving, but the pain, dear God, the pain. Her leg gave out, her knee buckled, and she went down.

2

Shit, shit, this isn't in the pattern.

Allie Hart crouched next to Mira and nearly gagged on the stink in the barn. Manure, urine, dirt, blood. Even though she smelled worse things than this daily in ER, she had to cover her mouth and nose with her hand. She felt for a pulse in Mira's neck. There. Quick and steady. Allie rolled her onto her back and shone her flashlight on Mira's thigh, where she'd taken the bullet. A dark stain spread across the denim. The bullet probably hadn't come out the other side. That was bad. No exit wound spelled infection. Infection meant complications. And complications meant more trouble, more possible glitches in her plan. She would have to remove the bullet and she sure as hell couldn't do emergency surgery here.

And what about her head? Had her head struck the ground first when she'd fallen? Allie shone the flashlight on Mira's face, saw a scrape on her cheek, but no other injuries. She moved her fingers expertly across her forehead and into her hair, looking for bumps, swellings. She ran her hand across the back of her neck and over the first couple of vertebrae, then raised her eyelids and checked her pupils. Everything looked okay. Except for the bullet. And the bleeding.

"Get her into the car," she murmured. "Wrap the

wound to stop the bleeding, pump her full of antibiotics. Drive. Get where you're going." That part of her plan wouldn't change. Once she arrived at her destination, she would do the surgery. She'd been planning to lay low for a few days, anyway, and Mira would be able to recuperate enough so that she could travel.

Allie hooked the flashlight to her belt, slipped the gun in her jacket pocket, and slid her hands and arms under Mira and lifted her. A hundred and fifteen pounds, give or take a few. Not a problem. She had lifted patients in ER who weighed twice as much. The car wasn't far.

The larger horse was going nuts, whinnying, kicking at the walls of the stall. Allie hurried out the closest door and moved quickly up the slope of land to her Land Rover. She had removed the rear seat before she'd left home, so there was plenty of room for Mira. Allie laid her on a blanket on the floor. She cuffed her left wrist to one of the metal rings that usually served to keep the rear seat in place, covered her with a blanket, and ran back to the cabin.

Grab the suitcase, she thought. Make sure she wiped off any surface she might have touched. *Hurry, hurry.*

The snow was coming down harder, big fat flakes that would make driving through the mountains perilous. But she didn't have to drive quickly, she reminded herself. She had time.

But Mira doesn't.

Okay, she would get out of town, pull off the road, tend to the bleeding, give her drugs. She had all sorts of drugs with her, antibiotics and painkillers, drugs to bring you up and take you down, drugs to kill you. Drugs weren't the problem. The goddamn bullet was the problem.

This isn't in the pattern. This wasn't part of the plan she had spent months hammering together.

But Mira hadn't left her a choice. She'd been running and a bullet was all that would stop her. It had seemed so obvious at the time. But now, nothing seemed obvious. Nothing seemed easy. Nothing seemed to be the way she'd envisioned it.

She hadn't intended to shoot the others, either. But at the time, they had gotten in her way and the only obvious solution had been to shoot them.

She took long, deep breaths to calm herself.

Inside the cabin now. The silence wrapped around her. Allie's gaze moved slowly through the front room. She hadn't touched anything in here. The only objects she'd touched were the handles on the dresser drawers. She yanked a dish towel from the rack in the kitchen, hastened down the hall and into the bedroom. She wiped vigorously at the handles, at the edges of the drawers, then returned to the kitchen, grabbed the suitcase off the floor, and went over to the front door. She had rapped on the wood, but her gloves had been on then.

She briefly shut her eyes, envisioning those few moments when she'd stood outside the door, when she'd stepped inside the cabin, and afterward. She hadn't touched anything else, she was sure of it.

I'm outta here.

The road down the hill from the farm was already slippery, treacherous. But the Land Rover could negotiate virtually any terrain and she reached the bottom of the hill quickly and made it to the two-lane road without mishap. Her plan had been to avoid the interstates and, considering the snow, that still seemed like a good idea.

She headed west toward the Great Smoky Mountains National Park, where she could pick up any number of country roads. No one would pay any attention to a car that turned off a country road and into the trees. She wouldn't need more than twenty minutes to bandage

Mira's leg and pump her so full of drugs that she would sleep through the night. Any infection that might be festering would be under control by morning.

But if the bullet had chipped a bone or hit a major vein and there was internal bleeding . . .

Then she would deal with it, just as she dealt with every trauma that came through her ER on a given night.

Heat poured out of the Rover's vents. Allie unzipped her jacket, removed her gloves, and reached into the cooler on the passenger seat for a bottle of water. It was important to stay hydrated in times of stress. And B vitamins would help. She opened the glove compartment and removed one of the many plastic packets of vitamins inside. Each travel packet contained a potent B complex, eight hundred milligrams of vitamin C, a hundred milligrams of zinc, twenty-five thousand units of A, and Pycnogenol, another antioxidant. She swallowed the pills, then reached into the cooler again and brought out a bottle of green tea in liquid form. Another good antioxidant. She squirted an eyedropper full into her mouth, tightened the cap, and put it back into the cooler. As soon as she could, she would start Mira on a regimen of antioxidants.

Her vitamin habit was well known around the ER. Most of the other docs on staff thought she was a bit odd because of it and gossiped and made jokes about it behind her back. But the hospital's chief of staff had become a convert when his daughter's face had required forty-eight stitches after a biking accident and Allie had recommended topical vitamin E six times a day instead of plastic surgery. Today the daughter didn't have a scar on her face.

Thanks to her diet, vitamins, and exercise, Allie, now forty-one, had a pulse rate of 52, a blood pressure of 110/62, and a cholesterol count of 152. She could run five miles in thirty-two minutes, which she did three times a week, and could bench-press four repetitions of 135 pounds.

She'd gotten her younger brother started on vitamins when he was in middle school. *Don't go there. Stay focused. Keep driving.*

But now that she had admitted him into her consciousness, she couldn't get him out. Tears welled up in her eyes, her foot pressed down against the gas pedal, and the speedometer leaped past sixty and climbed. The tires screeched as she took a turn.

Talk to me, she begged him.

Sometimes he did. Sometimes when she drove to work, he rode in the passenger seat with her and commented on the scenery, on their brother Keith's wild and pointless life, and he always looked just as he had when she had last seen him, a twenty-nine-year-old Olympian god. Or like a Viking. But tonight he wasn't talking. Tonight the cooler occupied the passenger seat and the blasted snow came down harder and faster and the woman began to groan in the back of the Rover. Tonight she was alone with the consequences of a plan that had developed some major glitches.

Allie slowed and turned on her high beams, looking for a road that led into the woods, a place where she could stop and take remedial measures that would keep Mira from bleeding to death or dying of septicemia in the back of her car. If she was going to die, she would do so when Allie was ready, and not a second before.

The thought made her smile. Right about now, Sheppard would be returning with the teens from their little sojourn to town. It wouldn't be long before he discovered that his life had been turned inside out like a dirty sock. Then that feeling of helplessness would seep into his bones and it would grow, minute by minute, hour by hour, day by day, just as her own helplessness had metastasized all these years.

Payback, Sheppard. Now eat your heart out.

3

1

Sheppard felt a strange contentment as he drove the van through the unfamiliar streets of Asheville, trying to find his way out of town and back to the farm. Ricki was curled up in the front seat, her nose tucked into her tail, dreaming whatever dogs dreamed, and in the back, Annie and Tess talked animatedly about Harry Potter's latest adventures. Both girls had read the five books in the series at least twice and considered themselves experts on the world of wizardry. They debated the ins and outs of Quidditch, whether Dumbledore was actually 150 years old, and how badly they both wanted to visit Hogsmeade, the magical town that was the equivalent of a school field trip for the young Hogwarts wizards.

In Sheppard's much younger days, he and his friends had spent endless hours discussing Tolkien's Middle-earth and young Frodo's impossible quest. He supposed every generation had certain books that shaped their lives and wondered what book it would be for Annie's children.

Mira constantly gave him books from her store—galleys and advanced reading copies from publishers, hardbacks that were about to be remaindered, and special books that she thought he would enjoy. The books that fell into the special category covered a vast range of topics and genres, from quantum physics to metaphysics,

from Harry Potter to Beatrix Potter. He read at least part
of everything she passed on to him, not because he enjoyed all of it, but because he knew it was important to
her.

He turned onto the narrow road that led up the
mountain and eventually branched off to the dirt road
that led to the Stevens property. The snow was coming
down faster now, a messy slush that caused the van to slip
and slide as it climbed. He hit the high beams, shifted
into a lower gear. The van didn't have four-wheel drive
and these mountain roads had taken a toll on the engine. It squealed and strained, complaining every inch
of the way.

At the top of the hill, Tess said, "Hey, they didn't leave
the porch lights on for us."

"Maybe the power went out," Annie said. "Because of
the snow."

"Even if it did, we have backup generators. Besides, I
see lights upstairs."

On the passenger seat Ricki suddenly sat up and
whined. Sheppard wondered if she was whining because
she knew she was home or for some other reason. As he
pulled up in front of the rambling old farmhouse, the
dog started pawing at the door, trying to dig her way out.
She whined, growled, and then began to howl, a mournful sound that spooked Sheppard so deeply he told the
girls to stay in the van.

Even Annie didn't protest.

As he got out, the retriever leaped past him and loped
toward the house, Sheppard hurrying along behind her,
his weapon out, his mind racing. Snow stuck to his hair,
his lashes, and melted against the back of his neck. The
dog barked and pawed at the front door. Outside in the
yard the other dogs now joined in, an agitated cacoph-
ony. He paused at the door, where Ricki now crouched,

growling and snarling, ready to spring, and turned the
knob slowly.

It wasn't locked. The door swung inward.

Ricki tore inside, barking. Then the barking stopped,
both inside and outside the house, and the silence was
somehow worse, seeping through the dark interior like
some sort of toxic gas. Sheppard paused just inside the
door, listening. He heard the hum of the fridge in the
kitchen, water dripping from a faucet, the click of
the heater as it came on, all the small, vital heartbeats
of the house. Whoever had been here was gone, he
thought, and backed up to the wall and flicked the
closest light switch.

The front room looked undisturbed. "Ramona?" he
called. "Jerry?"

His voice echoed, the wooden floor creaked beneath
his feet. He found Ricki in the kitchen, whimpering, cir-
cling Jerry, who was flat on his back, a bullet through the
center of his chest. "Jesus," Sheppard whispered, and
crouched beside him.

Blood covered his chest, was smeared across his arms,
his hands, his face. His eyes were wide open, his face
seized up with shock, surprise. He looked like he was
dressed for bed—sweatpants, T-shirt, thick socks. Sheppard knew he was dead, but touched the side of his neck
just the same, hoping against hope that he might feel
the faintest pulse. But there was nothing. He gently shut
Jerry's eyes. The dog pawed at Jerry's leg and made soft,
pathetic sounds that broke Sheppard's heart.

He didn't have to go far to find Ramona. Sprawled at
the top of the stairs, she'd been shot in the back. She obviously had been running from someone and the trail of
blood that led from midway up the steps to where she
had finally collapsed said she had lived long enough to
crawl. Sheppard moved quickly into the bedroom, where

the bedside lamps were on, books lying facedown on either side of the bed, as though Jerry and Ramona had been reading when they were interrupted. He yanked two quilts off the bed and ran back into the hall. Tess and Annie must never see this, he thought, and quickly covered Ramona with one quilt, then tore down the stairs to cover Jerry with the other. Then a crushing wave of despair and terror gripped him.

Mira, in the cabin. He raced back outside, where the girls now stood by the van's sliding doors, waiting for him, looking scared.

"In the van," he snapped.

They scrambled back inside and Sheppard sped up the dirt road toward the cabin, his fear so extreme he couldn't think beyond what he might find in the cabin. He couldn't think clearly enough to answer the girls' barrage of questions. *What's going on? Why're the dogs howling? Where're my parents? Where's Ricki?*

He slammed on the brakes, barked at the girls to stay inside, with the doors locked and the engine running. When he entered the cabin, his weapon was drawn. Wood crackled and hissed in the stove. A blanket lay across the recliner. Mira's handbag hung on the back of a kitchen chair. He took in these details in a single, sweeping glance and dread rooted in his bones.

Sheppard moved carefully down the hall, into the bedroom. Nothing disturbed. The closet door stood slightly ajar and he opened it all the way with the toe of his shoe. It looked as if clothes had been grabbed in a hurry, hangers every which way, some on the floor of the closet. He and Mira had slid their suitcases under the bed after they had unpacked, but when he got down and peered under, hers was gone.

He turned slowly in place, struggling against the incomprehensible. Had she heard the shots in the house and taken off into the woods? Possible. But then why would she pause long enough to pack a bag and not take her purse?

Sheppard hurried out into the living room again. She'd been sitting in front of the stove when they had left and had moved to the recliner. That was why the blanket was there. Mira's container of vitamin C and a bottle of water rested on the end table. He knelt and looked under the chair for her shoes.

No shoes.

He hastened back into the bedroom and checked the closet again. No shoes. She'd worn sneakers here and had complained that her feet were cold and that she needed to get a better pair of shoes for this climate. Had she brought any other shoes with her? It seemed that she had, a pair of loafers, and he went over to the closet again. Yes, okay, the loafers were hidden by a T-shirt that had slipped off a hanger.

If she had packed the bag, then it was possible she had taken one of the Stevenses' cars and escaped in it. But their vehicles had been parked at the side of the farmhouse. *The horses.* Would she have ridden away on a horse, lugging her duffel bag? The absurdity of the image drove him into the recliner, fists balled against his eyes, terror pouring through him.

His arms dropped to his sides. *Think, think.* He got up, paced into the kitchen, and saw Annie's cell phone half-hidden under the newspaper he'd been reading earlier. It was on, his cell number in the window, with a message that there wasn't any signal. He quickly scrolled to the Call List menu. Mira had dialed his number at 9:03 P.M.; it was now 10:28. So all of this had happened in the last hour and a half.

But where the hell is she?

If she had run, she would have her cell phone and her

handbag. He hadn't found her cell, but he'd found her purse. Even if she had been terrified, she would have taken these two items.

Screams erupted outside and Sheppard shot to his feet and exploded out of the cabin. The van's doors were open, the engine still idling, and in the backwash from the headlights, he saw Annie racing up the road from the stable, her hair loose, flying out behind her, screaming his name. "Come quick," she shouted. "There's . . . a . . . a dead man in the stable, Tess is freaking out, and the horses are going wild!"

He grabbed Annie by the shoulders. "Calm down, okay? I need for you to be calm, Annie. I need help."

"O-o-okay," she said breathlessly, her eyes wild. "I . . . the guy . . . one of the stable guys . . . he . . . he was shot in the head, Shep."

"I want you to go up to the cabin and call 911, Annie. Can you do that for me? Give them this address. Tell them there're multiple homicides."

"M-m-multiple?"

"Not your mom," he said quickly. "I think she took off, into the woods. It's Tess's parents, in the house. Tell them an FBI agent is on the scene, but that he needs local help. Will you do that for me?"

"Yes."

Calmer now. Focused. She had a job to do.

"Then get back into the van."

"Got it."

He paused long enough to turn off the engine, but left the headlights on so that he could see. He raced toward the barn and, in his peripheral vision, caught sight of Ricki the retriever dashing through the snowfall, answering Tess's frantic screams. Just as he reached the barn, the large black horse shot out the doors and thundered down the road. Tess stumbled out behind the horse, her face ravaged, and threw her arms around the dog, holding on as though she were drowning.

Sheppard spoke to her quietly, gently, until she stopped sobbing, then told her to go up to the cabin with the dog, where Annie was, and wait for him there. She nodded, wiped her hand across her nose, but tears still streamed down her cheeks. "Hernando," she managed to whisper. "He's . . . he's down there. Dead. I . . . I don't know where Miguel is."

"Miguel is the other guy who works in the barn?"

"Hernando's brother."

"Okay. I'll find him. You just wait up at the cabin with Annie and Ricki. The police are coming."

Now that she had been given a specific task, she calmed down, just as Annie had, and loped toward the cabin with Ricki trotting alongside her. Sheppard stepped into the barn, found the wall switch, and a bright, naked bulb came on, swinging slightly in the cold air, casting erratic patches of light across the floor, the scattered hay, the open stall door. The miniature horse snorted and pawed at her stall floor and stuck her head over the top of her stall, eyeing him with considerable wariness.

The dead man—Hernando—lay on the floor, shot through the head. Sheppard stepped over him and opened the door to the tack room. There, slumped against the wall, lay another man, probably Hernando's brother. He had fallen into a rack that had held bridles and stirrups, and some of them now lay across his thighs and were strewn around him on the floor. Blood tracked down his face from the corners of his mouth, and as Sheppard neared him, the man wheezed and coughed and his eyes fluttered open, glazed with agony.

"*Ayúdame,*" he whispered.

"*La ambulancia ya viene.*" Sheppard jerked a heavy horse blanket off the rack and covered the man's legs

with it. He unzipped his jacket halfway, exposing the
dark red stain that spread across the front of his sweatshirt, then zipped it back up to keep him warm. He kept
talking to him in Spanish, reassuring him that he was
going to be okay, that help was coming. "*Quien hizo esto?*"
Who did this?

The man's lips moved, but nothing came out. His eyes
fluttered shut, then open again, and he groaned and
Sheppard repeated his question and leaned closer. The
man murmured something.

"*No te entiendo,*" Sheppard said, and took the man's right
hand in both of his own and told him to move his index
finger if the answer was no or to blink if he didn't know.

Was it someone he knew?

The finger moved. No.

Was it a man?

A blink: he didn't know, probably hadn't see the person.

Sirens shrieked in the distance. The wind blew snow
through the open barn doors, the miniature horse
snorted and whinnied. Blood streamed more freely from
the corners of the man's mouth and Sheppard heard
Mira's voice in his head: *They're messengers. . . . Owls are
thought to carry the souls of the recently deceased. . . .*

Did he hear gunshots?

The finger didn't move. That was a yes.

How many shots? One? Two? Three?

"*Tres,*" he whispered.

Three.

Had he seen a car?"

"*Sí.*" A sibilant hiss.

The man coughed and blood sprayed from his mouth.
Sheppard knew he was drowning in it, that blood was filling his lungs, and that he wasn't going to last much
longer. And because he suspected the man was Mexican
and because most Mexicans were Catholics, he started

saying the Lord's Prayer in Spanish, and the man died with Sheppard still holding his hand.

2

"I need to go up to the house," Tess said softly, moving toward the cabin door, where Ricki whimpered and pawed to be let out.

"No." Annie grabbed her arm. "Shep told us to stay here."

Tess looked at Annie, her face ravaged. "I—I need to be with my mom and dad."

Multiple homicides . . . Tess's parents. Annie clutched her arms tightly to her body, terrified that if she moved, if she spoke, the shudders tearing through her would rip her body apart. She couldn't get the sight of the dead man out of her mind, and the longer she stood there, doing nothing, the more vivid the image became. Now his face changed to that of Tess's parents, then shifted again to the face of her mother. She finally pressed her fists into her eyes and struggled against the possibility that Shep had lied to her, that her mother was inside the house with Tess's parents, lying there, bloodied, dead. *And alone.*

"I'm going," Tess said, and threw open the cabin door and took off into the snowfall, Ricki racing alongside her.

Annie hesitated a moment, the image of her mother's face burning like the sun in her head, then ran after them, her own fear shoving her forward faster, faster, until she passed Tess. *Please don't let Mom be in there. . . .*

Sirens wailed. In moments the cops would be here and if her mom was in the house, they would whisk her body away and . . . A sob exploded from her mouth, she pounded up the porch steps and paused at the door, her heart racing, her eyes burning from the cold.

Ricki barked and whined and pawed at the door. Annie touched the knob, but couldn't bring herself to turn it, to open the door. Once she opened it and went inside the house, she would know for sure whether her mom was dead. As long as she didn't open it, she wouldn't have to know. Tess lurched to a stop behind her, breathing hard, and lunged for the door, but Annie turned quickly, blocking it with her body.

"We can't go inside. Shep told us to stay in the cabin."

"Get out of my way. It's my house."

"We can't—"

Tess shoved her hard and hurled open the door, screaming, "Mom? Dad?"

The shudders tore through Annie again. She felt as if her bones were shattering, her organs collapsing, and she gasped and doubled over at the waist. Then she snapped upright and ran into the house, shouting for Tess, her eyes darting here, sweeping the front rooms for some sign of her mother.

Then Tess's shrieks ripped apart the silence in the house, shrill, horrid sounds chopped up with panic, horror, the incomprehensible. Annie found her halfway up the stairs, cradling her dead mother's head in her lap, and the sight of it, of Ramona Stevens's lifeless body, filled her with such profound horror that she just stood there, staring, unable to make sense of it. Tess seemed beyond help. She wailed and shrieked and rocked her body back and forth, her hands smoothing her mother's hair off her cheeks.

Annie broke loose from her paralysis and raced up the stairs to the second floor, shouting for her mother, praying that Shep had been telling her the truth, that her mother wasn't here.

No one was on the second floor.

As she ran back down the stairs to check the first floor,

cops suddenly poured through the front door and two of them tried to restrain her. She kicked and bit and wrenched free and made it into the kitchen, where the dog was draped over Jerry's body, whimpering and licking his face.

"She's not in here, Annie," Sheppard said, hurrying over to her.

Annie spun around. "Then where the hell is she? We have to look for her, we have to go into the woods and search for her. She could be out there, shot and bleeding and dy-dy . . ." She choked on the word, couldn't bring herself to say *dying,* and then she collapsed into Sheppard's arms, sobbing and clinging to him and he scooped her up in his arms and carried her outside.

3

Midnight. Snow blanketed the ground and the stuff was still coming down. It cast a strange and terrible silence across the farm and within that silence, Sheppard's stomach churned.

He stood at the cabin window, Ricki the dog curled up in front of the stove, Annie asleep on the couch behind him, and Tess asleep in the bedroom, both of them knocked out by whatever a paramedic had given them. His breath fogged the glass, and every so often he ran his palm over it in tight circles, clearing a space so he could see outside.

The road between the cabin and the farmhouse still buzzed with activity. Powerful searchlights illuminated the falling snow and cops and forensics people moved through it like figures in a Kafkaesque nightmare. Mira had been gone now for between an hour and a half to three hours. The longer he stood here, waiting for someone to come in and tell him he was off the hook, the farther away Mira got and the harder she would be to track. He didn't have any idea what the holdup on this end was about.

He had given a lieutenant his badge number, his boss's cell number, his partner's cell number, and the number for the bureau's Miami office. Annie had confirmed his story: they had been in town and the girls had gone rock climbing at a place across the street from the Laughing Seed, the vegetarian restaurant where they'd had a bite to eat, and then they'd gone to Malaprop's Bookstore and bought a couple of books and videos. He'd shown the lieutenant the receipts, the merchandise. What the hell more did they want?

Annie had been able to call 911 from the cabin phone, but otherwise it didn't work and neither his cell nor Annie's picked up a signal. But even if he could call out, who would he call and what would he say? *Four people are dead and Mira's gone.*

Gone where?

The possibility that she had run into the woods when she'd heard the gunshots was clearly ludicrous, and she obviously hadn't ridden out of here on any horse. If she'd been wounded, then it hadn't happened in the cabin. He had searched the place for bloodstains and found nothing, nothing at all. In his heart he believed she was still alive, he *felt* that she was.

But alive where?

The cabin door opened and a man in jeans and a navy blue pea coat walked in, snow blowing in behind him. He had a buzz cut, a clean-shaven jaw, and, except for his clothes, looked like some businessman from Wall Street. He shut the door, glanced at Annie asleep on the couch, at the dog curled up in front of the stove, then at Sheppard and extended his hand.

"Kyle King." He spoke as quietly as he had shut the

door. "No relation to Martin Luther or Stephen," he added with a quick, winning smile. "I'm with the bureau in Charlotte." A firm, businesslike handshake. "Your badge number and alibi check out."

"It took them an hour and a half to figure that out?"

"Blame the mountains. At best, cell phones up here are erratic, and if you toss in a snowstorm, well, then the land lines don't work very well, either. I was in Asheville and they asked me to run your badge number and check out your story. Fortunately, the phones at my hotel are still working." He shrugged off his coat and fitted it over the back of a kitchen chair, then ran his hand over his buzz cut, brushing out the melting snow. He gestured at the pound of Cuban coffee on the kitchen table. "You mind if I make some of that? Christ, I haven't had real Cuban coffee since I don't know when. You look like you could use a cup, too."

"I need a search party," Sheppard said. "Not coffee. My fiancée was taken by the person responsible for these killings."

"How do you know that? We're still searching the woods. It's possible she ran off."

The soft, even pace of his voice snapped Sheppard back into the here and now. This King guy was good, Sheppard thought. Very good. He knew the drill. *Hi, I'm your buddy, I'm your friend, we're bureau brothers, and we're in this together. Now tell me everything you know.*

He wasn't doing this because he doubted Sheppard's alibi, so there had to be something else at work here. Maybe he knew something about the killer's MO or perhaps forensics had passed on some piece of vital information already. Whatever the reason, Sheppard didn't have time for games.

"Here's the deal, Agent King. I came back here, the dog was howling before the car stopped, and I had a bad feeling. I told the kids to stay in the van and went into the house." Sheppard went on from there, the abbreviated version, and ended up his story with the Mexican workman dying as he gripped the guy's hand. "We've lost time here and the more time we lose, the harder it will be to find the killer and Mira."

The pot was now filled with Cuban coffee and King, who was in no apparent hurry, brought over two mugs, set them on the table. "You take anything in your coffee?"

"Not tonight."

"Then, please, sit down. We're going to be here awhile. The snow has closed the interstates to the Georgia border and the perp can't go west because the interstates there are closed, too. He won't be getting far before sunrise."

Sheppard sat down reluctantly and suddenly his body felt as if it had been filled with cement.

"A relative will be here by morning to pick up the Stevens girl and, hopefully, the horses, dogs, cats, chickens, and whatever else is here." King filled the two mugs and pulled out the other chair. "I spoke to your boss, Baker Jernan, and to your partner, John Gutierrez. He'll be up here as soon as he can get a flight out. He said to tell you he'll be in touch with Nadine and that he'll make sure your cat is fed."

Sheppard couldn't help himself, he laughed at that. It was exactly something that "Goot" would say. It also meant that Goot was bringing Nadine, since she was the person presently feeding his cat, and that he would now be saddled with finding someone else to feed not only his cat, but Mira and Nadine's cats as well.

"Your boss said he's ready to send as many people as we need up here."

Sheppard noticed the *we*. "I need forensics information."

"I've got some preliminary stuff. Very preliminary. What's Mira's blood type?"

Mira. Her name rolled off King's tongue with familiarity.

"A Positive."

"Yours?"

"Same."

King nodded, withdrew a Pocket PC from his shirt pocket, and tapped this information into it. "The Stevenses both had O Positive blood. The two men found in the barn both had AB Positive. There was also A Positive blood found. Not a lot of it, but enough to suggest that whoever it came from was wounded. And since you don't look wounded, this could indicate that Mira was injured."

"The forensics people do the typing on-site?"

"The mobile forensics unit is relatively new. Tell me about your relationship with the Stevenses."

Sheppard sipped at the coffee, set it down, sipped some more. He had known Jerry Stevens since they'd shared an apartment together when they were both college students more than twenty years ago. He had been Jerry's best man at his wedding, when he'd married Ramona, and was technically Tess's godfather. The friendship now amounted to male bonding through e-mail and Ma Bell and a reunion when the spirit moved them.

"I understand your fiancée is allegedly psychic. Tell me about it."

"How would you know that?"

"God bless the Internet."

"Then you know her background with law enforcement, so there's not much to tell."

Silence. Sheppard finished his coffee and glanced toward the window, where the outside lights still illuminated the falling snow, then looked back at King as he spoke.

"So the question is this. If Mira is as psychic as the stories I read seem to suggest, then isn't it possible that she'll attempt to communicate with you or her daughter in some way?"

The question was so totally out of whack for an FBI agent that it threw Sheppard for a moment. Was this part of King's game or was it an honest question? He decided to give King the benefit of the doubt, at least for the moment. "Yeah, it's not only possible, it's likely. But she was feeling sick when we went into town. She thought she was coming down with the flu or something. And when she's sick, her abilities don't work very well. And if she's wounded on top of it . . ." His voice cracked with emotion and he shut up and looked quickly down at his empty mug.

"Is her daughter psychic?" King asked.

"Yes. But she's also a kid. It's erratic."

"What about Mira's grandmother?"

"Yes. But she's in her eighties."

"So you're saying that psychic abilities have age limitations."

Another out-of-whack question. Sheppard, irritated now, leaned forward. "I'm saying that I've known this woman more than five years, have seen her do amazing things, come up with astonishing information, and I've seen her daughter and her grandmother in the same light. But this ability isn't something you conjure at will. This is the twilight zone, Mr. King, and Rod Serling isn't here to give us the real-time scoop."

King raised his cup to his mouth, drank down the entire mug, set it down. "The snowfall should taper off by three or four. Tess's relatives should be here by breakfast and the phones should be working by then. I'm going to bunk up at the farmhouse. Get some sleep, let's see where things stand when the sun comes up."

With that, King pushed his chair back, stood, and shrugged on his pea coat again. "We'll find her, Mr. Sheppard."

"Shep," he said.

"Kyle."

They shook hands again and when King opened the door to leave, Ricki lifted her head and gazed after him, then looked at Sheppard, who said, "It's okay. You're staying here with us. Go back to sleep."

Ricki lowered her head to the floor and shut her eyes, and Sheppard wandered back to the smaller bedroom, feeling as though his life had come unraveled at the seams.

August 1989
Tybee Island, Georgia

1

The noises of the marsh rise and fall around them, as immutable as the cycles of the tides, of light and darkness. They listen raptly, trying to identify every sound. She has been out here by herself plenty of times at night, sneaking out of the oppressive house to breathe the air of freedom. But she has never before listened so closely to the music of the marsh.

"Frogs," he says.

"Fish jumping," Lia says.

"Scared fish?" Dean asks.

"Restless fish."

They are sitting at opposite ends of an old rowboat, their bare feet pressed together. She loves the heat and pressure of his feet, the shape of them, the summer roughness. It's late, way past midnight, and her parents believe she is asleep. She crept out of her bedroom window an hour ago, when she heard Dean's whistle echoing across the marsh, and he picked her up at the dock that juts out from her backyard. Now they are deep in Tybee's salt marsh, intruders stealing time together. Now and then he drops the paddles into the water to steer them deeper into the tall reeds. But mostly, they drift.

"Restless for what?" he asks. "What would make fish restless?"

Lia shrugs. "I don't know. Maybe the same things that make people restless."

"Hunger?"

She flexes her toes against the bottom of his feet. "Naw, they're well-fed fish. There's plenty of food in this marsh. I think they need a change of scenery. Maybe it's the tug of the ocean tides that makes them jump."

"You mean, the marsh fish are tempted to head into the At-lantic?"

"Yeah. Yeah, that sounds right."

He leans forward and runs his fingers over the tops of her toes. "You make me feel like that, Lia."

When he touches her, she feels a hunger so deep it scares her. She is fifteen years old. She first saw Dean two months ago, in June, while walking on a Tybee beach at sunset, hoping she would spot a pod of dolphins just offshore, and he fell into step beside her.

"Hey," he said. "You live across the marsh from me."

She remembers that she looked over at him, that her breath hitched in her chest, and that for moments she felt so tongue-tied she said nothing at all.

She recognized him, of course. Every teenage girl on Tybee knows who he is. He looks like an Olympian god, his father is a famous cancer researcher, he's a rich kid from Miami. "Yeah, so?" she finally managed to say.

"I've seen you out in the marsh late at night," he said. "You always seem to be looking for something."

"Dolphins," she told him. "They sometimes come into the marsh when the tide is high."

"And now?" he asked.

"They sometimes swim along the shore at sunset."

And right then, she told herself that if they spotted a pod of dolphins, if she saw even a single dolphin, it would be a sign. A good sign. A moving-forward sort of sign.

"I'm Dean," he said.

"Lia," she replied, and he smiled and so did she, and yes, they saw a pod of dolphins and that was how it started.

Now here she is. Here they are. It's August, the air steams even at this hour. The moon is sliding down low in the sky, no one can see them. She wants him, he wants her, what could be simpler? It's not the first time. It won't be the last. His mouth presses against hers and she unzips his shorts and they slide down inside the old rowboat and the rest of the world goes away.

They are careful. They are loving and lustful—but careful. He pulls out of her before he comes, and much later, as he is rowing back toward her dock, it occurs to her that pulling out isn't safe enough to suit her. "You know, maybe we should use condoms. Or birth control pills or something."

"Is this a safe time of the month for you?" he asks.

Is it? She isn't sure. Her mother, a religious woman who probably hasn't had sex since Lia was conceived, has never talked to her about this sort of stuff. What she knows has come from books and friends, and right now, she can't remember details. She can't remember when she had her last period or when the next one is due.

"I'll have to check," she replies.

As they near her house, she begins to cry, she can't help it. The tears simply leak from her eyes and roll down her cheeks and she says, "Listen, I don't want some silly fucking thing out in the marsh, okay? If that's what you're looking for, Dean, then just go find someone else."

He brings the paddles into the boat. "Is that what you think this is?"

"I don't know what this is."

Dean sits forward, his face very close to hers, his fingers traveling up her arm, to her shoulder and down again, and then up her arm to her chin. "I love you."

He says the words softly, brings his mouth to hers, kisses her again. Already, she has a hickey on her neck and must remember to cover it up before she goes inside her house. Her mother notices everything. She pulls back. "I have plans. I have dreams. They don't include this. You."

"Bullshit," he says, and kisses her again.

Lia's arms tighten around his neck. She feels compelled to tell

*him about her silly, social-climbing mother, and her emotionally
detached father. She blurts how she is the only child and therefore has no reality other than a child of their creation. Then they
are sliding down in the boat again, making love again, and she
is terrified her parents will hear the shocking resonance of her
body as she comes.*

2

*Dean's sister is visiting. Allie the big shot, the brains of the
Curry family fortune, that's how she sees herself. She'll be
twenty-eight in November and is doing her residency in ER medicine. She thinks she knows everything, that she is smarter than
their old man, smarter than God. He can't stand being around
her, can't stand the grating sound of her voice as they sit around
at dinner.*

*Allie dominates the conversation, bragging about her resi-
dency, about her new husband, her new home, her wonderful
life. Then she and their father get into one of their discussions
about the cancer drug he pioneered. Dean already knows the history, the particulars, that the drug made the Currys rich. He's
pleased that the drug saves lives, and yes, having money is
great, but the conversation bores him to death. He pushes away
from the table—and conversation abruptly stops.*

"Where're you going?" his mother asks.

"Out." To meet Lia on the beach. Lia, the sun in his universe.

"But I just got here," Allie says.

*"And you'll be around for four days," Dean replies, and picks
up his dishes and carries them out into the kitchen.*

*He hears the low, muted tone of their voices and knows they're
discussing him. Sure enough, Allie comes out into the kitchen
and leans against the counter, watching him. "So you've got a
girlfriend."*

She's fishing for information. He recognizes the ruse. "I do?"

"That must be it, for you to run off like this."

"I go out every night."

"But I rented a couple of movies for all of us to watch."

"Allie, in case you haven't noticed, I'm not twelve anymore. I don't feel like watching movies with you and Mom and Dad."

"If Keith were here, you would."

"I doubt it." He grabs his wallet and keys off the kitchen table. "See you tomorrow," he says, and escapes the house before she can say another word.

His black Trans Am, parked in the driveway, is wedged between Allie's car and his father's. Trapped, he thinks, and knows it was deliberate on Allie's part. This is the kind of shit she does. And now the front door opens and she comes outside.

"Guess you're not going anywhere so fast," she says with a smirk on her face.

"Move the car, Al."

She tosses him the keys. "You move it."

The inside of her car smells of perfume and leather. It's a BMW, spotless, not a speck of dust or a crumpled wrapper anywhere. He starts it up, revs the engine, and peels out of the driveway while Allie stands on the front steps, watching him. Then he slams the car into reverse and speeds back up the driveway, dust and gravel flying up, pinging against the sides of the car. He screeches to a stop inches from his father's back fender, gets out.

Allie marches over to him, her face like stone. "That gravel better not have dented the paint job," she snaps.

"Catch, Al." He hurls the keys at her.

She misses and they hit the ground. "Pick those up," she demands.

"Fuck off." As he strides past her, she grabs his arm and he wrenches around, jerking his arm free, and moves his head just in time to avoid the slap he knows is coming. He catches her forearm and grips it tightly. "Don't you dare."

She pulls her arm free. "Your problem is that you never had enough discipline when you were a kid, Dean."

He explodes with laughter. "Looks who's talking."

"I think it's time you got your car taken away from you."

"Yeah? And who's going to do it, Al? You?"

"Dad will, when I tell him you're out every night with your girlfriend."

"Dad didn't buy the car. I did. He doesn't pay the insurance. I do. Go back to your life and let us get on with ours, Al."

With that, he gets into his Trans Am and speeds away.

3

Lia is putting away stock in the storeroom of Mr. Barker's convenience store, where she has been working all summer. It's cool and quiet back here and she has time to think, to plan, to jot notes in her journal. She and Dean are trying to figure out how they can steal away for a night before he and his family return to Miami. She can tell her parents she's spending the night with her friend Molly, but if her mother calls Molly's house to check on her . . . Well, let her call. Molly's parents will be gone this weekend and Molly just won't answer the phone.

Yes, it can work.

She will make it work.

Mr. Barker sticks his head into the storeroom, his soft moon face beaded with sweat. He has been outside, unloading a truck of supplies. "Lia, your mom is out front."

"My mom?"

"Your mom." He gives her a sympathetic smile. Mr. Barker doesn't like her any better than Lia does. "She looks like she's on her way elsewhere," he whispers. "She probably won't stay long."

Lia nods, puts her journal into a cabinet, and goes out to see her mother.

She's all dressed up, her mother is, her plumpness jammed into one of the expensive dresses she wears when she's off to meet with her Savannah church group. Her hair is puffy and stiff with hair spray, she wears too much jewelry, and a cloud of perfume sur-

rounds her. She's paging through one of the tabloids Mr. Barker sells. It occurs to Lia that her mother's name, Susan Phoenix, doesn't fit her. She looks like a Dottie Smith. Or a Greta Jones.

"What is it, Mom? I'm kind of busy," Lia says.

Her mother quickly drops the tabloid into the rack. "What filth this newspaper contains," she says with a small grimace, fingering the large cross around her neck. "Why does Mr. Barker even carry these tabloids?"

"Because they sell."

"I just wanted to let you know I probably won't be at home when you get off work. The church group is having a charity sale today and your father won't be home from work until much later this evening."

Lia immediately thinks how perfect this is, how it will give her and Dean time together. "Okay. I'm going to spend the night at Molly's."

"This is the first I've heard about it."

"I just talked to her."

"You need to clear these plans with me first, young lady."

Yeah, yeah. "Okay, so can I spend the night with her?"

"I suppose it's all right. How will you get over there?"

"The same way I always do. I'll ride my bike."

"All right, but I want you home early tomorrow. You've got a million chores to do."

"Fine. Whatever. See you tomorrow."

Lia turns away, but her mother takes her roughly by the arm. "Now, just a minute, young lady."

"Hey, you're hurting my arm," Lia says loudly, and other customers in the store glance their way.

Her mother releases her arm. A bright pink flush creeps up her neck, into her cheeks, and her eyes shrink to dark points of light. She's embarrassed and pissed, Lia thinks, and tomorrow or next week, she'll make Lia pay for this public display.

"You will not speak to me in that tone," she hisses.

Lia crosses her arms and glares back at her, her insolence de-

liberate. "Have a great day, Mom. A nice charity sale. A fine lunch." *Lia pauses.* "Is that better?"

Her mother purses her lips, rocks forward onto the balls of her feet, and jabs her finger into Lia's cheek. "You will not be spending the night out. You will be at home after you leave work. And I'll be calling the house to make sure you're there."

Lia knows that now she is supposed to beg, to apologize, that her mother, in fact, is waiting for her to do exactly that. It's her power game and has been going on between them for as long as Lia can remember. "You don't own me." *Lia spits the words, then turns away and hurries back toward the storeroom.*

"What will they do when they come home and you're not there?" Dean asks.

They are lying naked on a double bed in a hotel room on the island one over from Tybee. "I don't know. I don't care."

He lifts up on his elbow and leans over her, caressing her face, her breasts. She rolls onto her side and puts her arms around him, drawing him close. "I can't stand the thought of your leaving," *she whispers.*

"Me either," *he whispers back, and tightens his arms around her.* "But I've got the car. I can drive up here on long weekends."

"My parents watch me like hawks, Dean."

"We'll get around it. In March, I'll be eighteen. We can get married."

"But I won't be eighteen for another two and a half years. My parents would never consent to my getting married."

He runs his fingers through her hair. "We'll work it out. Trust me," *he says softly.* "I'll call you, we'll write letters, and I'll kidnap you if I have to."

Then he nibbles at her ear and suddenly they are both laughing and rolling around on the bed, hitting each other with pillows.

Suddenly the phone rings, startling them both. Dean bolts up-right. "Who could that be?"

"Molly. But don't answer it. She'll leave a message."

A few minutes later, Lia picks up the message. "Hey, Lia, it's me, Molly. You'd better get your ass home. Your mom called here and left a message. She says if you're not home in an hour, she's calling the cops."

"Will she really do that?" Dean asks, frowning.

"Yes. Shit. I hate her. And my dad lets her get away with it just to keep the peace between them." And she presses her fists into her eyes, struggling to hold back tears.

"We can't risk this," he says, taking her gently by the shoulders. "Not now. I'll get you home."

4

Dean drives like a maniac, his fear for Lia so great that even when he pulls up in front of Molly's house, he doesn't want to let her out. "We can run away tonight," he says.

She shakes her head, gathers her beautiful blond hair in her hand and pulls it over her shoulder. "No. No, we can't start a life together like that. It'll be okay, Dean. They'll just rant and rave and leave me alone. Really." She touches her palm to the side of his face. "Just come by the store tomorrow, okay?"

"I will. What time?"

"I'll be there at ten."

"Okay. I'll be watching your house from the dock. Signal me when it's all over."

Then she gets out of the car and he watches as she hops onto her bike and pedals madly up the street, her hair flowing behind her, a pale cascade. He follows her until she turns down her street, then she glances back and lifts her arm, waving.

Minutes later, he's on the back dock, staring across the marsh at her house. The lights blaze over there. Shadows move against the blinds, the curtains. On still nights sounds travel easily across the marsh. But the windows at the Phoenix house are closed up, the AC is on. He can't hear a damn thing.

Behind him, a screen door creaks and bangs shut. He knows by the rhythm of the footsteps that it's Keith. "Hey, man, you okay?" Keith asks, settling next to him on the dock.

"Sure. When did you get in?"

"A while ago and I'm already itching to split."

Dean laughs. "I know just what you mean."

"Mom and Dad are at each other's throats, Allie's bitching about how 'the Family' isn't a unit anymore, it's falling apart . . . you know, all the same shit."

"Why the hell doesn't she just leave? All she does is create tension. She supposedly came for four days and she's been here a week."

"Listen, I'm thinking about selling the chartering business and buying a boat and getting out of the States. Mom and Dad are always poking around in my life, Allie is constantly in my face. . . . You want to come to Panama with me?"

Three months ago, Dean would have leaped at an opportunity like this. But now his life is more complicated. He has plans for college, for him and Lia. Keith, who is eight years older, has owned a boat-chartering business in Miami since he graduated from college three years ago and has no personal ties to hold him here.

"I can't. I got early acceptance at Stetson. I'm starting there in January."

"You've got a girl, that's why not."

"That too." He glances over at Keith. "Did Allie tell you that?"

He makes a disgusted sound. "Let's talk about something else. Like how about if I drive up to Stetson with you sometime this fall to look over the campus?"

"Would you?"

"Goddamn right. Mom and Dad will be too busy. We both know that. And Allie would drive you nuts."

Dean looks back at Lia's house. The lights still blaze, she hasn't signaled him. How long has it been? Ten minutes? Fifteen?

"So who's the girl?"

"I knew her in Greece. And in Ecuador in the sixteen hundreds."

Keith gives him an odd look. He doesn't subscribe to Dean's beliefs, but he usually listens with an open mind. "How do you know?"

"Dreams, mostly. Then I went to this medium in Cassadaga who confirmed it. He said it's going to be difficult for us this time around, but . . ." He shrugs. "We can overcome whatever happens."

Keith knows about Cassadaga. Dean has told him about the village of mediums just north of Orlando, a strange and wonderful place where he will take Lia soon.

"Keep the relationship to yourself, man. You know Allie. She'll do her best to break it up if she finds out."

He speaks from personal experience. "Why is that, do you think? Why should she give a shit?"

"Misery loves company, I guess. The more miserable we are, the closer we stick to the family roots. At least, I think that's how she figures it."

"I think it's more complicated than that."

"Hey, she's a control freak, Dean. She thinks she runs the family. You, me, Mom, Dad, with Allie at the head of the clan. That's how it's always been."

"Even when Ray was alive?"

Keith shrugs and gets up to go inside for another beer. Dean stays where he is, watching Lia's house.

5

Lia waits for the explosion she knows will come, waits with her stomach in knots, inside the privacy of her bedroom. Neither of her parents spoke a word to her when she came into the house. They couldn't very well say anything because neighbors are visiting. They can't look bad in front of other people.

She has showered, changed clothes, and now she is stretched out on her bed, the TV on, and winces when she hears the neighbors' car pulling out. Minutes later, banging on her door, her mother shouting, "Lia, open this door immediately."

Lia hesitates, then goes over to the door, turns the lock. Her mother blows in, her cheeks red from whatever she's been drinking, and slaps her across the face so hard that Lia stumbles back. "You intentionally disobeyed me," she yells. "You're grounded, do you understand me? Grounded for the next two weeks."

She stands there, puffing with rage, eyes bulging in their sockets. Lia hasn't moved, hasn't said a word. Her hand is pressed to the spot where her mother slapped her. The skin stings and aches.

"I asked you a question, young lady. Now answer me."

"I speak English. I understand what grounded *means."*

"Don't you get smart with me," her mother shouts, and moves toward her again, hands balled into fists.

Lia grabs a chair and thrusts it at her mother. "Don't come near me, you hypocritical bitch. You call yourself a Christian? What do you think your little church buddies would think of you if they knew you beat your daughter? Huh?" She doesn't raise her voice. She doesn't have to. These words possess such power that her mother stops where she is, fists raised.

"What the hell's going on in here?" Lia's father storms into the room, sees his wife's raised fists, sees Lia holding the chair, and lifts his hands, patting the air. "Time for everyone to calm down here. We'll talk about this in the morning, Lia. Susan, out." He stabs his thumb at the door.

"Out? She lied, she disobeyed us, she—"

"Out," he barks, and takes her by the shoulders and marches her out of the room. Then he pokes his head back in. "Lock the door, Lia. She's had too much to drink and we both know what that means."

Lia nods, barely able to hold back tears, and the door shuts. She rushes over to it, turns the dead bolt, and collapses against it, sobbing.

Sunday
December 28

4

1

Mira stirred awake, sluggishness clinging to her like Velcro. Wood crackled in the stove, the air smelled of sweet smoke. Just the floor lamp was on, casting a pale globe of light against the floor. Shadows pooled in the corners of the room. She wondered how long she'd been asleep.

She peeled the blanket away from her legs and went into the kitchen for a bottle of water. The stove light was on, a bulb so dim it belonged in some Third World country where every hotel room was lit by no more than forty watts. The Advil she'd taken earlier seemed to have kicked in. She didn't feel as sick now, but she felt strangely uneasy, disturbed, and didn't know why. She helped herself to a bottle of water from the fridge, spun the cap, and stared at the blackness that swam in the kitchen window. It deepened her unease.

The wind pushed branches up against the window and they scratched at the glass like tiny mice clawing to get in from the cold. Where did the goats and the chickens and the cats go when it snowed? Even though Ramona obviously loved the horses, she hadn't impressed Mira as the kind of woman who would bring farm animals into the house.

It bothered her that she hadn't picked up anything at all on the Stevenses. It wasn't as if she could read everyone she met, of course, but in a situation like this, she should have picked up *something*.

In fact, the longer she stood here, the more *wrong* everything felt.

The clock on the wall told her it was nine o'clock. Sheppard and the girls should be arriving shortly, she thought, and hoped it would be very soon. She didn't like being in the cabin alone, another oddity. Usually she enjoyed solitude regardless of where she was. As she plucked Annie's cell phone off the kitchen table to call him, a powerful déjà vu swept through her, a sensation so strange and unsettling that she went utterly still, struggling to make her way back to the source of it.

A dream? Was that it? Had she dreamed being alone in this cabin at some point in the past? Or was it the act of picking up Annie's phone that she had dreamed? Suddenly she flashed on herself racing down the hill outside, headed toward—*what?* Mira squeezed her eyes shut, trying to pick up more, to see more, but it was as if a door had slammed shut in her head.

She opened her eyes. The clock's hands hadn't moved. How could that be? Even the second hand wasn't moving. She went over to it, plucked it off the wall, turned it over. It had a battery, it was even ticking, but the hands didn't move. She shook it, figuring the hands had rusted or gotten stuck to something. But the hands still stood at 9:02. Her unease bit more deeply and she turned slowly in place, taking in the cabin's front room, the chair where she'd been sitting, the wood-burning stove. Shadows oozed around the furniture. She had been sitting in the recliner when Sheppard and Annie had left and had awakened there. Then she'd come into the kitchen, where she stood now.

Wrong, something's very wrong with this picture.

She turned her attention to the cell phone, punched

out Sheppard's cell number, but nothing happened. No ringing, no signal, no light. The phone was as dead as the clock. She picked up the receiver on the cabin phone and got a busy signal—and another wave of déjà vu crashed over her. "Jesus," she whispered. "What's going on?"

Mira pressed her palm to her forehead. The skin felt warm, but not raging hot. A low-grade fever. So it wasn't as if she were delirious and locked up in some weird fever vision. She pinched her arm, felt it. Okay, she wasn't delirious and she was definitely awake.

Then why didn't anything feel right?

She decided to walk up to the house to talk to Ramona and Jerry. She would use their phone, too, to find out when Sheppard would be back. She needed some company, that was all. Maybe Ramona would have green tea. Hell, maybe Ramona had beer or wine. A cold beer would hit the spot right now.

She went over to the chair and put on her shoes. Her Florida running shoes. Tomorrow she would have to go into Asheville to get some shoes better suited to the weather. And while she was at it, she would buy a heavier jacket and socks, too.

Just then, there was a knock at the door. It startled her, her head snapped up—and a sense of familiarity coursed through her again. She shook off her apprehension, certain that it was Ramona or Jerry at the door. Ramona knew she hadn't been feeling well and probably had brought over homemade chicken soup.

Mira went over to the door, unlocked it. As she opened it, the logs in the stove hissed and crackled and snow blew into the cabin, a wind-driven snow that prevented her from seeing more than six inches in front of her. No one was at the door. Either she'd imagined the knock or the wind had hurled something against the door.

Yeah? And what kind of something would that be, Mira? A snowball? An animal? A rock?

"Ramona?" she called, just to be sure.

The storm swallowed her voice, the wind wrapped around her legs, and suddenly Mira saw something moving through the wall of snow, off to the left. It looked like the darting beam of a flashlight. "Jerry?" she shouted. "Ramona? Shep?"

She stepped outside, hugging her arms against her, and then two figures emerged from the snow, as though the storm had given birth to them. The man in front raised his head.

Mira knew that some sort of noise escaped her, an explosive sound, a sob of horror or shock or both, and she wrenched back, blinking hard, certain that she was hallucinating, that she was locked in some feverish delirium. Her legs moved of their own volition, feet scrambling back, back, to put distance between herself and the door, through which the man now walked.

"Mira." He spoke softly, in a voice she remembered clearly, and then he smiled and she knew it was Tom, tall and handsome in jeans and a parka and a funny knit cap pulled down over his head.

Her heart seized up and they rushed toward each other, and when his arms came around her, he felt real, solid, and smelled of snow and wind and miracles. She didn't care if this was a hallucination, a mirage, or some cruel cosmic trick. When he kissed her, she tasted the moisture of the storm on his mouth and the eleven years since his death vanished in a flash. It was as if her husband had never left.

Mira pulled back, drinking in the sight of his face, her fingers peeling the knit cap off his head and sliding through the damp softness of his hair. Real, all of it real, tangible. "How—"

He touched his index finger to her mouth. "Remember the story we used to tell Annie about Jiminy Cricket? That anything's possible if you believe?"

Mira laughed and wept and ran her hands down his back, up his neck and into his hair again. The last time she had seen him, he'd been a teenager in the Keys in 1968, a kid who had somehow recognized her even though she wouldn't enter his life for decades. Now here he was, dead but not dead, and talking to her about belief and Jiminy Cricket.

"All these years, I've tried to find you. To go wherever you are. I kept hoping I'd sense you nearby. But you . . . you . . ."

She choked up and suddenly thought of how guilty she'd felt the night she'd accepted Sheppard's ring, as though she were betraying Tom, and how many times she had put her emotions on hold because of her memories of Tom, and of how many nights she'd cried herself to sleep, wishing that she could change what had happened, that she could bring him back. Now here he was, walking in from a snowstorm like he'd been gone a day instead of eleven years, and what she felt right then was anger.

"What the hell have you been doing all this time?" she burst out. "Why didn't you at least give me a sign, a nudge, something, Tom? My God. What do you do over there all day, year after year? You could have at least visited Annie and me. You could—"

"I told you this wouldn't be simple," said a voice on the other side of the room.

Mira spun around and there stood the second figure she'd seen, a tall young man with blond hair, leaning against the now-shut cabin door. He looked as though he belonged on a wild, powerful horse, galloping through the mist on the Scottish moors or leading a band of Vikings into battle. "Who're you?" she demanded.

"A friend," the man said, and came toward her, his hand extended. "The name's Dean."

Mira looked at his hand, at his face, a part of her terrified that if she touched him, Tom would vanish and everything would go back to the way it had been moments ago. "I don't understand," she said quietly, backing away from Dean. "I don't understand what's going on."

Dean's arm swung to his side. Tom tightened his grip on her hand. "It's okay, Mira. He's not the enemy. He's one of us."

"And what's that mean, exactly? That I'm dead?" She looked helplessly at Tom. " Is that it? I'm dead and you've come for me?"

"No, that's not it at all. We need a favor."

"A favor." She let out a clipped, dry laugh. "Eleven years of silence and now you show up for a *favor?* Christ, I can't believe I'm hearing this." She pulled her hand free of Tom's and sank down onto the couch. "I can't believe I'm having this conversation with a dead man. With two dead men." She looked at Dean. "You're dead, right?"

"For nearly a year in your time."

"Oh. Great. I don't remember you from before. When Tom was alive."

"I didn't know Tom when he was alive. Friendships are formed in death just as they are in life, Mira."

"Uh-huh."

"What do you think Tom's been doing all this time?" Dean asked. "Hanging out on clouds? Goofing off? Floating around your house, hoping you'll sense his presence? He's been making a death for himself. That's what you do when you're gone, Mira. You create something on the other side."

For some reason, she'd never thought of it like that. Despite all her years as a psychic, she had never considered what Tom might be doing as a spirit, except feeling the same raw grief and loss that she felt. She'd thought of him only in relation to herself and to Annie and the life they'd had together. The realization that he might have a life just as real to him on the other side as their life together had been here shocked her. Maybe he had a wife, children, pets, the whole suburban nine yards.

"Nothing has changed in what I feel for you, Mira." Tom sat next to her, put his arm around her shoulders. "Nothing will ever change that. But your life here needs to move on." Then, more quietly, he added: "Sheppard is a good man, Mira."

"I know he's a good man. I don't need you to tell me that." *But that's not the point.*

"You're right. That's not the point," Dean said, apparently reading her mind. "We made a mistake doing this, Tom. It's not fair to her."

"I'll decide what's fair to me," she snapped. "So what's the favor?"

Dean paced across the living room, his movements like that of a cat, infinitely graceful—and restless. Tom now sat so close to her she could feel the heat of his body. Could you make love when you were in spirit? Could you feel that kind of desire? *Don't go there.* Right. Best not to think about the strangeness of it all or the possibility that she might be in a loony bin in the real world, strapped into a straitjacket, howling at the moon.

"In the same way that you need to move on with your life," Dean said, "people in my family need to move on with theirs."

And the second he said this, it all rushed back to her. Answering the cabin door. The babe with the gun. Her mad race to the barn. The shot that brought her down. She grabbed onto Tom's hand, clutching it as if to root herself, to keep her *here,* wherever here was. But the cabin flickered, blurred, flickered again, as though they were all inside a hologram that had begun to decay or dissolve, revealing the reality behind it.

"Dean, we're running out of time," Tom said.

"I'm asking you to allow yourself to be used as an intermediary," Dean said. "Your abilities will propel events in directions my sister hasn't foreseen. It's the only thing that might stop her. And in the end, this would bring closure for my family."

"You're asking me to bring closure for the woman who *shot* me?"

"I'm asking you to try to stop her so that the rest of my family can get on with their lives."

"And what kind of guarantees do I have that I won't die in the process?"

"None." No hesitation, no lies, just the blunt truth.

"Well, hey, that's comforting. And what kind of help can I get from you?"

"As much as we're able to offer."

"But basically I'm on my own?"

"I can't guarantee anything, Mira," said Dean. "The same rules still apply. We all have free will. You may consent to help, then change your mind, and that's fine. It's your choice."

"Are you in the market for a deal?" she asked, sitting forward.

"A deal?" He laughed, genuinely amused by this. "What about karma and good deeds and spiritual evolution? That's all part of this package, you know."

"I'm talking about one favor for another."

"That's kind of unorthodox, Mira," said Tom.

"And this isn't?" She ran her fingers through his hair again, memorizing the texture of it, the contour of bone and skin against her fingertips. "I want to see you one last time, Tom. When I can remember it."

Tom took her hand and brought it to his mouth and kissed her palm. "We can do that."

"Consider it done," Dean agreed.

Mira wrapped her arms around Tom and buried her face in the curve of his shoulder, and . . .

. . . Her body exploded with pain, her teeth chattered, she was burning up and freezing cold at the same time, and she shrieked, *"I changed my mind, I changed my mind. . . ."*

"Jesus, be quiet. I'm doing the best I can," a female voice said. "I had to stem the bleeding. And this is the second time I've had to stop. You're one tough lady to knock out. Now be still. I'm going to give you another shot. Do you understand what I'm saying?"

Say-ing, say-ing, say-ing. The words bounced against the inside of Mira's skull, amplified 5 million times, pulverizing her bones. "Help me, please. . . ."

And something sharp pricked her arm and everything went white and silent and she was gone.

2

Visibility was practically zero, I-26 was closed. Allie was now on yet another county road, a miserable two-laner that was getting her nowhere fast. She couldn't risk pulling into a parking lot or even a campground, not with Mira in the back of the Land Rover, and if she kept driving, she wouldn't be moving much over thirty miles an hour. This road would lead to another that eventually would get her to I-85, which would take her into northern Georgia, but for all she knew, I-85 was shut down, too. Static filled her radio, a frequent occurrence here in the mountains, so she couldn't even get a weather report.

Her best chance, she thought, was to find a place to pull

off similar to where she had stopped twice to tend to Mira, a dirt road deep in the woods. She had her sleeping bag with her, a cooler filled with food and water—how bad could it be? She would sleep for a few hours in the car and when the snow stopped, she would be on her way again. Her plan had a little flexibility built into it.

The main problem with this plan was Mira's injury. The longer it took to remove the bullet, the more likely it would be that infection would deepen and spread. Even with the antibiotic Allie had given her, Mira's immune system would continue to try to expel the invader. But she couldn't do anything about that now.

She slowed to twenty-five miles an hour, turned on her high beams, and leaned forward, eyeing the trees that lined her side of the road. The good news was that the trees were pines, so the foliage would offer additional protection. But the deeper you went into the woods in this part of the country, the greater the likelihood of meeting some backcountry hicks or neocon survivalist types who might consider a woman traveling alone to be fair game.

But she was armed and was a crack shot. Yeah, she certainly had proven that beyond a shadow of a doubt. Two through the forehead, one in the chest, the other through the back. But they had seen her, would have been able to describe her, what choice had she had?

None. No choice. Of course not. Sheppard hadn't left her any choice.

Allie slowed, pulled off onto the shoulder of the road, lowered her window. Snow blew into the car, into her face. She squinted, trying to gauge the distance between her and the woods. A hundred yards? One hundred fifty? But more than the distance, she worried about whether the snow out there was deep. With the wind blowing as it was, even four inches of snow could drift, and if the Rover got stuck, no telling when she would get out and Mira would die. And that wasn't in the pattern. In fact, the pattern included a beginning date, today, and an end date of January 1, 2004. She had to remain within that time frame. The pattern demanded it.

She raised the window, gulped from a water bottle, and debated this thorny issue, weighing the pros and cons. The wipers whipped back and forth, the metronomic rhythm lulling her into false complacency.

Decide, decide.

Lights flashed behind her. She lowered her window halfway, swiped her palm at the side mirror. An elemental horror filled her. A cop, where the hell had he come from? He was pulling up behind her, no siren, red lights flashing. The lights threw an eerie glow against the falling snow, so it looked as though it were snowing blood.

She glanced quickly around at Mira and reached back and pulled the blanket up over her face. Now only the top of her head showed. She didn't move. _My roommate. She's sleeping._ She plucked her gun from her purse and tucked it under her thigh, just in case. She slipped her license and registration out of her wallet, grabbed the map and spread it open against the steering wheel.

You're a doc, your license says so, relax, it'll be fine. You're lost, that's all.

She lowered her window all the way. More snow blew inside. The cop moved toward her as if against an inexorable force, and stopped next to the window, his trooper hat pulled down low over his forehead so the wind wouldn't whip it away. "License and registration, ma'am."

Allie passed them through the window. "I'm lost." Her heart hammered, a pulse beat hard at the side of her neck. "I'm trying to get to Atlanta."

He held a flashlight up to her license, glanced at her, at the registration, then passed both back through the window. "You got way off track, Dr. Hart. You're on sixty-four." He passed her license and registration back through the window, then shone his flashlight at her map. "May I? I'll trace your route to Atlanta."

Allie turned the map toward him, trying not to think about Mira, about what she would have to do to the cop if Mira suddenly came to. But the cop's death would be *Mira's* fault. He used a pen to trace her route to I-85 and Atlanta. The map flapped in the wind, snow fell across it and instantly melted.

"This road here," he said, tapping the map, "will take you into Highlands. There you turn south to Seneca, take a right, and drive until you see one twenty-three. That'll take you to the interstate. But if I were you, I'd stay in Highlands for the night. All the interstates are shut down on account of the storm, but should be open by sunrise."

"How far is Highlands?"

"Six, seven miles tops. I just came outta there awhile ago. Had to escort some lost tourists to the motel. Try the Holiday Inn. They still have rooms."

"Thanks. Thanks very much." She took her map, started to raise her window, but he shone his flashlight inside the car. "What's that?"

The beam brushed the top of Mira's head. Her heartbeat slammed into overdrive, she felt the shape of the gun against her thigh. "My roommate. We've been taking turns driving."

"She's one sound sleeper," he remarked.

"She was pretty beat. We've been driving since we left Maryland."

"Well, you take care, Dr. Hart."

"Count on it."

She raised her window, sat back, squeezed her eyes shut. *This wasn't in the pattern, either.*

Allie dropped the gun back into her purse and waited for the cop to pull back onto the road. She watched his lights in her rearview mirror, a smear of illumination against the back window. Mira stirred, muttered something, and fell silent again. The cop made a U-turn in the middle of the road and drove off in the opposite direction.

She turned onto the road again, her mind shrieking, over and over gain, *Not in the pattern, not in the pattern,* that same insipid voice making a racket worthy of a two-year-old. She shook her head, trying to silence it, and it finally shut up. Stopping anywhere was now out of the question. She would drive as long as she had to drive to get to where she was going.

And by the time the sun came up, she thought, she and Mira would be in a safe place and Sheppard would be waking up inside his nightmare.

5

Great, sweeping gusts of wind blew up the Coosa River and slammed into the Rover, making it shudder. Snow swirled in the beams of the headlights and the wipers whipped the stuff into sloppy half-moon drifts on the windshield. Visibility was about two feet, if that, and Allie had to lower her window to see the houses along Riverside Road. There weren't many on this stretch of it, perhaps five, each with two to three acres of land, and all of them hidden behind snow-draped pines.

Just ahead, she spotted her brother's blue-and-gold mailbox. She tapped the Rover's brakes and turned down the steep driveway. The headlights struck the gorgeous cedar A-frame, a place Keith had bought eight or nine years ago and which he used for a month or two during the summer. He also owned a place in Key West, a condo in Aspen, and, of course, the catamaran, where he spent most of his time. She had no idea where he was sailing at the moment and didn't really give a shit, as long as he stayed away from here.

She pulled up in front of the three-car garage and suddenly wondered what she would do if he was here. But the notion was ludicrous. Keith detested the cold. During the winter he was usually sailing around the Caribbean, the rich, irresponsible gringo playboy with his *chiquitas,* living the Jimmy Buffett life. Thirty-nine-years old, living off his trust fund, and he still didn't know what he wanted to be when he grew up.

From the glove compartment, she retrieved the garage door opener and house keys that Keith had sent her a couple of years ago. *If you ever want to get away from ER, stay at my place.* Generous, she thought, and figured the generosity mollified his guilt that he did absolutely nothing to share the responsibility for their father's affairs. In Keith's world, tending to an elderly parent was woman's work.

The garage was so huge it was large enough for the Rover, for the pale yellow refurbished VW bug, circa 1969, that Keith used when he was home—his stab at being an ordinary Joe; and the trailer and hitch she'd been storing here since Keith had left last summer. She drove in, lowered the garage door, and kept the headlights on until she found the light switch on the wall near the door. She unlocked the door to the house, propped it open with the cooler that held perishable groceries, then hurried inside.

The place was spacious, three thousand square feet of wood and glass, with tremendous picture windows that faced the river. Fortunately, the windows were covered by custom-made plantation shutters that would give her plenty of privacy. The living room looked as though it had been imported from some Latin American country—Mexican tile floors, Hispanic art on the brightly colored walls, and furnishings from Panama. She suspected that the plantation shutters also had come from Panama, Keith's favorite home away from home. The house was cold, so she turned on the heat to warm up the rooms until she could gather wood for the potbellied stove in the kitchen.

She fastened the chain on the front door and went into the hallway off the kitchen to unlock the door to the basement, where Mira would be staying. When she'd come up here to drop off the trailer, she also had prepared the basement. She had brought in bedroom furniture, installed blinds on the four small windows, and tinted the shatterproof glass. She had put in a small fridge, hooked up the sink so it now had hot and cold running water, and had removed everything that could possibly be used as a weapon. She had scrubbed down the adjoining bathroom and put fresh towels in the linen closet. Aromatic bars of soap scented the air with a touch of mint. It wasn't the Waldorf, but it would be comfortable enough for a few days. And when Keith returned, he would find his basement vastly improved.

The immediate problem, though, was that she needed a sterile area for the surgery. The best she could do was Keith's massage table, which she brought out from under the stairs, where the washer and dryer were. She set it up to the left of the bed, so that it would be close to the sink, and wiped it down with Lysol spray. She didn't have a surgical gown, but she had a clean white smock that would serve the same purpose, surgical bootees and gloves still sealed up in plastic. She would shower in the bathroom and put on the bootees and the smock in there. Although she didn't have an IV pole or any kind of IV drip, she had surgical instruments and plenty of drugs and bandages with her. She would have to use the floor lamp and Keith's desk lamp for light. None of this was ideal, but it would have to do.

Once the basement was set up the way she wanted it, Allie hustled back upstairs. She pushed the cooler over to the fridge, then made several trips back and forth from the Rover to the house, unloading everything except Mira. She piled her belongings and Mira's duffel bag at the foot of the stairs, removed her own shoes, but not her socks, and finally returned to the Rover to get Mira.

Allie lifted the rear door of the Rover and her breath

hitched in her chest. "Shit," she hissed. The bandage wrapped around Mira's thigh had soaked through with blood, her breath rattled as she breathed, and when Allie lifted her off the blanket, she could feel the raging heat of fever through her clothes. Massive infection, she thought.

She ran into the house with Mira in her arms and raced down the basement stairs. *I waited too long, should've done it hours ago, shitdamnfuck. . . .*

Mira groaned and twisted her head. Allie started down the steep basement steps, moving carefully so that she didn't trip. Fifteen steps. The third and eighth steps from the top creaked. The basement was thirty feet and eight inches long and twenty-two feet and three inches wide, but that didn't count the space under the stairs, where the utility room was. Each of the four windows measured one and a half feet wide by two and a half feet long. The glass in the windows was a foot thick and shatterproof. The bathroom was nine feet long and six feet wide. The flooring was decorative concrete and the walls down here were concrete and four feet thick. The basement was soundproof and virtually impenetrable. There was one way in and out, up the stairs and through the door at the top.

She knew everything there was to know about the basement and the house and even the property. She knew the quickest route into the nearest town, Prescott, four miles away, and had made it her business to know who lived in the houses closest to Keith's. She knew how long it would take to drive to her final destination, as long as the weather was good, and she even had an alternate route in the event that she needed it. She'd done her homework.

For a year now, gathering this kind of information and feeding it into The Plan had been her second job. In the event that Plan A looked as though it were doomed to failure, she had Plan B to fall back on. Granted, it wasn't as fully developed and detailed as the primary plan, but the main points were fleshed out and, if she had to, she could implement it quickly.

From the very beginning, Allie had understood that not everything would unfold according to the way she'd envisioned it; being an ER doc had taught her that. But she hadn't counted on Murphy's Law kicking in quite this early in the chain of events. It was like preparing for an appendectomy only to find when you got in there that the patient's body was riddled with cancer.

Still, this entire venture required her to be flexible, to change directions on a moment's notice, to make snap decisions, something she'd always done well in her professional life, but had avoided doing in her personal life. When you worked in ER fifty or sixty hours a week, she thought, then in your free time you craved solitude, peace, stability, and, most of all, predictability.

At the foot of the stairs, she worked the sock off her left foot with the toes of her right foot, then vice versa. She padded barefoot across the floor and set Mira on the massage table, now covered with a sheet and a large sterile pad. She scrubbed her hands at the small aluminum sink, then gave Mira a shot of Midazolam, just enough to knock her out completely for about thirty minutes.

For an anesthesia, she planned to use Ketalar, the marketing name for ketamine, a disassociative anesthetic used on both animals and humans. As a painkiller, it was a popular choice in dentistry and for pediatric burn patients. Its disassociative properties also made it popular on the street as a recreational drug and some users whom she'd treated in ER reported out-of-body and near-death experiences that they believed to be of a spiritual nature.

She cut off the left leg of Mira's jeans, just as she had done earlier with the right leg, then unzipped them and slipped them off. She deposited them in the trash can. So much blood. *Hurry,* she thought, and went into the bathroom.

The hot water was very hot and Allie stood under the scalding needles with her eyes shut. The heat relaxed her muscles and drove out her fatigue. She had taken a couple of amphetamine tablets shortly after her run-in with the state trooper and could still feel the edginess in her blood. She could live with it. In a sense, the last twenty-four hours had been like medical school—sleep was a luxury and your body learned to function on catnaps, an hour here, fifteen minutes there. Your brain and nervous system existed in a heightened, edgy, and myopic state of awareness.

She could do this.

She had to do this.

Mira would die only when *she* determined it was time. On January first. No sooner, no later.

She didn't use a towel to dry off. She ran her hands over her skin to get off the excess water, then sat on the edge of the tub and slipped on the white smock, the bootees. Only then did she let her feet touch the floor. At the sink she scrubbed up again, snapped on latex gloves. Then she returned to the main room.

No, the area wasn't sterile. Yes, bacteria were everywhere. But it was the best she could do under these circumstances. And Christ, truth be told, it was probably cleaner down here than any hospital.

She tried not to dwell on bacteria. She opened her med kit, filled a sterile glass jar with alcohol, and dropped each instrument into the jar. She took out a digital thermometer and touched it to the inside of Mira's ear. Her temperature was 103.8.

Fuck.

She prepared an injection of Ketalar and another of a

penicillin derivative. She worried about using the Ketalar on a woman who was allegedly psychic. Despite her extensive research, she hadn't been able to find any information on whether the physiology of psychics differed from that of normal people. About the only thing she'd discovered was that many of them seemed to be overweight and had health problems; Mira definitely wasn't overweight and from what Allie had been able to determine, she didn't have any chronic health problems.

She wasn't convinced the woman was psychic; she'd sure as hell missed the boat on her own situation. But given the newspaper accounts she had read, the stories she had heard from Mira's clients in Lauderdale, and the police records she'd gotten about the investigation that had brought her and Sheppard together, she had to at least consider the possibility.

The only inkling she'd gotten that Mira *might* be psychic had happened in the cabin in Asheville, when Mira had said, *You're a doctor.* But it was possible she'd figured that out based on the questions Allie had been asking her. Even so, she worried about the effects of the ketamine, that she was hours too late on this surgery, that the infection had gotten hold despite the antibiotics, that the rattle she'd heard in Mira's breathing spelled pneumonia. She worried that in addition to the bullet wound, she would need to deal with pneumonia and other infections, that Mira's entire system was collapsing.

She unwound the bandage from Mira's thigh and laid bare the bullet wound.

She wasn't sure when she became aware of the pounding upstairs or how long it had been going on. But she knew she had to investigate what the hell it was because it sounded as though it had a human source—someone slamming a fist against the front door.

Allie stripped off her gloves, tossed them in the trash, and raced into the bathroom. She grabbed a terrycloth robe off a hook on the door and flew up the stairs, taking them two at a time. Before she reached the front door, she realized two things: she still wore surgery bootees on her feet and light crept in through the slats in the plantation blinds.

She stripped off the bootees and stabbed her fingers through her hair, messing it up worse than it already was messed. She tied the robe at her waist, took a couple of deep breaths, and opened the door with the chain still on. A tall, muscular guy stood on the porch, hands jammed in the pockets of his parka, his cheeks ruddy from the cold.

"What is it?" she snapped.

"Sorry to bother you, ma'am. Is Keith Cunningham home?"

She was so tired that it took her a moment to remember that years ago her brother had changed his last name from Curry to Cunningham. "No. I'm his sister. Who're you?"

"Nick Whitford. I . . ."

She didn't hear the rest of what he said. Her tired brain flipped through its meticulous filing cabinets of information and came up with a very brief bio: Keith's neighbor, the guy who watched his house while he was gone. *Shit.* "Oh. Right. Keith's neighbor. Hold on." She shut the door, smoothed her hands over the robe, removed the chain, and opened the door again.

"I'm really sorry to bother you." He sounded sincerely apologetic. "But when I unlocked the door and found the chain on, I got a little worried because Keith isn't due back for a few months."

Be nice, be charming. You don't need trouble from this guy.
She stepped onto the porch and shut the door behind
her. "I'm Allie Hart, Mr. Whitford."

She extended her hand and he took it. She liked the
texture, the heat that radiated from the skin, the perfect
strength of his grip. In fact, she liked everything about
Whitford's appearance. He stood six feet or a bit over,
weighed about 180, she guessed, and had hair the color
of walnuts, with a neatly trimmed beard beginning to
gray. He held on to her hand a little longer than necessary and she realized that the chemistry she'd felt was
apparently mutual. She usually had had a visceral effect
on men; they either detested her on sight or were completely taken in by her looks.

"Sorry I was so rude," she said, folding her arms, hugging them to her chest. "I thought you were selling
something."

He laughed; Allie liked the way it lit up his eyes.

"I drove most of the night through that storm. I
thought Keith was going to be here." *Careful, don't say too
much.* "I should've known better. His schedule is never
predictable."

"My understanding is that he wouldn't be back until
the ice on the river is thawed. That usually happens in
late March or early April."

"That sounds like Keith. I haven't spoken to him since
Thanksgiving. I think he was around Virgin Gorda then."

"He checked in with me a couple days before Christmas. From Balboa, Panama."

She nodded. "That sounds about right. The Balboa
Yacht Club. That's one of his favorite spots. I'll give him
a call and have him call you, Mr. Whitford." She smiled
again. "Just so you know I'm his sister and not some
squatter."

Whitford's smile dispelled the gloomy morning light.

"He never mentioned having a sister, but you look like him—not the hair, but in the eyes and mouth."

Well, she didn't like that he saw similarities in their appearances, but what the hell. They were related, after all.

"Basically, I just make sure the house is sound, that the driveway is plowed, that the pipes don't freeze, that kind of thing. I've been plowing driveways, if you'd like me to do yours."

"That'd be great, thanks."

"And I left some wood for the stove at the side of the house. How long are you going to be around?"

"A couple of days. I'm just on my way home."

"Then I'll keep plowing and dropping wood by. You want me to keep picking up Keith's mail?"

"It's probably best that way."

"So where's home?"

She detested questions like this. "Macon," she lied.

"Pretty place."

You can go now. She began to feel a discomfiting pressure behind her eyes and a weight against her spine: Mira and her unfinished business inside the house. But she didn't want to be too abrupt and arouse his suspicion. "Is that your dog?" she asked, pointing down near the river.

He glanced back. "Yes."

"Rottweiler?"

"Rottweiler and shepherd mix."

"It's gorgeous." Gorgeous, except that Allie detested dogs.

"Bristol," he called, and whistled.

The dog, 130 or 140 pounds of solid muscle, trotted toward Whitford, tail wagging. But as he neared them, Bristol dropped to his haunches, bared his teeth, and emitted a menacing growl. "Hey," Whitford snapped. "No."

The dog looked up at Whitford, tail wagging again,

but eyed Allie with considerable wariness. *Bristol knows. He knows I've got a secret stashed in the basement.*

"Sorry. He usually doesn't act that way." He looked down at the dog. "Go to the car. Go on." Bristol wandered off, tail between his legs. "I don't know what's gotten into him."

It was what parents usually said when their toddlers ran wild through restaurants, airports, hospital corridors. She smiled politely, another moment of silence passed, then he said: "I bet you're cold. I'll get going on your driveway. Have a good day. If you need anything, my number's on the fridge."

"Thanks."

She opened the door and slipped quickly back into the house. She leaned into the door, fists balled against her chest, blood pounding in her ears. Mr. Nosy Neighbor, she thought. Good-looking, but a potential problem. He seemed to be the type who would drop by daily, asking if she needed anything or just to chat and pass the time. A lonely, nosy neighbor, the worst kind.

But he sure was nice to look at.

Nope. Not this trip. He's not in the pattern.

Allie put the chain back on the door and hurried back into the basement. She had finished stitching up the wound and had given Mira another injection of antibiotics. Now she put a dressing on her thigh and wrapped it. She made up the bed with clean sheets and a heavy blanket, and secured the restraints on either side of the bed. She didn't want Mira to try to walk when she came to and the restraints seemed to be the best alternative. She lowered the massage table until it was even with the bed, put on the brakes, and slid Mira onto the bed. Her patient murmured, groaned, and Allie put the restraints around her wrists and ankles.

By the time she cleaned up her instruments and

mopped the floor, she was so beat she could barely see straight. She still had to put away the food that was in the cooler and eventually would have to go into Prescott for groceries. But for now, she was finished down here. She took one last glance around the basement, turned off all the lights except for a couple of night-lights, then stumbled upstairs and locked the basement door.

As she emptied the cooler, she heard the drone of the plow outside. But the noise seemed distant, unconnected to her and her immediate affairs. As long as she didn't give Mr. Nosy Neighbor any reason to be suspicious of her, she would be able to stay here until Mira had healed enough to travel. She had planned on staying here, anyway, she reminded herself, so in that sense the overall Plan hadn't changed. Only details had been shifted around.

As soon as her head hit the pillow, she fell into a sleep like death.

6

Balboa, Panama

Keith Curry lay sprawled on the bunk in the cabin, his head throbbing to the steady, irritating beat of Latino music that poured out of his cell phone. The phone was on the bedside stand and he knew that if he rolled over to reach for it, the massive quantities of tequila and beer that he'd consumed last night would roll through his stomach and surge into his esophagus and he would puke. He kept hoping that whoever it was would give up and call back later. Or would give up and never call back.

The ringing finally stopped, but its phantom echo pounded inside Curry's skull. The cabin's AC clicked on and the blissfully cool air washed over his body, soothing his hangover. He wondered if he dared move enough to dig the bottle of aspirin out of the bedside drawer. Even if he mustered the courage to move, though, he would have to swallow the aspirin and he didn't think he could swallow anything right now. He had some papaya enzymes in that drawer and maybe if he chewed a couple of them and then went back to sleep for a while he would wake up nearly as good as new.

Still on his back, he inched to the left, careful not to move his head too suddenly. The boat rocked in the gentle Pacific swells, a sure sign that the tide was rising, and the contents of his stomach seemed to rock right along with it. He extended his left arm, got the drawer open, stuck his fingers inside. He couldn't see the contents of the drawer without raising his head and there were too many bottles inside to do it strictly by touch. He scooted slowly up against the pillows, raising himself inch by painful inch. The throb in his forehead tilted into his left temple and hammered relentlessly.

Finally he was sitting high enough to see into the drawer, but it was so jammed with shit that he couldn't distinguish one bottle from another. Angry, he swung his legs over the side of the bunk, jerked out the drawer, and turned it upside down on top of the bed. *Stuff* tumbled out: bottles, pens, pads of paper with phone numbers and e-mail addresses jotted on them, wads of dollar bills, a pair of pliers, a wrench, rubber bands and paper clips, an extra cord for the laptop, CDs . . . *Christ.* Everything that had no other home ended up in this drawer.

Curry pawed through the bottles, found the papaya enzymes and the aspirin, but by then it was too late. His stomach heaved and he leaped off the bed and ran for the head. He made it, but barely.

You sorry sack of shit. The voice of his old man always came to him at moments like this. *You're wasting your life.* And behind this came the voice of his sister: *You're such an incredible idiot.* Or: *Grow up, Keith, face it. You'll never amount to anything.*

Curry pushed to his feet and went over to the sink. He turned on the cold water, held a washcloth under it, then pressed it, dripping wet, against his face. He felt a little better afterward, and cupped water in his hands and sipped it, washing the sour taste out of his mouth. He found a bottle of papaya enzymes and Advil in the medicine cabinet and helped himself to half a dozen of the first and two of the last. They had become his staples in life, both of them remedies for hangovers.

He caught sight of himself in the mirror: vivid blue eyes that were—on better days than this—his best feature, blond hair that had grown a bit too long these past months, a blond beard that looked ragged, and a weathered face that carried a lot of emotional baggage. Born with good looks, health, and intelligence, he had abused all three with a kind of relentless determination, as though it were his mission in life.

"Welcome to another day in paradise," he muttered, and got into the shower, wondering exactly what day it was.

The curious thing about living in Panama was that he lost track of time here. It wasn't just the booze, although that helped, but that the entire country seemed to exist in a permanent warp where the passage of days held no more importance than the current government administration. Life bumped along, following the familiar grooves of cultural habits and patterns. Poverty and corruption flourished, cheap booze and even cheaper drugs flowed, boats entered and left the canal, and the Pacific tides rose and fell, marking off his life in twelve-hour periods.

He knew he'd met a new woman last night, that they'd done some serious drinking together, but he couldn't remember her name or her face or what had happened to her when he'd left downtown Panama City to return to the yacht club. He didn't have any idea how he'd gotten back here. Had she been American or something else? He couldn't remember that, either. Women came and went from his life with a regularity as predictable as the tides.

Most of them were nomads, like Curry, except that a few of them owned the boats on which they traveled. They usually worked on the vessels, hitching rides from

Europe and Asia and the States and ended up here in
Balboa while they waited for their turn to go through the
canal. Many were headed west to the Galápagos, Easter
Island, Australia, a route Curry had taken four or five
times. Others headed south for Brazil or east to the Ca-
nary Islands, the coast of Spain. They generally went
where it was warm and the living was easy.

Some came for that easy living, others were drawn by
the weather. But nearly all ended up here because of the
canal, a passage of fifty-one miles that took you from one
ocean to another in about ten hours and shortened your
voyage by about eight thousand miles.

Twelve years ago when he'd first sailed down here, a
gringo in his late twenties, he'd fallen in love with the
easy living. It was rather like a seductive woman who got
under your skin and into your blood. Now, it was simply
the country that he loved, the passion and warmth of the
people, the hot, sultry air filled with music, and, of
course, the proximity of the oceans.

The Balboa Yacht Club stood on the west side of the Pacific entrance to the Panama Canal, just south of the
Bridge of the Americas. North latitude 8 degrees 56 minutes, west longitude 79 degrees 33 minutes, for anyone
who cared. The place had changed considerably since
he'd first come here. Twelve years ago, the clubhouse,
restaurant, and the open-air bar never closed. It rocked
with music, noise, chaos, and people from all over the
world. Expatriate Americans sat around drinking tequilas
and cheap Panamanian beer, trading gossip and stories
and tales of paradise in Ecuador, Tahiti, New Zealand.

Much of the old life at the Balboa ended on February
18, 1999, when the clubhouse, bar, and restaurant had
burned to the ground. He'd been moored here that night
and had awakened around three in the morning by the
choking stink of smoke. The fire was so far along by then

that even the *bomberos*—the firemen—couldn't stop it. By the time the sun had risen, the place was nothing but a smoldering, blackened heap. Then, two years later, 9/11 had happened, just one more nail in the Balboa's coffin.

In the last several years, though, some of the old spirit had returned as travelers had taken to the sea again. The clubhouse, bar, and restaurant had been rebuilt and the number of boats that moored here increased every month. Curry, who lived here at least six months out of the year, was now considered an old-timer. He knew his way around the considerable bureaucracy, was rich, and spoke the language like a native. And he had plenty of government contacts who were always on the take for the almighty buck.

He supposed that was why he'd found a wad of money in the bedside stand. Bribes. At least once or twice a week, he bribed someone for something—a good table, faster laundry service, a new parking sticker for his VW, faster service on the boat, faster this, better that. Money got things done here.

As soon as he was dressed, he pocketed the bills, then went into the galley. It looked wrecked—beer bottles everywhere, ashtrays overflowing, someone's shorts and a bikini bathing suit top on the floor, dirty dishes stacked in the sink. Sticking upright in a plant was a large, fat spliff with a blackened tip that whispered, *Smoke me, Keith. C'mon, Keith, get a little high, start your day off right, and I promise I'll make you feel better.*

He plucked the joint out of the plant and set it inside a large conch shell in the window. Before he tackled the kitchen, he needed to eat something. A mango, he thought, and plucked out the largest and the ripest one from a basket on the counter. He peeled and ate it over the sink, delighting in the feel of the warm juice sliding down the inside of his arms.

His cell phone rang again. He washed off his hands and went into the cabin to answer it. Every time he got a call from the States, *Unknown caller* appeared in the window. There were only a handful of U.S. callers for Curry: his housekeeper in Key West, his sister in Savannah, a couple of women in various parts of the States, his stockbroker in Miami, a property manager in Aspen, the guy in northern Georgia who looked after his riverside home.

"It's hot and sticky in Panama this morning," he said as he answered his phone. "This is Keith."

The person on the other end laughed. "Well, it's colder than a witch's tit here in Prescott this morning. Hey, Keith, it's Nick Whitford. Can you hear me okay?"

Whitford owned the bed-and-breakfast half a mile upriver from Curry's place. For the last six years, he'd been taking care of homes along the river that were owned by part-timers like Curry. He picked up mail, plowed driveways, checked pipes, did whatever people asked him to do. It had turned into a nice sideline business for Whitford, especially in the winter, when business at his bed-and-breakfast was slow.

"Like you're next door, Nick. Don't tell me the damn pipes burst again."

"No, nothing like that. We had quite a bit of snow and I went over to your place early this morning to check the pipes and what all, but the chain was on the door. Turns out your sister's staying there. I just wanted to let you know. I think she's going to call you, too."

My sister? "Could you, uh, describe her, Nick?"

"Brunette, five foot eight, I'd guess, slender, reminds me of Catherine Zeta-Jones. Gorgeous, Keith. Absolutely gorgeous."

Shit. It's her. Curry hadn't spoken to Allie since . . . *when?* He couldn't remember. "How long's she been there?"

"She said she'd driven most of the night through the storm, so I guess she's been there since before sunrise."

Driven from where? For what? Alarms shrilled in his head. His sister never had taken him up on his open invitation to use the riverside house or his place in Key West when he wasn't there. This break in her patterns disturbed him. But then, she'd disturbed him for as long as he remembered.

"Did she say how long she's going to stay?"

"A few days. Is there a problem, Keith?"

Maybe. But not a problem Whitford could do anything about. "No, it's fine. But you should keep picking up my mail and plowing the driveway. Did you get the latest check?"

"I did, thanks."

"Listen, Nick. Let me know when she leaves. She's an ER doc, high-stress job, you know? She's probably burned out and won't do much of anything except sleep and relax."

That was a lie. His sister never relaxed. Even when she slept, Curry imagined that her mind churned, struggled, argued, fought, plotted, and strategized. When you mixed a classic type A personality with a compulsive-obsessive, it spelled control freak.

"Kind of check up on her, will you?" Curry asked.

"Sure thing. I'll check in on her tomorrow. So how's Panama treating you?"

Whitford always asked this question. It was part of his repertoire and had voyeuristic overtones, Curry supposed, since Whitford rarely went anywhere. His wife had died some years back, shortly after they'd bought the bed-and-breakfast. And a woman like Allie would chew this guy up for breakfast and spit out his remains without blinking. "The living's easy, Nick. Hot and easy. Is it still snowing?"

"It's stopped for now. But they're predicting another two inches tomorrow sometime, then a major cold front. We're going to have some power outages, for sure."

"Could you make sure Al has firewood?"

"I already put some by the side of the house. I didn't know you had a sister. You've never mentioned her."

"We've never been close."

"Yeah, I've got a sister like that," he said with a laugh. "But Allie is one beautiful woman, my friend."

Watch your step, Nick. "Yeah, she is. She's also tough as nails. Hey, I'll check in with you tomorrow."

"You take care, Keith."

After they disconnected, Curry tackled his kitchen with a vengeance, the conversation with Whitford eating away at him. He kept imagining Al in his house, cooking on the stove, using the washer and dryer, watching TV, relaxing—and nothing added up. His sister rarely cooked, didn't do her own wash, watched maybe one TV show a year. Aside from two failed marriages and occasional intense affairs with basically nice men like Whitford, her life was about work and responsibility. It was about the ER and tending to their father, and when their brothers and mother had been alive, it was tending to them as well.

When Al *tended*, when she was fully into her responsibility mode, she sought to control everything and everyone in much the same way that she probably controlled her ER. *Do this, do that, we're going here, going there.* And when people didn't comply, her face muscles tightened, her eyes darkened, the air around her seemed to crackle with static discharge. But that was just the surface stuff. Her need for control went deeper than that.

When he had decided to sell his business in Miami, Allie had grilled him about his plans. *Where're you going?*

What're you planning to do? Why're you leaving? What about the family?

Yeah, it always came back to that. The Family. As though the Currys were a kind of Mafia where bloodlines were everything. But from the time Curry had been very young, he'd never felt what she had about the Family. She was older than Curry by just two years, but the differences between them might as well have been two hundred years. Dean used to remark that Allie probably had been grown up at the age of four, with her life planned out, her career goals set, already prepared to assume the mantle of responsibility of their old man's brilliance.

No one lived up to his sister's expectations.

No one, not even their parents.

For a while, it looked as if Dean might be the one who would surpass Allie's expectations, but in the end he had broken away from the Family more radically and permanently than Curry himself. All Curry had done was change his last name to Cunningham—the name by which Nick Whitford knew him, and left the country.

None of this answered the central question: why was she at his place on the river?

And suddenly he snapped upright, jerked open a drawer, and went through the papers inside, searching for a calendar. The date, what the hell was the date?

He snatched up his cell phone and scrolled to the date: *Sunday, December 28.*

She said she'd driven most of the night through the storm, Whitford had remarked.

Yesterday was December 27, the thirteenth anniversary of Dean's sentencing.

Curry leaned back against the edge of the counter and knuckled his eyes. *She blew, she finally blew.*

And did what?

Ridiculous. She was stressed, ER had finally gotten to

her and she had taken some time off. Good, that was what she needed. But even as he thought this, an image surfaced in his memory of Allie a year ago Christmas, the last time Curry had seen her. They'd been sitting in their father's room at the nursing home, trading gifts, when she'd suddenly said, *In two days, it will be twelve years since Dean was sentenced.*

Dean the bean, their father had said, smiling stupidly.

Someone should pay for it. She said this with such vehemence, looking straight at Curry, that he'd been shocked into muteness.

Let it go, Al, Curry finally managed to say.

And Allie had exploded, accusing him of deserting Dean, of never visiting him, of fleeing the country right after the trial and divorcing himself from the entire family. It was all true. Every goddamn thing she'd said was true. But when he'd fled, he'd done so with the desperation of a man who had no other choice.

Hey, he was sorry the old man had lost his mind. But their relationship had sucked from day one. The old man never liked Curry very much because he was conceived after he and Curry's mother had separated, during a night of weakness and lust. But once Curry's mother was pregnant, his father had felt obligated to move back into the house and try to make a go of the marriage. Curry was a constant, thorny reminder of where the old man's life had diverged, where doors had slammed shut, where his options had shrunk.

Dean, born eight years later, had been the golden boy, a brightness in Bill Curry's life that had coincided with the FDA approval of a drug that he had developed that now saved millions of lives each year and fed the Curry family coffers. Little Ray, born eighteen years after Allie, was the late-life child, a shock, a surprise, and a delight to everyone—except Allie. *Why not Allie?* He didn't know.

Had never known. Maybe it was just the vast difference in their ages, or that Ray had been a reminder of her inability to conceive. One summer afternoon when Ray was just five, he had dived off a diving board in the family pool and had never come up.

That event, Curry knew, had marked the beginning of their mother's addition to pills, which had culminated in her suicide shortly before Dean's arrest. Now here they were, a disintegrated family, with just the old man, Allie, and himself left to remember. Except that the old man could barely remember who *he* was, much less who anyone else was. What the fuck, he thought. The Kennedys didn't have an exclusive on family tragedies.

So when Curry punched out his sister's cell number, he did so for many reasons—guilt, curiosity, and a morbid fear that she finally had cracked like a nut. But the bottom line was that the bonds of blood were the most difficult to sever.

"Dr. Hart."

Her voice sounded as though she were drugged or emerging from a place so far underwater that he would need gills to get there. "It's Keith."

"Oh. Hey. Keith."

"I just wanted to wish you a belated merry Christmas. Did you and Dad get the package I sent?"

"Yeah. We did. Thanks. We opened gifts on Christmas Eve. Did you get our package?"

Had he? He didn't remember. He couldn't even remember if he had celebrated Christmas. "Yes, thanks. I got a call from the guy who takes care of my place. He said you were staying for a couple of days. You okay?"

"I meant to call you. Sure, I'm okay. I just needed some time off from work. It gets nuts in the ER during the holidays. I hope it's all right. I mean, I had the key and the garage opener you sent and . . ."

"It's fine. I'm glad someone is using the place. Nick said he left you some wood for the stove. Did you find it?"

"I got in kind of late. I haven't been outside yet. I turned on the electric heat. I'll pay you for the utilities."

"Forget it. The heat needs to be used sometimes. So how's your love life these days, Al?"

"It sucks. How's yours?"

"The same."

She laughed, but it was a biting, caustic sound. "Oh, c'mon. All those gorgeous women passing through."

"More men than women."

"So now you're gay? Is that what you're saying?"

Curry rolled his eyes. For such a bright woman, his sister could be dense at times. "That's a statement about statistics, not about my sexuality."

"Maybe I should come down there for a visit."

"You'd find a job in a heartbeat. Doctors are in short supply."

"A job's not really the issue, though, not for the Currys."

Silence. The past ticked between them. "Why is that, do you think?" he said.

"The easy answer is because we have trust funds. The deeper answer is tough to find."

"Childhood stuff? We were ignored? We were pampered? We had to live up to a legend? We had a few tragedies? We never went to church?"

She laughed and this time it sounded genuine. "Church? What the hell does church have to do with anything?"

"*Church* is the wrong word. We never had a *spiritual* focus."

"Dean seemed to."

Yes, he did, but his spiritual focus had been so far *out there* that Curry had never understood what the hell Dean had believed—Buddhism, paganism, Spiritualism,

Taoism, New Age-ism . . . he had studied all the *isms*. And even now, Curry couldn't say for sure what this pastiche of spiritual searching had amounted to. "Dean was too young to know what the fuck he believed."

"And what do *you* believe, Keith?"

That my head aches, that I want to get off the phone, that maybe you haven't cracked up yet and I'm just paranoid. Or maybe you've cracked big time and you cover it well. "I believe in right now," he said. "What about you?"

"An eye for an eye, that's what I believe."

Uh-huh. Yeah. Great. What the hell did *that* mean? Was it evidence that she'd cracked? "So, how's Dad?"

The abrupt change in the conversation seemed to throw her. It was a moment before she replied. "About the same."

"Is there anything I can do for him? Audiobooks? A new TV? Music?"

The silence at the other end was thick enough to choke a giant. "He has everything he needs, Keith. He's well taken care of."

"For five grand a month, he should have naked women dancing in his apartment every night. He should have a fully equipped lab, a voice-activated computer, caretakers at his beck and call."

"I don't see you up here looking for alternatives." She sounded defensive now. Tight-lipped. Anal. "I don't see you making nursing-home visits."

"Hey, I've told you before, Allie, I'd be glad to bring him down here. He'd like it here."

"Yeah, right. He's in diapers, for Chrissake. Most of the time he can't feed himself. He couldn't live on a fucking boat."

"He's mobile, he loves the water, he loves to fish. He'd do fine."

"You're dreaming, Keith. You don't know the first thing about Alzheimer's. He cries all the time, he—"

"Of course he cries. *I'd* cry if I were living in an institution. *I'd* be on happy pills for depression. Jesus, Allie, medical science doesn't have all the answers."

The line bristled now with hostility, resentment, none of it new. "Look, a visit from you once in a while would do him wonders."

"He doesn't remember me, what's the point?"

When she spoke again, her voice could hurl the Sahara into the next Ice Age. "Let's not go there."

"Yeah, let's not," he snapped, and pressed the disconnect button.

It's not my business.

The instant the line went dead, he reached for the fat spliff, lit it, and smoked the entire thing.

7

1

The Stevens property covered twenty-five acres of rolling, snow-covered hills, most of it heavily wooded. To Sheppard, it seemed like a forest primeval, filled with dense shadows, unseen perils, and secrets hidden for centuries. The terrain was so utterly alien to what he was accustomed to that he doubted if he would recognize a lead even if it reared up and bit him on the nose.

He, Annie, King, and half a dozen local cops searched the woods for hours. They traipsed through the trees on foot, following the barking hounds, fanning out like a small army on the march. By the first hour, his feet had turned to blocks of ice. By the second hour, he knew it was hopeless. If Mira had escaped on foot, she was beyond his ability to help her. By the third hour, every instinct he possessed screamed that whoever had killed Jerry, Ramona, and the two farmhands had taken Mira—not on a whim, not randomly, but that the person had come specifically for her.

But why?

Every investigation always started there, with a motive. If you could figure out the motive, you could usually get a lead on the perp. But what could possibly constitute a motive for nabbing Mira? Her disappearance didn't qualify as a kidnapping. There had been no ransom requests, no notes left at the scene. Besides, she wasn't rich. But if you

Googled her name, dozens of links came up, many of them related to her bookstore and author events and the rest related to her work as a psychic. He supposed it was possible that some nutcase grabbed her because he wanted winning Lotto numbers or the name of the next hot stock or commodity, but that struck Sheppard as a real stretch.

The other possibility was much darker and something he didn't really want to contemplate—revenge, toward him. For the last twenty years, he had worked in some facet of law or law enforcement—as an attorney, a homicide detective with the Broward County Sheriff's Office, and two stints with the bureau. He had investigated hundreds of cases and worked alongside other cops and agents on hundreds of others. It wouldn't be a stretch to imagine that somewhere along the line he had pissed off a perp or a perp's family and that person now intended to make him pay for whatever he'd done. Payback definitely qualified as a motive.

A new wave of despair washed through him. Out of all these hundreds of cases, how the hell could he possibly narrow this down to a single case, within a time frame that would make a difference?

"Shep?"

He glanced down at Annie, who had fallen into step next to him, with Ricki, the Stevenses' retriever, close at her side. It looked as if the dog was staying here with them for the time being because Ricki had refused to leave with Tess's aunt, who had picked her up much earlier this morning. She had taken away the other two dogs and the helpers who had accompanied her would be moving the horses, goats, chickens, and cats by this evening.

"You tired?" he asked.

"I'm fed up," she said quietly. "Mom isn't here. We're wasting our time. We need to be doing something different to find her." She pulled off the knit cap she wore and her beautiful black hair sprang free. "We need a plan."

"I'm open to suggestions."

"Hey, you're the cop."

She sounded like her mother now. "But you're the psychic."

Tears welled in her eyes and she blinked them back and looked quickly down at the ground. She might sound like her mother, he thought, but she was a fourteen-year-old kid scared out of her wits.

"Yeah, right. I'm the *daughter* of a psychic, there's a difference."

"That's not what your mom says."

"You know what else she says, Shep? That if you're too close to something, you can't see it. That's how it is for us right now. For you as a cop, for me as the daughter of a psychic. Maybe Nadine will be able to pick up something." She paused and cocked her head, listening to the barks of the hounds echoing throughout the woods. "And I'm not going back with her. I'm staying here with you."

"Not a good idea, Annie."

She stopped and glared at him, a hand on her hip, her voice sharp, defensive. "Why the hell not?" Her breath was visible in the cold air. "I can help, you know. She's my mom. I'm connected to her. All that time when I was in—in . . . that room, back in . . ."

Back in 1968, he thought, and wondered why she couldn't say it.

". . . back a long time ago, I could *feel* her, I knew she was close by."

Sheppard felt her terror, her uncertainty, her helplessness. These emotions were his own as well. "I'd be constantly worried about you," he said. "I'd be trying to concentrate on the investigation, but I'd be worried about where you were and how—"

"What bullshit!" she exclaimed. "You're talking like I'm eight years old and that I'd be running around outside, making snowballs and getting into trouble. You think I'd be in the way."

"That's not true, Annie."

But even as he said it, he knew that it *was* true, that she'd hit it exactly. It showed in his face and he knew that she saw it. A sob exploded from her and she slapped her hands over her mouth and stumbled away from him, back through the woods, Ricki trotting along after her.

What's Annie going to think about our being engaged? Sheppard had asked Mira the night he'd given her the ring.

She'll be ecstatic.

And she had been.

But she wasn't now.

He stood there beneath a thicket of pines, hands jammed in the pockets of his jacket, and watched her receding figure in the shadows, against the backdrop of snow and barren trees. Christ, but he'd just made a mess of things.

"That looked unpleasant," remarked Kyle King as he strode toward Sheppard.

"I blew it."

"Easy to do with a teenager. I've got two of them. A boy and a girl. She'll get over it."

"She doesn't want to go back to Tango with her great-grandmother."

"You can't blame her for that. Her father's dead, her mother is missing. . . ." He shrugged. "In her shoes, I wouldn't budge."

"She'll be in the way."

"I doubt it. I think she'll do whatever you ask her to

do. Right now, you're the closest thing she has to a dad. What time does the flight get in?"

"Around three."

With both Nadine and John Gutierrez on it. Goot would be bringing case files; Nadine, he was sure, would bring anger—at him.

"Then that gives us about four hours. I just got word that the coroner arrived. Let's see what he can tell us."

"The autopsies are finished?"

"They were given priority, Shep. The Stevenses were well liked in Buncombe County. They were involved in the community. Every summer they hosted a fund-raising drive for the shelters in town—for the homeless, for battered women. Those two workers who were killed? They were here on a work-study program of some kind that the Stevenses had organized in conjunction with a local junior college."

Sheppard wasn't surprised by any of this. Jerry had been an idealist when they'd met more than twenty years ago and he apparently had held on to his ideals. So why, in Mira's scheme of things, would two people who were such forces of good in their community choose to die like this?

We choose it all, Shep. The circumstances into which we're born, our parents, even the way we die. . . .

But in his view of things, life—like death—was a wild card. Shit happened. Tragedies and triumphs were equally random. If free will existed, then it did so in very small doses. *Today I'll fill my car with gas at $2.87 a gallon. I'm going for a swim. I'll have a tuna fish sandwich for lunch.* Much of the time, life seemed to be one grand hurricane of indifference. If you got in the way, you were blown away. Jerry and Ramona had been in the wrong place at the wrong time.

He and King walked toward the house in silence, Sheppard blowing into his bare hands and wishing he were back on Tango Key, where the temperature was probably a solid eighty degrees, with a blistering wind blowing out of the east. King broke the silence first.

"Is there anything in Mira's life that would lend itself to a kidnapping?"

"No."

"How about in your own life, Shep?"

"In what sense?"

"A vendetta. Revenge. Someone just itching to get even."

Sheppard laughed. It had a cutting bite to it, that laugh, but at least the emotion that engendered it was genuine. "C'mon, you've been in this business long enough to know the answer to that."

King paused on the rear porch of the house. "Is there any particular investigation or arrest that springs to mind?"

"No, nothing. Nothing that stands out. But we're talking twenty years here. And that would mean the killer had been watching us, that he'd followed us up here from Florida, that he saw me leave with the kids."

"It would imply that he was watching from somewhere close by."

"There're plenty of places out there where he could hide." Sheppard opened his arms wide, the gesture taking in the entire twenty-five acres of woods and hills.

King ran his hand over his buzz cut. "Twenty-two years ago, I was a beat cop in Chapel Hill. We got a call that a big narcotics deal was going down in a warehouse outside of town. We were there, ready. There was a kid, sixteen maybe seventeen years old. He had a sawed-off shotgun and he pointed it at me. I can still see his face, Shep, the wild panic in his eyes. He was shouting, jabbing at the air with that shotgun, and adrenaline was pumping through me and I—I blew him away. Afterward, we discovered that the shotgun wasn't even loaded. The press had a field day and the kid's father promised that he would get me even if it took the rest of his life. I still look over my shoulder."

"There's nothing like that."

"Have you ever put away the wrong guy?"

"Probably. But again, no one particular case comes to mind."

It was a relief to get inside the house, where it was warmer. Sheppard stripped off his jacket and held his hands close to the wood-burning stove in the corner. Even if he'd wanted to, he couldn't avoid looking at the chalked silhouette of Jerry's body. His blood still stained the hardwood floor.

"A cleaning service is coming in today to scrub down the house," King said, noticing Sheppard's discomfort.

Two men came into the kitchen and King introduced them as the head of forensics, Vince Oglethorpe, and the coroner, Bruce Polsten, both of them MDs. Oglethorpe was short and plump, Polsten tall and thin, an Abbott and Costello team. The four of them settled at the wooden kitchen table, with Sheppard facing Jerry's silhouette.

Oglethorpe got right to the point. "We've got some preliminary results, Agent Sheppard, but I'm not sure how helpful any of it is going to be."

Sheppard had his notepad ready, his mini cassette recorder on. Although he had a good memory, he couldn't trust his memory now because—as Annie had pointed out—he was too close to this. "Anything you can tell me could be helpful." He needed information that would allow him to see the events as a series of sequential images, a kind of mental movie that he could slow down, speed up, or pause as needed. As Mira had pointed out a number of times, this information would feed into his left brain, then his right brain would use it to gain the larger picture of the perp's motives.

"It's impossible to determine who was killed first—the workmen or the Stevenses."

"The Stevenses and the guy in the barn were killed first," Sheppard said. "The man who survived long enough to talk said he heard three shots."

"Then the murders happened very close together, within five or ten minutes of each other," Oglethorpe went on. "But let's say, for the sake of speculation, that the Stevenses were first. It seems likely that Mrs. Stevens answered the front door—"

"Why does that seem likely?"

"Because of where she was found. She was obviously running up the stairs when she was shot in the back. We know she and her husband were waiting for you to get back from town with the girls, so perhaps she heard a car coming up the road, thought it was you, and opened the door to greet everyone."

"And Jerry would be in the kitchen at this time?"

"Right," said Polsten.

"I don't agree," Sheppard said. "I think Jerry answered the door and Ramona came down to see what was going on."

Polsten looked uncomfortable. "Yes, well. Mr. Stevens's stomach contents indicate that he'd snacked about five minutes before he died. An apple and some sort of bread. Mrs. Stevens hadn't eaten for at least three hours, probably since dinner."

"So either Jerry or Ramona opens the door thinking it's me and instead one or the other sees the killer."

"With a gun aimed at one of them. A nine millimeter," Polsten said. "They were both killed by nine-millimeter Parabellum bullets. Mrs. Stevens took two bullets, one that punctured her left lung and another that severed her spine."

It was the same ammo that Sheppard's 9mm P226 SIG Sauer used. Granted, nine millimeters were fairly common, but his antenna twitched. *Coincidence or intent?*

"Whoever answered the door sees the gun," King said, picking up the thread of the story now. "We think it was Ramona. She turns and races for the stairs and the killer shoots her. Jerry's in the kitchen and he hears it."

Oglethorpe nodded. "We think the door between the kitchen and the living room was shut. There's a gouge in the wall that corresponds exactly to where the knob hits when the door is open. If a full-grown man is exploding through the door and it slams against the wall, it would account for the hole in the plaster."

So Jerry heard Ramona shouting or heard shots and he hurled open the door and it slammed into the wall. . . . The movie ran in Sheppard's head now, following the sequence of events as Oglethorpe described them.

"He sees the intruder and throws up his hands to pat the air or to protect his face—"

It sounded like something Jerry would do. "How do you know?"

"In addition to the bullet through his head," Polsten said, "a bullet grazed the outside of his right wrist. The wound was consistent with what you would find if the hands were raised. He must have had his hands slightly to the right because that bullet grazed his wrist and took out a chunk of skin but missed the rest of his body. We found it in the doorjamb. He probably stumbled back, clutching his wrist, and the intruder shot him again when he was close to the refrigerator."

"What about the workmen?" Sheppard asked.

"Nine millimeter. Both of them."

"Were they shot in the barn?" Sheppard asked.

"The one you found in the tack room was definitely killed in there," Oglethorpe replied. "The other man was probably shot in the doorway of the barn and managed to stumble back a ways before he died."

"Wouldn't the horses have spooked, though? They were in the barn when we got back."

"They probably did," King said. "But the stall doors were locked and the black horse didn't get out until Tess had unlocked it."

"As you know," Oglethorpe went on, "there was no sign of a struggle in the cabin, no blood, and we picked up a lot of partial prints. The blood in the barn . . . I believe Agent King told you about that."

Right. The type A. Since Mira was the only type A on the property last night, the blood was probably hers. "Anything else?"

"Two things, actually," said Polsten. "There were two sets of tire tracks outside the cabin, up close to the trees—those from your van and those from an SUV. The Stevenses don't have an SUV, so it's likely the killer is driving one."

Hey, great, Sheppard thought. The killer and millions of other Americans.

Oglethorpe now spoke again. "Up where your van was parked last night, there were a lot of footprints. We got casts for them." He opened his briefcase now and removed two lightweight casts of shoes. "Try this on for size, Agent Sheppard."

Sheppard held it to the sole of his shoe; the fit was perfect. So this cast was from his footprints last night.

"Size eleven?" asked King.

"On the nose."

"What about this one, Kyle?" Oglethorpe passed him the second, smaller cast.

King took it, held it between his fingers. "Size nine or so. A shorter, lighter person."

Oglethorpe grinned. "Kyle's got a great eye for details like this. Male or female?"

"Tough call." King shook his head and handed the cast back to Oglethorpe. "Not enough detail in the cast."

"Blame the snow for that," Oglethorpe said. "We were lucky to get what we did."

"So, gentlemen," King said, pressing his palms to the table. "That leaves us with a few more details, but no motive."

"It's possible that Ms. Morales witnessed the murders," Polsten said, "and the killer took her because of that."

"Possible, but unlikely," King replied. "Why take a hostage? It would be easier to kill her."

Sheppard suddenly hated these men for discussing Mira in front of him as though she were just another victim. But as soon as he thought this, he realized they considered him a professional—in other words, a man who could detach from his emotions and do whatever had to be done. The door to his heart slammed shut.

Oglethorpe sat forward, his pudgy hands folded carefully on the table in front of him, the backs of them dimpled. His nails were cut neatly, trimly, and seemed inordinately clean, as though he sat around in the evenings picking at them with a nail file. "Had Ms. Morales ever met the Stevenses before?"

"No."

"Then what could possibly connect Ms. Morales with the Stevenses, Agent Sheppard?"

"Me," he replied.

2

Annie sat in the barn with Ricki, her legs crossed lotus style, her eyes shut, her breathing soft, even. She struggled to make her mind a blank, the way her mother and Nana Nadine had taught her. She had hay clutched in her right hand that she'd plucked from the barn floor where her mother's blood had been found. She hoped it would create a connection to her mom, but so far, nothing had happened.

Total silence. It scared her. Even in the worst of times, like when she had gone through the black water mass, she'd been able to connect at some level with her mother and vice versa. She didn't want to think about what that might mean and hoped it was because of the drug the paramedic had given her last night to calm her down. Drugs screwed up the psychic wires. So did trauma. It had to be that. She refused to accept any other explanation. Maybe when Nadine got here, they would try this together and boost each other's psychic signal.

Shut up, shut up. Blank your mind.

Gradually her mind became a white screen, but instead of providing information, it grew thick and heavy with dark shapes that she knew were corpses. Jerry's body. Ramona's.

A gust of cold wind blew into the barn, chilling her, and Annie's eyes snapped open. "Shit, shit, it's not working," she muttered, and tossed the handful of hay onto the floor.

A great wave of fear rose up inside her, tears rolled down her cheeks. Ricki whimpered and moved up closer to Annie, licking her face, trying to comfort her. She wrapped her arms around the dog's neck and buried her face in Ricki's silken fur, her shoulders heaving with muted sobs.

Distantly an owl hooted.

8

"Hey, can I hitch a ride into town?"

Keith Curry glanced over at the young woman who had opened the passenger door of his VW. A gringa knockout. Her thick blond hair blew in the wind and she caught it with one hand and pulled it to the side so it fell over her right shoulder. Her mouth was probably the most perfect mouth Curry had ever seen, neither too large nor too small, a seductive bow shape that begged to be touched, caressed, kissed. High cheekbones. Blue eyes large enough to swim in. Her skin was tan, but not burned, not abused, not the sort of skin that would look like a wrinkled prune in ten years. She hadn't been down here long, he thought.

She was thin, with curves in the right places. She wore a halter top, with a cotton shirt over it, a wise move in downtown Panama, where the Latino men figured that a gringa with her boobs hanging out was an open invitation. Instead of the usual short shorts that the boater women wore, this woman wore white Capri pants. Also smart. Not too much leg showing.

"Sure, hop in," he said.

And she did. She slid into the passenger seat with her large shoulder bag, a bag of laundry, and shut the door. He backed out of the parking space and turned out of the yacht club and headed toward downtown Panama City.

"You don't remember me, do you?" she asked.

He nearly laughed. At the moment he felt fortunate that he remembered how to shift the VW. The spliff he had smoked back on the boat had been Panamanian Red, so potent and yet so mellow that Curry would be perfectly content to sit on a bench somewhere and watch the sun make its solitary journey across the sky.

"Should I?"

"We talked last night."

And it hit him. This was the woman he had spent hours with at the bar last night, deep in conversation about Christ-knew-what. "The bar," he said.

"Good. Very good." She smiled. "But my name slipped away."

"My own name slipped away," he said with a laugh.

"The dope we smoked on your boat is what did it. I actually stood there watching people drop into Never-Never Land. One guy thought he was Peter Pan and tried to fly. He climbed onto the deck railing, spread his arms, and promptly fell into the water and sank. Someone had to dive in to keep him from drowning."

Curry had absolutely no recollection of this event. "Was I there when this happened?"

"Definitely. You were going to go in after him, but someone else grabbed your shirt and told you to forget it. Then this French woman opened up a bottle of wine and that was it for me. I left."

"We talked about Peru. About the Incas. Machu Picchu."

"Now it's coming back." She laughed and brought her beautiful bare feet up against the glove compartment. "You're Keith and I'm . . ."

"Faye. You're Faye. Let's see. I think you told me you

came up from Chile on the *Caleuche.*" The ghost ship of Chilean folklore permeated the culture of a mystical island called Chiloé, where the residents believed not only in ghost ships, but in mermaids. "You seemed surprised that I knew about the legend."

"Not too many Americans do."

"Right after nine/eleven. I just wanted to get as far south of the States as possible, so I went through the canal and sailed down the western coast of Chile. Chiloé was my last stop. I spent nearly two months there. I even went out to the bridge one night where there had been sightings of the *Caleuche,* hoping for a glimpse of it."

"You don't seem the type."

"I'm not." Ghosts and things that went bump in the night belonged to the world his younger brother had inhabited. But there was something about Chiloé's magic that had gotten under his skin. "When were you there?"

"Last year."

"So how did you *really* get to Panama?"

"American Airlines. I'm visiting a friend who's sailing to the Galápagos. I've been staying on his boat at the Balboa."

"And headed where?"

She shrugged and turned her head toward the open window. The wind blew through her magnificent hair again. "Nowhere. This is just time out."

"From?"

"Life."

It was the sort of answer that hinted at some personal tragedy or story, a rather common occurrence down here. She removed a joint from her shirt pocket, lit it, offered him a hit, but he shook his head. She stabbed it out in the ashtray and slipped it back into her pocket.

"I need to get back to the States, but all the flights are

booked because of the holidays, so I figured the least I can do is my laundry."

"Exactly where I'm headed," he said, admiring the perfect shape of her legs, her feet, her toes. He had never met a woman with prettier toes.

"Ever eaten at the Caribe?" she asked.

He shook his head. He'd gone drinking at the Caribe and had made a dozen deals at the bar, but no, he'd never eaten there. "Nope, never."

"My treat," she said.

What a switch, he thought. Most of the people with whom he ate lunch or dinner or had drinks expected him to pay.

As they entered the traffic nightmare that led into downtown, Curry downshifted and prepared himself for a considerable wait. The wait usually sent his blood pressure soaring. But today he was content to sit back in the company of a beautiful woman, pop a CD into the player, and let the cool air from the AC vents blow in his face.

They both kept their windows shut against the endless clouds of black smoke that spewed from the exhaust pipes of the cars around them. Most of the cars on Panamanian streets were old and battered, had no clean-air contraptions on the engines, didn't use unleaded gas. Horns blared constantly and no one bothered using blinkers. Cars scraped up against their neighbors or rammed into them from behind, but few drivers stopped. Insurance here was unknown, so as long as no one was hurt, why bother stopping? That only invited the police and trouble.

During the thirty minutes it took them to get into town, they talked about American music and books and movies, about countries they had visited and would like to visit, but neither of them got very personal. That was the boating way. *Don't get too close too quickly. Keep your heart shut up in the closet.* After all, the person you slept with tonight could be headed for New Zealand tomorrow.

He parked behind the *lavandería* that had been washing and ironing his clothes for twelve years and he and Faye went inside. The air here was hotter than it was outside, a steaming jungle of fabrics and plastic. A window AC unit clattered noisily, emitting a pathetic spray of cool air that the steam rapidly swallowed. A thin layer of condensation covered the counters, the windows, and the faces of the young women who greeted him as *Don Keith,* as though he were the gringo equivalent of Don Quixote.

Good to see you, Don Keith. Of course we can have your laundry done in an hour, Don Keith. And the young lady's, too? As always, he passed a generous tip to the laundry manager and to the teenage girl who actually ironed his clothes.

Once they were back on the street, walking to the Hotel Caribe, Faye remarked, *"Don* Keith. That means you're a big deal here."

"Only because I give good tips and I'm a regular."

"How long have you been here in Panama?"

"Off and on for twelve years."

"Twelve *years?* That makes you a genuine expat."

"Only for five or six months of the year."

"You don't have to work?"

What a loaded question, he thought. "I had a chartering business in Miami that I sold for a lot of money. Then I made some good investments during the dotcom boom." That was true, as far as it went, but he didn't add that his initial money came from a trust fund his old man had set up years ago. "What about you?"

"I invested five grand in Yahoo when it was in its infancy and sold it during the dot-com boom."

Good looks, brains, and what else? he wondered. "So what's next?"

She laughed. "Fun and adventure for now. In January I find out if I got a job I've applied for."

"A job with?"

She glanced at him and he saw twin reflections of himself in her sunglasses. "You ask a lot of questions, Keith. But you don't offer much information in return."

He shrugged. "Habit, I guess. What do you want to know, exactly?"

"It was just an observation."

They reached the Hotel Caribe and the doorman greeted them both as though they were celebrities. "Either this isn't your first trip to Panama or you come to the Caribe frequently," Curry said as they entered the hotel.

"Both. It's my third trip here."

The Caribe wasn't the largest, plushest, or most expensive hotel in Panama, but for pure Latino atmosphere, it was the best. Native artwork, most of it by the Cuna Indian tribe, hung on the walls. There were tapestries from Mexico and Guatemala and wooden carvings from Ecuador, Peru, and Colombia. Venezuelan music played softly in the background. Native plants burst from huge clay pots, and bougainvillea vines climbed the iron gratings that separated the lobby from the dining room and bar. Everything about the place invited intimacy. But as they sat at a softly lit corner table, Curry suddenly felt like a tongue-tied teenager on his first date.

The weed, he thought. Either he'd smoked too much of the stuff or it had something in it.

In fact, as a waiter came toward them, the entire room listed to the right, everything blurred, and he suddenly felt as though he couldn't pull enough air into his lungs. Voices, music, all the sound in the room faded, boomed, echoed, and pulsed. Violent tremors seized him, then wrapped around him, picking up speed and intensity until he heard a soft *pop*—and found himself high in a corner, somewhere near the ceiling, staring down at the table where a man and a woman sat. A second man brought drinks and a basket to the table. A small, ancient woman with a shawl over her head shuffled toward the table, her spine bent like a straw, so she moved huddled over, as if with a permanent deformity. She spoke to them, then leaned forward, looked closely at the man at the table, and raised her arm, pointing directly at the ceiling.

Curry heard another *pop* and suddenly he was back at the table, inside his body, shocked to realize the man he'd seen was himself. The ancient woman held his chin in a tight, uncomfortable grip. "*Now* he is with us," she said in Spanish, and slapped her thigh and emitted a laugh like a witch's cackle. "Too much loco weed, my friend," the old woman went on, easing her huddled body into a chair between Curry and Faye. "It does strange things to the mind, no?"

"Keith, this is Milagro, a very good friend of mine and something of a legend here in Panama."

"She lies," the old woman said now in heavily accented perfect English. "I am no legend. I am myth." She laughed again, a noise like lightning crackling through dry trees.

"Legend, myth, whatever," Faye said with a smile. "Among the locals, she's known as Soul Seer."

What a crock, Curry thought, the old woman's face fading in and out of focus. In a moment when he saw her clearly, he realized that her skin was a rich, deep black, like bitter chocolate, and that despite the apparent age of her body, her face was practically unlined. The shawl slipped off her head and her dreadlocks tumbled out. She wore very dark sunglasses and carried a cane. She was blind. He suddenly felt so uncomfortable in her presence that he barely stifled a powerful urge to leap up and run. It wasn't her blindness that bothered him, but the sensation that despite her blindness, she could see into the very center of his soul.

She pushed the glasses back onto the top of her head. Instead of dark pupils and irises, her eyes were a thick, milky white. "Horrifying, isn't it?" she whispered. "In the days in Haiti when Papa Doc was in power, the Tonton Macoute were tyrants. They burned my eyes because I refused to tell them what they wanted to hear." She leaned forward and touched her cool, thick-skinned hand to the back of Curry's hand, and he felt a kind of electric current racing through him, energizing him. "Now," she said, removing her hand, "we are connected, you and me." Then she began to speak in very rapid French, her sightless eyes turned on Curry's face.

Faye, leaning forward, hanging on the old woman's words, translated. "'We have before us a soul that in several recent incarnations struggled against domination by others. A primary purpose of this life is to gain independence from the very people who dominated him in the past. However, he has taken this purpose to extremes, shirking responsibility for his own actions. Innocent people already have died, and unless he does what is right, there will be more death. There are secrets here, deep secrets carried for many years that must be confronted if the soul is to move forward so that it can fulfill its enormous potential.

"'Two women, we see two women, one badly injured, the other powerful and vengeful. No names, we aren't permitted to see their names. Names are blocked from our sight. Death, vengeance, secrets. Quick. Quick. Choices must be made. A woman from the village of spirits will help unravel the final secrets. . . .'"

Curry snapped out of the horror that had paralyzed him and shot to his feet so fast that his chair toppled and crashed to the floor. He ran for the door, the inside of

his skull on fire and his legs moving of their own volition, carrying him toward fresh air, bright light, the
noise of traffic and humanity, away from the relentless
sound of the old woman's voice.

He exploded through the front door, collided with a
couple on the sidewalk, but didn't stop, didn't slow
down. He ran, his shoes slapping the pavement, until he
reached his VW. He threw himself inside, turned on the
engine, and sat there with his hands clenched against
the steering wheel, his eyes squeezed shut, the doors
locked, the air blowing against his face.

There are secrets here. . . .

Shit.

Someone should pay for it. . . .

His eyes snapped open, he pushed in the clutch,
shifted into first gear, and swerved out of the parking
space. He drove like a Panamanian, whipping through
traffic, squeezing between cars, tires slamming over
curbs and through potholes. By the time he reached the
Balboa, his thoughts were sliding through a well-oiled
groove, the same groove that was true now and forever
more: *It's not my business.*

9

1

Mira's eyes opened to a dim light and complete silence. She could turn her head, but her arms and legs were strapped down. Although her left leg came up an inch or so off the mattress, she nearly passed out from the agony in her right leg, which was also strapped down.

She screamed and it came out as a pathetic whimper, then a silly gasp, then a stifled sob. Bile surged in her throat and she knew that if it came up, she would drown in it, suffocate in her own vomit. Panicked, she managed to raise up just enough—and threw up all over herself. Then she collapsed against the mattress, her mouth tasting horribly sour, her body burning up. She squeezed her eyes shut against an assault of tears, certain that if she cried, her nose would clog up or the tears would drip down her throat, and she would choke.

"*Rose!*" she shrieked.

Footsteps, pounding somewhere above her. Mira lifted her head slightly, saw a flight of stairs on the other side of the room, geometric shapes of light spilling across it, and now someone tore down the stairs.

"Get me out of here," Mira shouted.

"Calm down, Christ, calm down."

Mira blinked and the wacko's face came into focus. "Whatever you're giving me makes me sick."

"It's probably from the anesthesia. I'll have to get some clean sheets."

"What anesthesia?"

"I had to put you out for surgery."

Surgery? My God, what did she do to me? "What the hell did you do to me?"

"You need to calm down or you're going to get sick again."

"Untie me. Un . . . What's *that?*" she demanded, eyeing an instrument in Allie's hand.

"A digital thermometer. You touch it just inside the ear. You've never seen one of these?"

Mira blinked again, saw the thermometer. *My eyes don't work, my legs don't work, my arms don't work. . . .* Her head dropped back on the pillow, she shut her eyes. Her chest felt as though it were filled with broken glass.

"I'm going to touch the thermometer to the inside of your ear," Allie said.

"I'm having trouble . . . breathing."

"Shit," Allie hissed, and quickly untied the straps that had been holding her arms down. "Look, I want you to sip this and swallow a couple of aspirin. I'll lift your head and—"

Mira's eyes snapped open. "Don't touch me. You've already done enough damage. Aspirin will make my stomach worse."

Allie stepped back. "I was going to lift your head so that you can take some Advil. It shouldn't bother your stomach. You've got a fever."

Advil. Fever. Right. Yes, Advil was a good idea. "How high's my fever?"

"High."

"How high?"

"Nearly a hundred and four."

Mira struggled to calm herself, to sound rational. But

she couldn't think straight, it hurt to breathe. All she wanted to do was curl up and go to sleep. "Just give me the Advil. I'll take it. And don't give me any more of what you gave me. It makes me sick."

"We already had this conversation. You got sick because of the anesthesia. But the antibiotic doesn't seem to be working, so I'm going to try something else."

She helped Mira sit up and handed her a bottle of cold water and a container of Advil. It looked like the real thing and so did the two tablets she shook into her hand. She swallowed the tablets with a sip of water, then capped it again and rolled the cool bottle over her face, her arms, not only because it felt so good but because she was trying to buy herself a little time. *Think, think.* Her mind stumbled along, struggling to piece together a plan, a move, an escape route, something, anything. Her arms were free, but her legs were still strapped to the bed, so it wasn't as if she could leap up and run for the door.

Allie removed the straps on Mira's left leg. "You need to keep that right leg immobile for a few more hours." Her nails brushed the skin on Mira's leg, but she couldn't pick up shit from fingernails.

"Who's Rose?" Allie asked.

"What?"

"When I came in, you were shrieking for Rose."

Rose, Rose. It seemed that she should know this name, but there wasn't any time to think about it. Allie was turning, saying something about food, that Mira should eat some solid food, and Mira saw an empty syringe on the bed stand. A voice inside of her head whispered, *Do it, do it, do it now!*

Her fingers closed around the syringe, then she lunged forward and sank the needle into the fleshy area between Allie's shoulder blades. She shrieked, her arms flew behind her head, hands grappling to reach it. She stumbled, lost her balance, and crashed into a tray on wheels. It flew back across the floor and Mira lurched forward, clawing at the strap that secured her right leg to the bed.

Her fingers fumbled, her fever raged, her vision blurred, her breath exploded from her mouth. The strap—white, thick, made out of some sturdy material—gave a little and she jerked her leg to the right, the left, the pain biting so deep that her peripheral vision darkened and she nearly passed out. Then her leg popped free and she swiveled her butt against the mattress and slammed her left foot against the bedside stand. It rolled back across the floor and struck Allie just as she was rising. She fell back into the wall and slumped to the floor.

Mira stood, weight on her left leg, her good leg, and grabbed onto the railing to steady herself. Stairs. She would get to the stairs, somehow get up those stairs and through the door and out of the house and to a car or to someplace where she could hide. *You will not pass out, you will not pass out, you will not . . .*

First step, second . . . *Don't look back. . . .* She gripped the railing with both hands and, dragging her leg behind her, pulled herself to the third step, the fourth. She wore a hospital gown and socks, her teeth chattered, she could barely see, her chest burned and ached with every breath she took. But the door was closer. She would get to that door. She could see the wall just beyond it. She could smell her freedom, smell . . .

A horrible weight fell against her, trapping her body against the stairs, smashing her injured thigh against the edge of a step. She felt the stitches popping and a hot rush of blood. Allie grabbed her by the hair and yanked her head back. In the seconds before she plunged a needle into Mira's neck, she saw her own body hanging from the branch of a gnarled tree like a bloody slab of beef, skin flayed, in long, precise strips.

2

Allie pulled the syringe out of Mira's arm, wrenched away from her, and sat heavily on the edge of a step. Her chest heaved, beads of perspiration tracked down the sides of her face. She looked at the spent syringe, at the drop of ketamine glistening at the tip of the needle, and hurled it across the room. She rubbed her hands over her face, the puncture between her shoulder blades stung. No telling what kind of bacteria rioted in there now. And had the needle gone deep enough to scrape against bone? Had it chipped a disk?

A wave of despair shuddered through her. How had she come to this? A nosy neighbor, a botched surgery, and four people dead. Until last night, her professional life had been about the Hippocratic oath. Heal, rescue, save. On the rare occasions when her father snapped out of the deep throes of the Alzheimer's that had governed his life for the last six years, he begged her to kill him. *Just gimme a shot, let me go.*

She'd never been able to do it—and yet she had killed four people because they had seen her—*they were witnesses*—they had been in the way. She'd had no other choice. She had shot a woman to stop her from escaping and had driven her into another state and fucked up the surgery to remove the bullet from her thigh and had given her the wrong antibiotics. Now infection raged through her body, and what probably had been a cold or the flu had turned into pneumonia.

But Mira hadn't left her any choice, either. When she'd been running last night, the only obvious way to stop her was to shoot her. What else could she have done?

Maybe it was time to shift into Plan B. But both plans required moving Mira. If she moved her, Mira would die. If she didn't move her right away, she would improve enough so that she could travel.

But why travel if she could kill her here just as easily?

Allie didn't want to kill her here. It wasn't in the pattern of either Plan A or B. In her head she could see the pattern, like a map of interconnected roads and highways, cities and towns, a grid, the topography of a new world, the world *Allie* had created. And in that world, Mira couldn't die here, in a home connected to Allie's family. She had to die in one of two possible locations.

In Plan A, Allie would take Mira to a wooded area in Cassadaga, near Spirit Lake, and hang from her an old live oak. In Plan B, Allie would take Mira to a now decaying farm in High Springs, Florida, where she and her family had lived at one time, and string her up on a tree she and her brothers used to climb. Both places held special connections to Dean and in either place she could take her scalpel to Mira's body with the precision of the surgeon she was.

Allie pressed the heels of her hand against her eyes and forced herself to breathe deeply—in, out, in, out, over and over again until she felt marginally calmer. She stood, reached down, turned Mira over. Heat radiated from her skin, her breathing sounded ragged, blood soaked the bandage around her thigh.

She's going to die before morning.

Unless Allie repaired the damage to her leg again and got her the right drugs.

But that would entail going into town with a prescription she had written. She could do that in this state, she was licensed here. But the town was small, just fifteen thousand people, and that meant the pharmacists would know the local docs, would know that she didn't belong.

But so what? She didn't intend to stay. As soon as Mira was strong enough to travel, they would leave.

Back off, back off, you're leaping, don't go there yet.

First things first: that was what her father used to tell her when he was still sane, before her mother had died, before, before . . .

Before Dean . . .

Before Ray . . .

Allie shook away the pervasive gloom that had invaded the basement and took hold of Mira's forearms. She heaved her upward against her own body and moved her dead weight down the stairs to the bed.

Once Allie had Mira back on the bed, she washed up, put on latex gloves, and removed the bandage from Mira's thigh. The stitches had torn. It took a while to pick out the ripped threads, cleanse the wound, and put in new stitches. She bandaged the wound again, removed the soiled hospital gown, and dressed Mira in one of Keith's flannel shirts. It would keep her warm, but make it easy for Allie to check the wound.

She stripped off the latex gloves, then strapped down both of Mira's arms and legs again. The restraints had frightened her, but if Mira moved around too much, if she tried to escape again, it would only prolong their stay here. Restraints were necessary.

Allie placed the intercom box near Mira's right hand so she could push a button when she needed to use the bedpan. Off came the top sheet, the only one with vomit on it. She replaced it with a fresh sheet and covered Mira with a thick, clean blanket.

Now. The mess. She had to clean up the huge mess. Everything disposable that was soiled with blood went into the garbage can. Later, she would remove the trash bag and take it to the dump. She put the soiled sheet and hospital gown into the washing machine under the staircase and started a wash. Then she moved everything away from the bed—the hospital tray, the nightstand, even the floor lamp. She used Clorox to mop the floor, washed her hands, and checked Mira's temp again. It had dropped a bit and would continue to do so for the next four hours. But as soon as the Advil began to wear off, the pneumonia would push her temp through the ceiling again.

She was tempted to give her another shot of ketamine to keep her sleeping through the night. Instead, she trusted nature to do its work, and turned her attention to her own problem.

The spot between her shoulder blades where Mira had stabbed her with the needle still ached and stung. Since she couldn't reach it to swab the area with Betadine, she swallowed a couple of Augmentin tablets to cover whatever nasties Mira's body fluids might contain.

What else? Have I forgotten anything?

She looked slowly around. The bed where Mira lay was off to the left side of the stairs, and a chest of drawers with a lamp stood nearby. On the other side of the room was a sitting area—futon, coffee table, entertainment center, even a PC and a printer. She had long since uninstalled the Internet software from the computer, so that wouldn't be a problem. Keith also had an office upstairs that was much grander. Why a man who didn't work needed two offices was beyond her, just one more incomprehensible detail about her brother.

Allie decided she had done everything she could do, and turned off the overhead light. There. Much better. The glow of the floor lamp in the corner funneled light up the wall toward the ceiling, where it spread like pale, melted butter.

"Sleep tight," Allie said softly, then hurried up the stairs and locked the basement door behind her.

Moments later, she stood in the darkened kitchen, hands balled against her chest, trying to still the panic that fluttered in her chest like some small, trapped bird. Her head ached, she was starving, she could smell Mira's blood on herself. She wanted to go upstairs and shower and fall into bed. But if she did that now, Mira would be dead by morning.

Change clothes and get moving.

The town of Prescott, Georgia, lay four miles northwest of Keith's home and the river. She remembered coming here once years ago, long before the events that had clearly marked her life into "Before" and "After." It had been a family vacation, Mom and Dad and her two brothers driving forever in the camper. The five of them, that perfect number. Ray hadn't come along yet, so she must have been around fifteen, Keith had been thirteen, and Dean had been five. They had settled in a campsite on the other side of the river that had long since been replaced by expensive homes.

Back in those days, the campers didn't have satellite dishes and the TV reception was filled with static when it came through at all. So Allie and her two brothers had spent their days rafting on the river or swimming in a shrouded lagoon they had found farther downstream. Her memories of that summer vacation seemed idyllic to her now and she wondered if Keith felt the same way. It was the only explanation for why he had built his expensive retreat here rather than on St. Bart's or Saba or on one of the other exotic Caribbean islands that he visited so frequently.

She followed the two-lane road into town, relieved that it had been plowed, but dismayed by the temperature displayed in the digital window just above her head:

19 F. Although it was supposed to warm up into the low thirties tomorrow, snow was predicted. How much snow? How long would it snow? The cold front from Canada was definitely pushing southward, but due to prevailing winds at higher altitudes, no one could say for sure how far south it would push. So here she was, on the night of December 28, with a January 1 deadline staring back at her from the future, and she couldn't say with any certainty whether she would make it.

No. She would make it. One way or another, she would get to Cassadaga or to High Springs by her deadline.

Leave now. Tonight. It was a lovely thought, but she knew Mira wouldn't survive the trip. Even if she did, Allie hadn't finished outfitting the trailer yet and hadn't picked the campground. Best to stay put until December 31, then drive like hell.

Prescott still looked as it had thirty years ago, like a throwback to the 1950s. The main street was more than 130 feet wide and lined by businesses and shops that were, even now, mostly family owned. She supposed that when you were born in Prescott, you lived and died here as well.

The brick courthouse that she now passed, a designated historic landmark, had been built in the early 1800s and was still in use. It shared the block with another landmark, the Prescott train depot, circa 1836. Some years back, it had been converted into a restaurant and a local-history museum. Five or six years ago, when she and her second husband, Steve, were still getting along, they had come up here for a long weekend.

As a history professor, he was fascinated by old towns and had insisted on eating in the depot restaurant and going through the museum. Allie found most American history boring, but the Mound Builders who had occupied this land more than a thousand years ago intrigued her.

They were known for their advanced agricultural techniques and she believed that they, like the Maya and the Incas, had known a great deal about medicinal herbs.

She had traveled to many countries in search of information on medicinal herbs and now had an impressive library of information on the subject. At her home on Tybee Island, she had one large, sunlit room where she grew herbs. She often used them on herself—as immune boosters, for energy—and had experimented on her father, hoping that some combination of herbs would arrest the progress of his Alzheimer's. She had at least two herbs in her arsenal that would work more efficiently on Mira's pneumonia than any drug. But since she hadn't anticipated pneumonia as a complication to her little mission, she hadn't brought any herbs, so here she was, pulling up in front of Calvin's Drugstore.

Allie drew a brush through her dark hair, put on lipstick, and pulled her prescription pad out of her purse. She quickly wrote out a prescription to herself for amoxycillin. One dose of it would have saved the life of Muppet creator Jim Henson, she thought, and Mira would get much more than that.

The inside of the drugstore looked like any Walgreens or Eckerd at home, with one exception: the lunch counter along the far wall had red and black twirling stools that had dated back to *Leave It to Beaver.* An overweight man was the only customer.

Allie walked over to the pharmacy window and a dour-looking man said, "May I help you?"

"I'd like to fill this." She handed him the prescription.

He looked at it, at her. "You on our computer?"

"No, I'm not."

He looked up at the clock on the wall, one of the large, round, ugly clocks that Allie associated with elementary school. The hands stood at 9:15. "Don't know if I can fill it before we close."

Allie glanced around. "But I'm the only customer."

"Reckon so, ma'am, but it takes time to get you entered in the computer and all and to clear the prescription through your insurance company and—"

"Then I won't go through my insurance company." She brought out her medical license and her driver's license and set them on the counter. "I'm the physician and the patient. I've got a terrible sinus infection."

He poked at his glasses and frowned as though this were the most unusual request of his entire career. He glanced from her photo to her face, then back at the medical license. "You're from Tybee."

"Right."

"But you're in Prescott."

She was ready to strangle this idiot. "And I'm on my way to New York, but won't get there without something for this sinus infection."

"Uh-huh." He looked again at the clock on the wall. "Reckon I can fill this before we close. Give me five minutes, Dr. Hart."

"Thanks." *Moron.*

Behind her, the lights blinked once, twice, a signal that the store was about to close. *Hurry up, hurry up.* The pharmacy phone rang and the man answered it. The lights blinked again. The fat man who had been at the counter now shuffled up next to her and said, "Ma'am, we're about to close." He had a name tag on his shirt that identified him as the store manager. *Shit shit shit.*

"I'll just be a minute. He's filling my prescription."

"Jobie, you goin' to be able to finish that script in the next two minutes?" the manager called. "I need to get home on time tonight. The wife's been spittin' bullets about these late nights."

Spare me morons with no social skills, no public-relations skills, and minimal intelligence. I will not scream. I will not act in a way that will cause him to remember me. I will stand here quietly, waiting.

"One minute, Carl," the pharmacist called back. "I'll be done in a minute."

The manager smiled at Allie, his fat cheeks dimpling in the corners of his mouth. "We close promptly at nine-thirty every evening, ma'am."

He's a postal employee in disguise. "Right," she murmured.

"We just can't have people sailing in here at the last minute every night and expecting us to remain open."

"I understand." *One more word outta you, fatso, and that's it. I lose it.*

"Here you go, Dr. Hart." The pharmacist handed her the medication. "Do you have any questions about it?" Then he laughed at his own snafu. "Well, no, of course you don't. That's $7.80."

She handed him a ten and he rang up the sale. But as the cash drawer popped open, he sighed. "I don't have enough change."

"That's fine. Keep the change."

She picked up the bag and practically ran toward the door. The fat manager opened it for her. "Our hours are eight A.M. to nine-thirty P.M., ma'am."

She stopped, turned, and stared at him so long that he blinked repeatedly. "Let me give you a piece of advice, my friend. You're badly in need of public-relations skills. The people who come in here are the ones who keep you employed. I'm calling your boss to file a complaint about the way I was treated here. And then let's see what kind of bullets your wife spits when you lose your god-damn job. Have a great night."

With that, she walked out into the cold, empty street, feeling so incredibly good, so wonderfully optimistic, so perfectly in control, that she laughed out loud.

10

1

Mira's grandmother, Nadine, sat on the living-room floor across from Sheppard, her salt-and-pepper hair tumbling over her shoulders, her slender legs folded in a perfect lotus position. She turned the pages in one of the files that John "Goot" Gutierrez had brought with him, one of Sheppard's old cases—hell, they were all his old cases. The rustle of the pages and the hiss and snap of logs in the stove were the only sounds in the room. Annie had fallen asleep on the couch next to Ricki the dog, Goot had run into town for some groceries, and Kyle King had left earlier.

Nadine hadn't said much of anything since Sheppard had picked her and Goot up at the airport. Even though she had hugged him hello, it had been an obligatory hug, that of a woman toward the man to whom her grand-daughter was now engaged. Sheppard knew that in Nadine's eyes, he always would be the bastard gringo step-son. Yes, he enjoyed moments of reprieve, moments when Nadine accepted him fully. Those moments, though, were few and far between and he suspected that from here on in, those moments were history. She was pissed and he knew that, sooner or later, she would let him have it. Might as well get it out of the way, he thought.

"Stop blaming me," he said suddenly.

Nadine raised her head, removed her half-moon–shaped glasses, and glared at him. Fire poured into her dark eyes and she leaned forward, elbows resting against her knees. When she spoke, her voice was sharp enough to cut diamonds. "You and your macho world, your world of guns and supposed justice are responsible for this, Shep. Some . . . some *loco* has taken Mira and it all comes back to this." She waved the file in the air, papers spilling out of it, then slapped it against the floor and rose in a single, fluid motion. "Your world disgusts me," she spat, and went into the kitchen.

Sheppard squeezed the bridge of his nose and dropped his head back against the cushion of the chair behind him. He rubbed the aching muscles in his neck and thought back to the first time he had met Nadine. Lauderdale, the bookstore she and Mira owned. He had gone there looking for information about a deck of tarot cards, leads in a murder investigation that ultimately had involved Mira. In those days, Nadine's hair had been cut short and she had limped slightly from a broken hip some months earlier. Even then, she hadn't looked her age, had taught yoga, been a full-fledged vegetarian, and had deplored violence of any kind. Even then, she had radiated a mysterious presence, as if she saw and understood things that no one else did.

She had lived in the apartment above the bookstore, a woman alone with her mystical inclinations and her prodigious talent. She had outlived two husbands, most of her five children, and was closest then—as now—to her eldest granddaughter. Her roots were Cuban and her spiritual beliefs were an amalgam of Buddhism and paganism. She claimed that her intuitive abilities had waned with age, but Sheppard knew otherwise. When she was plugged in, she was nearly as good as Mira.

He pushed to his feet and joined her in the kitchen.

She was sitting at the small wooden table and stared out the window at the falling snow. Sheppard helped himself to beer from the fridge, sat in the chair opposite Nadine, and turned the cap on the bottle of Coors. "Every year, Nadine, crime in this country accounts for more death, injuries, and loss of property than all the natural disasters combined."

Her eyes met his. He had her attention, but not much else.

"Annually thirteen million people are victims of crime. That amounts to about five percent of the population. Of these, a million and a half to two million are victims of violent crime. Rape, murder, assault, kidnapping. I don't create these statistics. These are facts."

She raised a bottle of cold water to her mouth, sipped, set it down. "Violence attracts violence. There's no other law, Shep. You live by a violent code. Every cop does."

"It's not that simple and you know it."

"I'm not saying it's simple. I'm saying that we create change a step at a time, one person at a time, one set of beliefs at a time. In my ideal vision of the world, everyone has access to the necessities—food, shelter, education, medical care, the pursuit of happiness, and prosperity. Give people those things, and your statistics shrink dramatically. I'm not saying that crime vanishes overnight, but that the motive for crime is drastically diminished. As beliefs change, experience changes."

"None of that eradicates revenge, Nadine. Or crimes of passion. Or greed."

She cupped the bottle in both hands and shook her head. "Revenge is born of a festering wound. If the system is changed, there are no wounds because there are no injustices. Crimes of passion are born of anger and greed. If people have equal access to the necessities, anger and greed become practically nonexistent. You're a cog in the wheel, Shep. So is Goot. Find another line of work, something that feeds into a vision of potential rather than a vision of cause and effect—and your life will change." She paused. "And so will Mira's because of her feelings for you."

Sheppard sat back, disgusted, angered, offended. "The world hasn't caught up to your vision, Nadine. Politics is corrupt, we have a president who stole the election, we're now a colonial power that invades sovereign nations for oil profits and lies about what they're actually doing, and we have a nation still so traumatized by nine/eleven that they're terrified of speaking out. The Bill of Rights has gone south, three million people have lost their jobs, we have racial profiling, and every neighbor has become a suspect. So don't talk to me about utopias, okay?"

She smiled. "A rebel in the bureau's midst. You'd best keep your political views to yourself, Shep. Or you'll find yourself railroaded out of a job."

"It won't be the first time." In 1992, after Hurricane Andrew, his letter of resignation to the bureau detailing what he'd seen and experienced in the aftermath of the hurricane's devastation, had prompted a visit from Department of Defense officials. They had told him he was suffering from posttraumatic stress and that he could seek treatment at the government's expense. Sheppard had gotten the message, all right, and had fled the country with his secrets about the true horrors of Andrew.

"Look, I didn't come here to argue about the differences in our worldview. But I'll tell you this. Mira is gone because of choices *you* made in the past. This is about *you*, not her. She's just a pawn. And that's what you need to be looking for. Who hates you enough to try to hurt you through her?"

Just then, the door opened and snow and wind blew inside as Goot returned with bags of groceries. He kicked the door shut and hurried in, griping about the cold, the snow, the whole weather mess outside. "That road up here is so slippery now, I'm lucky the van made it."

He set the groceries on the counter and proceeded to put them away. If he noticed the tension in the room, he didn't comment. Sheppard and Nadine sat there a moment longer, eyes locked in mortal combat, then she pushed away from the table and got up.

"Juanito, you complain too much," she muttered, and headed down the hall. "Tomorrow we need to organize this effort. I'm going to bed."

As she left, Sheppard said, "She's right. We need lists—names, places, years. We need a systematic way of sifting through all these cases."

"I'm with you, amigo. But right this second, I need food. I need Cuban coffee. I need *arepas,* black beans, and rice. How about you?"

"I need sleep." Sheppard put a couple more logs in the stove and weaved down the hall to the bedroom where, twenty-four hours ago, he and Mira had been making love when the Stevenses' arrival interrupted them.

2

Allie drove slowly along the icy road out of town, wishing that she hadn't stopped for groceries. She had gone into an all-night Kroger and been shocked to find a long line of shoppers at the only register that was open. Most of them seemed to be buying booze and staples, perhaps stocking up for the next storm. She probably had gone overboard on the food, but better to do it at night, on the outskirts of town, than in downtown Prescott during the day. This way, she wouldn't have to go into town again before she headed south.

As she turned down Riverside, the headlights impaled a man walking at a brisk pace along the side of the road. Nick Whitford. She wanted to believe that she was slowing down because it would be too *un*neighborly not to stop; nothing aroused suspicion faster in a small town than an unfriendly stranger. But the truth was that she was attracted to Whitford.

Allie drew alongside him and he glanced up and waved. She lowered her window. "It's awfully cold out, Mr. Whitford. You want a ride back to your place?"

"I'd love one. Thanks."

He hurried around to the passenger side and ducked as he got in. He immediately pulled off his gloves and blew into his hands. "I certainly appreciate this, Dr. Hart."

"Allie."

He smiled at that. "And I'm Nick."

"How'd you know I'm a doctor?" She didn't recall telling him that.

"Keith mentioned it."

Of course he would. But she wondered in what context he'd mentioned it. "He said he'd spoken to you." There. That just let him know that she, too, had spoken to her brother. "Which way is your place?"

"Oh, that's right. You don't know where I live. You need to make a U-turn. I'm about half a mile east." He held his hands up to the heat that blew out of the vents. "I was chasing whatever got into my garbage, trying to get a good look at it. I lost it in the trees and didn't realize I'd come so far."

"Was it a raccoon?"

"That's what I thought at first. But this looked like a bear cub. That's when I decided I'd better give it up. Wherever there's a cub, there's a mother bear."

"*Bears?* Around here?"

"I spotted one a couple years back, a full-grown brown bear on the other side of the river. But it's rare."

"I thought bears hibernated during the winter."

"They do, but they come out from time to time. Could be that the mother or the cub or both of them are sick. Could be haywire weather patterns that drove them out." He shrugged. "No telling. Did you find the firewood I left at the side of the house?"

"I did, thanks. It beats electric heat."

"Cheaper, too. I'll drop some more wood off tomorrow morning."

She didn't want him just dropping by. "You don't need to make a special trip."

"It's not a special trip. I drop off bundles of wood a couple times a week at certain houses along the river."

"I can pick mine up now. I actually need it tonight, what with this cold front."

"Well, it's bundled and ready to go. I'm up here on the right."

She slowed and turned into a long, curving driveway that led to a two-story Victorian house. A floodlight on the lawn illuminated a sign that read, NICK'S BED & BREAKFAST. "This is gorgeous," she said.

"Business booms in the spring and summer and isn't too shabby in the fall. But as soon as the temperature drops, the place is dead. My wife and I bought it seven years ago. She died a year later. It's really too big for me to run by myself, but I've gotten rather fond of life up here. Park in front of the garage. That's where I keep the wood."

A widower. Lonely. Nosy. *Back off, back off.* The spot where Mira had stabbed her began to ache and throb, a reminder that she should stick to the plan, that she needed to get back to Keith's so that she could give Mira her first dose of amoxycillin. She stopped in front of the garage and they both got out.

Wind whipped off the river and whistled through the eaves. She zipped up her leather jacket and followed Whitford into the garage. Bundles of wood were stacked against the wall closest to the ATV. "How many do you want?" he asked.

"How many can you spare?"

"You can have the lot if you smile."

It was an unexpected remark and such an obvious come-on that she laughed. Her laughter sounded as self-conscious as she felt. "Better?"

He grinned. "You won the lot."

She laughed again and went over to stand against the stack of wood, holding the bundles in place as he reached for the top two. Barking erupted inside the house and Whitford's monster dog suddenly exploded through the lower half of the door, a pet door, and went straight for Allie. Whitford dropped the wood to grab the dog's collar, Allie wrenched back, and then the pile of wood was on the move and crashed to the floor of the garage.

In her haste to get out of the way of the tumbling wood, Allie stumbled and fell back into the ATV. She landed hard against the front seat, air rushed from her lungs, and for seconds she lay there, unable to draw a breath, to pull air in, panic shrieking inside her. It seemed that her vision dimmed, that her brain turned to mush, that her hearing began to fade. Whitford grabbed her hands and pulled her up, out of the ATV and to her feet, and she sucked desperately at the air, pulling it deeply into her aching lungs.

"Are you okay?"

"I—I . . ."

Whitford held on to her shoulders, his body so close to hers that she could smell the wood on his hands, the distinctly masculine scent of his skin. She heard the dog's wild, frantic barks inside the house and noticed that the glass storm door was now shut, preventing the pet door from swinging open. And then they were pressed together, hip to hip, mouth to mouth, their hands roaming, hungry, desperate. Something happened deep inside her body, she felt it, the violent shifting of a tectonic plate that released a volcanic eruption of desire. It seared through her like some white-hot flame, purging her of every other thought, desire, need.

They fell back against the front of the ATV, his fingers struggling with the zipper on her jeans, her hands yanking on his belt. He grabbed her by the shoulders, pulling her up, his mouth crushing hers again, and they moved like awkward dancers toward his truck. Her skin burned from the inside out. Her breath exploded softly against his mouth, his neck.

She tore open his shirt, the buttons popped off. He rolled her jeans down over her hips, discovered she wore no panties, and drove his fingers up inside her. Her pleasure didn't build slowly; it burst through her like fireworks, burning new afferent pathways in her brain, wiping away memory, sound, sight, obliterating everything except the need for more. She ground her hips against the exquisite pressure and her back arched over the hood of the truck and his mouth slid in a kind of free fall down the center of her and between her thighs. When he slipped his tongue over her, she cried out and her hands locked in his hair, holding him there, and then she was gone, swept away in a wave of pleasure so intense that she thought she blacked out. The next thing she knew, he was inside her, her legs wrapped around his waist, his hands supporting her, and it was starting all over again.

They slipped down the hood to the floor of the garage. Their damp bellies and thighs slapped together and waves of heat and desire rose from every part of her, from the pit of her belly and the space between her toes, sweeping upward over her face and the crown of her head. She threw her arms back, her hips, then wild, violent shudders seized her.

Afterward, she twitched like a splayed frog and inhaled the cold, sweet air. A weird sort of peace settled through her. He ruined it by running his hands over her hair and caressing her cheek and whispering how wonderful she was, how beautiful, and she just wished he would shut up and disappear.

Allie suddenly thought of Mira and the amoxycillin. *How long have I been here? How much time have I lost? Suppose she died? Suppose . . .*

"I have to go," she murmured, and pushed him away and quickly sat up. Her clothes, where the hell were her clothes?

"What's wrong?" Whitford asked.

"Nothing's wrong. I just have to go. I'm expecting calls from my staff in the ER. I completely forgot about it."

"Oh."

He sounded mortally disappointed and got to his feet. He gathered up his clothes and quickly pulled on his jeans, shirt, and shoes. Both of them seemed inordinately modest now, turning their backs on each other to finish dressing, one commenting on the chill wind that blew through the garage, the other remarking on the dog's continued barks. She helped him pick up the wood that had fallen and stack it back against the wall. He carried two bundles out to the Rover for her and as she shut the door, he said, "I'd like to see you again, Allie."

"Sure." She didn't want to get into some heavy, drawn-out conversation.

"Breakfast tomorrow?"

"I don't plan on getting up before noon, Nick. I'll call

you." She got into her car before he could say anything else and backed out of the driveway.

Mira looked bad. Her breathing was shallow, ragged. She was sweating profusely because the aspirin had lowered her temperature, but she still had a fever of 101.

"Mira, wake up, c'mon," Allie said, touching her shoulder. "You need to swallow this."

"Water," she murmured.

"I've got water. I'm going to lift your head up. You need to take a sip and swallow these two pills."

Allie slipped her hand under Mira's head, but because her arms were still strapped down, she couldn't raise up on her elbows and started to cough. Allie quickly removed the straps and helped her sit up. "Slide the pill between your lips. Great, that's great. You're doing just great."

"Hurts to breathe," Mira whispered, and started coughing.

When the coughing spell had passed, Mira opened her eyes, looked at Allie, and frowned. "Who're you?"

"I'm Allie."

Her eyes slipped to Allie's left. "I know you."

"Right. I'm Allie."

"No, not you. Him." She lifted her arm and pointed to Allie's right. "That man."

Goose bumps raced up and down Allie's arms and her head snapped around. But no one was there. Of course not. "There's no one in the house but us, Mira. Look, you need to take this other pill. Then you can use the bedpan."

"I remember you!" Mira exclaimed, still looking at something to Allie's left. "Your name is . . ."

Shit, she's raving.

"Take this pill," Allie said again, slipping the tablet between Mira's dry, chapped lips. "That's right. Here's some water." She slid the bedpan beneath her. "Use this."

Mira sipped from the bottle of water, swallowed, coughed, sipped some more. Allie removed the bedpan, set it aside, and lowered her head to the pillow. She realized the temperature in the basement had turned significantly cooler. It had its own thermostat and she remembered checking it before she'd left, making sure it was set at about seventy-five degrees. But the temperature in here now felt at least twenty degrees colder than that and it definitely hadn't been that cool when she'd come down here a few minutes ago.

When she exhaled, she could see her breath in the air. Great. That was all she needed. No heat. She would have to move Mira upstairs and that would entail greater risk. Especially now.

Breakfast tomorrow?

Nick Whitford had been the day's major mistake. But Christ, it had felt so good.

So give him your number and tell him to call you after the new year. Then you can fuck your little brains out, and what difference will it make?

None. Except that she'd told him she lived in Macon . . .

Oops, I told you the wrong city.

. . . and she didn't want a relationship. She wanted sex. She wanted his body. She wanted hours of sensuality and no ties, no expectations.

And why's it so damn cold in here?

Allie went into the bathroom to empty the bedpan. It wasn't at all cold in here. Why not? The bathroom was on the same thermostat as the rest of the basement.

When she returned to the main room, the temperature felt as though it had dropped several more degrees. Mira was propped up on her elbows, eyes focused on an empty spot in the room. She was smiling stupidly. "I went to the library," Mira said.

"Right." Allie pulled the sheet over her.

"I sat where J. K. Rowling sat," Mira went on, nodding, her smile widening, her cheeks damp, flushed, her eyes glazed with lunacy.

Allie considered giving her another shot that would knock her out for the rest of the night, but she was afraid of overdosing her. "Hey, Mira. I'm right here." She waved her hand in front of Mira's face, but she didn't notice.

"Your name. Right. Your name. It's . . . Dean. That's it. Your name is Dean."

Jesus God. Allie, shivering now, jerked back from the bed. Goose bumps covered her arms, crawled up her neck, and a tongue of ice licked its way along her spine. Her heartbeat slammed into three digits, sweat rushed from the pores in her skin. She caught movement in her peripheral vision and spun around.

Nothing.

And now Mira was humming to herself, nodding *yes, yes,* and said, "The library, right, uh-huh."

She's talking to someone.

Someone Allie couldn't see.

To Dean.

She lurched forward, pushed Mira back against the mattress, quickly secured the straps around her arms again. The cold was almost unbearable now. Mira would die in this cold, die before the plan was finished.

Allie ran across the basement and into the utility area under the stairs. She threw open the cabinet doors and brought out two more blankets, thick blankets, winter blankets. She raced back into the main room—and stopped, gaping, clutching the blankets to her chest.

There, right next to the side of Mira's bed, was a

shape. She couldn't tell what the hell it was, except that it seemed to be growing up from the floor, drawing the cold into itself, as though the cold gave it substance. And then the shape drifted over the mattress, elongating, shrinking, adjusting itself to the length and width and shape of Mira's body.

Mira jerked—her limbs, head, torso—and her face contorted, one side of her mouth puckering, the other side widening, so her mouth looked like a clown's. Then her eyes shut, snapped open, shut, and snapped open again and looked straight at Allie.

The blankets dropped out of Allie's arms.

Mira raised her head from the pillow, the tendons in her neck straining. Her mouth moved. "Don't do it, Al," she said in Dean's voice. "Not in my name."

With that, Mira's head collapsed against the pillow and Allie whirled around and ran for the stairs, her shoes pounding against the basement floor. She took the stairs two and three at a time and burst through the door at the top. She slammed it shut, fumbled with the key in the lock, turned it, heard the click, and backed away from the door, blinking hard, shivering, arms clutched to her chest.

Not in the pattern, not in the pattern, not not not . . .

And when she couldn't go any farther, when her spine was up against the opposite wall, she slid down it to the floor, jerked her legs up against her. She wrapped her arms around her legs, pressed her head against her thighs, and shook uncontrollably.

November 1989
Cassadaga, Florida

1

Dean hurries downstairs, anxious to get on the road. It's nearly two and it will take him at least five hours to get to Disney World, where he's supposed to meet Lia. With traffic, it may take even longer. Every moment he delays is one less moment he will spend with her.

He heads into the kitchen to post a note on the corkboard for his parents, informing them where he'll be—DeLand, looking for an apartment near Stetson for when he starts college in January. He's leaving Ian West's number in Cassadaga in case they want to get in touch with him. Which they probably won't. Usually they don't care where he goes or what he does, as long as they know how to get in touch with him.

But when he comes into the kitchen, his mother is there, struggling with something at the counter, her back to him. "I thought you were at the lab," Dean says.

She whips around, an unopened container of pills in one hand. "You startled me. I can't get this damn thing open. Can you do it?"

"I thought you took those only at night, Mom."

"I'm feeling kind of stressed about Allie's dinner party."

Dean sticks his note on the corkboard, then goes over to the counter and opens the container of pills. Ever since little Ray's death four years ago, his mother has been romancing sleeping pills the way other women romance their lovers. At first, she took them only at night. Now she seems to take then all day long and often combines them with booze. Recently she has been coming home from work early, before Dean gets out of school, and is usually out of it by dinner. Mothers with addiction problems are probably the only family thing that he and Lia have in common.

"What're you doing home so early?" she asks as he hands her the opened container of pills.

"I told you. I'm going up to DeLand to find an apartment."

She frowns, struggling to remember. At one time, his mother was a pretty woman, with a mind as sharp as cut glass, and her impeccable appearance like a trademark. But the pills and booze have changed all that. She is fat now, sloppy, and indifferent to how she looks. Her mind doesn't function like it used to.

"You didn't tell me that," she says finally.

"I did, Mom. Look, I've got to hit the road." He gives her a quick hug.

"But what about Allie's party? It's her anniversary. She thinks you and Keith are going to be here."

"I've got other plans. See you Sunday."

He hurries out the door before she can say anything else, tosses his bag in the back of the car, and realizes he has left his camping gear in the garage. He raises the garage door and hastens inside, gathering up the gear—the tent, sleeping bags, pillows, the grill, and a cooler of food. His heart soars at the thought of seeing Lia—the first time since August.

For the last two and a half months, they have traded dozens of phone calls and letters, with Lia's calls and letters going through Mr. Barker's store. He is their messenger, their Hermes. Since Dean has his own phone line and pays the bill, he always calls her. So much sneaking and planning, he thinks, but nothing worked out until this opportunity came up last week. Lia and some friends are going to Disney World and someone's older sister and her friends are chaperoning them. Lia will leave the group for two days. It will just be the two of them.

When he shuts his trunk, his sister's BMW is pulling into the driveway. Great timing.

Allie swings out, still dressed in her ER greens. She's holding a large tray of food. "Hey, Dean," she calls.

He waves, gets quickly into his car. She's the last person he wants to talk to right now. But she can't stand being ignored and strides over to the car. "I hope you'll be back by six. We're having a dinner party. The family, a few friends."

"Mom didn't mention it. I'm off to Stetson for the weekend. To find an apartment for January."

She whips off her shades. As usual, her eyes look enraged. "You can't do that. This is a special party. It's my one-year anniversary."

"Exactly. Your anniversary, Al. Not mine."

"Do Mom and Dad know you're going?"

"Sure. They're glad to get rid of me."

"But you're only seventeen years old. They're letting you drive all over the state."

"I'm not your kid, Al. Butt out. Besides, my driving record is better than yours. Dad said that last speeding ticket of yours was—what? A hundred bucks and change?"

Her mouth purses with annoyance. "I was in a hurry."

"Yeah, well, so am I. Enjoy the party." He raises his window and takes off.

She will make a stink with their parents and his father will say the usual thing, that Dean is old enough to make his own choices. She and their mother will commiserate about how permissive Dad is and by then Mom will be so out to lunch she won't remember a word of the conversation. Even if this weren't his weekend for meeting Lia, he wouldn't attend the party. He dislikes Allie's husband, a surgical resident as arrogant as she is.

It shouldn't be this big a deal, but of course it is because he's striking out on his own rather than doing something with the Family.

He drives hard and fast, music pounding from the radio, and pulls up in front of Lia's motel at exactly eight o'clock. And there she is, waiting outside, just as she said she would be. Her hair is loose, her long legs tanned. Nearly three months and she is still the most beautiful thing he has ever seen.

She runs over to the car, her bag banging against her hip, and scoots inside and off they go. But he makes it exactly two blocks before he pulls into a gas station and takes her into his arms. His senses are flooded with the fragrance of her skin and hair, the softness of her hungry mouth, the shape and feel of her. They break apart and just look at each other. "Forty-eight hours together, can you believe it?" she whispers.

"But is it safe?" he asks.

"It should be. Molly's older sister says as long as I'm back by five on Saturday, when they're leaving, she's fine with it."

"Five it'll be."

They drive half an hour north to a campground about a mile from Cassadaga. Their campsite is secluded, tucked back under huge banyans and live oaks, and that first night they do little more than talk and make love. It's the longest time they have been alone together, Dean thinks, without the threat of discovery hanging over them.

Late that night, they lie in the tent, on top of the sleeping bags because it's unseasonably warm. Night sounds surround them, the air is redolent with the scent of smoke. He tells her all about Cassadaga, preparing her for the strange wonder of it. "There's only one other place like it in the country, a sister community in upstate New York."

"And everyone who lives there talks to the dead?"

"Most of them." He tells her about his friend Ian West, a medium who has lived and worked in the village for fourteen years, a man she will meet tomorrow. "He's an incredible medium. You'll see."

"Tell me more about the history."

The history of the town dated back to Iowa in 1875, he

continues, when a medium named George Colby held a séance at the home of a friend. His Indian guide, Seneca, came through and told him to travel to Eau Claire, Wisconsin, where he was supposed to contact T. D. Giddings, a Spiritualist. Once he was in Wisconsin, Seneca promised to give him more instructions. Colby, who was single, in his late twenties, packed up and split.

"You have to kind of wonder about a guy like that," she says. "Was he nuts? My mother would think so."

Dean laughs. "I think Ian would say that Colby had a lot of faith in what he received as a medium. But it gets weirder. In Wisconsin, Colby met up with Giddings and held another séance. Seneca described a wilderness of high bluffs, lakes, hills, and told Colby and Giddings to head for Florida. So they did. They institutionalize people for less than that. But this was 1875 and the Spiritualist movement was gathering steam. When you hear Ian talk about it, he talks about spirit with a capital S."

"So is this like blind faith?"

"No. Ian studied this stuff most of his adult life. He's the youngest medium they've ever had in Cassadaga. When he did his first reading for me, he tuned in on my grandfather. Described him, talked like he talked . . . It was eerie."

She turns onto her side, pulling her pillow closer to him. "Tell me more about this Colby guy."

"They headed south, Colby, Giddings and his family, on trains and then steamboats. They got as far as Blue Springs, a frontier town surrounded by subtropical forest, that was supposedly close to their final destination. There they held another séance and Seneca instructed them to start walking into the forest. So they did. And we're talking about thousands of acres of wilderness covered in pines, scrub brush, palmettos, and riddled with all kinds of reptiles and insects. It must've seemed like another planet to these two guys."

After a few miles of arduous hiking, Seneca told them to

stop. Colby glanced around and saw everything Seneca had described in that first séance in Iowa. This was the spot where Colby and Giddings were supposed to build their Spiritualist camp.

"Colby built a home on the shores of Lake Colby—which was later moved to a place you'll see tomorrow, at the edge of Spirit Lake—and Giddings and his family built their home close by. Colby eventually got a government deed for seventy-four acres, but he didn't do much of anything else for eighteen years."

"How come?" she asks.

"No one really knows. In October 1894, a dozen mediums signed the charter for the Southern Cassadaga Spiritualist Camp. The charter states that the camp was to be a nonprofit association that promoted Spiritualist beliefs in the soul's immortality."

"You think Mr. West would read for me, Dean?" She sits up, hugging her knees against her.

"Sure. "

"My dad's mom—Nana Honey—died a few years ago. Maybe he can tune in on her."

Then she tells him about Nana Honey, how she buried money for Lia in her backyard and put money in a college trust fund for her that her parents can't touch. "She always called it my freedom money. She said someday I might need it to get away from my mother."

Dean snaps forward. "Lia, this is perfect. Part of my trust fund will be available to me when I turn eighteen. With that and the money you have, we won't be struggling financially. We'll have my car. We can live together in my apartment at Stetson."

"Unless my parents are looking for me."

Unless, what if, maybe . . . he hates the uncertainty, the unknowns. He draws her back against the nest of sleeping bags and holds her while she falls asleep. Outside, the night sounds rise and fall with a strange, steady rhythm.

2

The road climbs and dips over a series of shallow hills, and everywhere Lia looks, there are pines, thick and green and tall. A hush suffuses the morning air. Lia is certain that if Dean stops the car, she won't hear a sound.

Now, coming up on her right, she spots a large two-story stucco building that looks as if it were transported here from the Mediterranean. Along one side runs a wide porch lined with rocking chairs. "That's the Cassadaga Hotel," Dean says. "We'll park there and walk around."

As they walk, Dean explains that the town actually has two distinct areas, a rebel camp—psychics who broke off from the association—and the Spiritualist camp. It lies to the south of 430A, the road they came in on, and to the west of and behind the hotel. And here, the crooked little houses look like they were shipped in from Cape Cod, and in front of nearly every home is a sign with the psychic's name and specialty on it. Reverend So and So, medium or clairvoyant, reader or astrologer. And over there, Spirit Lake glimmers like a blue eye in the warm November light and that old house at the edge of the marsh is the Colby place.

But all of that aside, Cassadaga feels like home to her in a way no other place except Tybee ever has. It isn't just the marsh that surrounds Spirit Lake, but the very texture and feel of the air, as though magic hums just beneath the surface of everything. She feels safe in this strange little community.

"I love it," she says softly. "Let's live here."

"Once I start at Stetson, Ian has offered to let me use the Colby house if I want. Maybe we can live there together."

It frightens her when Dean talks like this because it means she would have to run away from home. As bad as her home life is, as much as she detests her mother, the idea of being a runaway appalls her. Yet, if she had Nana Honey's money, if she and Dean had a place to live, she could study for her GED while he was going to college. If she could get her GED by the time she was sixteen, she could be finished with college by twenty and be done with law school at twenty-four. This idea appeals to her, to get an early jump on life, to make something of herself earlier than her peers.

Dean points at a two-story yellow house at the end of the street. "That's where he lives with his wife, Heather, and their eight-year-old son."

As they get closer, Lia gets a good look at the place. It reminds her of a house in a fairy tale—a crooked screened porch, odd little windows, a side yard filled with lush, colorful plants. A fountain shaped like a swan has vines growing around it. The sound of the water soothes her.

Ian himself answer the door. He's a tall, Ichabod Crane–like man, with thick, dark hair and large eyes the same deep blue as the Pacific. His eyebrows seem to be perpetually raised and his forehead is deeply lined. He exudes enthusiasm and although his voice isn't loud, it seems to boom when he greets Dean. He doesn't bother shaking Lia's hand; he hugs her hello as though she is already a member of the family. She has never felt so welcome anywhere.

They settle in his living room. It's crowded with things—statues, figurines, magazines, and books everywhere, old photos on the walls, plants that billow in the bright sunlight that streams through the many windows. And there's a strangeness about the air here, a kind of hush that quivers just beneath the chaos, the friendly mess. Spirits?

As Ian brings in drinks and snacks, Lia wonders if he's tuning in on her, if he's seeing spirits. Is that how it works?

"Who's Honey?" Ian suddenly asks.

Well, she thinks, that answers her question. "My grandmother."

Ian sets the tray on an end table, cocks his head as if listening to something Lia can't hear, then nods and sits down. "She says the house is going to be sold and that you should dig up what's buried in the yard and hide it at your house."

Lia looks quickly at Dean, who holds up his hands. "I didn't tell him anything. I swear."

"Whose house is going to be sold?"

"Honey's house." Now his eyes are fixed on the space just to the right of Lia's head. "Susan will never understand. Don't deceive yourself about that."

Her mother. "She won't understand what?"

"Who you are. Who you and Dean are together, she says. It's best not to fight her, but just to follow your heart."

Nana Honey used to say those very words to her whenever Lia was torn about something. Follow your heart. *She's too stunned to speak, to ask any more questions. She smooths her hands over her shorts, her thighs, as if to assure herself that her body is real.*

3

While Heather is showing Lia the library, Ian leans close to Dean and speaks in a soft, hushed tone. "I'll try to tell you what I need to tell you before Lia comes back. For years there have been predictions, Dean, made by a variety of psychics here in Cassadaga, about a violent series of events that involve a Curry, a shepherd, and a mirror. These events happen near water, and begin in 1989, with a Romeo and Juliet romance. They culminate early in the new century, in a year that adds up to six. That would be 2004. My feeling is that you're the Curry the predictions speak of, and that you and Lia are the Romeo and Juliet."

Dean has heard a lot of strange things from Ian, but this is one of the strangest. He doesn't know what to think. "What or who are the shepherd and the mirror?"

"We don't know yet."

Every day there are thousands of violent events, crimes, victims, and perpetrators. Why would this particular series of events show up in a prediction? And how many other Currys are there in the world? Probably hundreds. "If I'm the Curry, why would there be psychic predictions involving me?"

"I don't know."

Something in Ian's tone of voice, in the way he suddenly lowers his eyes, tells Dean that Ian not only know the answers to this question, but that he knows far more than he's revealing. "So what am I supposed to do with this information?"

"That's up to you. I'm just passing it along."

"What kind of violent events?"

"I don't have the specifics. These predictions are contained in something we call the Book of Voices. They go back nearly a century. The ones I just told you about have come from many different psychics over the last ten or fifteen years. The predictions are sealed when they're submitted, and up until last year, no one saw them but the secretary of the association. She has been trying to put them into order for probably thirty years now. Last year she had a stroke and the president of the Cassadaga Spiritualist Association asked for four volunteers to help with the organization. I volunteered."

"May I see the book?"

"Sure. But I think we should wait until we're alone."

Dean mulls it over for the rest of the day—while he and Lia are swimming in a nearby sinkhole, while they're breaking down camp so they can move into the Cassadaga Hotel for the night, and finally mentions it to Lia over dinner at the hotel. She listens without interrupting, then sets down her fork.

"Romeo and Juliet? But our families aren't warring. Our families don't even know each other."

"I guess it's more of a metaphor."

"Well, fuck the metaphor. I'm not going to be anyone's tragedy."

"Hey, don't get so mad, Lia."

"I'm not mad."

"You sound mad."

"I'm tired." She pushes back from the table. "I'll be up in the room."

Dean sits there awhile, alone, mystified by Lia's behavior. When he looks up, Ian is hurrying through the restaurant door. "Dean, you just got a call from your brother. Heather

took it. Your mom had a nasty fall and is in the hospital."
He withdraws a slip of paper from his shirt pocket. "Keith
said to call him at this number. You can use the phone at the
house, if you'd like."

His brother's car phone number. "I'll use the pay phone." He
calls from the old-fashioned phone booth in the lobby and Keith
answers immediately.

"Hey, Keith. What's going on?"

"Mom had too much to drink on top of the pills she probably
had taken, too. She slipped in the bathroom. They think she's got
a concussion. Allie's checking her out now. I don't think it's all
that serious, okay? But Allie insisted I call you. If you're with
your lady love, stay put. Mom's not going to pass away. This is
just more of Allie's control shit."

Maybe, maybe not. If he stays here and his mother passes
away, how will he live with that? On the other hand, if Keith's
theory about Allie is right, he knows how it will be, all of them
in the waiting room at the hospital, Allie ranting about their
mother's drinking, chastising everyone for not watching her
more carefully. He knows. And forget it. He wants no part of it.

"How come you're on the car phone?"

"I came out here to smoke a joint. It's the only way I can deal
with all that shit."

"If you want some company, I'll come. Otherwise, tell Allie
you couldn't get in touch with me."

"Don't worry about me. I'm heading home in about five
minutes."

"Great, so you never got in touch with me."

"You got it."

Dean returns to the restaurant and tells Ian about the call.

"You made the right choice," Ian says. "I don't feel she'll pass
over from this injury."

Again Dean has the feeling that Ian knows more than he's
saying.

"Your sister . . . is she a brunette?" he asks.

"Yes."

"Quite striking in appearance?"

"So I'm told."

"She's . . . I don't want to be too blunt about this, Dean."

"Be as blunt as you want."

"She's bad news." His eyes have glazed over. *"There's a strong past-life connection here. I don't know the years, I can't see that. But the relationship was obsessive on her part."*

"What was the relationship?" Even as he asks, a part of him dreads knowing.

"Lovers. She killed you in a fit of jealous rage." He blinks, rubs his eyes. *"There's more material on this, but I'm unable to see it for some reason."* He pauses, frowns. *"Who was Ray?"*

"My youngest brother."

"He's dead."

"Yes. Four years ago. Why?"

Ian now describes Ray, a small boy with blond hair, his parents' delight, bright and mischievous. *"He's trying to communicate something, but I can't get it."* He shakes his head. *"Perhaps another time."* He reaches over and pats Dean's arm. *"I need to get back to the house. A client's coming."*

"I'll walk outside with you." Dean pays the bill and they head outside.

The air has cooled somewhat. The scent of the marsh mixes with the fragrance of night-blooming jasmine, gardenias. The silence out here seems to stretch forever through the darkness.

"There's more to those predictions than you told me."

Ian tucks his fingers into the back pockets of his jeans. *"We aren't meant to know everything,"* he says quietly. *"Mediums and psychics aren't gods. Our impressions are filtered through our own consciousness, Dean. That's why some predictions are wrong."*

"But?"

Now Ian looks over at him. On the planes of his face, a bat-

tle rages between light and darkness. Dean senses his reluctance to pursue the matter. "I need to know, Ian."

"Yes, I realize that. But this places me in somewhat of a moral dilemma, Dean. I don't like meddling in other people's lives. But when a prediction remains consistent over time and comes from several different psychics who don't know anything about the other predictions, then I pay close attention. You're going to father a child who becomes important in the spiritual evolution of Cassadaga. That's the big picture. And I think that's why the name Curry appears in the Book of Voices." He clasps Dean's shoulder. "I really have to get going. We'll talk tomorrow."

And then he's off, striding at a swift pace through the dark shadows of the Cassadaga street, and Dean stands there, struggling to absorb what this strange, gentle man has said. And suddenly he is very afraid.

4

It's the Friday after Thanksgiving and Lia is having her first gynecological exam. At her mother's insistence. It's humiliating. She knows this has nothing to do with her health and everything to do with her mother's suspicion that she is not a virgin.

After the exam the doctor and the nurse leave the room and Lia dresses, fighting back tears, fighting back rage, fighting back every emotion she has ever repressed. She can hear her mother and the doctor talking next door, in his office, and as soon as she sees her mother's face, she knows the doctor has informed her that Lia is not a virgin. To a woman like her mother, she thinks, this is tantamount to a one-way ticket to social ruin and scandal, and what if the priest at the church finds out?

She doesn't say a word to Lia on the drive back to Tybee. But as soon as they pull into the driveway, she turns to Lia and demands to know the boy's name.

And she refuses to say anything.

Her mother grabs her by the shoulders and strikes her so hard across the face that her lip splits open and starts to bleed. She strikes Lia again. And then Lia shoves her back hard enough so that her head hits the window. "If you ever hit me again, I'll kill you."

Lia leaps out of the car, slams the door, and runs into the house. Over dinner no one speaks. But her mother is drinking heavily, knocking back one vodka after another.

Later that night, she hears her parents shouting, glass shattering, doors banging open and shut. Then the car peels out of the driveway and she knows her father has left. She leaps off her bed and pulls her dresser in front of the door. It's already locked, but the dresser will give her additional protection. Her mother will be too drunk to break the door down.

She huddles on her bed with a flashlight, scribbling a letter to Dean, telling him she can't stand it any longer, she's ready to run away. She'll mail it tomorrow at work. She desperately wants to talk to him, but her mother has long since removed the phone from her room. Then the banging begins, the shouts, the curses, the madwoman is at her door.

Lia presses pillows against the sides of her head and closes herself in the closet.

Her bag is packed, Nana Honey's money inside. Tomorrow she will run.

The banging stops. Her mother has passed out.

Daylight. Knocking at her door. Polite raps. This is her father. "Lia, hon, please let me in," he says.

She pushes the dresser away, unlocks the door. Sobbing, she throws her arms around his waist. "You left me alone here with her. She was crazy."

"I know," he says, patting her head. "Ssshh. It's going to be okay." Then he pulls back from her slightly. "She's going into an institution to dry out. But the only way she's consenting to go is if you stay with your grandmother for a while."

"But that's in upstate New York. I don't want to go there. And why should I leave? She's the nutcase."

"Honey, I swear, it'll only be a few months. I just need to get your mother into this place, then we can work this out."

She argues, she sobs, but her father is as intractable as a concrete wall. And then he drops the bomb. She's leaving today. This afternoon.

On the way to the airport, her father stops at Mr. Barker's so Lia can pick up her final paycheck and give her notice. She breaks down in front of Mr. Barker and begs him to mail a letter to Dean. "Or if he calls, tell him I'll call you with a forwarding address, so I can get his letters. Would that be okay?"

"Aw, Lia, honey," Mr. Barker says. "You know I'll do anything to help you out." Lia gives him the letter to Dean and as he walks outside with her, he slips it through the mailbox slot.

Monday
December 29

11

1

Sheppard snapped upright in the recliner, his heart hammering. Goose bumps raced up his arms, the hairs on his arms stood up, a kind of electrical current zipped through him.

His eyes darted around the front room, through the dim glow cast by a night-light. Goot: sacked out on the couch. Ricki the dog: curled up in her usual spot next to the stove. The laptop: still on the floor with dozens of file folders. Annie and Nadine: in the bedrooms. Nothing stirred. The only sounds he heard were logs crackling in the stove, an occasional sigh from the dog, and Goot turning in his sleep.

Yet his body screamed danger. He dug his SIG out from between the cushion and the side of the chair and quickly stood. He crossed the room, stood to the side of the door, listening. He turned the dead bolt carefully, then the knob, and pushed the door open. A biting cold blew through the open doorway and the scent of fresh snow, pine, and smoke swirled into the room. Sheppard eased himself around the doorjamb, gripping his weapon with both hands, and stepped outside.

He swung right, left, sighting along the barrel of the gun. Nothing. Wind whistled through the branches of the trees, snow flew into his face and melted instantly on his skin. A light burned in the Stevens' kitchen window, the light Kyle King left burning, he said, so the souls could find their way home.

Sheppard shut the door to the cabin and stood against it for a few minutes, the cold eating up his bare feet, his bare arms, his bare heart. His arms dropped to his sides. He didn't know what had spooked him, what had caused his body to slam into adrenaline overdrive. But now the adrenaline was rushing out of him and he felt old, used up, and totally useless.

The hours they had spent sifting through old cases, collating information, and making endless lists had amounted to nothing. He had slept for a few hours in the bedroom, then gotten up and gone back into the living room to work alone. But even in solitude, the math didn't change. It all amounted to one big fat zero.

This is about you, not her, Nadine had said. He agreed with her. The fallout. But that didn't make the task of finding leads any easier. Anyone he had put away could be a potential suspect. And if you included wives, husbands, lovers, and family members who might hold a major grudge against an arresting officer, then his possible suspects numbered in the thousands.

The MO didn't fit anything in his current caseload, but it could fit any number of investigations he'd conducted over the last two decades. Every day people disappeared. Some never turned up, others turned up dead, some had clear motives and ransom notes, others didn't. The longer it took him to find a lead—any lead, however insignificant—the colder her trail got for police methods and for a sensitive like Nadine, who might be able to pick up some emotional residue.

He suddenly heard screaming inside the cabin. Annie screaming.

Sheppard whipped around, barely aware that he had walked over to the Stevens house in his bare feet, without a jacket on, and raced back to the cabin. As he burst through the door, lights came on, Nadine was shouting, Goot was shouting, Annie was shouting, Sheppard was shouting—and the dog was barking. It sounded like a Latino family celebration, emotions running high in Spanish, then English, then in Spanglish, a weird combination of the two.

As Sheppard reached Annie's bedroom, Nadine and Goot were already there, firing questions at Annie, and Annie was huddled on the bed, her arms wrapped around her head, as if to protect herself from the verbal assault. Ricki leaped onto the bed and pushed her snout against Annie's thigh. Sheppard's arms flew up and he waved the gun around and yelled, "*Time out! Hey, time out, people!*"

Silence. Annie peeked out from between her arms, leaped off the bed and ran over to him. She threw her arms around his waist, clutching him tightly, burying her face against his thin cotton T-shirt. Sheppard quickly tucked the gun in the waistband of his jeans and brought his hands down against her soft, tangled hair.

"Jesus, give her a chance to say something," Sheppard admonished the other two.

"Where the hell were *you?*" Goot demanded to know.

"I thought I heard something outside." His arms now rested against Annie's back. "You okay, Annie? What happened?"

She slowly tilted her head back, looking up at him. "Mom . . . Mom was here." Now she stepped away from him and faced Goot and Nadine. In a stronger voice, she said, "I felt her here. She kissed my forehead. She was OBE."

"OB what?" Goot asked.

"Then you wouldn't feel her kiss you," said Nadine.

"Hello," Goot said. "Could someone please tell me what's going on?"

Goot always talked with his hands; one moment they were in midair, palms open, as though supplicating the gods, and the next second they were fixed to his hips and then his fingers were running through his hair.

"It means out-of-body experience," Sheppard replied, drawing on knowledge he hadn't realized he'd had.

Nadine shook her head and leaned against the wall. "And it's something Mira has never been able to produce at will. If you felt your mother kiss your forehead, she wasn't OBE, Annie."

"You already said that, and she *was* OBE," Annie argued. "I know what I felt."

"Excuse me," Goot said, his hands flying around now, unrooted, wild. "Please explain *out of body* in ten words or less."

"*Carajo,*" Nadine murmured, running her hands over her face.

"It's when the soul or spirit leaves the body." Annie paced restlessly around the room now, Ricki on the bed, watching her. "It's what happens in near-death experiences. It's what happens sometimes in meditation, during sex, in pain, in heightened states of awareness."

Goot looked blankly at Annie, then rolled his eyes and ran his hands over his face. "Oh, yeah, that explains it all."

Sheppard went over to the other bed, sat at the edge of it, and rubbed his frozen feet. He listened to Nadine's explanation about OBEs. Even though Goot came from a family of Cuban *santeros*—practitioners of a mystical religion that involved trance states and all sorts of odd rituals—his eyes glazed over. Sheppard could see it. Goot honestly didn't have a clue what she was talking about.

"He doesn't get it." Annie plopped down on her bed. "He just doesn't get it."

"Hey, I get it." Goot sounded irritable and angry now. "The soul goes and does its woo-woo shit. But it's also possible, Annie, that you were dreaming."

"I was *not* dreaming," Annie shot back. "I know the difference between a dream and what I experienced."

Nadine gathered her long salt and pepper braid behind her head and, in a soft, patient voice, began to speak in Spanish. This time she kept her explanation grounded. She told him the story of Robert Monroe, a radio executive who, in the late '50s, began having spontaneous out-of-body experiences. He would stretch out to nap, she said, and would sometimes experience a cocoon of vibration around his body, and suddenly he would be *elsewhere*, flung out of his body like a wad of paper from a rubber band. Monroe, a left-brain type, thought he was crazy and undertook an exploration of what was happening to him.

Eventually his experiences became a book, *Journeys Out of the Body*, and he went on to establish the Monroe Institute, where people could learn to do what Monroe did. "The CIA became interested in Monroe's work and its psychic spy program, Stargate, actually grew out of his discoveries."

The book Nadine mentioned was one that Mira had given Sheppard way back in the early days of their relationship. He had read a chapter and thought it was so far *out there* that he hadn't finished it. Mira had given him two other books by Monroe as well and he hadn't read those, either. He felt ashamed of that now, of his unwillingness to dive into the unknown with an open mind.

"El espíritu se va," she finished with a flick of her wrist. *The spirit leaves.*

Goot obviously understood this. "Spirit walking," he breathed.

"Finally," Annie said, obviously exasperated.

Nadine continued. "Monroe mapped states of consciousness, Goot. He described it as being on an interstate and getting off at certain exits to see what was there. One of the spots he found, which he called Focus 21, was a place between this world and the next, where it was possible for the living to visit the dead. He also traveled to parallel worlds. I remember one scene in particular that he described, where he ended up in a place with two suns."

"So what's it mean?" Goot asked. "Why's Mira spirit-walking?"

"To tell us that she's alive," Sheppard replied. *Or because she's dead,* he thought, but didn't say it. "She's trying to communicate with us. I know that I felt something out there in the living room. It's what woke me."

Goot combed his fingers through his hair. "We need more than spirit walking, amigo. We need directions to where she is."

Nadine jerked her thumb over her shoulder. "It's in there. In those files. And when it gets light, Annie and I need to do our own spirit walking. Down to the barn, into the house. C'mon, *mi amor.*" She put her arm around Annie's shoulder. "You come sleep with me."

Annie got up from the bed, a teen in her cute frog pajamas, and Ricki followed the two women into the other bedroom.

"So?" Goot asked. "You slept enough?"

"Yeah, let's go to work."

2

Annie lay awake beside Nana Nadine, her arm hanging over the side of the bed, fingers sliding through Ricki's fur. She knew that what she had experienced had not been a dream. Her mother had been here, in the cabin, and no one and nothing would convince her otherwise. But it didn't mean she was alive.

She turned on her side, trying not to let her fear overpower her. If her mother could come to her, then why couldn't she go to her mother and get the kind of concrete information that Sheppard needed to find her? Annie didn't know if she could do that alone, but if she and Nadine attempted it together, boosting each other's signals, they might be able to do it.

"Nana Nadine," she whispered. "Are you still awake?"

"And thinking the same things you are."

Annie raised up on her elbows. "I have an idea."

"Me too. We should divorce Shep."

Annie understood that Nadine was furious with Sheppard, that she blamed him for what had happened to her mom. But she didn't want to talk about her fury. She wanted results. "If you and I can combine our energies, we can locate Mom and get the information Shep needs to find her. I think we should try it."

Sheets rustled. Nadine sat up, turned on the bedside lamp, looked at Annie. Her salt-and-pepper hair hung over her shoulder in a single thick braid, her sleepy dark eyes regarded Annie with a mixture of love and puzzlement. "It's extremely difficult to get details like locations, road names, towns, the kind of thing you're talking about, *mi amor.*"

"Okay, so we should try for anything that Shep might be able to use. But we need to try it together. We'll be each other's booster rockets."

"We should get sleep so tomorrow we can read the site in the barn."

"We can still do that. But right now, let's try this. Like you and Mom taught me."

Nadine thought about it a moment, then leaned against the headboard, folded her legs lotus style, and picked up the pad of paper and pen on the bedside table. She set the items between them on the bed. "You remember how you're supposed to breathe?"

"Sure."

"Okay, move up next to me." She patted the mattress.

Annie scooted up to the top of the bed, leaned back against the headboard, and she and Nadine joined hands. They began a yogic breathing exercise that Nadine had taught Annie when she was four or five, alternate nostril breathing that brought both hemispheres of the brain into sync with each other.

"We're asking for information about Mira's whereabouts," Nadine began in a quiet, even voice. "As I begin to count backward from ten, our levels of relaxation and receptivity increase threefold with each number. *Ten . . .* we're feeling very, very relaxed and that relaxation moves up through the soles of our feet and into our ankles, our calves. . . . *Nine . . .* the relaxation now slips up into our knees, our stomachs. . . ."

Annie knew that Nadine used this technique for self-hypnosis, that she had tapes of her own voice that she listened to on nights when she couldn't sleep. And what a wonderful voice it was, smooth and silky, warm and safe. Annie felt herself slipping down, down, down, until she was no longer aware of Nadine's voice, of the numbers, of anything except the noise of her own breathing.

An open elevator door appeared on the inner screen of her eyes. She stepped inside; the doors shut. Although there was no sensation of movement, the numbers lit up overhead, and when one burned brightly, the doors opened and Annie stepped out into moonlight.

Everything seemed blurred, indistinct, and she sensed her monstrous fear crouched in the peripheral shadows, ready to leap out at her and tear her to shreds. *I'm safe, nothing hurts me here.* Her vision suddenly cleared and she saw moonlight glinting against a frozen river. To her right, barren trees, branches gnarled like arthritic hands in the moonlight. To her left, tall pines. She turned slowly until she was facing a house.

Wooden, an A-frame. Large.

Her mother, she knew, was inside that house.

She moved toward it, looking for any identifying numbers, landmarks, something concrete she could bring back to Shep, but didn't see anything. This house was in the middle of nowhere.

Annie went up to the steps to the front door and wondered how she was supposed to get inside. She wasn't sure about the rules of the place where she traveled now. Maybe there weren't any rules. Maybe the rules were the same. She turned the knob and the door creaked open and she slipped into a spacious living room. Moonlight streamed through the top of the picture windows. Art on the walls. Colorful furniture.

She called to her mother in her mind, and a soft, feminine voice said, *She's in the cellar.*

Annie's head snapped toward the sound of the voice and a short woman with shiny black hair walked out of the shadows. Was this her fear in human form? Annie tensed, but then the woman spoke. *I'm Rose. Can you remember that? Rose. It's important, honey.*

I need an address, Rose. For this place. I need something tangible.

River, Rose said. *Northern Georgia. Now quick, there's not much time.* And she gently clasped Annie's hand and they instantly were in another room, a basement, that was what it felt like to Annie. Her mother lay on a bed, arms and legs strapped down, her hair so damp it was plastered to the sides of her head. *She operated on your mother,* Rose said. The sight of her mom like this, so still, strapped down, held prisoner, shocked

Annie out of the state of mind where Nadine had taken
her and she suddenly snapped forward, gasping for
air, her eyes wild, startled. The room was utterly dark
and Nadine's soft snores rose and fell in the quiet.

What's going on?

Terrified, Annie fumbled for the lamp switch and the
light flared and Nadine rolled onto her back and Ricki
lifted her head, yawning sleepily. "Why's the light on?"
Nadine murmured.

"You—you turned it on earlier. When we were talking.
When we decided to boost each other's signals, when
you did the countdown for the hypnosis."

Frowning, Nadine lifted up on her elbows and shook
her head. "Annie, after you swore your mother was spirit-
walking, you came in here with me and we went to sleep.
I didn't do any hypnosis, *mi amor.*"

"You did. You even said that we should divorce Shep."

Nadine sat all the way up now. "No, I didn't say that.
But it sounds like a good idea."

"You picked up the pad and pen and put them between us. Here. On the bed." Annie jerked back the
covers. No pad, no pen.

"They're here." Nadine gestured at the bedside table
and, yes, there they were, a yellow pad and a blue pen.

"Oh, my God," Annie whispered, and rubbed her
hands over her face. "I was dreaming within a dream.
And I saw her, Nana Nadine. I saw my mom. Strapped
down. In a basement." She tried to hold the images in
her mind, of the house on the *frozen river,* in the moonlight, in *northern Georgia.* And Rose, a woman named
Rose. *Can you remember that? It's important, honey.*

"What else?" Nadine asked.

Annie's hands dropped away from her face. She
glanced over at Nadine, scribbling frantically on the yellow pad. "I—I don't know. There was other stuff, but I

can't remember. Mom . . . Mom looked bad," she finished in a whisper, and began to cry.

Nadine gently cupped Annie's face in her hands. "You did great, Annie."

"But it's not enough information for Shep to find her."

"It's a start."

12

Mira woke, sheathed in sweat, the stink of her body thick in the air. The T-shirt that she wore stuck to her skin, her hair clung to her neck, her wrists felt glued to the straps. And her legs. She knew they were strapped down, that she was beneath a house somewhere, like in a cellar or a basement, that the wacko had operated on her, that she had been *elsewhere.*

With Annie?

It felt right, but she couldn't be sure. She didn't seem to be sure of much of anything at the moment.

The sweat.

My fever broke.

If she was on the mend, then why didn't she pick up anything from the straps? The bed? The sheets? The pillows? Everything that touched her should have been communicating something to her, information about this crazy woman, about her motive, about who and what she was.

Gone, it's gone.

Mira pressed her palms flat against the sheets and shut her eyes. She lay there for a few moments, adjusting her breathing, waiting for an image to surface, for information to pour into her, waiting for an inner shift. Instead, her physical body seized her attention—a full bladder that ached, discomfort and a nagging throb in her thigh, a growling stomach, the pressing need to get up and move around.

Why couldn't she pick up anything psychically? How could she get through life being half a person? *How?*

Deep breaths, calm down. Fabric wasn't the best conductor of psychic energy, and whenever she was sick, her abilities faltered. This was just a temporary glitch. She needed to take care of her physical needs first, but to do that, she had to get the wacko down here.

Mira cleared her throat, preparing to shout for Allie, but then heard the door at the top of the stairs opening. She lifted her head and in the dim glow of the nightlight, saw the wacko's legs. A light flared. "Rise and shine, Mira. I bet you're starved." She set a tray on the nearby counter.

Mira glared at her. "I'm hungry, I need to use the bathroom, I'd like to take a shower, and these sheets are filthy." She noticed that the wacko wore latex gloves and a white smock over black pants and a white pullover sweater. She also wore makeup and had fixed her lustrous black hair so that it fell over her shoulder in a single thick braid. Except for the gloves, she looked as though she were dressed for work.

"Definite improvement. The amoxycillin is doing the trick. I'm going to unfasten the straps." She reached under her sweater and brought out a gun. "If you try anything—anything at all—I'll shoot you. Clear?"

"I speak English."

With her left hand, the wacko unfastened the straps on Mira's arms and legs and not once did her hands touch Mira's body.

She stepped back from the bed, the gun aimed at Mira. "Okay, you can sit up."

Mira pushed up slowly on her elbows, the wretched smell of her own body nauseating her. Her head spun, pain flared in her thigh. She glanced around at the bathroom, way on the other side of the room, and didn't know if she could make it that distance under her own steam.

"I don't know if I can walk all the way to the bathroom."

"You're going to have to. I'm not touching you."

And why not? Mira wondered. Had she picked up something on wacko last night and blurted it out? If so, it meant her abilities weren't totally gone. But why couldn't she remember any of what she'd said? "I said something to you?"

The wacko emitted a sharp, ugly laugh. "That's not the half of it. You can eat first or go to the bathroom, your choice."

"The bathroom, a shower, then I'd like to eat."

She started coughing, a wet, hacking cough, and Wacko, using the end of the gun, pushed a box of Kleenex toward Mira. "Wipe your chin."

Mira no longer thought of this woman as having a normal name. In her mind her name was now "Wacko." In fact, maybe she didn't have a gender, either. Maybe that pretty face and dynamite body were just part of her disguise. In that case, she could be described as "the wacko," a genderless being, a kind of human mutant no less horrifying than Gollum in *Lord of the Rings*. Gollum had once been a hobbit but had been corrupted so deeply by the power of the ring that it had changed his physical appearance. What had corrupted Wacko?

"You need to move around today and get that fluid out of your lungs."

"I need something to hold on to."

Wacko pressed her foot against the bottom of the bedside table and it rolled toward her. "Use that."

While Wacko kept her foot pressed against the stand,

Mira grabbed onto the edges and pulled herself up. She immediately felt light-headed and clutched the edges of the stand to steady herself. "Whatever I said to you must've really spooked you," Mira remarked.

"Let me just put it this way. I had my doubts about whether you were psychic. Now I don't doubt it at all. You made a believer out of me."

Mira nearly laughed at the irony. The wacko believed she was psychic and seemed terrified that Mira might see something when, in fact, she couldn't pick up squat. She felt the way a conjoined twin would feel after separation surgery, as though her soul had been torn out of her.

"Go on, get that thing rolling," Wacko said. "Your toothbrush and toothpaste are on the sink and there's a fresh towel and clothes on the rack. While you're in there, you can remove the bandage and just drop it in the wastebasket."

"What about when I shower? Can my thigh get wet?"

"Sure. Just don't use soap on it."

Mira pushed the stand slowly across the basement. The muscles in her legs cried out, her stomach cramped, her lungs still didn't feel quite right. "I had pneumonia, right?"

"You still do. But by tomorrow or the next day, you'll be feeling a hundred percent better."

"And my leg? Is that going to be a hundred percent better, too?"

"If you don't tear the stitches out again."

"Did your bullet hit anything major?"

"You're the psychic, you tell me."

And under ordinary conditions, she would be able to do that. But nothing had been normal since she and Shep and Annie had left home. The only thing she could say with any certainty about her health and her body was that her fever had broken.

"Everything feels okay," Mira replied. "Except that I hurt all over."

"That's normal with pneumonia."

Despite the gun the wacko had, Mira didn't feel that she was in any immediate danger—i.e., that it was safe to use the bathroom, take a shower, and eat. The big question was what would happen after that. Why was the wacko dressed up? Was she leaving the house? *Is she planning on taking me with her?* The possibility filled Mira with dread. *Need to find a way outta here.*

On her way to the bathroom, she took in all the details of the basement—the placement and size of the windows (too small to squeeze through), that there didn't appear to be another door, the alcove under the stairs that housed a washer and dryer, the desk with the computer on it.

With an Internet connection?

Doubtful. Wacko was a fucking nutcase, but she was smart and functional. She had found an ideal hiding place, had handled Mira's medical emergencies, and she knew how to shoot a gun. She apparently had a plan that had been in place for a long time and had fine-tuned it. The only psychic information she remembered picking up on Wacko was that she was a physician and intended to hang Mira and skin her alive.

And that's the key to understanding all this.

The stand pressed up against the jamb of the bathroom door and Mira leaned against it, resting. "You watched us for a long time before you made your move," Mira said.

"I plan well."

"You went through the glove compartment of our van when we stayed overnight in Savannah."

It was a guess. But she felt a certain smugness when

she glimpsed the expression that flickered, shadowlike, across the wacko's face.

"So what were you looking for, exactly?" Mira asked.

"A map or some indication of where you were going."

Mira remembered opening the glove compartment when they were driving between Savannah and Asheville because she was looking for the cell phone. The glove compartment lid was metal, one of the best conductors of psychic energy, yet she hadn't picked up anything at all when she'd touched the lid. Why not? She hadn't felt sick then. The scratchy throat and the sneezing had come along once they were in the mountains. She suddenly wondered if the loss of her ability was due to a delayed effect of having gone through the black water mass rather than to pneumonia.

It made a terrible kind of sense. After she had gone through the mass, her abilities had been so heightened, so extreme, it was as if she were plugged into some greater source and power. And for the last six months, that had been the case most of the time. Now, suddenly, she was unplugged and stumbling along at the opposite end of the spectrum, psychically blind, deaf, and mute.

The possibility that the condition might be permanent horrified her.

"Move away from the stand," the wacko said. "Use the jamb or the knob to steady yourself. That's right. See? You're doing fine."

Mira barely made it to the toilet.

Wacko didn't shut the door, but she stepped away from the doorway, presumably to give Mira some privacy. Mira moved toward the sink, holding on to the towel rack, then leaned into the wall to steady herself. A metal towel rack, a concrete wall. Metal and concrete held psychic energy, yet no images came to mind, no impressions, nothing at all. Practically on the verge of tears now, she grabbed onto the edge of the sink. *Porcelain.*

Nothing.

She yanked the washcloth and towel off the rack, ran the cloth under the cold water, and started to press it against her face—and stopped when she caught sight of herself in the mirror. She looked like someone coming off a weeklong drunk. Her hair was a filthy, tangled mess, her eyelids were swollen, her lips were cracked, and her cheeks had sunk. She pressed the wet cloth to her face, barely stifling a sob.

"Hey, you all right in there?"

"I'm—I'm going to shower now," Mira called back. "Is there shampoo?"

"In the shower. I've got an electric razor you can use after you shower. And that shirt you have on smells pretty ripe. I'll get you a clean one."

Mira dropped the washcloth in the sink, avoided looking at herself, and leaned against the wall again. She carefully unwrapped her thigh and nearly passed out. The skin looked as if Dr. Frankenstein had been digging around in her thigh with a filthy fork. It had turned a purple so dark that it could be black, and it wasn't just an angry bruise. It raged. At the edges, where the stitches were, the skin seemed puckered and raw and *stuff* leaked out. She brought her hand to within half an inch of the wound and felt the intense heat that radiated from it. Maybe the pneumonia was on its way out, but there was something seriously wrong with this wound.

She tossed the bandage in the trash can, turned on the water in the shower. She stepped inside and shut the flimsy plastic door—and great, heaving sobs burst out of her. Mira slapped her hands over her mouth to smother the sounds. *It's never as bad as it seems.*

Yeah, it was worse.

Steam drifted up around her, a thick jungle steam that she sucked deeply into her lungs. It eased the tightness in her chest and made it easier for her to breathe. As she breathed, she began to calm down. The hot spray melted away the soreness in her shoulders, back, arms. Despite what the wacko had said, Mira gently washed the wound with soap and rinsed it off. She shampooed her hair and took her sweet time about it, giving herself a chance to think.

But all she found were riddles. If the wacko intended to hang and flay her, why had she operated on Mira's leg or treated her pneumonia? Because she had to be conscious and aware when she was hung? Because she had to be aware when Wacko took a scalpel to her arms? Her legs? Because Allie had a certain time frame in mind? The answers to these questions, she knew, formed the core of Wacko's motive. Denied any psychic input and lacking basic information like where she was and how long she'd been here, Mira couldn't begin to fathom what that motive might be. But worse, her mind had seized on the image of her flayed body. Such terror clamped over her that for seconds she couldn't move or breathe.

Then a vague memory nagged at her, something about a library and a man who looked like a mythological god. Mira struggled to grab the memory, but it was a slippery little devil that kept getting away from her.

"You all right in there?" the wacko called.

"Fine, I'm fine."

Any second now, Mira thought, she would come in here, rap at the plastic door. Mira wondered if she could hurl it open hard enough so it would slam into Allie and knock her out. Probably not. And if it didn't knock her out, she would shoot Mira. She might not shoot to kill— *not time for me to die yet*—but she definitely would shoot to maim, just as she had done in the barn. Then there might be another surgery, more drugs, and her immune system would collapse. Forget it. Right now, she needed to focus on building up her strength and buying some time. She would eat breakfast, ask questions, observe.

Mira turned off the shower, stepped out, wrapped one towel around her body and another around her hair. She went over to the sink to brush her teeth. The mirror was steamed up, and as she reached out to rub a clear spot, lines began to appear in the foggy glass.

She jerked back, hugging her arms against her, and stared as the lines continued to appear. It astonished her, shocked her, but didn't frighten her. She simply stood there, fascinated by what she was seeing. Then it hit her. Letters, these were letters, but awkwardly formed, as though a small, invisible child were practicing his writing skills. Thirteen indecipherable letters—then the writing stopped.

ᴎ ᗺƎᗡ⅃ᴎⅎƎᴙ⋏⊃Ǝᗺ

Frowning, Mira moved closer to the mirror, tilted her head to the right, the left, then leaned way to the right and tried to look at the letters upside down. No good. She backed up a few steps, studying them, and when it hit her, she nearly laughed out loud. These were mirror-image letters. "Dean be careful," she murmured.

Some kid had probably stayed here recently and written these words on a mirror after taking a shower, and when the air steamed up again, the letters appeared. The big problem with this theory, though, was how many people wrote their mirror messages as mirror images?

She looked around uneasily and whispered, "Is someone here?"

She didn't know what she expected—an apparition,

a disembodied voice. Again, there was nothing. She decided the source was less important than the message: *dean be careful.* Or *be careful dean.*

Who was Dean? It seemed she should know that name, but she couldn't place it.

She heard Wacko saying something again, so Mira quickly rubbed her hand over the mirror, wiping away the letters.

"Just so you know, the glass in these basement windows is shatterproof. There's just one way in and out of the basement. That door." Wacko stabbed her thumb at the door at the top of the stairs. "The basement is soundproof. There's plenty of food in the fridge, fresh fruit and vegetables, vitamins, immune boosters. As soon as you finish eating, you should take another dose of amoxycillin, then a second dose in about eight hours. I've got a lot of stuff to do, so I won't be back to check on you until later."

She's leaving and doesn't want me to know it. Or she thinks I'm too stupid to get it. Or she's testing me.

"I set up a VCR with some movies and brought you some books, so you don't get bored. Boredom can be as much a killer as viruses, you know. And I didn't touch the VCR or the movies, not with my hands. In fact, I've cleaned this place so thoroughly that there's nothing human left in here for you to read, Mira."

Mira nodded. She just wanted the woman to get the hell out of here. She was sitting at the edge of the bed, consuming her first real meal in she didn't know how long. Granola cereal with fresh blueberries, an English muffin, a strawberry smoothie, a hard-boiled egg, slices of sharp cheddar cheese. She even had a mug of coffee. It wasn't Cuban, but it sure tasted good. She tried to eat slowly to prevent herself from getting sick, and paused in between each bite, savoring the taste of everything.

"What's the point of all this?" Mira finally asked.

"The point?" Wacko blinked rapidly, her gaze skipped around the room. The question seemed to have caught her off guard. "You have to get better, that's the fucking point."

"Beyond that."

Wacko moved closer to the other side of the table and squatted down so her face was even with Mira's, uncomfortably close. Mira could see every line in her face, the pinched wariness at the corners of her eyes, the fine lines that, in twenty years, would make her mouth plunge into a permanent grimace. And she could see the swirl of color in her irises, part green, part blue, part madness.

"Let's get one thing straight, Mira. I don't enjoy your company. I don't want to engage in conversation with you. I think you're an aberration of nature. A freak. For my purposes, you aren't a human being, you aren't even a woman. You're a symbol."

What Mira heard in her voice wasn't just hatred, but a specific hatred born of some deep, festering wound that demanded vengeance, an eye for an eye, something of almost biblical proportions. "Gee, I was just thinking the same thing about you. I know your name is Allie, but I think of you as Wacko—capital *W*—or as the 'wacko.'"

"'Freak' and 'Wacko.'" She actually smiled. "It sounds like a vaudeville act."

Yeah, but in vaudeville, no one was held captive. And Mira suddenly knew she was here because of Sheppard, because of their relationship. This woman intended to get even with Sheppard by hanging Mira and skinning her alive. And she would hang her because—what? *What's the answer?*

Be careful dean. "Who's Dean?" Mira asked.

Allie wrenched back as though she'd been burned—then rage poured into her eyes and she grabbed Mira by the hair and jammed the barrel of the gun up under her jaw. Mira didn't move, didn't breathe. "If I pull the trigger," Allie hissed, "the bullet will blow apart the lower half of your face, pulverize your brain, and you'll be dead before it exits through the top of your skull. You are not to say that name, think that name, breathe that name. You understand me?"

Mira's psychic circuits blew wide open.

She's driving with the windows down, a warm breeze blowing through her hair. Dean sits in the passenger seat, saying nothing. His head is turned away from her, toward the water, the Miami skyline.

"Christ, talk to me, Dean."

He turns his head slowly, as though it's painful for him to look at her, and as always, she is struck by the exquisite beauty of his face. "I don't have anything to say."

"Is it true? You're married? You're married and you didn't tell any of us?"

He doesn't say anything.

"Who is she? Can she help our defense? Were you with her the night of the accident? Is she your alibi? Where the hell is she?"

He runs his palms over his thighs, shakes his head. "Allie, Allie. There's so much you'll never understand. This isn't about me, okay?"

She swerves to the side of the road, slams on the brakes. Her face is livid when she grabs his jaw, forcing him to look at her. "The reason you aren't rotting in jail while you wait for trial, Dean, is because you're out on a bond worth nearly two million bucks. Dad and I put up the money. We deserve answers."

"I didn't ask you to put up the bond." He pulls his head free of her grasp. "I asked you to butt out and you didn't."

Her arm swings back and his arm flies up and he grabs her wrist before she can strike him. He grips it so hard that it hurts. "Listen carefully, Al. You don't call the shots in my life. I do." Then he throws open the passenger door and gets out and starts walking.

Wacko backed away from Mira, her face frozen in shock. "How—how . . . ," she stammered.

Mira realized she had spoken what she'd seen, that she'd blabbed it all. She couldn't pick up anything on Wacko by touching objects she had touched; the contact had to be direct, immediate, and then it was explosive.

And now the wacko's hands shook as she raised the gun, her mouth moved and no sounds came out, and in an instant of strange and surreal clarity, Mira saw her finger tightening against the trigger. She hurled herself to the floor and, a heartbeat later, an explosion rocked through the basement.

"Don't you ever say his name," Wacko shrieked, and fired into the mattress, the ceiling, the wall, one deafening blast after another.

She ran over to where Mira lay, curled up in a ball on the floor, and kicked her savagely in the ribs. *Be careful dean* went south. Mira reared up and grabbed onto Allie's leg . . .

. . . and she and Nick are locked together on the floor of the garage and she moans and writhes

and the wacko danced about like a stork, an amputee. . . .

. . . Nick's mouth is on her . . . Nosy Neighbor, Divine Lover . . .

Then Wacko lost her balance and crashed backward, into the bedside stand. She gasped, her arms flailing in the air, and the stand rolled and she struck the floor.

Mira scrambled toward her on her hands and knees, her ribs on fire, explosions of pain in her thigh, and threw her body across Wacko's legs . . .

. . . little Ray, gone today, little Ray, who will pray? And she's kneeling over a child's body that lies next to a swimming pool, hair wet, beads of water glistening against his lifeless body. . . .

. . . and scooped up the fallen gun. She pushed the barrel up against her neck and ground it into the skin until Wacko gasped. Until her eyes widened. Until her mouth formed a perfect O.

"Don't," Mira said, her voice like nails against chalkboard.

Wacko's body went slack, but her eyes turned to granite and Mira could see her own reflection in the pupils. "Do what you did last night. Make your eyes roll back in your head. Speak in my dead brother's voice. C'mon, Freak, do it. And then pull the fucking trigger."

Mira's finger ached to apply pressure, to press the trigger and just be done with it. But she couldn't. She knew she couldn't. She couldn't take a life. And her hesitation, brief as it was, gave Wacko all the room she needed. She jackknifed her legs, her feet slammed into the back of Mira's neck, knocked the gun out of her hand, and it skittered across the floor. Wacko leaped up, scooped the gun off the floor, and backed away from Mira as she lay there, her neck feeling as though it had been severed from the rest of her body.

"You should've shot me"—Wacko's voice trembled—"while you had the chance."

Mira raised her eyes and watched Wacko back away, shaken. "And bring myself to your level? No thanks."

"You and Sheppard deserve each other. You're both assholes."

"Now I'm a psychic freak asshole. Hey, that's good." Mira remained on the floor, on her side, rubbing the back of her neck. She realized that as long as she didn't make any threatening moves toward Wacko, she probably would be okay. Her best defense, in fact, was that Wacko seemed to be terrified Mira would read her psychically.

"Hot sex with Nick, *Nosy Neighbor, Divine Lover.*" Mira spoke softly, evenly. "Considering the number of laws you've broken, that was careless. Risky. But even killers get horny, I guess. Even Wacko needs sex. Bundy needed sex. Richard Speck too. So if you need sex, then some part of you is still human, right? But Nick, that could be your biggest mistake." And now she sang in the same small voice she'd heard seconds ago. *"Little Ray, gone today, little Ray, who will pray?* Who's Ray, Wacko?"

"Shut up, Freak." She looked as if she'd been punched in the stomach and couldn't draw in her next breath of air. Then she was moving backward up the stairs, biting at her lower lip.

Mira stayed where she was, rubbing her neck, and moments later the door slammed and the lock turned with a sharp, echoing click.

13

It's not my business, not my business, my business, business.
. . . Keith Curry woke to the worst hangover of his life, his
mouth moving to the words that he heard in his head. He
lifted his arm and glanced at his watch: 7:27 A.M.

He reached blindly for the bedside stand and patted the
surface, looking for a joint he was sure he'd left here last
night. Odd, that he could remember that, that he could
remember rolling the damn thing, taking a couple of hits,
putting it out and crashing. Odd because he couldn't recall much of anything else that had happened.

He found the joint, lit it, puffed on it several times, then
ground out what was left and fell back against the
pillows—and into a dream. Allie was in his face, shouting
at him, accusing him of not giving a shit about Dean,
about the Family, about anyone except himself. And in the
dream he agreed with her completely, he was a no-good,
selfish fuck and he refused to spend his life trapped in
Miami or on Tybee, fretting about the Family.

Then the dream suddenly faltered and skipped and
he was racing into his parents' house, past the paramedics, the police, following his mother's wails, and he
exploded through the patio doors to the chaos around
the pool. There his sister was kneeling over little Ray, trying to resuscitate him, shouting at the paramedics to get
her some epinephrine, fast, she didn't have a pulse.

Curry came to suddenly, gasping for air, unable to breathe, his brain locked in a wild, white panic, and he knew that he was dying, that he had finally had one too many drinks, one too many joints, one too many lost nights in paradise. He flipped onto his side and slammed his fists against his chest, as though he could jump-start his lungs or his heart or whatever was wrong. Suddenly the air in the cabin felt like Vail in January and the cabin exploded with whiteness and Dean emerged from the whiteness. *Please help, Keith,* he implored, and then he threw himself over Curry's body and air rushed into his lungs and he sucked and coughed, sucked and coughed, and collapsed against the pillows again.

He breathed in. Breathed out. In and out, again and again, until his head started to clear. *What the hell just happened?*

Curry could make out the geometric shapes on the ceiling caused by the light that spilled through the venetian blinds. He could hear the long, mournful bleat of a boat's horn, coming into the yacht club's slip. He tasted the sourness of last night's binge in the back of his throat. But he wasn't hung over.

Impossible. Seconds ago, he definitely had been hung over, thought he was dying, couldn't breathe, and he'd seen Dean. *Please help, Keith.*

The joint, of course. He'd taken a couple hits off a joint and fallen back to sleep and now it was hours later. He looked at his watch: 7:27. His watch had stopped.

"Shit."

He threw off the sheet and sat up. His head didn't spin. He didn't feel like puking. The alarm on the night-stand appeared to have stopped, too, and at the same time. 7:27.

Okay, jig's up, Curry. You're dead and the momentous event happened at precisely 7:27.

So, could a dead man brush his teeth? Wash his face? Walk? He got up and went into the head, aware of how his bare feet felt against the floor. If he was dead, why did the floor feel real? Why did his body feel real? Could a dead man taste toothpaste and feel water against his face? The toothpaste was mint, the water was cold.

He emerged from the head, convinced now that he hadn't died. In fact, he heard noise in the galley and smelled coffee. From the bundle of clean laundry he'd picked up yesterday, he pulled out gym shorts and a T-shirt and quickly dressed. He never locked the boat at night; few people did. In this community, *"mi casa es su casa"* was the rule of the land. Even so, this was a bit much, some boater in his galley, making himself right at home.

Curry paused in the doorway and took in the sight of the gringa knockout, moving with utter ease around the galley. Her magnificent blond hair was caught up in a ponytail and she wore a sleeveless cotton dress that hugged her hips, revealed her magnificent legs, the curve of her breasts, the soft, slender lines of her neck and arms. She was barefoot and he kept staring at her perfect feet, her ten perfectly sculpted toes.

"Make yourself at home," he said.

She looked around, those huge blue eyes of hers neither startled nor apologetic, and her lovely mouth swung into a smile. "Hungry?"

"Starved." He went over to the table and sat down. "Smells fantastic."

"I'm not much of a cook, but I make a really tasty omelette." She put one on a plate with a slice of papaya and a corn *arepa.* "Coffee?"

"You bet." Curry couldn't remember the last time a woman had made him breakfast. "So tell me what your fortune-teller pal said after I fled the Caribe."

"That you'd had too much to smoke." Faye brought the

coffeepot and her own plate over to the table. "That you're self-destructive. That you're a man of many secrets."

"A rave review," he said, and cut into the omelette.

It was already warm and sticky in the galley and she reached back and turned on the counter fan and opened the galley windows wider. "It's going to be a scorcher today."

"Does your watch work?" he asked.

"Yeah. Why?"

"My watch and my alarm stopped. What time do you have?"

"It's just after eight."

How was it possible that within a span of just twenty-four minutes, he was now sober? And why had his watch stopped? *And why did I dream of Ray?* He'd had that same dream before, which was really more like a replay of what had actually happened on that black day in 1985. He'd gotten a frantic call from his old man that something had happened to Ray, and by the time he'd gotten to the house, it was too late—Ray was dead.

"So let me guess. We were together last night and you stayed here," he said. "And I was so drunk I don't have a clue what happened."

Her beautiful mouth twitched with annoyance. "Don't flatter yourself, Keith. We went barhopping, you drank too much, and I drove you back here and got you to bed. But I sure as hell didn't stay. There's nothing worse than screwing a guy who's drunk." She leaned across the table, arms resting against the surface, and smiled. "But I have to admit, you look damn good for a guy who put away so much booze he could barely walk."

"That bad, huh?"

"What do you remember?"

He thought about it. "The early part of the evening is clear. You were drinking Dos Equis with a twist of lime. I was drinking rum. We were dancing. I remember thinking that you dance well, but was wishing the music was slower so I could hold you close." *Shit, fuck, what am I saying?* The first rule in his world was to never, never confess what you felt about a woman. But now that he'd started, he didn't want to stop. "I remember sitting outside at one bar, under the stars, just you and me and the sultry air. My hand was on your thigh. Your dress was very short. We were, uh, kissing."

"We were?" She frowned, her magnificent eyes guileless. "Are you sure?"

Curry reached out, touched his hand to her chin, and leaned forward and kissed her. A chaste kiss, as far as kisses went, but the shape and texture and taste of her mouth were so exquisite that he knew if he died in the next ten minutes, that would be okay. To kiss a mouth like this. Christ almighty. "I think it was like that," he said, pulling back slightly.

She gave him the strangest look, as if she suddenly understood something about him that had escaped her before. "You're right. That's exactly how it was—"

"And then I screwed it up by getting loaded," he finished.

She shrugged, their eyes locked. Hers reminded him of sunlight on the Pacific waters just outside the galley windows, an incomparable and impossible fusion of one element with another. "You just redeemed yourself," she said quietly.

He didn't have any snappy comeback to that. Her piercing gaze made him squirm inside, as though his skin had shrunk and was now too small for his bones, and he looked quickly down at his plate and finished up his omelette. She scooted back her chair and got up. She brought the pot of coffee back to the table and refilled their mugs. "You don't seem like a Cunningham," she said suddenly.

"What's that supposed to mean?"

"Well, remember Richie Cunningham on *Happy Days*?"

"Ron Howard."

"Yeah. But that character he played was always up, happy. Ever since, I've associated Cunninghams with that character and you don't seem so up and happy. I mean, you do now, but not usually."

"I didn't realize you even knew my last name." He didn't remember telling her that. But hell, he didn't remember half of what he'd said to her.

"Everyone around here knows your last name," she said with a laugh. "'The party's at Cunningham's boat. The best music is at Cunningham's.' No one has to say anything about what slip you're in or what kind of boat you own. Cunningham this, Cunningham that. I know that you sailed to New Zealand with a couple of Aussies. I know that you sailed to the Caribbean with a couple of women from Spain and a guy from Barbados. You fund children's clinics in Panama; you have a lot of military and government contacts; you're an expat but you speak the language like a native. I've heard all the boating stories, Keith, and I'm sorry, you're not a Cunningham."

Gorgeous, smart, and insightful to boot. "You're right. I'm not. I changed my name from Curry before I left the States twelve years ago."

She winked an eye shut and her index finger shot out at him. "See? I learned a lot from TV."

He had the feeling then that she was playing with him, teasing him, and then she broke the moment by getting up and clearing the table. She stood at *his* sink, washing off *his* dishes, on *his* boat, and yet *he* was the one who couldn't think of anything to say.

"Why'd you change your name?" she asked.

"To separate myself from my family."

"They're so awful?"

"It's a long story." He got up to get more coffee and for moments they stood side by side in the galley, their elbows brushing.

"Do you have a dish rack?" she asked.

"Down here." Curry stooped to open the cabinet under the sink. As he straightened up and set the rack on the counter, the sweet scent of her hair and her skin filled his senses with such a profound desire that he needed to touch her. He ran his fingers across the back of her neck and along the seamless line of her jaw. She scooped suds off the top of what she was washing and touched the end of his nose and dotted each cheek and his forehead with more suds.

Curry skimmed suds out of the sink and dabbed them lightly all over her face and they both laughed. He touched his soapy hand to the back of her neck and brought her face toward him and kissed her. Nothing chaste in this kiss. Their mouths opened, her soapy hands slid into his hair, his left hand dropped to the small of her back and over the beautiful curve of her ass, and her dress hiked up, and she pressed her magnificent body up against him and slid her hands down inside his gym shorts.

Even though the air steamed with the heat their bodies threw off, the silk of her panties felt as cool and light as mountain water against his hands. Curry slipped his hand between her thighs and she leaned back, gripping his shoulders, arching her back against the pressure, her mouth slightly parted, her eyes locked on his and filling with tears.

Then she suddenly twisted away from him and ran her hands over her clothes, smoothing them back into place.

"This is moving a little fast for me," she said, her voice husky, thick, choked. "I didn't come here for this."

Blew it, I blew it. "I'm sorry . . . I didn't mean to upset you."

"It's not your fault. You just remind me of someone."

Curry wasn't about to touch *that* one.

She turned back to the sink, to the dishes, to the dish rack. After a few uncomfortably silent moments, she said, "Keith, I need to get back to the States."

He felt relieved to talk about something else. "You didn't buy a round-trip ticket?"

"No. I stupidly thought I could get a cheaper fare by buying a return ticket here."

"I liked your *Caleuche* story better."

"Yeah, me too." She glanced up at him and smiled. "I'm on standby for three different flights. I heard you've got connections, that you can get back to the States whenever you want."

He laughed. He could just imagine where this rumor had gotten started, deep in some pot-infested cabin where nomadic gringos sat around trying to impress women who looked like Faye. "My *connections,*" he said, "are always purchased. Not outright—a hundred bucks here, a thousand there, five grand for some local cause, everything under the table. To get a flight out between Christmas and New Year's Day is practically impossible. You'd be better off finding a boater who's headed back to the States."

"So you can't help me?"

"I doubt it."

"Christ," she said softly, biting at the side of her nail.

"Well, there's a military guy I know. He's done me favors in the past." *Please help, Keith.* Maybe it was time to see if his sister actually had blown her cork. "I'll see if I can get us seats on a military transport plane."

"*Us?*"

"I need to get home, too," he said, and wondered if he

would regret the words the moment he stepped on American soil.

She broke into a smile that could light up half of Manhattan. "I really appreciate this, Keith."

"But you have to understand. These aren't direct flights, okay? They go via Havana, Mexico City, Guatemala, Caracas . . . no telling."

"That's fine. Where in the States do these flights usually land?"

"Miami, Orlando, Atlanta, it varies."

"Any of those would work."

"But because this is the capital of 'Mañana Land,' Faye, these plans could fall through. That's what happens at least fifty percent of the time."

"It means we have a fifty-fifty chance of getting back to the States. That's better than I have on standby."

"Let me grab my cell phone and we'll get going."

"*We?*"

We, us. "Hey, you're going to plead your case. These military guys are always suckers for a beautiful woman's sob story."

"Should I change clothes?"

No. "Something a little more modest."

"Less legs? Less boobs? A hat? Sunglasses? Be specific."

"Less legs, less boobs, but be imaginative."

She looked amused. "I'll meet you in the parking lot in five minutes. Should I have my bag with me?"

"No. These flights usually leave at night. We'll have plenty of time to get back here."

She started out, her straw bag over her shoulder, then turned, came back to him, and cupped his face in her hands and kissed him. Not the kiss of an innocent, he thought, and definitely a kiss that promised to finish what had begun here. "Just give me some time," she said softly. "See you in five minutes."

When she met him in the parking lot exactly five minutes later, she looked like something off the pages of a fashion magazine. Seductive, but not crass, a gringa with class.

14

Light the color of pus filtered through the cabin windows, a faithful reflection of Sheppard's mood. Even two mugs of Goot's Cuban *café con leche* didn't do much to lift his spirits and it didn't banish his fatigue. His eyes still felt as if they'd been scrubbed with gravel and put back sideways into the sockets.

Since Annie's hysteria three or four hours ago, he and Goot had made little progress. They didn't have any idea what they were looking for. They couldn't name it, tag it, categorize it. Yet, last night, both of them had felt certain that they would recognize *it*, this quality, this critical element, when they saw it. Now he wasn't at all sure.

"Shep?"

He glanced up as Annie sank down next to him on the living-room floor. "What is it, kiddo?"

"After I woke everyone up last night and went into Nadine's room, something weird happened."

Weird. Okay, that was business as usual for the Morales family, he thought. "Weird how?"

As she started explaining, Sheppard picked up a legal pad and scribbled notes. A house on a frozen river. Northern Georgia. Mira in a basement or cellar, strapped down to a bed. A woman named Rose. It didn't seem like much information, but his years with the Morales family had taught him to pay attention to the smallest details, regardless of how insignificant they might look.

"Who was this Rose person?" he asked.

"I don't know. But she said it was important to remember her name."

"Goot, do we have anyone in these case files named Rose?"

He was already doing a search on the laptop. "A perp?"

Sheppard looked at Annie and she shook her head. "She wasn't a bad person."

"Anyone, Goot," Sheppard said. "Family members, relatives, friends connected to any of the cases."

"We haven't finished compiling all the names yet," Goot said. "But I'll keep searching."

Nadine brought breakfast plates over to the kitchen table and, as they all sat down, announced that she and Annie would like to read the barn after they ate. "We'd like to start here at the cabin and follow the path that Mira took."

Eighty-two years old and she could sleep for a few hours and then function. Sheppard was forty years younger and felt like warmed shit on toast. The secret, he thought, had to be yoga and good genes. Nadine had practiced yoga for fifty years or more, long before it had become popular with baby boomers. She looked twenty years younger than she was, had a body so flexible that on a good day she could do a backflip that would send Olympic competitors in gymnastics back into training.

So right after breakfast, they all retreated to the outdoors. Kyle King had arrived by then and he had the equipment they needed to wire Nadine and Annie for sound. He, Goot, and Sheppard hung back as Annie and Nadine began their descent down the shallow slope of the hill toward the barn.

He sensed, as he had so many times in the past since he'd met Mira, that he was superfluous in the grander plan. He believed this plan had more to do with women than with men, that perhaps the ultimate energy in the universe was feminine, not male, and that anyone with a dick would be playing a very small role in the world that was evolving. He had read two science fiction novels like that, both of them written by women and recommended to him by Mira.

In *The Shore of Women,* author Pamela Sargent saw men as the threat against a walled city in which only women lived. In *The Blue Place,* author Nicola Griffith hadn't included a single man. The entire novel took place on another planet populated only by women.

There was suddenly no doubt in his mind that regardless of how long he knew Mira, whether they got married or simply continued as they were, Nadine would remain the matriarch of this family and he, Sheppard, would still be the bastard gringo son. Especially now.

"Neither of them has said a thing," King whispered.

"It means they haven't picked up anything," Sheppard replied.

"If one of them says something, won't that influence the other?" King asked.

"It could," Goot answered. "But that's not necessarily bad."

Sheppard nodded and licked snowflakes off his lip. "But what usually happens is that what one says feeds into the impressions of the other."

"They become like one mind," Goot said.

"Sounds like bees," King remarked.

"I taste something hot," Annie said, and the men fell silent.

"Like pepper," Nadine added. "Hot peppers. Jalapeños."

Annie reached for her grandmother's hand. "That's it exactly, Nana."

"She had a fever," Nadine went on.

"A raging fever," Annie agreed. "But what I taste is different than a fever."

"What the fuck does *that* mean?" King asked.

"Nothing yet," Sheppard said.

"Scared, I'm scared." Nadine spoke and she sounded breathless. She moved very fast. "Screaming for help. Where're the dogs? Where is everyone?"

She and Annie now broke into a run and raced through the door of the barn, and Sheppard broke away from King and Goot to catch up with them. The horses and the goats were gone now, but the smell of animals lingered in the barn, thick odors that assaulted Sheppard—the ripe stink of manure, the sweetness of hay, the powerful smell of the earth. Nadine and Annie were sitting on their heels, near the spot where Mira's blood had been found, their hands still joined.

"She fell here," Annie said softly.

Sheppard hadn't told them anything about where Mira's blood had been found.

"Someone else was here, too. She fell over a body," Nadine added.

"Hot, my mouth is so hot," Annie went on.

Nadine stood, pulling Annie to her feet. They stood for a moment in the quiet, their breaths visible in the cold air, their free hands clenched tightly over the earring each one held. Mira's earrings. Then Nadine let go of Annie's hand and dropped into a crouch. In a voice that sounded nothing like her own, she said, *"Why'd you run? Why? It's not in the pattern."*

"What the hell's *that*?" King asked.

Sheppard shrugged. He didn't have a clue.

"If she starts to move, get out of her way," Goot said. "Because she won't see you."

"Get her into the car," Nadine continued in a voice that wasn't hers. *"Wrap the wound to stop the bleeding. Pump her full of antibiotics."*

Annie seemed to realize what was happening and quickly stepped out of the way. Nadine stooped over and went through the motions of picking up something—or someone—and then walked fast, her arms curved in front of her.

Nadine was now inside the killer, who was carrying Mira. It was bizarre to witness; not only had her voice changed, but she moved differently, her spine straighter, her stride longer. Instead of going through the front of the barn, she went out the rear door, the closest door, and Sheppard and Annie hurried after her, with Goot, King, and the dog falling in behind them. Annie took Sheppard's hand.

"She's hooked into the killer, Shep," Annie whispered. "I could feel the energy there, waiting for one of us to claim it, but it scared me. The energy is so powerful. But Nadine's not afraid of anything."

"You did great, Annie. You okay?"

Her head bobbed once, then she fell silent. Ricki trotted alongside Annie and every so often she reached down and ran her fingers through the retriever's fur.

"What do you mean by powerful, Annie? Is it like electricity? Powerful in that way? Or like wind? What?" *Tell me, help me understand.*

She thought about this, her shoes crunching over the snow. "In history class we saw a film about the bombing of Hiroshima. It's that kind of energy."

"Is it the killer's energy that's like that or the energy of the event?"

"I can't separate them in that way. Nana Nadine can, Mom can, but I can't do that yet."

"When you saw your mom last night, in that dream or whatever it was, how'd she seem?"

"Sick. She looked bad."

Shit. "Can you describe Rose?"

Annie thought for a moment. "Black hair, really pretty. Like I said before, she isn't bad."

Her answer didn't tell him enough. What he really wanted to ask was what, exactly, had she experienced? A dream? An out-of-body experience? Telepathy? Clairvoyance? What the hell was he supposed to call it?

Ridiculous. He should know by now that he couldn't attach labels to the phenomena in Mira's world.

At the top of the slope, just past the cabin, Nadine stopped behind King's Explorer. Sheppard gestured for him to open the back of the vehicle. Once the rear door swung upward, Nadine leaned over and put the body—Mira's body—in the back. Her hands were busy—moving as though she were unfolding a sheet or a blanket, pulling it up over the body, tucking it in around the feet. She climbed into the back of the car, reached into her jacket pocket. Sheppard couldn't imagine what she held when she removed her hand from her pocket and didn't have a clue what she was doing. He was tempted to question Nadine, as he sometimes did Mira when she was in this state, but was afraid she might snap out of it if he spoke.

"The killer handcuffed Mira to something on the floor," Goot whispered.

A pit tore open in Sheppard's stomach.

Nadine scrambled out of the Explorer and stood still for a moment, her face lifted into the air like a dog who has caught an intriguing scent. She walked fast toward the cabin, through the door, down the hall, and into the bedroom. *"What'd I touch?"* she muttered, and looked wildly around.

Back up the hall, into the kitchen. Nadine grabbed a dish towel and returned to the bedroom. She wiped down drawer handles, surfaces. She stuffed the dish towel into her jacket pocket and practically ran back up the hall and into the living room. Every gesture that she made, every movement, suggested haste, but attention to details.

Outside again, she hurried over to the Explorer, King's Explorer. He looked worriedly at Sheppard. "She can't drive in this condition."

"I'll drive," Sheppard said. "Everyone else get in the back. One of you help Nadine into the passenger seat."

Annie helped her into the car and everyone else, including the dog, piled into the back. Sheppard could tell from Nadine's silence and her focused concentration that she was completely immersed in an altered state, but that she was aware of how easily that focus could be broken. She sat quietly, staring straight ahead, her palms flat against her thighs.

As he headed down the steep, crooked road that led away from the farm, the wipers whipped back and forth across the windshield, clearing a half-moon in the accumulated snow on the glass. At the bottom of the hill, Sheppard stopped and glanced at Nadine. "Which way?" he asked.

"I'm outta here," she said in that strange voice that was not her own. *"West. Two-lane roads. Interstates could be closed."*

Goot leaned forward and fit a mini digital recorder between the driver and the passenger seats. It was on, getting it all. He had worked enough with Mira to appreciate the importance of a record. Sheppard headed west, the wipers making a rhythmic, mesmerizing noise. The road led through a wooded area, past a small, frozen lake shaped

like an eye. A couple of ice-skaters sped across the ice, surreal figures in the light snowfall. At an intersection three
miles later, Sheppard caught the red light and stopped.

If he headed due west as the compass read, he would
enter a hillside neighborhood. If he turned right, he
eventually would end up on I-240, the Asheville bypass
that fed into I-40. If he followed I-40 west, it would lead
him into Asheville, then the Biltmore estate area, and
then onward toward the Smoky Mountain National Park.

"Which way, Nadine?"

"*Mierda, lo perdí,*" she spat.

She'd lost the trail.

"Pull off to the side of the road, Shep."

He pulled onto the shoulder and Nadine threw open
the door and stepped outside. She turned slowly in
place, arms bent at the elbows, palms upward, facing the
sky. Then she brought her hands out in front of her,
palms facing outward, and kept turning, turning. She
looked, Sheppard thought, like some ancient warrior,
knees slightly bent, body positioned for defense. The
wind blew through her hair.

"What's she doing?" King asked.

"Trying to pick up my mom's signal," Annie said. "But
I don't think she can do it here."

Annie got out and she and Nadine appeared to be arguing. Sheppard watched them, his eyes aching from
lack of sleep, and wondered what Annie could possibly
say to stubborn Nadine that would get her back in the
car. Again he was struck by the reality: Their world was
not his world. At best, he was just a visitor, a tourist, a guy
passing through.

"So we know they were headed west," Goot said, studying a map spread open in his lap. "We know the killer
wanted two-lane roads because he thought the interstate
might be closed."

"There're dozens of two-laners through the national park," King said. "We need more specific information."

"South," Nadine said as she and Annie got back into the car. "The destination is south, but she had to go west to get there. South to northern Georgia, someplace by a river, that was what Annie got last night."

"The Blue Ridge Parkway goes through the Smoky Mountain National Park and was shut down by ten that night," King said. "If this guy went south, he would take two-lane roads that skirted the park so he could get to the Georgia line. There, he could connect with I-75 or I-80. As for rivers . . ." King shook his head. "There're dozens of rivers in Georgia. But at least we know the general direction now."

"Weren't those interstates closed that night by the snowstorm?" Goot asked.

"For a while. But the North Carolina stretches shut down first."

"He?" Nadine frowned and turned around in her seat. "Who're you talking about?"

"The killer," Goot and King replied simultaneously.

"The killer," Nadine said, "the person who has Mira, is a woman."

15

The power of Mira's own fear shocked her. For the longest time after the basement door slammed shut, she stayed where she was, on the cold, hard floor, too terrified to move. She was sure Wacko would know about it and would burst through the basement door to kick her some more. She wondered if this was how political prisoners felt, particularly those Americans who had no access to legal counsel and were interrogated off U.S. soil.

Wacko's departure had to be a trick. After all, Mira thought, she hadn't been handcuffed, strapped down to the bed, drugged, or immobilized in any way this time. She was free to move around the basement—and yet, her fear paralyzed her.

She finally rolled onto her back and sat up. She stared at the basement door, but it didn't fly open. Wacko didn't appear. There were no surveillance cameras down here.

Mira moved slowly, prowling back and forth in front of the stairs. Her ribs hurt, her thigh hurt, every goddamn part of her body hurt and every step required enormous effort. She finally grabbed onto the staircase railing and began to climb.

She wouldn't break any speed records. She tested each step for creaks before she put her full weight on it. She counted the steps, engaging her mind in this useless act to allow her intuitive self greater freedom. But that self seemed to be out to lunch again. Even though wood usually held psychic residue, nothing about Wacko surfaced.

At the top of the stairs, she pressed her ear to the door, listening. She didn't hear any sounds. She brought her hand to the knob, turned it, pushed. Locked. Definitely locked. And why didn't she pick up any impressions from the metal knob?

Because you're now half a person. Get over it and get out of here.

She started back down the stairs, paused, sat down on the fourth step and turned, peering between the steps to the space under the staircase. A good hiding place. But she didn't want to hide. She wanted to escape.

At the bottom of the stairs, she eyed the small, supposedly shatterproof windows on the other side of the room. A soft light now filtered through them. Even if Wacko had lied about the glass being shatterproof, the windows were too small for her to fit through and much too high to reach without standing on something. However, if she could reach a window and break one, she could scream and her screams might be heard by someone passing by. Maybe heard by Nick? Where did Nick live in relation to this house? It seemed like a long shot. But she had to try.

Mira opened one of the cabinet doors, looking for something she could use to hit the window, to try to break it. She picked a can of black beans. She set the can on the hospital tray, lowered it as far as it would go, almost even with her knees, pressed down on the brake to keep it in place. Then she swung her good leg over it, straddled the hospital tray as she would a horse, and released the brake. She pressed her bare feet to the floor to move the table.

The edge of the table bumped up against the wall and

Mira maneuvered it until it was parallel and pressed down on the brake again. She reached under the table for the lever and raised it to its full height. Then, moving carefully, she brought her feet up onto the table and slowly raised up into a crouch and finally to her full height, the can of beans gripped in her right hand.

She set the can on the windowsill and rubbed her palms against the cold glass, trying to clear a space so that she could see outside. But the tinting on the window was too dark to make out much of anything except bushes. She picked up the can and drew her arm back and whacked the glass. No cracks, no fissures, not even a hint of weakness. It was like trying to dent steel with a toothpick.

Even so, she whacked it twice more. The can ruptured at the seams and black juice sluiced down the inside of her arm. Disgusted and frustrated, she dropped the oozing can, moved into a crouch again, brought her legs down on either side of the table, lowered it, and released the brake.

Okay, so Wacko apparently had told her the truth about the glass.

And now that she had wasted untold minutes or hours or however long this had taken, she would have to clean up the mess. She scooted back toward the bed, then over to the counter, finding it easier to get around like this than walking. She drew up next to the counter, dropped the can into the trash, grabbed a roll of paper towels, and wiped off the juice.

Now what?

She helped herself to a bottle of water and an apple from the small fridge and sat there, drinking, munching, thinking.

Shatterproof glass, nothing in the basement to use as a weapon, one exit. Maybe she could break through the door somehow. Yeah, right. And what the hell would she use? Another can of beans? She already knew Wacko had locked the door when she'd left; Mira had heard the click of the dead bolt.

Forget the door, forget the windows. Was there another exit here that Wacko didn't know about? Unlikely. But she had to look.

Mira pressed her bare feet against the floor again. She pushed herself away from the counter, past the bed, toward the computer on the other side of the room and into the alcove. Here she hit the wall switch and a dim overhead light came on. She put on the table's brake and got off. Washing machine, dryer, hamper. *Nothing, nothing.* "Shit, suppose there was a fire down here and the main door was blocked? How would anyone get out?"

She planted her palms firmly against the top of the washing machine. A *metal* washing machine. *Give me something.*

No, no, this was wrong, she decided. She never got anywhere by demanding. She had to go back to the basics. *Inhale right nostril, exhale left nostril, five times on one side, five times on the other, clear the mind, be calm, be calm.* She had learned this technique from Nadine when she was five or six, and when all else failed, she returned to it like a homing pigeon. *The will controls the mind,* Nadine always told her.

The shift in her consciousness was subtle this time, no shocking impressions, no blazing lights, no urgent rush of information. Instead, her body seemed to hum like a tuning fork. Well, it was a start, right? It was more than she'd felt in a long time from just touching an object.

Mira twisted her bare feet against the floor, one way, then the other, three times, six, grounding herself. She visualized a circuit of light around her body, heels to hands to skull, until she was surrounded by the circuit, encased inside of it. . . .

Bright sunlight against water.

Warm boards under my feet.

Thick letter in my hand.

No last name, just a first name and an address on Tybee, a convenience store. Should I read the letter? I want to, I want to know. But that's something Al would do, so I refuse. Ha-ha, Al, too bad, Al, fuck you, Al. . . .

Mira pulled her hands away from the washing machine and felt like cheering. It worked, she could still read objects. But apparently she could only read objects related to the man who owned the house, not to Wacko. Even so, it was costing her. Already, sweat seeped from her pores, the pain in her leg had awakened, her body ached, the rattle in her lungs had grown more pronounced.

Tell me, Nadine's physician had once asked. *How is the physiology of a psychic different from that of other people? Or is there any difference?* It was the one question that Wacko apparently hadn't considered and now Mira was paying for it.

Mira couldn't speak for other psychics, but she knew that for herself, Nadine, and even Annie, some drugs could complicate a physical ailment, making it worse. Certain types of drugs could send their spirits soaring—and leave their bodies back here on earth to wallow in shit. The three of them were sensitive to certain types of foods and additives, something a doctor would tag as an allergy, but it was about assimilation, not allergy. Bottom line? There were pronounced differences, but it might not be related to anything psychic. It could just be genetic.

Regardless, her thigh was a mess, her lungs—though

improved—still sounded as though she should be on a respirator, and she was getting nowhere fast down here in the basement.

Use what you've got. Right. Okay. Use it even though what she had was running at about an eighth of its usual power. Mira rubbed her hands against her T-shirt, then rubbed them together hard and quickly, working up a heat. So who was this man? Wacko's uncle? A cousin? Brother?

Brother.

She brought her hands to the surface of the washing machine again.

Two men, one standing, one sitting. They look like Vikings, both handsome and blue-eyed—

She pulled her hands off. She *recognized* the younger man, she knew that face. But from where? She fought to retrieve the memory, but the only thing she got was a fragment of something weird, of herself with Tom and this man, the younger Viking. Still, she was pretty sure she'd never met this guy.

This sort of thing had happened to her occasionally in the past when she glimpsed the face of someone who hadn't entered her life yet or, even more rarely, the face of someone she later discovered was dead. Mira brought her hands slowly to the washer.

The older man paces restlessly around the room. "This is wrong," he bursts out. "I'm going in there now to speak to your attorney, to tell him—"

"No." The younger man shoots to his feet. "You promised,

Keith. You gave me your word that you wouldn't bring her into this."

"These bastards are building their case to convict you for something you didn't do, Dean, and they need to know you've got an alibi. They need to hear it, from her. What the fuck's wrong with her, anyway? If she loved you, she'd be here."

"It's not that simple." Dean sinks into the chair, brings his fists to his eyes. "She's underage. A runaway. Her parents would take away the baby and—"

"The baby? What baby?"

"Forget it. At the most, I'll get three to five years. I'll do the time. And once I do the time, I'm free to live my own life."

The older man—Keith—grabs his brother by the shoulders. "What baby? Who is this woman, Dean? Where is she? What the fuck is going on?"

And just that quickly, the vein dried up. Even though she kept her hands to the machine, nothing else came to her. She moved her hands to the top of the dryer, to the cabinet doors, to the plastic hamper. Disappointment, terror, panic: all of it poured through Mira. She rubbed her hands over her face, her eyes, and squeezed back the hot sting of tears that threatened to fall.

She slung her good leg over the table again, pushed herself out of the alcove, paused at the computer. She really didn't think Wacko would be this careless, but she was out of choices, out of ideas. Her ability, the one thing she had been able to count on always, now seemed capricious, whimsical, as unpredictable as the weather. She didn't know why, didn't give a shit about reasons, didn't have the energy to puzzle through it.

Mira dismounted from her silly wooden horse. She plugged in the computer, turned it on. While it booted up, she jerked open drawers in the desk, looking for the phone cord. She found it in a bottom drawer, under a supply of paper, still in its wrapper. She tore open the wrapper, connected the cord to the computer, and plugged it into the phone outlet. When her fingers touched the keyboard, it came to her, an entire scene, a mother lode of information. . . .

Keith, pacing. Dean, standing with his back to a wall. And now a third man in a three-piece suit hurries into the room with Allie.

"We need to talk, Dean," this man says. "Allie tells me you're married, that there's a woman who can provide an alibi—"

"I've told you everything, Jim. Allie's dreaming."

Allie looks helplessly at Keith. "He's married, he told me as much. And you've known about it all along and never said a goddamn thing." Hysteria makes her voice crack. She sounds like a shrew.

Keith looks away from her, down at his shoes, and says nothing.

The lawyer paces. "Dean? You want to say anything more?"

"Nope."

Allie's explosion sweeps through the room like a hurricane. "For Christ's sake, Jim. Use it anyway. Say it. That way the jury hears it. Dean was with his wife the night of the accident."

"But I don't know that," Jim snaps.

"You're fired," Allie shouts, her entire body shaking, her face bright red.

"Go fuck yourself," Dean hisses, and looks at the lawyer, at Jim. "I'm guilty of what they say I did. It was my car. I was there. I ran. The rest . . . everything else I told you . . . it's bullshit, Jim. That's all you have to know. And you're not fired."

Allie shouts that he's lying, that he's lying to protect this woman, this whore, this . . .

***

Gone. Mira brought her hands down hard against the keyboard, begging the keys to give her more, to finish the story, to tell her what she needed to know to escape. But nothing else came to her. She was like some prospector from the Old West who hits a vein of gold, only to find that the vein has gone dry two inches later.

But now the desktop screen was up. Her eyes flicked across the icons. Not a single online service. She brought the cursor to the start button, left-clicked, scanned the column of options that appeared.

Nothing.

Frustrated, Mira pushed away from the computer, got back on her silly wooden horse, and looked around the room for something else she could read. The refrigerator? The cabinet against the far wall? She had touched both, but she'd been looking for information on Allie, not her brother.

She scooted the table across the room, dismounted again, put on the brake. She crouched in front of it and placed her hands on the door. . . .

Hundreds of people file through a room where a small coffin is displayed, the lid open. Men and women weep openly, a woman at the front is overcome with grief and collapses. . . .

The funeral of a child, the brother Ray. No, she didn't want to experience that. "Take me elsewhere," Mira said quietly, and brought her hands to the fridge again.

***

The two brothers, Keith and Dean, sit on a tall diving board that overlooks a massive swimming pool. It's lit at the bottom and now, in the dark, resembles some pristine pond in paradise.

Keith lights a joint, puffs, passes it to Dean. Sobbing drifts out into the night air from an open upstairs window in the house behind them. Keith shakes his head and blows out smoke. "I realized that we're a family who lives in total silence."

"You and I don't," *Dean says.*

"We do, but not as badly as the others."

"Everyone talked when Ray was here."

"Not enough. Allie always interfered."

"I wish she would go away forever," *Dean remarks.* "She thinks she's my mother."

"She thinks she's everyone's mother, even Mom and Dad's."

Dean opens a cardboard box he has carried up to the diving board with him. "You read?" *he asks.*

"Yeah."

From the box, Dean removes a flower from the funeral, a slightly withered red rose, a key chain with a panda dangling at the end of it, a little house made of Legos, and Big Bird. "You first, Keith."

Keith picks up the red rose and tosses it out over the pool. "For you, Ray," *he says quietly, and they watch the rose as it tumbles down toward the gleaming blue water.*

Dean picks up Big Bird, whom Ray loved so much. He presses it between his hands, then hurls it out over the pool. They finish the joint and are about to toss the last two items when Allie's shrill voice shatters the quiet.

"Dean, what the hell are you doing at the top of that diving board? Get down from there this instant!"

"Chill out, Al," *Keith calls down.* "He's up here with me."

"And that's supposed to reassure me?" *she shouts.*

"Let's jump," *Dean says, giggling from the pot.*

"Good idea, man." *Then, more loudly:* "Hey, Al, we're coming down."

Dean stands, strips off his clothes, walks with great assurance to the tip of the diving board, and executes a perfect swan dive. Allie is shouting, Dean is laughing, and Keith strips down to his shorts, scoops up the remaining items from the wooden box. He runs to the end of the diving board, leaps, and pulls his legs up against his body so the splash will be huge. When he surfaces, Allie is standing by the side of the pool, her perfect clothes drenched, her face ravaged with rage.

Dean is doubled over with laughter at the shallow end. Allie marches toward Dean, grabs him by the arm, and slaps him so hard across the face that the noise seems to sting the air. Keith literally sees red. He scrambles out of the pool, runs toward the bitch, grabs her arm, and spins her around so fast she doesn't even know what has happened.

"Don't you ever touch him again," Keith hisses, and then he does something he has always ached to do. He swings and knocks her flat.

Mira kept her hands there a moment longer, but this vein had run dry as well.

But seeing Keith knock his sister to the ground had done something for Mira that nothing else had. She suddenly knew that her only way out of here was to catch Wacko by surprise.

16

The Lakeview Nursing Home sprawled across five acres of prime Savannah real estate and was painted a soft, inviting yellow. In the spring and summer, Allie thought, that color blended in with the blooming wetlands, the vast savannas.

But it was winter now and the wetlands and the savannas looked dead, the lake was frozen. In the winter, nothing looked like it should, which was probably why the curtains on the picture windows were closed and why the blinds in every room she passed were lowered. In this wing the patients lived in a perpetual winter, a nowhere land stripped clean of memory, their pasts as dead to them as the land outside.

Allie moved quickly through the hallway and the day room of wing A, carrying her father's food tray. It was too late for breakfast and too early for lunch, but he hadn't eaten anything today, the nurse had told her, except for a can of Ensure. So she had gone into the resident kitchen and prepared him a meal herself, using what was available. Now she would feed him. Now she would change his diapers. Now she would do for him what he had done for her when she was an infant, a toddler, the first kid in the Curry household.

Once upon a time there had been four kids in the Curry family. Once upon a time there were six Currys, one too many, so then there were five. Now there were only three: one who was permanently out to lunch, another who still didn't know what he wanted to be when he grew up, and herself, the only functional human being of the lot. *And I have got a shitload on my plate.*

In the day room, a woman whom everyone called "Jane Russell" rushed over to Allie, her black high heels tapping out a code against the tile floors. She was dressed in a designer wool suit and a knee-length leather jacket that probably had cost seven or eight hundred bucks. Flung around her neck was a beautiful wool scarf. Leather gloves covered her hands. The strap of an expensive leather purse hung from her shoulder.

Tagging along behind her was Jane Russell's entourage, several ladies in various stages of dementia or Alzheimer's who lived in the same wing. One of them, Lillian, had wild white hair and wore a bathrobe and Bugs Bunny slippers. The other was put together all wrong, left brow higher than the right, that glazed, distracted look in her eyes so common among Alzheimer's patients, her flab rolling out from under her halter top and shorts. She looked as if she'd crawled out of a bad novel.

"Honey, so good to see you," Jane Russell gushed, flicking her beautifully cut hair off the collar of her leather coat. "How've you been?"

"Just great, Jane," Allie replied. "How're things here?"

"So glad you asked." She was always scrupulously polite. She leaned forward, her tone of voice conspiratorial, hushed. "Where can we get a cab around here? We're due in the city for a play. No one gives me the right answer."

Lillian, the woman with the Bugs Bunny slippers, broke into hysterical laughter. "Yeah, right. My son took my money, too."

Jane rolled her soft brown eyes. "They overdosed her on the meds," she confided.

"You and your friends will freeze to death outside," Allie said. "It's cold out there."

"Oh, we'll do just fine. All we need is a cab, honey."

"The cab's waiting out front. I saw it on my way in."

A light winked on in Jane Russell's eyes. "Your father has been asking for Allie and Dean all day. I know you're Allie and I hope Dean's with you."

"Oh, he is. He is. He's on his way in even as we speak, Jane. You'd better hurry before the cab leaves. Down the hall, and take a right."

That would take them to the locked door.

Jane blinked, the lights in her eyes went out, and she turned to her companions. "We'd better hurry, ladies. You heard the honey here. The cab may leave without us."

And they shuffled up the hall, twittering among themselves.

Not long after Allie had moved her father into Lakeview, Jane Russell had come on to him. She had goosed him during a facility event and, later that night, a nurse had found her humping him in his bed as he slept on, oblivious to her overtures. Allie figured that in her day Jane had been quite a hot ticket, a lady about town with money to burn and a creature of her appetites, rather like Allie herself. But now Jane was deep in the throes of Alzheimer's, her slender hips wrapped in diapers, committed by her son, who had then stolen her money.

And she wasn't the exception. Her father, God bless him, was surrounded by nutcases like Jane Russell. No wonder he rarely had a coherent thought.

Allie hastened down the hall to avoid any more residents who recognized her—not as who she was, but just as a friendly face in the crowd, someone sympathetic to their cause, whatever that might be. A cab into Manhattan. A way out of the nuthouse. A large penis for some rest and relaxation. Welcome to the Alzheimer's wing of Lakeview, the place where men and women went quietly mad during the final years of their lives.

Room 33 was her father's. The staff had made a beautiful wooden sign with his name engraved on it—BILL CURRY, M.D.—that hung on the door. Next to it on the wall hung a shadow box filled with photographs of his life, one of the techniques used with Alzheimer's patients to stimulate their memories. It didn't seem to have much impact on her father.

She pushed open the door with her foot, already aware that he wouldn't remember she had been here for hours. "Hey, Dad, I've brought you some food."

The man who lay on the bed, an arm flung over his eyes, lifted his elbow and peeked out at her. "Who're you?"

"Your daughter," she replied, and set the tray on the bedside table.

"Hey, you're pretty." He raised up.

He wore boxer shorts and a silk shirt with a tie. His feet were bare. But his hair was still thick and white, and when he was dressed properly, he looked like the father she remembered, a strapping man, six foot three, broad-shouldered and handsome. The apple of her mother's eye.

But right now, he looked like what he was, a seventy-four-year-old man whose lights had gone out. A shell of a man.

"I've got some clam chowder, scrambled eggs, rye bread toasted just the way you like it."

"Not hungry," he said petulantly.

"Of course you are."

Allie helped him swing his legs around so he was now sitting up. He blinked his rheumy eyes, cocked his head as though listening to something she couldn't hear, and said, "Mother's here."

Mother was Allie's mother, not her father's mother, not

her grandmother. Her parents, in their later years together, had called each other by the roles in which they knew each other best: *Mother* and *Father,* as though these words were their names.

"Really. And where is she?" Allie asked, tucking a napkin into the throat of her father's silk shirt.

"Sitting next to me."

"Uh-huh." She dipped the spoon into the chowder. "And what's she got to say for herself?"

"She's very annoyed with you."

"And why is that?"

"She says you know exactly why."

"Oh? And what's she say, Dad?"

He cocked his head, as if listening. "The Dean business."

Just then, Allie felt a chilly breath of air on the back of her neck, as though someone were behind her, blowing on the back of her neck, and she suddenly thought of the shape she had seen next to Mira's bed and how Mira had spoken to her in what sounded like Dean's voice. *Don't do it, Al. Not in my name.* She obviously had imagined the entire thing, just as she now imagined that someone was blowing on the back of her neck. She looked around, but of course no one was there.

She rubbed her hand across the back of her neck, unable to shake off the eerie sensation that his remark had evoked in her.

"Who am I, Dad?"

"Our daughter. Allie. Firstborn."

Well, the lights had come on. She got several spoonfuls of chowder into his mouth. "And who're your other kids, Dad?"

"Ray, Keith, and Dean." He took the spoon from her, dished it into the bowl she held, and brought the spoon upward, missing his mouth entirely. The chowder dribbled down his chin, his neck, onto the napkin that covered the front of the shirt. "I never see the others. They don't visit me." And then he began to cry. "Can't do shit anymore. Can't remember. Useless."

Allie sat back, struggling to ignore his tears, the agony in his voice, the chowder that dripped down his chin. "Don't cry, Daddy," she said softly, and wiped gently at his chin, his jaw, the front of his shirt. "Hey, you know who I saw? Jane Russell. She and her cronies are on their way to the Manhattan theater district. They were looking for a cab."

A year ago, she and her father used to laugh about Jane Russell and her buddies. He called them "inmates." Now he frowned, his brow wrinkled like the skin of a prune. "Who's Jane Russell?"

"Oh, just a silly woman," she replied, struggling to keep her voice light, casual. "I think we should go out as soon as you finish lunch, Dad."

"I never go out anymore," he murmured, and opened his mouth like a small, hungry bird.

It took her a while to get him cleaned up and dressed in street clothes. Thank God he was still mobile and she didn't have to get him to a walker or into a wheelchair. All the years he had spent swimming his three or four miles a day in the family pool in Miami had paid off with mobility and a minimum of other health problems. His joints, eyesight, lungs, heart, kidneys, and liver were all in good condition. Only his brain, the organ he had valued most, was damaged.

In the beginning, when she first noticed how forgetful he was becoming, Allie had put him on Aricept, the so-called wonder drug for Alzheimer's in the 1990s, and had sent him to a chelation clinic twice a week. She had prescribed a strict regimen of vitamins and minerals and had hired a cook to prepare gourmet vegetarian meals. The combination of traditional and alternative medicine had arrested the progress of the disease. But in the end the disease had won, it usually did. She supposed there were Alzheimer's patients who had gone into remission, but she hadn't met one. Now here they were, she and her father, six years down the road, her mother dead, her only living sibling unavailable, and her own life trapped in chaos.

Drive, she thought, and drove—out of Savannah, away from the nursing home. She headed east toward Tybee Island, a spit of sand in the outer banks, a place she had called home for fifteen years. It wasn't the paradise she had known as a kid, when she and her family used to come up here for the summers, to the house where she now lived. Developers had moved in, walled communities had gone up, dirt roads had been paved, and Hollywood had discovered the place.

Celebrities usually spelled the kiss of death. Sandra Bullock had a home on Tybee and no telling who would be next: Keanu Reeves in his wraparound shades and long leather coat, Russell Crowe fighting gladiators and lions, Julia Roberts with her eighteenth husband. Her dad, of course, wasn't aware of the changes. Or, if he was, he didn't comment. His face was turned toward the open window, where the cool air carried the rich, complex smells of the salt marsh. Her father loved the marsh, always had, and at the moment everything about it seemed wonderful to her, too.

The weather was clear, sunny, with a temp of about forty, twenty degrees warmer than Prescott. No snow, just the usual line of tourist traffic, snaking across the string of islands and bridges, practically unchanged since she was a kid.

The house where she lived, where she had visited every

summer out of her first sixteen or so, had been a cabin in those days, three rooms and a kitchen barely large enough for the family and the pets that accompanied them. She and her brothers had fished from the rear dock, had rowed their rickety vessels into the marsh at high tide, and had walked the soggy marsh at low tide. They had rescued birds, stray cats, and had gone swimming with wild dolphins that had cruised along the shores of the island. When she thought of summer, she thought of these experiences, of the days before Ray had come along, when her family had been whole.

"Dad, how're you doing?"

"Oh, fine, fine," he said, his eyes still on the passing marsh. "I don't recognize shit. But it smells wonderful, doesn't it?"

"It really does. Are you cold? Should I shut the windows?"

"Only if you want to lose your hands." He laughed as he said it, something from the old days, when he was her father and not a patient.

May I touch it, Daddy? She would ask her father about some bug or flower or tree they saw on their nature outings.

Only if you want to lose your hands.

She laughed, too, and for a few moments she enjoyed the illusion that she was twelve and he was healthy.

"We should put the leather on the stove," he said suddenly, and glanced over at her, worried.

"What?"

"My feet are cold."

The window of clarity, she thought, was closing. Welcome to the world of Alzheimer's. Allie turned on the heat and the floor blower. "What do you remember about Dean, Daddy?"

"Dean ate a bean. Dean was lean. Dean was seen." He slapped his thigh and laughed and laughed.

"What about Ray?"

"Ray's the day. Ray went away." He sniffled and began to sob.

Allie passed him a pack of Kleenex and he busied himself with it, blowing his nose, wiping his eyes, then tearing the tissue to shreds. And when there was nothing left to tear and bits of Kleenex blew around the inside of the car like snow, his fingers worried at his jeans, pinching, smoothing, rubbing.

She had to make one stop before Tybee, a ramshackle restaurant on the water. She pulled into the dusty lot and parked at the back. "Dad, stay here, okay? I'll be right back."

"Here, dear," he replied. "I smell food."

"It's from YoYo's on the Marsh. We've eaten here a lot, remember?"

"Oh, sure," he replied vaguely, and she knew he didn't remember at all.

"Just stay put. I'll be back in five minutes. Promise?"

"Uh-huh."

Allie got out and went up to the scratched wooden rear door. She rapped three times and when it opened, the chain was on and a bearded man with bloodshot eyes peered out. "Yeah?"

"I'm here to see YoYo."

"And you are?"

"Allie," she said.

"YoYo," the man shouted. "Allie's here to see you."

"Let her in," a voice called back.

"Hold on." He shut the door, the chain clattered, then the door opened just wide enough for her to slip inside.

The room was meticulously tidy, with half a dozen computers set up against the far wall, and every available space taken up by shelves that held machine parts of every type and shape and variety. Speakers were mounted at the four corners of the room and early Beatles music surrounded her. At the far end of the room, a man in a wheelchair turned around and waved at Allie.

From the waist up, YoYo was a handsome, muscular man in his early forties, with a winning smile, frizzy dark hair, and tragic eyes. From the waist down, he looked 120, with shriveled legs that had been misshapen since birth. Allie had met him in the ER several years ago, when he had been brought in after a boating accident. She had saved his life and YoYo, being the kind of guy he was, had felt permanently indebted to her.

"Doc, just finishing up." He gestured her over. "Take a look."

Allie made her way between endless shelves of boating equipment, old computers and monitors, car engines, transmissions, and all the other stuff that YoYo fixed. He also owned the restaurant, but his first love was his repair shop.

She paused next to his wheelchair. From a drawer in a desk, he brought out her original passport, smoothed it open. "Now here's the new one." He plucked a duplicate from a shelf, smoothed it open. "Pretty damn good, huh?"

Allie picked up both passports, studying one, then the other. The original had her married name on it: Allison Hart. The new one identified her as Sandra Bedford. And Sandra had short reddish hair and dark eyes, the result of a wig and contacts that she'd worn the day YoYo had taken her photo. "Fantastic," she said.

"I have to admit, Doc, I like you better with long hair."

"Yeah, me too."

"And here's a license in Sandra's name."

"This is great, YoYo. I can't thank you enough." She

reached into her bag and brought out five grand in cash and three bottles of Quaaludes. "I think this is what we agreed on."

He gently kissed the back of her hand, then took the 'ludes, counted out three grand, and handed it back to her. "I can't charge you the full price. So when're you leaving?"

"I may not." Leaving belonged with Plan B and High Springs and at the moment she was sticking with Plan A. "But I want to be prepared. You know how it is. If Dad passes away anytime soon, I just want to disappear."

"I hear you, Doc."

"How're your legs behaving these days? You still have pain?"

"Now and then. But the acupuncture has helped. And the 'ludes," he added with a grin.

Allie dropped both passports and the new license in her bag. "You take care, YoYo." She hugged him quickly and left.

Her father wasn't in the car. He was strolling along the seawall, hands in his pockets, an old guy out for his daily constitution. Allie hurried after him. "Dad, c'mon, you need to get in the car." She took his arm and he yanked it free.

"Who're you?" he demanded.

"Dad, it's me, Allie. Your firstborn. Remember?"

The light winked on in his eyes. "Oh." He laughed. "Allie. You left me, honey. Why'd you do that?"

"I'm here now, Dad. C'mon, let's get in the car."

"Love the smell of the air here," he remarked, sniffing at the air like a dog.

She got her dad back into the Rover, then drove onward toward Tybee, worried about what her dad would do if she had to implement Plan B. Money for his care wouldn't be an issue and she could hire someone to come in once or twice a week to take him out. But it wasn't the same thing as family. With luck, though, it wouldn't come to that, she wouldn't need this passport or the license. Those items weren't in the current pattern. She just wanted to return to her job, to her house on Tybee, and continue on with her life, her brother's death vindicated.

But she had to be prepared.

And why's it so important, Allie? asked a small, niggling voice within. *Why's it so important to vindicate Dean's death?*

Because.

She shook the thought away and turned right on Campbell Street, a narrow road wedged between two salt marshes. It was shaded by huge trees that rose on either side, their lush branches reaching out across the asphalt, as if to shake hands. The homes along here were old, set back from the road, and everyone who lived here knew everyone else. At the very end of the street, a gate and wall had been erected, and behind it lay an expensive development, one of the least attractive signs of progress and development on the island.

As she turned into the driveway of 192, her father leaned forward and peered through the windshield. "Lori should be home now. She was going shopping."

Lori was Allie's mother, dead now for years. But she wasn't about to remind him of that. It would only bring on more tears. She felt mildly encouraged that he seemed to recognize the house, that he associated it with her mother.

"I thought you might like to sit out on the back porch for a while, in the sun. It should be comfortable out there. The tide will be high now. I'll get you the fishing pole."

"What's running these days?"

"I don't really know, Dad. I don't fish much."

"Hey, Doc, good to see you," someone called from the road.

Allie glanced around and saw Fred Pringle, the elderly neighbor who had lived here forever and watched the house while she was gone. "Hi, Freddie. I brought Dad out to fish a little."

Old man Pringle hurried over, his cat trotting alongside him like a dog. "Bill, good to see you, good to see you."

Her father smiled and nodded and said hello, but Allie could tell by the expression on his face that he didn't have a clue who Pringle was.

"Got some mail for you, Doc. Left it on the kitchen table. You back for good now?"

"No. I'm going back to the mountains to finish up my vacation. I just took a day out to see Dad."

"He don't remember me," Pringle said quietly, watching her father as he made his way through the side yard.

"It's nothing personal. Most days he doesn't remember me, either. Could you keep bringing in the mail till I get back?"

"Sure thing. You still returning after the new year?"

"Probably around the second of January." *Unless I go to Plan B.*

"You two enjoy your visit, Doc."

The stilted wooden house had changed somewhat over the years. Allie had put on a second story, adding two rooms, a second bath, and a balcony, and she had enclosed the downstairs porch in glass, making it a sunroom. Here were her herbs, her magical garden, which old man Pringle watered for her when she was gone. The dock where she took her father jutted out into the salt marsh, an alien, self-contained world of tall reeds and grasses, where water from the Atlantic rose and fell with the same rhythms that powered the oceans. Birds swooped through the light, gulls shrieked and pin-wheeled against the soft blue sky.

"You have a seat right here, Dad," she said, and pulled the wooden deck chair up close to the railing and helped him into it. The fishing pole, rusted and old and long unused, stood in the corner of the railing. She handed it to him and told him she would be right back with some bait that she had in the freezer.

"Over there," he said suddenly, pointing across the porch. "Dean had a girlfriend who lived in that blue house."

"Probably just some silly summer infatuation," she said.

"No, no, she came to see me."

Uh-huh, sure. "I'll be back in a jiffy, Dad."

He simply sat there, gazing off across the marsh, the pole clutched in his right hand, the fingers of his left hand pinching and smoothing and rubbing at his jeans.

On the sunporch she checked her dozens of potted herbs and thought they looked remarkably healthy. She leafed through the mail on the kitchen table, then checked her answering machine. The only message of any importance was from Keith, a call that had come in the night she was in North Carolina, at about the same time that Mira had opened the cabin door.

"Hey, Al. Call me when you get this. My cell should work, but if it doesn't, call the Balboa Yacht Club in Panama. I'm in slip fourteen." He rattled off a number, which she jotted down. "Just want to wish you a merry and a happy. I called Dad Christmas Day, but he didn't seem to remember who I was."

Hardly surprising. Her father hadn't seen Keith for a year. *Hey, Merry Christmas and Happy New Year and glad you're up there taking care of Dad, sis. Keep up the good work while I'm down here screwing my brains out and sailing around the world.*

What strange twist of genes or behavioral disposition had created such a disparity between her and Keith? They both had trust funds, yet he had spent the last thirteen years squandering his and living the high life while she had worked sixty-hour weeks. Why did she bother? She could be off living in Paris or New Zealand, or could plop herself down in the middle of the Amazon and research the vast, untapped potential of plants that might yield new pharmaceuticals. She didn't have to work.

But her work gave her life meaning, and who else would look after her father? *You love the adrenaline rush of ER*, Keith had once said to her. And it was true. But what was even more true was that she enjoyed playing God. In ER she held the power of life or death.

Her rage erupted suddenly, without warning. She jerked the phone out of the wall and hurled it across the room. It smashed against the kitchen table. She whipped out her cell phone, started punching out the number for the Balboa, then disconnected.

Can't. For all she knew, Nosy Neighbor/Divine Lover had called Keith again and told him what a wild ticket his sister was. He would wonder about that, her brother would, and if he stayed sober long enough, he would reconsider her story about why she had gone to his place on a frozen river for rest and relaxation. The last thing she needed was for Keith to show up at the house while Mira was still there, recovering . . .

From what? Who is she? What's wrong with her? What the fuck have you done, Allison?

She could *hear* Keith's voice, *see* the confrontation. He would even call her by her full name, *Allison*, the name he used when he was pissed. The night of Ray's funeral, he had called her that after he'd decked her, while she lay bleeding on the ground, her nose broken, her jaw dislocated. *Allison, if you ever lay a hand on Dean again, I'll waste you. Got it?*

They would get into it and every little thing that had gone wrong throughout the years would be dredged up, every accusation, hurt, betrayal. And in the end Keith would betray her.

Allie covered her face with her hands. Harsh, grating sobs exploded from her mouth despite her efforts to stifle them. She stumbled back, horrified at her outburst.

"Lori? Lori, hon?"

She whipped around. Her father stood there, still clutching the fishing pole in one hand, his other hand tugging at his jeans, which were unzipped and sliding down, exposing his pull-up diapers. Allie swiped at her eyes and hurried over to him.

"Christ, Dad, what the hell are you doing?"

"I—I have to use the toilet, and I . . ." A frown appeared between his rheumy eyes. "I . . . Where's Lori? You're not Lori. I thought I heard Lori in here."

She jerked his jeans back up, zipped them shut, took the fishing pole away from him, and set it against the couch. "If you have to use the toilet, it's right there." She pointed him in the direction of the bathroom.

"You're not Lori. Where is she?"

"Mom's dead," Allie snapped, and instantly regretted the words. Her father's face seemed to cave in, the features collapsing, eyes plunging into his nose, nose coming apart and crashing into his mouth, mouth sagging to his chin.

"That's a lie!" he shouted, and grabbed the fishing pole. "That's a goddamn lie, she's here, I just heard her. What've you done to her?" And he swung the pole.

It whistled past her head, the hook at the end whipping back and forth, nearly snagging the side of her face. Allie ducked and came up behind him and grabbed the pole out of his hand, shrieking, *"Stop it, Dad, stop it!"*

She kicked open the door to the sunroom and tossed the fishing pole through it. When she turned back to him, he looked beaten, his shoulders stooped, saliva sliding out of the corner of his mouth and onto his unshaven jaw. His expression was that of a man defeated by life who no longer knew how to fight back or if the battle was even worth it.

"Give me a shot," he begged in a broken voice. "Just give me a shot so I'll go to sleep and never wake up."

"Don't be ridiculous." She took him by the arm, sat him down on the couch. "I'll make you something hot to drink. Tea, cocoa, coffee, whatever you want."

He looked up at her, his face now draining of color, his eyes bulging in their sockets. A vein pulsed and throbbed at his temple. *"I want to die,"* he shrieked. And, with shocking rapidity, he leaped up and ran into the bathroom and slammed the door.

Allie stood still, his words slamming around inside her skull. *Deep breaths, calm down, you've been here before.* In fact, she'd been down this road so many times before that she'd lost count. It had started right after her mother's suicide, when her father was merely forgetful but aware enough to know that his memory was failing him. He'd made her promise that she would euthanize him when he reached the point where he could no longer function.

Oh, c'mon, Daddy. You're just a little forgetful.

We both know it's more than that, Allie. Just promise me that you'll do what I ask. When I'm a pathetic, drooling slob in diapers who doesn't know you anymore, just do it then.

Many times, in situations worse than today, she had almost done it. The ER had all the drugs she could possibly need to euthanize a patient, including the particular drugs used in most lethal injections for death row inmates. A shot of potassium chloride would induce cardiac arrest. Five grams of sodium thiopental—otherwise known as Pentothal—would kill him in about thirty seconds if administered intravenously. A hundred milligrams of pancuronium bromide, a muscle relaxant, could paralyze his diaphragm and lungs within a minute.

In the event of his death, there wouldn't be an autopsy; people in Alzheimer's units and nursing homes died all the time. Unless murder was suspected, their deaths were listed as "natural causes." She was a physician who visited him almost daily, the only remaining member of the family who did. Who would suspect?

Not a soul.

Nearly a year ago, shortly after Dean's death and a horrible moment of clarity in which her father had begged her to kill him, she had taken potassium chloride from the ER, fully intending to fulfill her father's wishes. She had driven over to Lakeview, where he had been slumped in a chair in the TV room, snoring loudly, and had gotten him back into his room. She had helped him change into his pajamas, gotten him tucked in, and as he had fallen off to sleep, she actually had brought the syringe out of her pocket.

And that was as far as she had gotten. She simply couldn't bring herself to do it.

But in the last three days, she had killed four people, was holding a woman captive, and the idea of ending her father's suffering didn't seem quite as terrible. But it couldn't happen here. Not in her home. Not now. Not today.

"Dad?" She knocked softly at the bathroom door.

"Go away."

"Dad, please unlock the door. Otherwise I'll have to remove it from the hinges."

"I'm using the toilet, for Christ's sake. Just give me some peace."

Allie listened at the door. She heard pages turning. He was looking through a magazine. She decided he was probably okay in there for a few minutes and hurried into the downstairs bedroom, into the closet. She brought out her medical case, the one where she stored all the drugs she could possibly need for emergencies, the case she should have taken to North Carolina with her. In here she had more Midazolam, Ketalar, antibiotics, and a number of barbiturates. She had syringes, IV supplies, a stethoscope, scalpels, sutures, and suturing needles, a regular ER supply case. Since she was in charge of the ER supplies, the losses wouldn't show up during the inventories.

She grabbed an empty bag from her closet floor, tossed it on her bed next to the medical kit, and packed some fresh clothes. She added a couple of heavy sweatshirts and sweatpants, heavier socks, winter shoes, a quilted jacket, clothes she usually didn't have to wear on Tybee. She zipped up the bag, picked up the medical kit, and returned to the front room.

Her father now wandered slowly through the kitchen. Except for a small addition on the south side of the room, which she had expanded to fit in a dishwasher, the kitchen was pretty much unchanged since she was a kid. The tiled counter over which her father's fingers trailed dated back to 1934, when the cabin was built. The glass panes through which he gazed out onto the dock and the marsh were the originals. Perhaps, in some dim pocket of his mind, the kitchen triggered memories of the past. She couldn't tell. She never could.

"Dad, we should get going."

"Going, going, gone," he murmured, and turned to

face her, tears brimming again in his eyes. "You promised me. You broke your promise."

She tensed, terrified that another storm would erupt.

"I'm *there*," he said desperately. "You know I am. I know I am. I'm *there*. *Look* at me." He threw his arms out at his sides, his expression was one of such profound torture and agony that she finally looked away.

Allie set her bags on the couch and went over to him, hugging him close, his body so thin and frail against her own that she knew she could break his neck with a single, swift wrench of his head. Never mind that it would be merciful, the right thing to do. She couldn't. *Not now, not yet, not here, not like that. It's not in the pattern.*

"C'mon, Dad, we'll stop for chocolates on the way back. Remember that great chocolate shop in town?"

Allie took his hand, slung the duffel bag over her shoulder, picked up her med kit, and together she and her father walked out to the Rover.

17

"I don't even know your last name," Curry said.

"You don't *remember* my last name," Faye corrected.

They sat in the Hotel Caribe, at a corner table where the lights were dim and cool air poured through the overhead vents. Samba music played softly in the background. Curry was sober, as straight as he had been in months, and she still looked good.

"Okay, so I don't remember. What is it?"

"What difference does it make?"

Good question, he thought, and the answer was a no-brainer. She was the first woman he'd met in years who intrigued him so much that he actually wanted to know her better, to have a relationship with her, wanted to love her and be loved by her. The feelings made him feel like a ninth grader with wild, raging hormones.

"You made me breakfast this morning," he said. "Now we're having an early dinner together. Tomorrow we'll be traveling on the same transport plane to the States. I should at least know your last name."

"Davis. It's Davis. But I bet you don't know the last names of half the women you've been with, Keith."

It was true. It was also necessary in the particular world that he lived in. "Most of the women I've known aren't like you. They don't know how to talk about anything other than themselves."

"You can't even remember our conversations."

"I remember enough of what we've talked about."

She laughed and sat forward, elbows on the table. "Yeah? Like what?"

My God, she was beautiful, but, there was no conceit in her beauty. She didn't flaunt it, didn't wear clothes or behave in a way that called attention to herself, that screamed, *Hey, notice me, aren't I something else?* But beneath that beauty lay a strange and mysterious current that he couldn't quite define. Whatever it was, he desperately wanted to dip his hands into it, dive into it, flow with it, be swept along with it.

"Well?" she asked.

"This is a test, right? If I don't answer five questions correctly, then you get up and leave. Is that it?"

"Naw, I'm just giving you a hard time, Keith. I'm curious what you're running from, that's all."

The conversation now veered into an area that made Curry distinctly uncomfortable. He disliked talking about his family, about the past. What was the point? It wouldn't change anything. "What makes you think I'm running from anything?"

She tucked her hair behind her ears and sat back, her index finger sliding around the rim of her water glass. "You don't drink or get stoned for pleasure. You seem to do both to forget."

Was he that transparent? He told her that 80 percent of the people in Panama were running from something—the IRS, FBI, Scotland Yard, a pissed-off spouse, social services, the Mafia. She just smiled and shook her head.

"Those reasons don't fit you."

"C'mon, I could be a serial killer on the run."

"Nope."

"Or a rapist."

"Nope."

"A bank robber?"

"Sorry."

He shrugged. "I'm here because I like the country and I don't want to deal with my family."

He was grateful that the waiter arrived just then with their meals, disrupting the direction of the conversation. There was cerviche, a way of preparing fish, with black beans and rice, baked plantains, and thick, rich cups of coffee. They ate in comfortable silence until she said, "By family, do you mean a wife or an ex?"

"I've never been married."

"No kids?"

"None that I know of."

"So, you're running from a parental situation?"

"I'm not *running*. I made a *choice*. And no, it's not parents. My mother's dead, my father's in an Alzheimer's facility. I had two brothers, but they're both dead. It's a sister, a control freak. It's just like your buddy, the blind seer, said. Domination by others—by my sister. That's the issue. My life is a hundred percent easier not having to deal with her." There. It was the most he'd told anyone about his family in years.

But Faye couldn't leave it alone. "Then why're you going back to the States?"

"I have property there. I should check in with my old man. What're you digging for, Faye?"

She shrugged. "I don't know. Just curious, I guess."

Curious, okay. He could buy curious. But he sensed there was more to it.

"Why'd you get so freaked out over what Milagro said to you?" she asked.

Because he'd been stoned. That was what he wanted to say. But it wasn't the whole truth. "I think my sister has gone over the edge, that she's the powerful and vengeful woman Milagro mentioned. And since she's staying at my place, it could implicate me. Bottom line. She isn't just a control freak. She may have come completely unhinged."

"Over what? How?"

He pushed his fish and plantains around on his plate and sat back. "Look, my sister's fucked up. I just need to deal with this situation. Now, how about if you list your questions on a sheet of paper and then I'll just answer them one by one?"

She tried hard to look guilty, but burst out laughing. "Okay, okay. You made your point. But everyone's family is fucked up in some way. My mother was into appearances, you know? In her mind you had to belong to the right clubs, hobnob with the right people, do the socially acceptable things, and the rest of the family had to toe the line. My father was passive, unless he got pissed off and then watch out."

"What'd he do?"

"Do?" She looked up from her plate, her lovely eyes shadowed with remembrances. "Most of the time he went along with my mother's agenda just to keep the peace."

"For work."

"Oh. He was an engineer. And he loved to fish. I was just sort of the sideline family business. When they discovered I was sleeping with my boyfriend, they sent me out of state."

"Hey, you went to law school. They must have supported your ambitions."

She nearly gagged on a bite of food. "I ran away from home when I was fifteen and haven't seen either of them since."

"Ever been married?"

Or, more to the point, was she married now? Even though she didn't wear a wedding band, married women in Panama, especially in the boating world, often removed their wedding rings.

"Yes. A long time ago."

"So where's your husband?"

"Dead."

Of all the things she might have said, he hadn't expected that. "Christ, I'm sorry, Faye."

She quickly lowered her eyes. When she spoke, her voice was way too soft. "Me too."

"How long has he been gone?"

"Long enough."

"Then what's pulling you back to the States?"

"I want to spend the new year with my daughter."

So there *was* family.

"And right after the new year, I should hear about a job I applied for as a translator for a criminal-law firm. But there're a lot of other qualified applicants. So . . ." She shrugged and finished off the last of her fish. "We'll see."

"You sound indifferent."

"Not at all. I've just learned to trust the flow of events."

" *'Que será será,'* " he said. "Like that?"

"Yes."

"Sounds fatalistic. Or like AA. You know, surrender and trust God."

She laughed and he loved the sound of it. Musical, yet not like any music he'd heard in the last twenty years. "It's not AA and it's not God. I guess I just trust the underlying order of things. I mean, how'd you feel when your brothers died? What'd you think was happening on a deeper level?"

He admired the slick and effortless way she did this, veering the conversation away from herself and back to him. "I avoided deeper levels." And regretted it now. "I didn't really know my youngest brother very well. He was the midlife surprise for my parents and was only five when he died. As for what I thought . . ." He shook his head. "Shit happens. There didn't seem to be any order about it at all." That wasn't quite true, but he didn't want to go there. He still remembered the night of the funeral when he and Dean had tossed little Ray's favorite things into the pool, their tribute to him. He still vividly recalled how great it had felt when he'd slugged Allie.

"And the other brother?"

Curry picked up his coffee mug, sipped, thought about it. "There was always something special about Dean. I felt like he had the bigger picture and I was just . . . I don't know, a pawn. Not his pawn, but a pawn. He believed in a lot of things that I felt were so far out there they weren't worth thinking about."

"Like what?"

"Well, he was part Buddhist, part Spiritualist, part pagan. A real amalgam. He believed in life after death, reincarnation, that it's possible for the dead and the living to communicate. A lot of stuff like that."

"And what do you believe, Keith?"

"It's all random."

And she set down her coffee mug, leaned toward him, touched his chin with her soft, cool fingers, then kissed him. A simple kiss. "Is that random?" she whispered.

"It could be hormones." He took her hand in his own, and they both laughed and then he ran his fingers through her hair, satisfying an urge he'd been feeling ever since the episodes on his boat this morning. He drew her face toward him and kissed her.

"This could be complicated." She pulled away.

"By?"

She ran her hands nervously over her slacks, tugged at the hemline of her shirt, went through her purse and brought out a pack of cigarettes. She lit one, sat back, and blew a smoke ring into the air just above his head. "It's a long story, Keith."

"I have time," he said.

"It basically amounts to the fact that you and I come from different worlds. I'm looking for answers and I don't know what you're looking for. Maybe a quick fuck."

He liked her bluntness, but her conclusion pissed him off. "That's right, you don't know. From my perspective, it looks like you were using me to get a free trip back to the States. Now that you've got it, things are conveniently complicated."

"That's not how it is at all." She sounded indignant. "You've got it all wrong, Keith."

"Yeah? I don't think so, Faye. I've met dozens of women like you down here. Some want money, others want a free place to crash at night, and others are just pure parasites. You wanted something a bit different, but basically you're cut from the same cloth."

She rolled her eyes, as if to make it clear that everything he said was absurd. "You're wrong, that's all."

"Then convince me otherwise."

"I don't have to convince you of anything, you sanctimonious prick."

And right then, all the old habits and emotional defenses kicked in. Curry knew that if he stuck around here much longer, this woman would suck out the core of his heart and the walls would cave in. He dropped bills on the table to cover their lunches. "See you at the airport tomorrow. If you want a ride to the airport drop by the boat."

With that, he left the restaurant, his bruised and empty heart crying out for her to convince him that she wasn't like all the others.

18

1

By five that afternoon, Sheppard was starting to see double. Nadine suggested he and Annie run down to the grocery store to get something for dinner, and Sheppard, grateful for an excuse to get away from the endless mountains of files, seized the opportunity.

Since Mira's disappearance, he'd left the farm only twice—yesterday, for a brief news conference that he and King had given in downtown Asheville, and right now. He felt a little guilty leaving Nadine and Goot to the paperwork, but knew that he needed a break, however brief, to begin processing all that he'd been reading. He also felt he owed the time to Annie. Not only had her mother disappeared, but she had seen the killing field—the Stevens bodies, one of the farmhands.

As he drove down the hill from the farm, the late-afternoon sun popped out from behind a bank of clouds and light burst against the windshield of the van. It seemed like nature's equivalent of a marching band. His gloom lifted enough for him to appreciate the beauty of the surrounding mountains.

The Smoky Mountains contained Asheville, embraced it, protected it like some ancient and mystical presence. However, the immediate landscape reflected his deeper mood—the ground frozen, the trees stripped of greenery, everything stalled in a kind of weather warp. Even during the worst months on Tango Key, he rarely felt as he did now, as though every step, word, and thought required extreme effort to break through a physical torpor.

On Tango he knew the names of the trees: banyan, buttonwood, mahogany, ficus, gumbo limbo, acacia. Here he had a kindergarten education when it came to trees, just pines and maples and oaks, and barely cleared second grade when it came to everything else. He felt so displaced and out of sync with his surroundings that it affected him on a primordial level. He just didn't function well.

Annie was seated next to him in the van, one of Robert Monroe's books open on her lap. She'd been reading him excerpts, but now was fiddling with the buttons on the radio, switching from one station to another, like some maniacal kid channel-surfing on satellite TV. He finally reached out and touched her hand. "Hey," he said. "You're making me crazy."

"I'm making myself crazy." She rubbed her palms against her jeans. "Shep, I need to know something."

"What station plays rap?"

She laughed, but it was a halfhearted laugh, merely courteous. "Well, there's *that*, yeah, but I've been wondering what's going to happen to me if Mom doesn't . . ." She paused, shook her head. "Nana Nadine is eighty-two years old, my dad is dead, my mom is gone. Nadine won't live forever and . . . and would you adopt me?"

Jesus, he thought. *Right to the point.*

"I mean, I wouldn't be any trouble, I'm a smart kid, and I know how to take care of myself. I'd live with Nadine until she . . . she . . ." Her voice cracked and she bit at her lower lip and quickly turned her face toward the window.

His heart broke like an egg, pieces of the shell scattered about. She'd lost her father when she was three and now, at the age of fourteen, it appeared that her

mother might be lost to her, too. "We'll find her, Annie."
The words echoed with a terrifying emptiness.

"I'm just saying . . . *if* . . ."

Sheppard squeezed her hand. "I consider it an honor
that you'd even want me in your life and you know I'd
make you mine in a heartbeat. Never worry on that account, Annie. But we both need to stop thinking such
dark thoughts. We're going to find her." *And the bitch who
did this.*

It had taken them hours of painstaking work to sift
through the hundreds of case files. Goot had brought
hard copies, CDs, and had downloaded many of the
cases from the bureau's computers. They'd divided the
cases into thirds and looked for those that either involved female perps or male perps with wives, girlfriends,
or female family members who might seek revenge for
what had happened to their loved ones. The last category was a judgment call that was largely intuitive.
Sometimes the presentence report had something in it
that raised a red flag. Other times a red flag might be
raised by the crime itself or by the family members' insistence on the perp's innocence.

Shortly before Sheppard and Annie had left the cabin,
they had narrowed the cases down to sixty-five possibilities.
Of these, they had eliminated more than twenty for a variety of reasons—the perp was still in prison or had died,
the girlfriend or wife had remarried, the possibly vengeful
sibling or mother or daughter had gone on to establish a
whole new life for herself. In some of the cases, Nadine
had been adamant that the person wasn't remotely connected to anything that had happened to Mira.

They now had forty-three cases, an alarmingly high
number when he considered that with each one, they
had to investigate the person's present status. Was he or
she still in prison, on work release, parole, or free? And

if the person was free, where did he or she live and work? They needed time frames, details, specifics. Nadine and Annie had taken copious notes on names and dates, crimes and locations and work, but so far, they hadn't found any perp named Rose or even any family member named Rose. With every passing hour, the trail grew as cold as the weather.

Moments later, Sheppard pulled into the shopping center where Ingles grocery store was. The first time Mira and Annie had seen the sign for the store, they both had pronounced it as *Inglés*, with an accent over the *e,* the Spanish word for English. When Sheppard laughed and told them it rhymed with Pringles, a conspiratorial look passed between them. *To us, it's* Inglés, Annie had said.

So that was how he said it now, making it clear he was a full-fledged member of the Morales club.

The shopping center was still festooned with Christmas lights and holiday decorations. Festive music drifted through the cold air and some of the trees outside had been strung with lights. It all depressed Sheppard and Annie sensed it; she took his hand as they crossed the parking lot. "We'll have her back before New Year's Eve," she said. "I feel strongly about that."

He immediately felt like a shit. Christ, he was the adult, but *she* was comforting *him.*

They headed up and down the wide, brightly lit aisles, selecting items from the list that Goot and Nadine had made. Annie and Sheppard added their own items. Each of them, he thought, was idiosyncratic about food, but Nadine beat them all. No meat products, no meat by-products, no meat-based soup, only soy. No fat, no cholesterol, minimal sodium. Yada-yada.

"I need yogurt," Annie said. "I'll meet you in the video section, okay?"

"Sure. And if you don't show up in five minutes, I'll have you paged."

She rolled her eyes. "You sound like my mom," she remarked, and veered away from him.

Sheppard stood there a moment, watching her, her words echoing in his skull. *Would you adopt me?*

Would he?

Absolutely.

2

Five minutes, that was all she needed. Five minutes alone, wandering through the aisles, puzzling over the soft, insistent voice in her head. *Go up aisle three.*

Whose voice was it? She didn't have a clue. Maybe it was more of a feeling than a voice, but her perceptions heard it as a voice. Or maybe she was going crazy. This seemed like a distinct possibility to Annie, lunacy at the age of fourteen—schizophrenia, multiple personality disorder—she'd watched all those movies on Lifetime. And she'd seen *The Three Faces of Eve, Pollock, Frida, Girl, Interrupted*, the fine edge of madness.

She clenched and unclenched her fingers as she turned into aisle three. Why this aisle? she wondered. She glanced at the sign above her head: crackers, sauces, cookies, pasta, jellies, peanut butter. That hot taste flooded her mouth again, the same hotness she'd tasted when she and Nadine had been reading the barn. But she didn't know what it meant, what it was. A food? Was it a food that the killer liked? Was it something that simple?

Slow down, look at everything carefully.

She felt a presence, it was the only way she could describe it, a sense that someone or something was peering over her shoulder. *Mom? Is that you?*

Annie paused in front of the vast selections of peanut

butter. The hotness had invaded her nose, it was all that she smelled. *Hot, spicy.* Forget the peanut butter. No brand that she knew of tasted hot or spicy.

Mom?

Silence from her mother. This was someone else. Something else. Annie glanced around uneasily and sidestepped down the aisle. Jellies.

Nope.

Pasta.

Nope.

Cookies?

She didn't know, but the Vanilla Wafers would taste good with ice cream, she thought, and grabbed a box.

Annie turned, eyeing the products on the other side of the aisle. The hotness had invaded her senses so deeply that her eyes now watered. Had Jerry or Ramona or the farmhand smelled something like this as they'd died? Had her mother smelled it as she'd fallen in the barn?

Tears burned as they spilled down her cheeks. Annie swiped at her eyes and blinked to clear her vision. *Don't cry like some stupid baby. Keep moving, right foot, left foot, down the aisle.* Had it been five minutes yet?

Mom? You there?

Nothing, nothing, nothing. But the hotness in her mouth was now so hot, so spicy, she knew she was close. Her eyes scanned the shelves. She clutched the box of Vanilla Wafers tightly to her chest. *Help me, please,* she thought, and wondered who she was pleading with.

And suddenly she felt it, a sense that she should stop. That she should look hard. That she should pay very close attention.

Sauces and spices and cooking powders. Dozens of varieties and types. Who made all this stuff? She suddenly felt as she did when she Googled a word or phrase and pages of sites came up. Who entered all the information? Whose busy fingers typed it all in? *Who manufactures all these sauces?*

Annie took a step to the right, scanned the shelves, took another step, and stopped. There. Eye level. "Holy crap," she whispered, and snatched a bottle off the shelf.

And then she tore up the aisle, the soles of her shoes squeaking against the polished floors, her urgency bursting in the center of her chest. Shep, where was Shep? Not in aisles four or five or six. Not in aisles seven or eight. *"Shep!"*

She shrieked his name, bellowed at the top of her lungs, and broke into a run, ignoring the furtive looks, the open, embarrassed looks, the frankly annoyed looks of other customers. "Shep, Shep, I found it, I know who it is, I found it!"

Then he was there, right in front of her, his eyes wide with worry and shock, and he took her by the shoulders and someone hurried over to them, to him, a tall, skinny man with a badge, a name tag, who snapped, "Sir, you need to contain your—"

Sheppard turned his hard, furious eyes on the skinny guy and whipped out his badge and shoved it in the skinny man's face and snapped, "Back off. Back the fuck off."

Then he tucked Annie against him and led her into the wine area and she thrust the bottle at him. "Curry. The name's Curry."

He jerked back as though she'd struck him, took the bottle from her. "Christ," he whispered. "Oh, Christ." And he backed right into a rack of wine and murmured, "Dean Curry. Vehicular homicide. Twelve, thirteen years ago. The judge was *Rose*, Annie. Rose Udell. She died a few years back. The old man was a cancer researcher. My God, Annie. Good work. Fantastic." And he hugged her hard.

Then he fumbled for his cell phone and called Goot, set the bottle of curry powder on a shelf, draped an arm around her shoulders, and they hurried out of the store, their groceries forgotten.

Winter—Summer 1990
Utica, New York/
Cassadaga, Florida

1

Lia's grandparents live on a country road outside of town, in an ancient Victorian house that smells of mothballs, dusty quilts, cat piss, and old age. The curtains hanging in the windows remind her of folds of fabric in a coffin. A fitting metaphor, she thinks, for how she feels most of the time, as though she is a corpse whose heart still beats, whose mind still thinks, and whose emotions are in a constant state of rage because she must pretend that she is dead.

At the moment she is trudging through the intense and bitter cold, making her way to the bus stop. The school bus will arrive around seven-thirty and she will get on it without speaking to anyone and no one will speak to her. She will eat lunch alone. Her classes bore her. At three-thirteen in the afternoon, she will board the bus again and around four will walk into her grandparents' kitchen to find a glass of milk and a plate of cookies waiting on the table for her. If her grandmother is sleeping, then she'll have about an hour to herself before one of her grandparents is in her face, asking questions about school, homework.

The only break in this routine is that on Wednesdays or Thursdays, one of her grandparents drives her into town to the drugstore or to Wal-Mart to buy stuff she needs for school. On Tuesday or Friday evenings, they go out and play bridge with friends and she has the house to herself. But even the breaks in the routine are routine and predictable. Lia has considered calling Dean or even Mr. Barker on one of these nights and reversing the charges, but she doesn't have any idea if Dean will be home or if Mr. Barker will be at the store. The only other choice is to send a letter for Dean to Mr. Barker and ask him to forward it. But whenever she goes into town with her grandparents, they watch her like hawks. If they saw her mailing a letter or using a pay phone, no telling what would happen. Dean doesn't even have an address for her because when she mailed him that last letter, she didn't have an address or a phone number for her grandparents' house.

But she has to try. She must be braver and take risks. After all, what's the worst that can be done to her? What can be worse than what her parents have already done to her?

"Lia, honey?" her grandmother says, covering the mouthpiece of the phone. "It's your mom."

"That's nice," Lia replies, without glancing up from the book she's reading.

"Don't you want to talk to her?"

"No."

Murmuring now in the living room as Lia's grandmother discusses the situation with Lia's mother. "Your mother insists that you get on the phone."

"Tell her to go fuck herself." Lia pushes away from the dining-room table and flees into the kitchen and then out the back door to the screened porch. It's freezing out here, pitch black. She hugs her arms against herself and struggles not to cry.

"Lia, you'll catch your death of cold out there," her grandmother says from the doorway.

"Are you off the phone?" she asks.

"Yes."

She goes back inside the house, her perplexed grandmother eyeing her as though she is some kind of mutant. Or part of an alien species.

"You shouldn't say the F *word, Lia. I should ground you for that."*

"Ground me?" Lia explodes with laughter. "Ground me from doing what? I don't do *anything, Grandma, except go to school. I don't watch TV. I have exactly one friend. I don't go out. About the only thing you can do is ground me from school. That would be wonderful. Please do that, please."*

Her grandmother regards her with an expression that falls somewhere between shock and regret. "I . . . I didn't know you were so unhappy, Lia."

"Unhappy? I'm miserable. I hate it here. I just want to go home."

"But you were . . . uh, that is, your mother told me you've had sex with someone. You can't go home. She's trying to prevent problems."

"She's the problem. *She's* the drunk. *She's* the kid beater. *Oh, forget it. Just forget it." Lia grabs her schoolbooks and runs upstairs and slams her door.*

Wednesday evening. Her grandfather drives her to Wal-Mart. He lets her out at the front of the store, and while he's parking, she drops a letter into the mailbox. She has a purse filled with change and knows exactly how she will get the time she needs to call Dean. She doesn't care if one of his parents answers. She can at least leave him a phone number and a day to call her.

"So what do you need, kiddo?" her grandfather asks.

"School supplies, jeans, a sweatshirt. I'll need to try on the clothes. Why don't you go shop and I'll meet you back here in about twenty minutes?"

"You don't mind? I need some things in the automotive section."

"It's fine, Grandpa. Really."

And off he goes. Lia watches him until he vanishes around the corner. Then she rushes back outside, the change jingling in her pocket, her heart pounding so hard she is breathless. She fumbles with the coins, her fingers are like wood. Ringing now on the other end. A man answers. She asks for Dean. The man—Dean's father, she guesses—gives her another number, different area code. Minutes tick by. She glances nervously at the front door of the Wal-Mart. Ringing, ringing. She squeezes her eyes shut, praying that he answers.

"Hello?"

And she bursts into tears, sobbing, barely able to say his name. Then he is speaking softly to her, begging her to calm down. My God, my God, he's been so worried, he says.

"My phone number," she manages to say, and spits it out. "Call Friday night. At nine. They'll be out. Let it ring twice, hang up, then call back. I sent you a letter to Mr. Barker's—"

"Lia, I've got my own place in DeLand. You're coming here. I don't know how, but we'll work it out. Believe that, okay?"

"I— I do. I have to go. My grandfather is inside the store. I'll be sitting by the phone Friday night."

"I love you, just—"

And the operator's voice breaks in. "Please deposit another fifty cents."

Just then, a hand reaches over her shoulder, disconnects the call. Lia whips around and her grandfather stands there, glaring.

"What do you think you're doing?" he demands.

"Calling my friend. What's the big deal?"

"What friend?"

"Molly. My friend Molly."

"You're not supposed to call anyone on Tybee. Those were your mother's directions, Lia."

"My mother's a drunk."

He looks stricken, her grandfather does. "Honey, I know your mother has got some problems." He gently takes her arm and leads her back inside the store. "But she means well."

What's the point of arguing? She has no rights, no say in the course of her own life. And right then, beneath the horrid glare of the Wal-Mart lights, she decides to run away from this place. She doesn't know how she will do it, but one way or another she will find a way.

She wakes to a heavy, leaden sky outside her bedroom window and her stomach in turmoil. She barely makes it to the bathroom before she throws up. Every morning it's the same thing—anxiety, sadness, and nausea. She can't eat the oatmeal her grandmother puts in front of her, and before she leaves for school, she has to gobble down saltine crackers and ginger ale.

"Lia, I forgot to tell you. Your parents called last night," her grandmother says. "They're coming up for a visit on February twenty-third."

This is supposed to make her happy? "Is she sober yet?"

"Your father says she successfully completed the AA program."

"That doesn't mean anything."

Her grandmother stands at the stove, hands on her hips. "You should give her more credit than that, honey. She's trying."

Lies, all lies. Everyone believes her mother's lies, even her father. But then, he lied to her, too. He swore she would be here only for a few months and she is certain it's going to be through the end of high school.

She locks herself in the bathroom and follows the directions on the pregnancy kit. A few drops of urine, mix it up with the stuff in the kit, then wait. She puts the container under the sink while she waits, then gets into the shower.

Naked, the water pouring over her, she looks down at herself. Her stomach and her boobs are larger. Definitely larger. And she hasn't had a period in three months. She doesn't have to be a doctor to know what this means. She knows what will happen, too, if her grandparents or her parents find out. They will send her somewhere for the duration of the pregnancy and make her give the baby up for adoption.

Lia begins to cry, to sob, and hates herself for surrendering to such despair.

When she finally gets out of the shower, she brings the container out from under the sink. The color is blue. It's official. She's pretty sure it happened that night in the tent outside of Cassadaga, when she and Dean didn't use protection. That means she's about three months pregnant and the baby is due in late July or August.

Dear God, dear God. She has to get out of here long before then.

2

Dean watches the clock and, promptly at nine, calls Lia's grandmother's house. He lets the phone ring twice, hangs up, calls again. Their signal. She answers on the first ring.

"They're gone?" he asks.

"Gone. It's safe to talk. It's a mile to the train station from school."

"How long will it take you to walk it?" he asks.

"Maybe twenty minutes. There's a train that leaves from the Utica station at one. It gets into Albany an hour later. I'll take a larger pack to school that day. I think February twenty-first is the best day. It's a Wednesday and on Wednesdays I usually go over to a friend's to study, so they won't even know I'm gone until around six or so, when they usually pick me up at her house."

"Perfect. I can meet you in Albany. Then we'll drive back here."

Dean, surrounded by maps and train schedules, explains the two options he has in mind. He can leave on February 19 and drive to Albany and be there on February 21 to meet her train. He would call her grandmother's house on the previous two nights, at eight on the nose, just so she would know things are on course. "You can just tell them it's someone from school, right? Isn't that legitimate?"

"Yeah, that'll be okay. I'll just be close to the phone on those two nights."

"The only problem is that we'd have to turn around and drive straight back to Florida. I could use my fake ID to gets us a motel room somewhere along the way, but that could be risky if your grandparents report your disappearance, which they undoubtedly will."

"I don't mind driving straight through," she says.

His other plan is to fly to Albany on February 20, so he could be there on Wednesday to meet her at the train station. But again, there's an age problem—no motel room, no rental car, unless he uses his fake ID. "I could ask Ian to drive up with me. He and I could get a motel room on the twentieth, meet you, then you and I can drive straight through and he can fly back to Florida. I'm okay with any of these. I just want to get you back here so we can get married, Lia."

She starts crying—not surprising. She cries a lot when they talk. He waits for her to calm down, then reassures her that everything will work out. Ian has offered them the use of the Colby house, he tells her, and his wife, Heather, has offered to tutor her for her GED.

"But . . . but there's a complication," she says.

What now? he wonders. There have been so many complications that neither of them foresaw. "What?"

"I'm pregnant."

Dean and Ian stroll across the campus, through the cool afternoon light. Dean unloads on him, and as usual, Ian listens without interruption, his expression unreadable. "Do you remember what I told you back in November?" Ian asks.

"That I'd become a father." The idea terrifies him.

He nods. "So now we know that a particular path is opening up—and other options are closing. It means there'll be other landmarks along this particular path that you should be alert

*for. In the meantime, though, I'd be glad to drive up there with
you and fly back after we meet Lia. She or both of you can stay
at the Colby place."*

*"Officially, she'll be considered a runaway, Ian. That could
get you into legal hot water."*

He laughs. "The only law that matters is that of the heart."

*They are headed to Dean's apartment, and as they're cross-
ing through the parking lot, Dean hears someone calling to him.
He glances around and sees his sister, getting out of her BMW,
waving.*

"Shit," he murmurs. "The wicked witch is here."

*Allie looks as though she's on her way to a meeting—business
suit, heels, her hair pulled back with tortoiseshell combs. She's
carrying a bag over her shoulder. Her eyes harden when she sees
Ian—not because she knows him, they have never met, but because he is here at all.*

"What brings you up this way, Al?" Dean asks.

*"I'm on my way to a conference in Jacksonville." Her eyes dart
to Ian and she extends her hand. "Hi, I'm Allie. Dean's sister."*

"Ian West."

"You're a student here?"

Ian laughs. "Hardly. Just a friend."

*"Ian's a medium," Dean says, a part of him hoping to shock
her.*

*"A medium?" Her brows lift, her mouth twitches into a cocky
smile. "Fascinating. Mediums talk to the dead, right?"*

*Ian, who knows how to handle people like Allie, seems
amused. "We actually spend more time talking to the living
than to the dead. I'd better shove off, Dean. Keep me posted."*

*He heads back toward the campus, where he left his car, and
Allie gazes after him for a moment, her eyes narrowed with suspicion. "What the hell are you doing hanging out with a
medium?" she asks.*

"He's a friend."

"You believe all that shit?"

Dean isn't in the mood for Allie and her opinions. "Look, if you came here to critique my life, Al, I don't have time for it. I've got two tests tomorrow and I need to go study."

She looks hurt now and gestures toward her car. "I just stopped to bring you a care package from home. It's in the car. Casseroles, chocolate chip cookies . . ." She shrugged. "You know Mom."

They walk over to her car and unload three bags of food. He's surprised his mother can stay off pills long enough to cook anything. "How's Mom doing?"

"Not so good. Very depressed. I put her on something new for the depression."

A new drug, another quick fix that fixes nothing, Dean thinks. "I spoke to Ray," Dean says.

Allie's eyes snap to his face. "What do you mean, you spoke *to Ray?"*

"Through Ian."

"Oh." She laughs. "Right. And what did Ray say, Dean? The weather's great over here?"

Her glibness infuriates him. "Actually, he said that Mom could be joining him shortly and someone needs to watch over her very closely."

Allie's face seems to be on the verge of collapsing. "That's not funny," she snaps.

"It isn't meant to be. Thanks for delivering the food, Al."

Dean hurries away from her, feeling dirty and soiled just by her presence.

Tomorrow Dean and Ian leave for upstate New York. Dean is staying in Cassadaga tonight so he and Ian can get an early start in the morning. He feels anxious, scared, and worried that something will go wrong on Lia's end.

But he spoke to her last night and she's ready, her plan is in place. It will work, he thinks. It has to work.

At dinner there's another guest, a woman named Jean, a medium here in the village. She is soft-spoken, pretty, unassuming. She doesn't seem to know anything about Dean except that he's a "family friend," as Ian puts it. But suddenly, over dinner, she looks at him and blurts, "You have an older sister. Stay away from her. She's a lunatic. With many, many secrets. There's another woman, younger. Her name starts with . . . hmm, an L; *yes, I think it's an* L. *A short name. She's . . ." And her eyes dart to Ian.*

"You didn't tell me, Ian. You should have mentioned this."

"Mentioned what?" Ian asks.

"These two, Dean and the L *woman. They're connected to the Voices."*

Ian doesn't say anything. Dean glances from him to Jean, waiting, his stomach tied in knots. He hears the grandfather clock in the den chiming seven. Jean leans forward and touches her soft, warm palm to Dean's arm. "Listen very carefully, Dean. In the spring your car will be stolen. This is a point where your future diverges, where several paths open up. If you don't report the theft to the police, the consequences for you are dire. If you do report it, the situation is improved—not greatly, there will still be challenges—but not nearly as severe as what will happen if you don't report it."

"Now just a goddamn minute, Jean," Ian bursts out. "You're frightening him. You don't have—"

And Jean of the soft voice, the gentle demeanor, slams her fist down so hard on the table that everything shakes—silverware, glasses, plants. Even the napkins tremble. "He needs *to remember this warning. He* needs *to be frightened."*

Ian starts to say something, but Dean stops him. "I want to hear this."

"You won't want to report the theft. You'll be trying to do the right thing, to protect this woman. But I'm telling, she's protected regardless. It's you *whose future diverges."*

"But what does a stolen car have to do with my future diverging?" Dean asks.

Jean shakes her head. "I don't know. I just see it as a decisive event."

"What do you see, Ian?" Dean asks.

"That the car will be stolen and that whoever steals it probably won't be caught. Beyond that, everything is subject to interpretation and free will. The choices that are made must be your *choices, Dean, no one else's."*

3

6:30 A.M. Snow is predicted for later today. Lia worries about that, about whether it will screw up her plans.

6:47 A.M. Lia's backpack is jammed with clothes.

7:07 A.M. She's scared shitless. So much can go wrong.

7:49 A.M. On the bus now. Speaking to no one. Scribbling. Nana Honey's money is buried down deep inside her pack, in her wallet, her purse, sewn into the pockets of her jacket.

9:01 A.M. She vomits in the girls' bathroom.

10:17 A.M. Math.

10:38 A.M. Bathroom, water fountain. Her anxiety is now so extreme that her stomach is churning again.

10:47 A.M. She is called into the guidance counselor's office. There, standing in front of the window, are her parents. They're here two days early. Of course. This is exactly the sort of stunt they would pull.

Her father looks as if he has swallowed several golf balls; he's incapable of speech, perhaps because he recognizes the shock on Lia's face. Her mother, decked out in her Southern tan, fingers the garish cross around her neck. She wears it like an emblem of her true intent—to punish the sinner. But she rushes toward Lia, her arms open, and embraces her daughter, a big show for the guidance counselor.

As her mother's arms close around Lia, she nearly suffocates in the stink of her mother's heavy perfume, her excessive makeup, in the horrors of her religious prejudices. Lia knows that her mother feels her belly, her weight, that at some level she's aware of the new life inside her. She acts overjoyed at seeing Lia, and gushes to the guidance counselor about how she and her husband arrived early and just had to see their little girl. She should get an Oscar, Lia thinks.

The moment the three of them are in the hall, where not another soul is around, Lia's mother sinks her nails into her arm and hisses, "My God, my God, what the hell has happened to you? You're fat, you're—"

"Knock it off, Susan," Lia's father says.

"Knock it off?" her mother shrills. "Just look at her—"

Lia whips around. "You're a mean, spiteful woman who detests getting old and has never had a single genuine emotion except anger and bitterness." She spits the words at her mother and takes a perverse pleasure in the expression that seizes her face, pinches her mouth, shuts down whatever iota of humanity is in her eyes. Her father, who is right beside her mother, just stares at Lia, his mouth falling open so far his chin nearly hits his chest. "Do something, Dad. For once in your goddamn life, stand up to her."

Then she wrenches her arm free and tears away from them, up the hall, running as fast as her pathetic legs will carry her. She explodes through the double doors, races down the stairs, and doesn't stop until she's off the campus, in an alley that runs between houses. She has to stop to catch her breath. Her side burns, her heart hammers. She pukes as she stands there. And in her head, the future shows itself to her, that her parents will find her, whisk her back to Tybee, and make her give up her baby.

She keeps moving, making her way in the general direction of the train station. Even though the sun is out, the air is so cold that when she breathes, it hurts. Sirens shriek in the distance. Maybe they aren't meant for her, but she can't risk it. She rushes into a convenience store and makes a beeline for the back, where the rows of refrigerators are. She grabs two bottles of water, a bag of chips, and a sub. The sirens are closer now, she dares a glance back at the windows.

Two cop cars race past, headed in the direction of the train station.

She waits a few minutes and wanders up an aisle where there are sunglasses and winter hats. She tries on several of both, makes her selection, and finally goes up to the counter. She no longer hears the sirens. She finds out the restroom is around back and she doesn't need a key.

Once she's inside, she turns on the light, locks the door, leans against it. She realizes she's half a mile from school, if that, and by now her mother has feigned hysteria and her father has given her description to the cops—what she's wearing, her age, how tall she is, her weight, the color of her hair. He is her mother's voice at times like this. So she quickly changes clothes, trades her coat for a heavy ski parka, tucks her hair under the hat, slips on the sunglasses. She studies herself in the mirror.

She hardly recognizes herself.

She's on the move again, but not running, not doing anything to arouse suspicion. Three blocks later, she hangs a right, then another left, working her way through neighborhoods to the train station. Two cop cars are parked at the curb, lights spinning, sirens off. She keeps her head down, jams her hands in the pockets of her parka, forces herself to walk normally. Where will she hide until the train leaves?

Lia gets inside the building without anyone stopping her. She heads straight to the window and buys a ticket to NYC via Albany. A train is leaving in twenty minutes. It will put her into Albany way too early, but she doesn't care. Albany is a little over ninety miles from here, from her parents, her grandparents, this school, this life that was forced upon her.

She's snuggled down in a window seat, her face hidden behind a book. By tipping the book slightly forward, she can look out the window. People boarding, conductors conducting, kids with parents, boyfriends with girlfriends, husbands with wives, brothers with sisters, friends with friends. Then she sees two cops talking to the conductor, showing him a photo. He shakes his head.

One of the cops points at the train.

Her train.

She looks frantically around for a bathroom, for a place to hide. But there's no time to get to the restroom. She puts her backpack on the seat beside her, drapes her jacket over it, pulls her hat down over her eyes, turns her face away from the aisle, lets the book rest against her chest. A young woman sleeping. She could be anyone.

She senses their approach, hears their footsteps, their voices. These sounds are strangely loud, magnified, as though her fear has heightened her hearing. Her heart seems to come loose in her chest and bangs against her rib cage. She resists the urge to lift her hat a little and peek out.

Minutes tick by. The conductor shouts, the train lurches forward. She finally peeks out from under her hat and sees the cops outside.

Relief pours through her and she begins to tremble, then shake.

She spots him instantly, standing in front of the train schedules. He looks wonderful, good enough to eat. Lia just stops and stares at him, taking in all the details, her mind snapping photographs of him, of these first few moments. He has a beard now and it makes him look older. He wears a leather jacket that fits him well. His jeans look old and beat up.

He must feel that someone is staring at him because he suddenly looks in Lia's direction. And looks again, frowning slightly. He's thinking that she looks familiar, but her disguise fools even Dean. She whips off her baseball cap and her hair falls free and his face lights up like a full moon. They don't just rush toward each other; they are pulled by a force so powerful it's like an immutable law of nature. And when they're inches apart, he reaches out and removes her sunglasses and she wants to leap into his eyes, drown in them. Then they're holding each other and laughing and spinning around, forgetting where they are.

4

On March 17, Dean's eighteenth birthday, Ian West marries him and Lia on the back porch of the Colby place, at the edge of Spirit Lake. It's the happiest day of Dean's life.

Several dozen people attend, residents of Cassadaga, and not a single member of either the Curry or the Phoenix family knows about it. Because Lia is an underage bride, Ian has somehow managed to get her a birth certificate that says she is eighteen, that her maiden name is Davis, so their marriage is legal and their child won't be born out of wedlock. It didn't matter either way to Lia, but this point was important to Dean. It means their child will have a claim on the Curry family fortune.

The one major glitch in all of this, of course, is that Lia's parents are looking for her, she has joined the FBI's ranks of missing children. If she's found, that birth certificate won't make a bit of difference. But Dean tries not to think about any of this—not now, not today.

After the ceremony there's a party at the Colby place. He and Lia moved into the house two weeks ago and are paying the association a modest rent. He will probably stay at his apartment during the week, while classes are in session, but will be here every weekend. They have planned to take a honeymoon this summer, before the baby is born and after classes have ended. He would like to take her to some romantic, exotic spot, but by then she'll be nearly eight months pregnant and the airlines won't allow her to fly. So they might drive somewhere—the Poconos, the Smokies.

He may have to talk her into this. Even though Lia has changed her appearance—short, dark hair now, and contacts that tint her eyes a soft brown—she's terrified that she'll be recognized and that her parents and the police will descend like a pack of wolves.

Now the Colby house rocks with music and more people, and Dean and Lia sneak away and make love in the shower. It may not be his sister's idea of a perfect life, but it sure comes close to his ideal.

The next morning, she's still in bed when he rises and dresses. He hasn't told her that his parents, brother, and sister are driving up to DeLand today to pay him a visit at his apartment. If he doesn't meet them there, if they get the idea he is living elsewhere, Allie will become the proverbial bloodhound and will track down the truth. She would turn Lia in, Lia would go back to the nightmare of Tybee, their baby would be given up for adoption, and Ian would be arrested for forging a birth certificate or harboring a fugitive. He can't risk it.

If he had told her the truth last night or even earlier in the week, they would have argued. And he just isn't up to arguing. Not about this, not about his fucked-up family, not about any of it. This is easier. Do it, be done with it, and he wouldn't have to see any of them for another six months.

Except Keith. He wants Lia and Keith to meet.

And so he steals out of the Colby house and walks into his apartment in DeLand forty minutes later. He cleans the place in a frenzy, rushes out to the grocery store for food, and by the time they pull in an hour later, he is ready for them.

They pour into his apartment with their boisterous greetings, their judgmental bullshit. His mother immediately moves through the rooms, running her hands over this piece of furniture and that, doing the dust test. His old man pages through his textbooks, and Keith just rolls his eyes and wants to know if Dean has anything to drink—beer, wine, vodka, it doesn't matter. Then there's Allie, zipped into her cold beauty, hugging him hello, big sis to little brother, and she says, "So where's your girlfriend, Dean?"

Silence.

"What girlfriend?" his mother asks.

"Dean has a girlfriend?" his father echoes.

"Sweet Christ," Keith murmurs, and heads into Dean's kitchen for booze.

Around noon, Allie brings in a veritable feast—a vegetarian soufflé, lasagna, breads made from whole wheat and pumpkin seeds, and yes, it's all delicious, Dean thinks, but every single detail has been orchestrated, planned out. The real mystery, he thinks, is why she bothers with any of them.

Over lunch Dean's mother knocks back one glass of wine after another, booze on top of the pills she probably has taken. Keith opens another bottle and becomes morose and silent while their mother sobs about Ray. Dean's father pontificates about the real causes of cancer, and Allie begins to grill Dean about his girlfriend. Why isn't she here? Doesn't she want to meet the family?

"Who said he has a girlfriend?" Keith asks. "And what fucking difference does it make to you, Al?"

"Keith, don's'fuc," their mother says, slurring her words, admonishing him as though he's ten years old.

"Fuck, fuck, fuck," Keith mutters.

"I'm just curious," Allie says. "I mean, we know you have girlfriends, Keith, we've met a few of them."

"And we know you have a husband, Al, whom we never see," Keith shoots back.

"He's working." She gets testy. "He had other commitments."

Dean gets up and walks out of the room, leaving them to their bickering, their dysfunctional behaviors, their bullshit. He goes down the back stairs and hurries up the sidewalk, grateful to be away from them.

"Hey, man, wait up," Keith calls, and runs to catch up.

"I'm going to move, then they won't know where I am," Dean says.

"Exactly why I'm going to Panama."

"What's her problem, anyway?"

"Her marriage is unraveling. So she turns back to the Family. It really bugs the shit out of her that you and I are blocking her out."

"Good, let her drive Mom and Dad nuts."

They walk in silence for a few minutes. "It's the same girl, isn't it?" Keith asks suddenly. "The one you told me about last summer."

Dean nods.

"Good for you, man. You may be the only one of us who can sustain a relationship."

"We got married."

"What?" Keith stops. "When?"

"Yesterday."

"Holy shit," he answers breathily.

"She's underage."

"Christ, then don't ever let them know."

"Only you know."

Keith holds up his hands. "Don't tell me anything else. It's not my business. But Christ, Dean, I'm glad for you." And then he throws his arms around Dean, hugging him close, and Dean is nearly overcome with emotion.

Dusk. They're finally leaving, his parents in one car, Keith in his car, Allie in hers. As his sister brushes her mouth against his cheek, she whispers, "You have a lot of secrets, Dean."

"You bet." And that's how it will remain, he thinks.

5

Lia and Heather, Ian's wife, are in Winter Park, window-shopping, looking for things for the baby. A girl. It will be a girl. Lia had an ultrasound last week and saw her daughter on the screen, a little thing floating in amniotic fluid like some sort of human fish. She has a large head, two legs, two arms, a thumb touching her chin. Lia could see her profile, her beautiful knees.

She has already bought a crib, a stroller, blankets, colorful mobiles, a diaper changer, all the essentials. Nana Honey's money has been well spent. Now she's on the prowl for wallpaper for the nursery, bootees, clothes, certain kinds of music. This is when it would be nice to have a mother with her. A real mother, a normal mother. Heather is like a surrogate mother, younger than her flesh-and-blood mother, but with the kind of soft caring and compassion that Lia needs right now.

"Does it hurt?" Lia asks suddenly.

"Does what hurt?"

"Giving birth."

Heather looks away from the store window and her celery green eyes come to rest on Lia's face. Her frizzy copper hair shines in the sunlight. "Yes, it hurts. But it's the sort of pain your body understands, Lia. Your body knows how to deal with it. During the most intense of my contractions when I was having Adam, I went elsewhere. I knew I was in pain, but it was as if I was in some other world.

"At some point the breathing they teach in Lamaze is beside the point. All you want is to get the baby out, to reclaim your own body. So you push and you shove and you become totally primitive in your need to expel what's inside. And the first time you look at this little miracle, your heart fills with a rush of love and . . . it's indescribable."

Lia hugs her quickly, grateful for her honesty.

"Dean will be there. You'll be fine. Trust me on this, honey."

They walk a little farther up the street and there, plastered to one of the windows, is Lia's photo. A photo taken the summer she was fourteen, when her hair was still long and blond. Beneath it are numbers to call, her vital statistics, her name, where and when she was last seen. A reward of $20,000 is being offered for information leading to her whereabouts.

Lia's knees melt like butter. She grasps Heather's arm to keep from falling. The world goes dark and opaque at the edges of her vision. Somehow, Heather gets her moving, up the street to where she has parked her car.

That night Lia logs onto GEnie, part of this new phenomenon called going online. It's a clumsy way to communicate through message boards, green letters against a black screen, something that universities have used for a long time. It's now becoming available to people outside the academic world. Ian claims that in this decade, it will transform the way life is lived on the planet and has told her to be prepared to invest in something called Yahoo. Right now, she doesn't give a shit about Yahoo or making money. At the moment she is searching for information about herself.

It takes a while, but she finally comes across a message board about missing children and there is her name, with all the information the photo had, and a plea from her father: "Lia, if you're reading this, please forgive me. I was wrong. I love you. Please come home."

Lia presses her fists into her eyes, breaks down, and cries.

May. She's as big as a whale and waddles when she walks. Now and then, she feels the baby, her daughter, moving around inside her, as if she's restless to get on with it, the business of being born, the business of living. Tonight, in fact, the baby moves as she and Dean are waiting to pay their bill in a restaurant in Orlando.

"Dean, she moved," Lia whispers.

And Dean, who seems oblivious to their surroundings, leans toward her big fat belly, cups his hands at the sound of his mouth, and says, "Hey, it's your dad, Natasha. We've got your room ready."

"Natasha?" Lia looks at him. "Where'd that name come from?"

"I don't know. Do you like it?"

"I love it. It's so . . . Russian or something."

Dean laughs and pays the bill; holding hands, they walk out into the spring night and discover that his car isn't where they left it. As they walk through the entire parking lot, an elemental fear seizes her. She knows about the predictions. She knows what the psychic Jean said to Dean.

"It's gone," she says. "We need to report it stolen."

Dean looks at her as though she has lost her mind. "Oh, sure, right. Just what we need. Cops. They'll take one look at you, Lia, and connect you to those photos. Forget the cops."

"You don't have to mention me. Call it in tomorrow. Say that you were with Ian. Produce the receipt."

"And the cops will come here and question the employees and find out I was here with a woman. No. Forget it."

"But Jean said—"

"I don't give a goddamn what Jean or any other psychic says, okay? I don't live my life according to predictions. I'm not reporting it."

"Fuck you," she shouts, and waddles away from him as fast as she can.

"Lia," he calls, and hurries after her.

He catches up to her, grabs her arm, she whips around. "You're deliberately doing what they said not to do."

"You don't understand. My family is rich and powerful and my sister will use that power and that money to squash you if she discovers you exist. You don't know how she is, Lia. You'll end up back on Tybee, our daughter will be put up for adoption, and that will be the end of you and me and Natasha. The end. No. I won't do it."

A kind of strange and eerie calmness comes over her. "I'm the problem, I'll remove myself."

"Yeah? And where the fuck will you go?"

"Someplace where I can't harm you, Dean."

But there's no place for her to go and they both know that. Her face collapses, she feels it happening, and then he puts his arms around her and says, "Let's go home."

6

Dean rents a car and drives to Miami. There he and Keith buy a new used car. He lies and says he sold his Trans Am and Keith believes him—why shouldn't he? On the registration he uses his father's address.

It will be okay, he tells himself, and keeps assuring himself of this as he registers for summer classes, as he drives to and from Cassadaga every weekend, as his wife's belly continues to swell.

And one night in early July, his father calls him in a panic. An FBI agent has just left the house, he says. "You're being indicted for vehicular homicide. What the hell's going on, Dean?"

Tuesday,
December 30

19

1

Sheppard felt as if he were playing a giant connect-the-dots game. It was just him and Nadine now, the two of them awake in the living room, Nadine on the Internet, searching for information, and Sheppard paging through the voluminous file on Dean Curry that he'd printed out from Goot's laptop.

Had Curry been released from prison? If so, where was he living? Where were his parents, his brother, his sister? And if he was still in prison, then what female in the immediate family or among relatives might seek retribution against Sheppard? Had he had a girlfriend?

After he and Annie had gotten back to the cabin last night, he'd sent an e-mail to his boss and to the bureau's liaison in the Florida prison system, explaining what he needed. He'd heard from his boss within an hour, advising him to do what he'd done, contact the liaison. But the office of the Department of Corrections wouldn't open before seven or eight in the morning, and even then, he might not get the information he needed. It was the Christmas holidays, the most difficult time to get anything from a bureaucratic organization.

As Sheppard paged through the file, the summer of 1990 came back to him with glaring clarity.

* * *

He was three years into his first run with the bureau, working sixty-hour weeks and beginning to feel trapped. His wife, working part-time as an attorney, complained that he was never around, that they never had any money, and what the hell was the point of it all, anyway? He wanted kids, she didn't. He hungered for travel, she wanted companionship. No matter what it was, they differed.

Then one night in early June, he'd come home earlier than usual from work and had found his wife in bed with another man. The following day, she moved out with half the furniture, half the dishes, one of the cars, and none of the debt—and moved in with her boyfriend across town. These were the events that preceded the call on June 9, reporting a hit and run on the Seminole reservation. Sheppard had tagged along with the agent who usually covered the reservation because he was going to retire shortly and Sheppard was to take over his territory.

A chopper flew them out to the site and when they arrived, paramedics were already there, working frantically on a young Seminole woman who'd been biking along the highway. She'd been struck from behind, hurled off the bike and into the air, and had landed on the banks of a shallow canal that paralleled the highway. She died within minutes of their arrival.

The car that had hit her, a black Trans Am, stood in the middle of the highway, the driver's door thrown open, the inside light still on, the engine still idling. The perp had leaped out of the car and taken off. Four choppers had searched the surrounding sugarcane fields, swamp, and the reservation for hours, but to no avail. Sheppard and his partner called in a tow truck and ground reinforcements with dogs. Sometime later, they had gone to the young woman's home to break the news to her family.

The car didn't have a tag, so tracing it through title ownership wasn't possible. Then forensics reported that they were unable to lift a single viable print from the interior of the car and the serial number that should have been on the vehicle's engine had been sanded off. Dead end. Armed with nothing except his instincts, Sheppard returned to the crime scene and began to work his way outward, back toward the reservation, the bingo halls, and then out toward the other side of the state.

The car had a nearly full tank of gas, so Sheppard reasoned that if the perp was coming from the west coast of Florida, he had stopped somewhere to fill up. The first gas station was about thirty miles from the crime scene. He obtained the purchase records and security videotapes for June 9, but they'd led nowhere.

He checked dozens of car dealerships between Key West and Jacksonville, trying to trace the make and model to the original purchase date, and finally tracked down the owner, a seventy-two-year-old man living on Miami Beach, who had bought the car in 1987 for his grandson. He located the grandson, then a grad student at the University of Miami; he said he'd sold the car a year after he'd gotten it to a female art student who worked part-time at Blockbuster in Lauderdale. He had the receipt to prove it.

It had taken Sheppard a week to track down the young woman. She supposedly had sold the car to a young man named Dean Curry. It had marked his break in the investigation, but when he'd gone to the address listed on the registration, he'd discovered that Dean Curry's parents weren't just run-of-the-mill Miami residents. William Curry was a medical doctor, a researcher and extremely wealthy man who had made the bulk of his money from a cancer drug he had pioneered. He and his wife were pillars of the Miami community.

It was William Curry's understanding that his son had sold the Trans Am in May, while he was completing his first semester at Stetson. Yes, of course Dean would have a record of the sale. Yes, Agent Sheppard could speak to Dean, William would call him immediately. But Dean hadn't answered his phone, and by the next morning Curry had hired a high-profile defense attorney for his son.

Sheppard remembered Dean Curry as a quiet, handsome young man who sure as hell didn't fit his concept of a hit-and-run driver. Dean claimed his Trans Am had been stolen the month before and that he hadn't reported the theft because "whoever had taken it had needed it more than I did." He and his brother had gone out and bought another car. The ease of wealth. The brother, Keith, who owned a charter boat business in South Miami, had confirmed that he'd gone with Dean to buy a car, but didn't know the Trans Am had been stolen. He thought Dean had sold it.

Sheppard felt Dean Curry was guilty of something, but wasn't convinced he'd been driving the Trans Am the night the young Seminole woman was killed. Besides, he had an alibi. An odd man named Ian West, a medium who lived in the village of Cassadaga, claimed he and Dean were having dinner in Orlando the night of the accident. According to West, Dean was studying Spiritualism and West was his mentor. But when Sheppard had pressed him to produce a receipt or a witness to the fact that he and Dean had dined in the restaurant on June 9, West came up short.

Even without a viable alibi, though, Sheppard couldn't make the intuitive leap that would connect Dean Curry to the crime. He just didn't fit the profile. He had graduated early from high school, with honors, and had gotten straight A's during his first semester at Stetson. He professed to be a Buddhist, had spent time at a Buddhist ashram, was described by friends and teachers as compassionate and genuinely caring. But by then, Dean had his high-power defense attorney, the media had decided the case was worthy of attention, and the state attorney was pressing for an arrest. Sheppard's boss, an ambitious prick who understood how the media game was played and undoubtedly envisioned a promotion in his own future, demanded that Sheppard go for the jugular. Sheppard wanted more time, but the politics had found an enormous momentum and he was overruled.

Since the Department of Corrections was closed for the night, Shep's first calls were to the number listed in the files for William Curry, the old man, and for the chartering business Keith Curry had owned in Miami. But it had been years, so it wasn't a big surprise to find that the old man's number was disconnected. Although someone had answered at the chartering business, Sheppard had been told that Keith Curry had sold out a number of years ago. He had a home somewhere in the Florida Keys, but spent most of his time sailing in the Caribbean.

Sheppard had checked information for the Keys, but didn't turn up any number for a Keith Curry. There was a brief reference in the case file to Dean's sister, Allison Curry, a woman Sheppard had seen only once, a knockout brunette who had slipped in and out of the courtroom with the slyness of a rat. In the files it was noted that she was a medical resident at Mount Sinai Hospital in Miami.

"Nadine, see if you can get into a site for the American Medical Association. I'm looking for Dean's sister,

Allison. She was a resident at Mount Sinai thirteen years ago. The AMA should know where she is or have a listing for her."

"Okay, but first let me print out this stuff I found on the Curry family."

"Anything on Dean?"

"Nothing significant. But the Internet was barely born in 1990. You calling Mount Sinai in the morning?"

"I'm calling them now."

"It's nearly one A.M., Shep."

"Yeah, well, maybe I'll get lucky."

Sheppard had to move closer to the porch doors to get a signal on the cell, and once he did, he called Miami information, punched out the number, and paced as a phone rang at the other end.

He listened to a long menu, realized he didn't know who to ask for, and pressed 0 for the operator. When a woman answered, he said, "I need to speak to whoever is in charge of the resident program."

"That would be Dr. Meltroth. But he won't be in until tomorrow morning, sir."

"Then I need the number for his answering service."

"Sir, I'm not allowed to give out numbers. If you could call back in the—"

He lost it. "Listen, lady. I'm with the FBI. This concerns a homicide and kidnapping. I need Dr. Meltroth's answering-service number or his home number. And I need it now."

"If you could leave me your badge number, sir, I would be happy to—"

"What's your name?" he demanded.

"Joan. Joan Flanders. If you would please . . ."

Sheppard spat out his badge number and cell number. "If you haven't called me back in ten minutes, I'll call the Miami bureau and someone will be at the hospital's front door before your shift is over, Ms. Flanders. Got it?" He disconnected, squeezed the bridge of his nose, and paced back into the middle of the living room, where Nadine gave him a disdainful look.

"What?" Sheppard exploded. "I'm not allowed to get pissed off? You're the only one around here who's allowed to get mad?"

She threw up her hands. "If anger's what it takes to make a breakthrough and find Mira, then go for it, Shep. And just so we don't have any misunderstanding, my anger isn't directed specifically at you, but at what you do for a living. That's what attracted this violence in the first place."

"Yeah, yeah. We've been there, done that, Nadine. Let's leave it alone for now."

He marched into the kitchen and helped himself to another mug of coffee from the pot Nadine had made to get them through the night. He stood at the kitchen window, sipping it and staring out the window, into the darkness.

"The problem with anger," Nadine went on, as if there had been no lapse in the conversation, "is that operators aren't going to put their jobs on the line for some maniac who calls in the middle of the night. And there's nothing on the AMA site for an Allison Curry. In fact, I can't even get into the site that lists members."

He suddenly felt as if his insides had been sucked out and his bones and spinal column were now collapsing. Sheppard sank into the nearest kitchen chair, his discouragement at an all-time peak.

And then his cell phone rang. Sheppard, still clutching it in his hand, pressed the answer button. "Agent Sheppard."

"This is Dr. Meltroth. Your badge number checked

out. Now, just what the hell is it you need to know at this hour of the night, Agent Sheppard?"

"I need to know how to get in touch with Allison Curry. She was a resident at Mount Sinai in 1990."

"Curry? Was she any relation to William Curry, the cancer researcher?"

"His daughter."

"My God, his daughter did her residency *here*? I had no idea."

"Internship or residency, I'm not sure which one. How long have you been at Mount Sinai, Dr. Meltroth?"

"Two years. But believe me, if any child of William Curry's had worked here, I would know about it."

Sheppard suddenly understood how difficult this would be. Allison Curry may have used another name—maybe a married name, maybe a pseudonym—to prevent being associated with her famous father or her infamous brother. Even though William Curry was unknown to *People* or *Extra* or the *National Enquirer,* he apparently was a legend within medical circles. "Do you have any idea how I can get in touch with William Curry?" Sheppard asked.

"The last I heard—and this isn't official, you understand—was that he died a few years back. May I ask what this is about?"

"Murder."

"Can you be more specific?"

"No. Would you happen to know about his sons? Where they might be?"

"His sons? No, I'm sorry. I don't. Let me check with the AMA. If William Curry's daughter is actually a physician, they probably will know about it regardless of what name she's using. And if they don't know, they'll at least know whether Dr. Curry is alive or dead."

"He was that big a deal?"

"Absolutely. Before Bill, certain types of cancer were terminal. You got it, your life became finite. Now some patients have a chance. We can extend their lives. We can give them *hope*. I may not be able to get in touch with anyone before tomorrow morning, Agent Sheppard. Should I call you back at this number?"

"Yes."

"I'll be in touch."

He disconnected.

"Well?" Nadine asked.

He told her what Meltroth had said. "Have you tried the Web site for the Department of Corrections, Nadine?"

"Of course I did." She logged off the computer, shut it down, and got up, stretching. "We're stymied until the sun comes up. Let's get some sleep. I'll be up by five. I'll wake you, Shep."

And then she did a strange thing, completely out of character. She put her arms around him, hugging him. "Go to bed."

Sheppard's eyes squeezed shut against an unspeakable pain. What had happened to Mira was the fallout of a choice he'd made thirteen years ago. *I'm responsible.*

Nadine stepped away and, because he was so much taller than she was, tilted her head back to look at him. "We'll get through this."

Then she wandered off to bed and Sheppard sat in the recliner, hands covering his face, his despair as unspeakable as his blame.

2

Curry and Faye stood in the passenger area at the Panama City airport, waiting for the pilot he'd hired to fly them to the States. Neither of them had said much, which didn't surprise him. After all, she'd made it clear at dinner last night that she considered him to be a sanctimonious prick and he had made it equally clear that she was a parasite.

He stood near the practically empty bar, watching CNN, and she sat nearby, paging through a book. Around eight last night, Curry had gotten a call from the general who had arranged the transport; the plane was needed elsewhere. Curry figured it was a lie, that the general was hoping for a big fat payoff. So it went in Panama. Curry thanked the general and immediately started calling pilots that he knew. He finally tracked down an Aussie who would be perfectly happy to fly him and Faye to Atlanta in his boss's Lear—for eight grand.

Now here they were, with their bags and their silences, and with any luck they would be in Atlanta in about five hours and would go their separate ways.

Curry ordered four bottles of water and two turkey sandwiches to take with him on the flight. While he waited for the bartender to get them, he glanced up at the TV and nearly swallowed his tongue. There stood Wayne Sheppard—older, bearded, looking haggard—giving a news conference about a quadruple homicide in Asheville, North Carolina, and the disappearance of a bookstore owner, Mira Morales, from Tango Key, Florida, on December 27. And right then, Curry knew just how far over the edge his sister had gone.

His thoughts raced, stumbled, came to a screeching halt, then stumbled forward again. If he called the feds and they stormed his house with choppers and a legion of cops, the Morales woman would die. He needed to speak directly to Sheppard. Curry would make him understand how important it was to get the woman out of the house before they blasted the place to hell.

If he tried the 800 number, it would probably connect

to a district FBI office. He would be handed off from one office to another, one clerk to another, and might never reach Sheppard. Forget that route, he decided, and quickly punched out Nick Whitford's number.

The phone at the other end rang and rang, then Curry lost the signal. He quickly moved to the long windows that overlooked the runway, punched out the number again. This time Whitford answered on the second ring. "Yes? Hello?"

"Nick, it's Keith. Can you hear me all right?"

"Yeah, a bit hollow, but I can hear you. Did you just call before?"

"And lost the signal. Is my sister still at my place?"

"She was out most of the day, but I saw her earlier this evening, maybe around eleven or so, on her way back to the house. We're supposed to have breakfast tomorrow. She's one hot ticket, Keith."

Shit. He's slept with her. "She's not what she appears to be, Nick. Now listen very carefully. She's holding a woman hostage in the basement. I need you to lure her out of the house in some way, and then go inside and free this woman. Her name is Mira Morales. Get her to safety and then call the feds. Tell them Allie is armed and extremely dangerous. They should contact Wayne Sheppard at the FBI."

Silence.

"Nick?"

He exploded with laughter. "This is a joke, right, Keith?"

"No, it's not a fucking joke. It was on CNN, a quadruple homicide in Asheville, North Carolina. She's killed four people, Nick. It's really important that you don't call the police until you've got Mira out of there. Do you understand what I'm saying?"

There was no trace of humor in Whitford's voice

when he spoke this time. "How the hell am I supposed to do that? It's nearly three in the morning. She's not going to come out in the middle of the night just because I call her."

Curry rubbed his aching eyes. This was a mistake. He shouldn't have called Whitford. He was just a guy who owned a bed-and-breakfast and had gotten taken in by a pretty face. "Okay, don't do anything. I should land in Atlanta in about five hours. It'll take me a few hours to get through customs and drive up there. I'll take care of it."

"Wait, man. Suppose she kills the hostage?"

"She won't do it at my place." Unless cops stormed the house and cornered Allie. "What's she driving?"

"A Land Rover. But there's a trailer with a hitch in your garage. Is that yours or hers?"

A trailer with a hitch. Of course. It made sense. His sister had planned this whole thing with exquisite precision. But despite her planning, things had gone wrong already. She would be rattled now, edgy, unpredictable, explosive. "Nick, just sit tight."

"Look, I think it's best to call the police, Keith. They know how to handle this kind of thing."

"*No.* It's too risky. Mira needs to be out of there before the cops are called. Trust me on this. I know Allie, I know how she is."

"Okay, okay. I just can't believe she—"

"You don't have to believe it. Just take my word for it."

"Listen, I'll watch the place. I'll be discreet. I know a spot across from the house where I can keep an eye on things without being seen. I'll let you know if I see anything or if she leaves or whatever."

"If I don't answer, it's because I'm in the air. But leave a message. I'll check my voice mail as soon as I land. Be careful, Nick. No heroics. She's dangerous."

"I know, man, don't worry."

But Curry started worrying as soon as they disconnected. He worried as he paid for the water and food, worried as the Aussie approached him and Faye and said they were ready to leave. And he worried even when Faye said, "Is there a problem, Keith?"

"Yeah." *You might say that.*

"Anything I can do to help?"

"No." The sort of help he needed fell in the realm of divinity, miracles. He was terrified that he had put Whitford at risk by calling him.

Once they were inside the plane, he and Faye sat on opposite sides and Curry quickly shut his eyes and tried to sleep. But even with his eyes closed, various scenarios played out against an inner screen in his mind and subsequently wormed their way into his dreams.

20

1

Allie stood in front of the bathroom mirror and proceeded to divide her wet hair into fourths, then into eighths, and clipped each piece together. She began cutting the longest sections first, just as her hairdresser had shown her, and worked her way around her head. The hair at the back was the most difficult and she had to pull it to the side to be able to cut it. She was using a pair of professional scissors that she'd bought from her hairdresser for two hundred bucks and change and the blades worked to perfection. After all, if she was going to change her color and style of hair, she intended to do it well.

Once her hair was cut to the length she wanted it, she draped her shoulders in a large towel and applied the Redken dye. The color and style would match the photo on her new passport and license, at least as close as she could get it. Even though the change was part of Plan B and she was still in Plan A, it wouldn't hurt to disguise herself.

Forty-five minutes later, she washed out the dye and blew her hair dry and stood back, studying her new image in the mirror. She liked it. The color was reddish, the style was windblown, sort of carefree, completely contrary to how she lived her daily life. She thought it made her look younger, too, and it was a close approximation of the photo on her new passport and license.

She cleaned up the mess, put on jeans and a long-sleeved shirt, pulled a heavy sweatshirt over it, and went out into the garage to do her last-minute check on the trailer. It was a used Airstream Bambi, nineteen feet long, with one double bed in the back, where she would put Mira, and a convertible dinette table, where she would sleep. The galley had a stove, oven, fridge, and sink, all of it snug and yet self-contained. She didn't need to hook up anywhere. It had its own fuel for cooking, its own lights and water.

When she'd bought it, the carpet was worn, the oven didn't work, the mattress in the double bed had been as flat as a dime, and the shower produced a trickle as thin and pathetic as that of a patient with prostrate problems. Over a series of weekends, before she'd brought it to Keith's place, she'd had everything fixed. All she had to do now was top off the water tanks and load up the cabinets and fridge with food. Essentially, the baby was ready to roll.

She went back inside the house, excited now that she was about to embark on the final leg of her journey, the last part of Plan A. Even though the hair change was intrinsic to Plan B and she was leaving earlier than she'd planned, she was pleased with herself for being flexible enough to incorporate it into her original plan. And maybe, when it was all over, she would choose the ending of Plan B as well, and flee.

Allie rolled the idea around in her mind, trying it on for size. She could see herself driving straight to the Miami airport and buying a one-way ticket to some exotic spot where she could start over again. If she could *see* it, then it was possible. If it was possible, then she could make it so. It held an undeniable appeal and made her feel liberated.

No more ER, no more responsibility, no more playing God, no more adrenaline rush.

Can I live with that?

Yes, yes, of course she could. She would contact a realtor and put her house up for sale, have her Savannah bank transfer money to a Swiss bank, and would make sure that her father was cared for.

Keith could do it, so why couldn't she? Where was it written that because she was the oldest, she had to assume all the responsibility? She was rich and still young enough to enjoy it. She could live anywhere, in comfort, for a very long time.

She finished packing her bag, cleaned out the fridge, and put the food into a cooler. She emptied the garbage and hauled several bags out to the trash can in the garage. She would pull the can out to the curb before she left and Nosy Neighbor/Divine Lover would tend to it on his rounds. Too bad that she didn't have time for another romp with Nick before she split, but it was probably better this way. Right now, she felt focused and he would only distract her.

She would bring Mira out right before she was ready to leave, which would be shortly after sunrise at the rate she was moving. Once Allie got her into the trailer, she would handcuff her to the bed. She didn't want to tranquilize her, but she would if Mira forced her hand. Mira hadn't been restrained since Allie was last down there yesterday morning before she'd left for Savannah. She intentionally had left Mira alone, isolating her, hoping the long hours of solitude would make her a bit more compliant.

When she was satisfied that the house was clean, with things exactly as she'd found them, she doused the fire in the stove and turned the electric heat to sixty-five. She put her jacket and purse in the car, removed her gun from her purse, and slipped it into her waistband, under the sweatshirt. She raised the garage door and drove the Rover out of the garage, then backed up until she was even with the trailer. She got out and connected the hitch, then pulled the trash can out to the side of the road.

She stood for a moment, breathing in the cold, brittle air. It would feel good to get some place warmer, she thought. Although Savannah and Tybee got cold in the winter, the proximity of the ocean made it a less piercing cold than this. But even Tybee couldn't compare with Florida in the winter. She shut her eyes for a moment, imagining what it would be like in Panama now, the eternal heat, the seductive scent of sea and salt and tropical lushness. Yes, she could get used to that very fast. Panama, then Peru, then into the Brazilian Amazon, with its wealth of untapped potentials. Then Europe. Hell, the possibilities were limitless.

But first things first. Time to get into the groove and slide into the pattern.

Now: Mira.

She went back inside the house, got out her gun, unlocked the basement door, switched on the stairwell light. She went down a couple of steps to allow her to see the basement, and spotted Mira in the bed, covers pulled up over her head. The VCR was on, volume low, *Sleepless in Seattle* playing, the light flickering eerily across the walls.

"Rise and shine, Mi—"

Hands suddenly grabbed her ankles from behind, the nails digging through her socks and into her skin, and she knew she'd fallen for the oldest trick in the book— pillows plumped up under the covers to resemble a body. A scream rose in her throat as she tumbled down the staircase, the floor rushing up to meet her, and her arms shot out to break her fall. She crashed to the floor, air *whooshed* from her lungs, she rolled, but it was too late. Mira rushed her from the side, shrieking like some ancient female warrior, and kicked the gun out of Allie's hand. Then she leaped.

Her feet struck Allie in the shoulder and sent her sprawling. Her chin smacked the floor hard, splitting it open. Mira pounded up the stairs, each reverberating echo a mockery, an abomination. She slammed the basement door, Allie heard the sharp click of the lock.

Gasping for air, blood pouring out of her chin, Allie scrambled to her feet and looked frantically around for the gun. She saw it lying on the floor against the far wall and lost precious seconds as she crossed the basement and scooped it up. Then she tore toward the stairs, a clock ticking loudly in her head. Thirty seconds, thirty-five. How many seconds would it take Mira to reach the road and plunge into the woods on the other side?

She still had to unlock the door.

Hurry, hurry.

2

Mira exploded out the front door, her bare feet sliding against the slippery porch, her lungs on fire, her injured thigh throbbing. She ran down the steps, but it was so profoundly dark outside that she couldn't see anything—no trees, no other houses, nothing but the cold, hard darkness. She wore only a long T-shirt and the cold bit at her naked arms and legs and wrapped around her bare feet so that within seconds, she couldn't feel them.

She stumbled along the right side of the house, scared shitless that her leg would give out and too terrified to scream for help because it would give away her position. The smell of trees and water and freedom filled her senses and shoved her forward faster, faster. Soon she would reach the road and other houses and cars and people. Except that it felt like it was the middle of the night. No traffic sounds anywhere. No human sounds. Nothing but the bone-numbing cold that poked into her sinuses like icicles and drove long, sharp nails into her ribs and encased her feet in blocks of ice.

She reached the corner of the house and bent forward, hands clutched at her waist, trying to catch her breath. She pressed her palms to her thigh, heat radiating against her hands. She heard a door slam shut behind her; Wacko was on the run now.

In the dim light that came from the partially open garage, she saw a Land Rover and, behind it, a trailer. *She's taking me somewhere.* Mira tore up the steep driveway in front of her, her rattling breath now cut to sharp, staccato rasps. Pain erupted in her thigh and at the back of her skull, an ache of mammoth proportions, and then her body sprang alive with agony, as though the headache were a signal to the rest of her organs to shriek in unison.

Near the top of the driveway, she stumbled but didn't fall, and when she reached the top seconds later, lights blazed, blinding her. She froze, her arms flew up to protect her eyes, her teeth chattered. Her tired brain struggled to make connections—how had Wacko gotten to the top of the driveway so fast? What was she doing in a truck?

But it wasn't Wacko who leaped out of the truck. It was a man and he dashed toward her. Mira lurched forward, screaming, "*Help me, help . . .*"and a dog started barking, then howling, and Mira practically fell into the man's arms. He quickly threw a jacket around her shoulders. "Jesus, it's true. You're the Morales woman. I need to get you outta here—"

"Coming," Mira rasped. "She's coming. Has a gu—"

"Step away from her, Nick," Allie shouted, appearing at the top of the driveway, blood streaming from her chin, down the front of her clothes. "Get back. Go on, move away!"

Just then, the dog leaped out the window and raced toward Wacko, snarling, snapping at the air, and Mira screamed, *"Run!"*

She grabbed Nick's hand and pulled him away from the lights. Wacko fired. The first shot struck one of the headlights and it exploded, spewing glass. The second shot sent the dog, howling, off into the trees. The third shot got Nick. He made a strangled sound as he stumbled forward and then he fell like a giant. Mira knew he was dead before he hit the ground.

She ran toward Nick's truck, its single headlight burning in the darkness like some lonely beacon, and scrambled behind the wheel. Shaking, her teeth chattering, Mira threw the truck into reverse, pressed her frozen foot to the accelerator, and tore down the slippery road in reverse, the truck sliding to the left, whipping to the right, to the left again. She slammed on the brakes, the truck skidded, the engine died.

"Oh, God, c'mon, start, please start." She turned the key, nothing happened. She jerked the gearshift into park, fumbled with the key, turned it, and her frozen foot hit the gas pedal. The truck shot forward, and in the glare of its single headlight, time seemed to slow. It was as if she were a child again, being pulled in a wagon by a friend, the world passing by at a leisurely summer pace. She saw Nick's dog creeping out of the trees to her left and the headlights of Wacko's Rover coming up the driveway to her right, and Nick's body laying in the middle of the road in front of her—and a man standing beside Nick's body, staring down at it.

Where had *he* come from?

"Get out of the way!" she screamed. "Run, she's crazy!" Mira banged her fist against the horn.

The man looked up and shock shuddered through her. The man was Nick, his expression puzzled, blood covering the front of his shirt. "Aw, Christ," she sobbed. "You're dead, Nick, you're dead."

Mira swerved to avoid hitting his physical body, his dead body, and suddenly he—his spirit, his soul, whatever she wanted to call it—was inside the truck with her. He looked real, but less solid than a living person, and when he touched her arm, she could feel it. But it wasn't the weight or texture of a hand she felt; it was a spot of extreme cold on her arm, as though someone had sprayed liquid nitrogen on her skin.

I screwed up.

His voice was a whisper in her head, the sound the wind made when it strummed the trees around the cabin.

I'm so sorry. Keith asked me to rescue you. But I couldn't believe what he was saying about Allie, I was watching the house, waiting to see if Keith was right. You're in Prescott, Georgia, I'm supposed to tell you that. Riverside Drive, on the Coosa River. There's a cell phone in the glove compartment. Get it now. She's going to try to ram you from the side.

Then he started to fade away. In seconds he was gone.

Mira snapped forward to open the glove compartment, but the door banged open on its own, as if Nick had helped it along. A light winked on inside and she grabbed the cell phone, a charger, and a Swiss Army knife. She stuck them in an inside pocket in Nick's jacket, which she wore, then gripped the wheel with both hands to maintain control of the truck, struggling to keep it from slipping and sliding. But driving on ice was as foreign to her as everything else here.

Time slammed into fast-forward again and the Rover

roared over the lip of the steep driveway, its headlights bearing down on her like some beast from the depths of hell. Mira jammed her frozen foot against the gas pedal and flew beyond the driveway and the Rover and raced up the winding road in the middle of nowhere.

Trees loomed on either side of her, a wall of pines covered with snow. Low-hanging branches slapped the windshield, leaving behind snow, pine needles, shit that muddied the glass and made it difficult to see. She hit the lever for the windshield wipers and the stuff smeared across the glass.

Oh God oh God, hurry, get outta here.

The Rover gained on her, coming up fast on her right, its headlights burning into the side mirror. Mira jerked the steering wheel toward Wacko, trying to force her off the road. The truck slammed into the Rover, jarring Mira to the bone. Metal scraped against metal, shrieking like an animal in pain, and the Rover tore along the shoulder, crashing over brush. Mira sped ahead, the truck's tires skidding, the rear end fishtailing, and the Rover pulled alongside her, neck to neck, and struck her. The vehicles crashed together, parted, met again, a duel of metal and screeching tires.

Mira suddenly slammed on the brakes and the Rover kept on going. She exploded with hysterical laughter that collapsed into equally hysterical sobs as she threw the truck into reverse and weaved down the road—and into a mound of dirt mixed with snow.

The rear tires spun impotently. Mira slammed the gearshift into drive, reverse, drive again, trying to rock the tires loose. In the windshield the rear red lights of the trailer sped toward her; Wacko was racing toward her in reverse. Mira threw open the door and leaped out.

Her bare feet sank into loose dirt, brush, thorns, and then the trailer rammed into the front of the truck and the open door swung back against her, knocking her to the ground. Before she could get up, scream, or do anything to protect herself, something hit her in the back of her head.

She sank like a stone through honey.

3

For long, terrible seconds, Allie couldn't get up from the ground, couldn't force herself to stand. She was breathing hard, blood still streamed from her chin, the world spun. *Not in the pattern, not in the pattern, shit, fuck.*

She finally rocked back onto her heels, dug her fingers into the snow, and pressed it against her chin. *Slow the bleeding.* The shock of the cold snow against her face steadied her vision, the world stopped spinning. But when she took her hand away from her chin, the snow was bloody.

Get her into the trailer, then worry about your chin.

Right. Of course. First things first. She slid her arms under Mira, lifting her, and stumbled over to the trailer, blood streaming down her neck, dripping on Mira. She got the door open, but had to stop before she could attempt the steps. Mira suddenly felt extremely heavy and Allie's arms trembled with the weight. *Move, move.*

One step. Two. Three.

Then she was inside the trailer, struggling to flip the light switch with her elbow. Even when she hit the switch, the light was dim. Allie stumbled through the bedroom door and dropped Mira on the bed. She was so utterly exhausted, so spent, that she sagged against the wall, sucking in air, shaking the tension from her arms.

What now?

Cuff her.

She rubbed her hands over her face, forcing herself to

think, and felt the warm stickiness of her own blood. The sight of it shocked her. It was *her* blood, not someone else's. *Cuff her now*, demanded an inner voice.

Allie pulled a pair of handcuffs out of her jacket pocket, cuffed Mira's right hand to the bed frame, then weaved through the doorway, slamming the door behind her. She grabbed her med kit from the counter and made a beeline for the bathroom.

Lights.

She flicked the switch and another dim light came on. *Why aren't the lights brighter? Is there a short?* She felt dizzy, winded, disoriented, and her thinking was fuzzy. She needed a hit of speed.

No, first she needed to stop the bleeding.

She yanked a towel off the rack, pressed it to her bleeding chin, and sat back on the toilet seat. She tried not to think about the truck outside, its single headlight still burning, or about Nick's body in the middle of the road, or about the blasted dog that had nearly attacked her or the fact that anyone who happened along Riverside right now would see all this. She would have to kill that person, he or she wouldn't leave her any other choice, just as Nick and the people at the farm hadn't left her any other choice.

Allie finally stood, moved to the sink, turned on the faucet. She splashed water on her face, washing away the blood, then pressed the towel to her chin. With her other hand, she rifled through the med kit. *What do I need?* Every day in ER, she dealt with emergencies worse than this, but she couldn't seem to remember what she needed to treat her own injury.

Betadine.

Right. Cleanse, stitch, cleanse, stitch.

No time for stitches.

She brought out the Betadine, gauze, a butterfly bandage.

Then she took the towel away from her chin and looked at herself in the mirror. In the seconds before blood started pouring from her chin again, she nearly passed out from the sight. A small flap of skin hung loosely, the whiteness of bone glimmering in the meager light. "Fuckfuckfuck," she murmured, and pressed the towel against her chin again, covering it, hiding it.

Deal with it.

Yes, okay, she could deal with it. She needed stitches, but there wasn't time. Gauze and a butterfly bandage would have to work until she got out of here, put some distance between herself and Riverside Drive.

But her hands shook, her chin kept bleeding, the stupid light kept fading in and out. She would need to hold an ice pack against her chin while she drove to reduce bleeding and swelling. *Or is it heat that I need?* My God, my God, this was basic, why couldn't she remember what to do?

Ice.

Sometime later, she moved out of the bathroom with her med kit tucked under her arm and her chin bandaged, a new towel pressed against it. She changed into clean clothes, turned off the lights, let herself out of the trailer. She padlocked the door from the outside and hurried over to the Rover. The cooler was on the backseat and she opened the lid and scooped out a handful of ice that she wrapped in the towel.

By the time she finally sped away from her brother's house, from Nick's truck and his pathetic body sprawled in the road, the sky was turning a dove gray. Even once the sun rose, it might be hours before anyone happened along this road and found Nick's truck or his body. In five or six hours, she would be out of Georgia and bound for her destination in Plan B.

Events had forced her to make the switch to Plan B. High Springs, then get out of the country.

As she drove, she kept the ice pack pressed to her chin and her window down. The cold air revived her, her mind was chugging along again. *A hit of speed.* She dug her hand into her purse, brought out her beautiful bottle of amphetamines, popped two. Just enough to take the edge off. Just enough to keep her going. Just enough to keep her awake for the next eight to twelve hours.

And once the speed kicked in, she began to play back everything that had happened, letting the movie run in her head. The big question was why Nick had been here at all, at this hour of the morning. Had he been spying on the house? On her? Or had he just been some insomniac out for a drive at precisely the right moment?

Or maybe Keith's suspicions had been aroused and he had called Nick and asked him to watch the house? *Did Keith betray me?*

As soon as she was on the highway, she punched out her brother's cell number. She reached his voice mail. "Hey, this is Keith. Your call is important to me. Please leave me a message and a number so I can get back to you."

Beep.

"It's me. Call me as soon as you get this."

Then she disconnected.

21

1

When Sheppard's cell phone rang at seven-thirty that morning, he'd been up for two hours already and had consumed enough coffee to take the edge off his fatigue. Goot, Nadine, even Annie, were at work on the laptops and the shrill of the phone stopped everything—talking, the tap of computer keys, even the thump of Ricki's tail against the floor. *Private* came up in the cell window.

"Agent Sheppard."

"Good morning, sir. This is Frieda Pollack at the Florida Department of Corrections. I understand you have a request for information?"

"Yes, that's right. I do."

"Your badge number, sir?"

Sheppard ticked it off, absurdly grateful that Frieda didn't have a rolling Southern accent, that she sounded, in fact, like a transplanted Yankee.

"Very well, Agent Sheppard. What can I do for you?"

He grabbed his legal pad, where he'd jotted all the pertinent information on Dean Curry—date of birth, Social Security number, date of his arrest, and anything else the DOC might need to track him down.

"I'm trying to find a man named Dean Curry. He was arrested for vehicular homicide on 7/7/90, and was sentenced on 12/27/90." *Twelve twenty-seven. Thirteen years to the date that the perp had snatched Mira.* How the hell had he missed that?

"Do you have a Social Security number, Agent Sheppard?"

He reeled it off and heard the tick of computer keys.

Then: "Okay. Curry, Dean. He was processed into the receiving station at Lake Butler on 12/28/90 to serve five years for vehicular homicide. He was sent to Indian River Correctional Institution ten days later. In June of '91, he escaped from Indian River. He was apprehended four days later near Orlando and received an additional fifteen years. As an escape risk, he was transferred to Raiford to serve out the remainder of his sentence. On January first of this year, he was, uh, found hanging in the prison laundry."

Jesus. That's it. The time frame. Dean was sentenced thirteen years ago on December 27—the same night Mira was snatched—and January 1 would be the first anniversary of his death. Sheppard suddenly heard the ticking of a very loud clock in his skull.

"He hung himself?" Sheppard asked.

"I'm checking, just a minute." More tapping of keys. "An attorney hired by the family demanded an inquest. In March of this year, it was determined that the hanging was murder. He was, uh, skinned alive."

Sheppard felt the air rush from his lungs. "Skinned alive? Jesus." Images filled his head, each worse than the one before it.

"Who hired the attorney?"

"The only thing these records show, Agent Sheppard, is that the attorney represented the family."

"What was the attorney's name?"

"Lawrence Rendall," she said. "With Rendall and Sons here in Tallahassee. I have a number here, sir."

"Great." Sheppard scribbled frantically. "What about a visitors' list? Would you have that information?'"

"Yes. Let's see. His parents, William and Lori Curry, his siblings, Allison Curry and Keith Cunningham, and friends, Ian and Lia West."

Sheppard took note of the brother's different last name and wondered about the Ian West connection. He was the oddball who had testified at Curry's trial, a medium from the village of Cassadaga, if memory served him. But who was Lia West? Ian West's daughter? Wife?

"Do you have any personal data on these people? Addresses? Phone numbers? Social Security numbers?"

"No, sir. We just keep the lists, none of the personal data. That would be in the actual file at Raiford."

It was a start. "Thanks very much for your time, Frieda. You have a happy new year."

"Same to you, Agent Sheppard."

He hung up, despair and fatigue like two warring factions in his body, and stared at what he already knew would be useless information. Just the same, he called the attorney's office in Tallahassee and wasn't surprised when he got a recording that the firm wouldn't reopen until Monday, January 5. He considered calling Meltroth, but figured he needed to give the doctor time to hunt down the information Sheppard needed. He needed to get outside, to move, to feel the cold against his face. He grabbed his jacket, slipped his cell phone in the pocket, and headed for the door.

"Can Ricki and I come with you?" Annie asked.

"You bet. C'mon."

Despite the cold, brittle air, it felt good to move, to feel the hard, solid ground under his feet. He moved fast, his shoes crunching over dead twigs, leaves, branches, and Annie kept pace with him. Ricki had darted ahead, following some fresh scent in the snow.

Salvation and redemption lay in continued movement, but he wished the movement were toward Mira rather than into a dingy woods. The metaphor didn't escape him. He knew the perp was connected to Curry, knew the perp's time frame, but didn't have any idea who the woman was or where she might be.

"Shep," Annie said, grabbing his hand. "I dreamed about . . . about the Stevenses last night. About finding them . . . in the house."

Sheppard paused and crouched so he was eye level with Annie. "I'm so sorry that you had to see that, Annie. I should have handled the whole situation much better than I did."

Her face scrunched up, tears brimming in her dark eyes, and she wrapped her arms around Sheppard's neck, hugging him. "It's not your fault," she whispered hoarsely.

He held her for a few moments, then Ricki bounded over and pushed her nose between them, breaking them apart. Sheppard straightened up, and as he and Annie moved forward again, she said, "What I meant to say was that I remembered something else Rose told me in that dream or whatever it was."

"What's that?"

"She said the woman operated on Mom."

Everything inside of Sheppard went utterly still. Operated on her, and intended to hang her and skin her alive. The full horror hit him. Even his heart seemed to stop. Then he blinked and the world snapped back into clarity. It was there all the time, right in front of him. Mira had been shot, Allison Curry had been a medical resident and probably was a medical doctor now. *The woman operated on Mom.*

Before he could say anything, his cell phone rang. The peal echoed through the cold silence of the woods and Meltroth's number appeared in the window. "Annie, let me get this call. Run back to the cabin and tell Goot and Nadine what you just told me. She's our perp. Allison Curry."

Her eyes widened, then she spun around and raced back through the trees.

"Agent Sheppard."

"It's Dr. Meltroth. I saw you on CNN last night. I figure your question is connected to the quadruple homicides in North Carolina."

"Yes, that's right."

"Okay, you have a pencil?"

"I do."

"William Curry is presently in an Alzheimer's facility called Lakeview Nursing Home in Savannah, Georgia." He gave Sheppard the address and phone number. "They don't have any record of an Allison Curry as a physician. The oncologist I spoke to was shocked when I mentioned that she was supposedly a physician. That means she either isn't one or practices under a different name. But someone must be paying Dr. Curry's bills. My advice is to call the institution and see what you can find out."

"You've been a tremendous help, Dr. Meltroth."

"Good luck, Agent Sheppard."

Like luck had anything to do with it, Sheppard thought, and quickly punched out information for Savannah. A few moments later, he was clear of the trees and listening to the ringing of a phone at the Lakeview Nursing Home in Savannah.

"Lakeview. How may I help you?"

"Hi. Is William Curry in?"

"He's at breakfast right now. Could you call back in about an hour?"

My God, still there, still alive. "I'll call back. But in the meantime, is your director in?"

"She'll be in about nine. Would you like her voice mail?"

"No, thanks."

Sheppard disconnected and ran back to the cabin. He didn't need to speak to the director by phone. It was just over three hundred miles to Savannah. If King could get a plane, he could be there in about ninety minutes.

His next call was to Kyle King.

Sheppard shoved clothes into his pack, aware that Goot watched him with a certain wariness.

"You need backup," Goot said.

"I need a ride to the airport and for you to drive Nadine and Annie back to Tango. Or you stay here with them."

"We can fly," Nadine said, ducking under Goot's arm to share the doorway with him.

"It's nearly New Year's. You won't get a flight." Sheppard had checked. There wasn't a commercial flight to be had anywhere on the east coast. "Besides, we can't leave Ricki here. She needs a home."

The dog, hearing her name, nosed in between Goot and Nadine, who looked down at her and laughed. "Well, I think *she* likes the idea. But Annie and I can make it back on our own."

Nadine had many admirable qualities, but driving wasn't among them. And this wasn't a trip to the grocery store. With pit stops and gas, it was fifteen hours, and at the rate Nadine drove, they would be lucky to make the drive in twenty-five. "Not in holiday traffic."

"Right," Goot agreed. "You two should stay here."

"You stay with them," Sheppard said to Goot.

"We should do what Shep says," Annie chimed in. "He's right."

Sheppard winked at her. "Thanks for the support,

kiddo." He zipped his bag shut, slung it over his shoulder. "I'm leaving now."

Nadine and Goot looked at each other and Goot rolled his eyes as if to say that argument was futile. But Nadine, who never hesitated to say what she thought, let loose with a stream of Spanish that amounted to a single salient opinion: Sheppard was the gringo bastard son, not related by blood, and what right did he have to decide who was going where? Mira was *her* granddaughter, Annie's mother. . . .

Sheppard, fighting back a rising tide of fury that he knew would completely sever his relationship with one of the two people Mira loved the most, cut her off. "I do this alone, Nadine. If I need Goot, I'll call him. King will be staying here too, trying to track down the doctor's brother."

The color bled out of Nadine's face. Her shoulders sagged. He had won this round, but at what cost? "Then listen to me closely, *gringo*. You have to think as this woman thinks, plan as she plans, and then you have to beat her at her own game. Mira isn't the point. *You* are. Remember that."

It was her way of telling him that all of this was *his* fault, that she blamed him, that it wasn't Sheppard the man with whom she had issues, but Sheppard the cop. He wondered, suddenly, whether she would like him any better if he sold insurance. "I know," he said, nodding, then bussed her quickly on the cheek, gave Annie a hug, and swept past them, Goot hurrying along after him.

2

"Keith?"

He didn't want to open his eyes, didn't want to talk to Faye, but it was just them and two other people on the plane, friends of the pilot, and he would have to say something to her soon anyway because they would be landing shortly. He opened his eyes and gazed into her lovely face.

"I really don't have much to say, Faye."

"You don't have to say anything." She set her large straw purse on her lap and reached inside. "I've been carrying these around for a long time." She brought out a thick legal-size envelope and set it on his lap. "I think it will help you understand some things."

"I don't need to understand anything."

"About your brother. About Dean."

"Dean? You knew Dean?"

She nodded.

He opened the envelope and took out a thick packet of letter-size envelopes. He recognized the ones on top, letters he had mailed to his brother's girlfriend, Lia, in care of a post office box in Lake Helen, Florida. "How did you get . . ." He stopped, looked up at her. "You're. . . . *Lia? The* Lia? *Dean's* Lia?"

"Lia Phoenix. Then after I ran away, I was Lia Davis. And then on Dean's eighteenth birthday, I became Lia Davis Curry."

And suddenly he was on that sidewalk outside Dean's apartment in DeLand so many years ago. *We got married. . . .* Curry felt as if he'd stumbled into some strange upside-down world where paths in time rushed together and converged in a single, explosive moment of understanding. The walls around his heart collapsed, a rift opened in the center of his being, and for moments he couldn't speak around the lump in his throat. He groped for her hand and she gripped it tightly and brought it to her cheek and pressed his knuckles against her exquisitely soft skin.

"He wanted us to meet," she said. "But time ran out. So I had to make good on that promise."

Curry wished he knew what to say. But all he could think of was the many times Dean had seemed on the verge of confessing something, of telling him the name of his mysterious girlfriend, and Curry had discouraged the intimacy, claimed he was better off not knowing. *It's not my business* had become not only his litany, but a way of life.

The lump in his throat began to dissolve. "Your daughter . . ."

She nodded. "Dean's. Born about three weeks after he was arrested."

"Fuck," he whispered. "Did Dean ever meet her?"

"Twice. Ian took Natasha with him once when he went up to the correctional facility at Indian River to see him. He was our mail carrier for that part of our lives. Then, when Dean escaped, the three of us spent four glorious days together. We were going to leave the country. But on the morning of the fifth day, he woke up and told me he was driving into Orlando and that he loved us and we couldn't go with him. I knew. I knew what it meant. Two hours later, they found him sitting in a café in Orlando and arrested him.

"After he got sent to Raiford, I visited him several times. I got put on his visiting list as Ian's sister. I wanted to appeal his case, to open the whole thing up again. I mean, I was Dean's alibi the night of the accident out on the reservation, but because I was an underage runaway, he refused to let me testify. He was afraid my parents would take me away, force me to give up the baby for adoption, and that Ian would be indicted for forgery or something, because of my phony birth certificate. When I turned eighteen, I wanted to open the case up again, but he refused. He knew Allie might still intervene.

Then he escaped and it was all beside the point because he got stuck with another fifteen years."

Curry felt as if a stake had been driven through his heart. "What a moron I've been. I was the worst kind of coward. I kept telling myself it was none of my business."

"No. You saved us. You delivered our letters, Keith, during that horrible time right after his arrest. I can never repay you for that."

Curry put his arms around her and drew her head toward his chest, and for a long time, they held on to each other, neither of them speaking.

"How did you find me?" he asked finally.

"The Internet. You wrote an article about the Balboa. There was a photo. I went to Panama twice before this last trip, looking for you. My timing was off. You were elsewhere. Then a guy at the Balboa told me you came when the snow flew and I left on the twenty-sixth and found you easily. I just wanted to meet you, to let you know the truth. It was something I had promised Dean."

"Allie has . . . She's killed some people."

"I watch CNN, too. I figured that much out."

"How?"

"It's complicated," she replied, then made her way slowly through a strange story about a set of predictions in Cassadaga. "We know these events end in a place near water or that has water in the name. For a long time, we thought the place was Spirit Lake in Cassadaga. That's where we were married. But shortly before I left for Panama, some new predictions were submitted for the Book of Voices about these events. Ian no longer thinks that Spirit Lake is the place. Free will is always operative, that's how Ian puts it. But all the predictions have been consistent about the reference to water, the violence, and that there's some sort of manifestation."

Curry was having a difficult time taking in any of this. "What's a manifestation?"

"Well, it can be different things. But for these predictions—and I'm quoting now—'the living meet the dead.'"

Dean's world hadn't been his, but it seemed it was about to become his in a major way.

3

Mira came to suddenly, heart slamming hard and fast against the cage of her ribs. *Monsters. Monsters everywhere.*

But she saw only the familiar contours of the cabin living room, heard the comforting crackle of wood in the stove, and realized she'd been dreaming. My God, but she was thirsty. She threw off the blanket, swung her legs over the side of the recliner, and padded into the dimly lit kitchen for a drink of water. As she opened the fridge and reached for a bottle of water, an electric sensation tore through her and she straightened up and peered at the clock on the wall, above the sink.

The hands had stopped at 9:02.

She spun around and there stood Tom, alone this time, holding his hands up to the stove to warm them. She wondered why a dead man would have to warm his hands.

I don't have to. But I like remembering what a fire's warmth feels like. He didn't speak the words aloud; they seemed to flow through the pores of her skin and into her head.

Do you miss it? Being human? Physical? she asked, going over to him.

He straightened and turned, facing her. *Sometimes. But I miss you and Annie all the time.* Tom took her in his arms and Mira clung to him as if a part of her believed that if she held him tightly, she would be able to make him flesh and blood again.

"Is this visit part of our bargain?" she asked, pulling back slightly so that she could see his face.

"I'm not here to say good-bye, Mira. I'm here to warn you. You have to come to, okay? And you better do it fast. You're going to need whatever time you've got."

She shook her head. "I don't want to come to. Monsters are outside."

As if to support her belief in monsters, the wind outside suddenly whipped into a howling frenzy. Branches slapped and clawed at the windows.

"There's only one monster," Tom whispered, cupping her face in his beautiful hands. "And you have to defeat her." Then he pulled his arms in toward his body and clapped his hands twice, loudly, right in front of her face . . .

. . . and she was with Sheppard, reading a crime scene, and the rope burns on a victim's wrist had materialized on her own. Sheppard had noticed. He had questioned her. He wanted answers . . .

. . . and she was inside the place in 1968 where Annie had been imprisoned, and as she moved through the room, her daughter's injuries had appeared on her body, mark for mark, bruise for bruise. Her body had absorbed the injuries, released them, and the physical marks had faded. Yes, okay, she got the message. It was something that had happened to her off and on throughout her life. So what?

"You turn the injury inward," Tom said. "But that same energy can be turned outward, Mira."

"I don't understand."

"You will," he promised, and she fell back into a dream.

In the dream a phone was ringing and people she couldn't see were shouting at her to answer it. Her eyes fluttered open. She was curled up on her side, on a bed.

A moving bed. *The trailer.* And it all rushed back to her, the basement and Nick and the truck. She heard the ringing again and realized it was coming from the cell phone in her pocket.

Nick's phone.

She dug it out of the pocket with her free hand, her left hand. The name Keith came up in the window. *Keith asked me to rescue you.* She pressed the answer button. "Yes? Hello? Keith? Is this Keith whose house is on the river?"

"Yes, this is Keith. Who's this?"

Mira raised up as far as the handcuff would allow and spoke so fast that she tripped over her own tongue. "Mira Morales. Your sister killed Nick, shot him. We're on the road somewhere, don't know exactly where. I'm handcuffed to a bed in a trailer. Get in touch with Wayne Sheppard." She spat out Sheppard's cell number. "Did you get that, Keith? Hello? Keith?"

"Still here, Mira. Hold on, just hold on. My friend is calling Sheppard now."

"Where are you?" she asked.

"I just landed in Atlanta airport. Can you describe the trailer?" he asked again.

Atlanta airport. What was he doing there? He lived someplace warm, somewhere distant. *The trailer, focus on the trailer.* She shut her eyes, trying to visualize those moments outside the house, when she was fleeing. "It's got a hitch. She's towing it with her Land Rover. I think it's silver, maybe twenty feet long."

"Do you have any idea where you are?"

"None. It was dark, the middle of the night when she shot Nick and knocked me out. Now it's daylight."

"Can you tell which direction you're headed?"

Mira glanced at one window, then the other. Blinds covered them, the light was pale, murky, and she guessed it was overcast outside. "Can't tell." But even as she said the words, information surfaced, impressions that had poured into her when she had grabbed Wacko's ankles. "Wait a minute. I think she's headed south, maybe into Florida, a place that was important in her childhood, before little Ray was born. And I picked up something about Plan B."

"Picked up? What do you mean?"

She realized she'd been talking as though Keith Curry knew that she was psychic. He obviously didn't know, and rather than tell him, she said, "I overheard it. And I know she intends to kill me to get back at Sheppard and then she's going to leave the country."

"Mira, Sheppard's cell phone is busy. I need another number."

Another number, quick, quick. But her brain felt sluggish and the base of her skull felt as though she'd been hit with a block of concrete. *Be calm.* Right. Calm. What a joke. She adjusted her breathing, shut her eyes, and Annie's cell number clicked into place. Then Goot's. She rattled off both numbers.

"Keep the phone on, but put it on vibrate," Keith said. "That way she won't hear it. Even if the battery's running low, just keep it on."

"I have a charger. If I can reach the outlet, I'll plug it in."

"I'll call you back in five minutes. If I can't get through for some reason, here's my number." He ticked it off, had her repeat it. "I'll give Sheppard this number, Mira. Is there anything in the trailer you can use as a weapon?"

"Nick had . . . a Swiss Army knife in the glove compartment. I have that."

"Good. That's good. Now listen. I don't think she'll do anything to you until she gets where she's going. She has a plan, she'll stick to it. But at the first opportunity you get, use that knife. It could spell the difference for you.

I'm going to get off now and call one of these other numbers. Don't worry, Mira. We'll find you."

But can you do it fast enough?

The line went dead.

22

Lakeview definitely lay at the expensive end of the nursing-home spectrum. Its location on a lake ringed with trees was no less impressive than its electronic doors and a lobby that spoke tomes about the income bracket of the residents.

Sheppard pulled up in front and got out. The chopper had landed on the rooftop of the FBI building in downtown Savannah and he'd been given a car to use and an offer of backup if he needed it. At the moment the only thing he needed was information.

He rang the doorbell and the electronic doors slid open. Even the air in here smelled rarefied, of fresh flowers and wood smoke from the fireplace. A large plasma-screen TV caught Sheppard's eye as soon as he entered; six or eight grand, he thought. The couches and chairs, all hardwoods with colorful cushions that matched the rug, had come from a designer showroom. The four speakers mounted on the walls looked like they had been made in some distant future and brought back through time. They emitted such exquisite sound that Sheppard felt as though music were rising up through the tile floors that graced the entrance and wide corridors. Original artwork decorated the walls, all of it as boldly colored as the pair of macaws in the cage near the far windows. There was also a cage with a pair of doves in it, and two black-

and-white cats strolled the area with all the grace of jungle cats. It made it seem as if Alzheimer's was a disease of the wealthy, the privileged.

He stopped at the desk and the young woman behind it flashed a charming smile. "Mornin'," she said in a chirpy Southern drawl. "What can ah do for you?"

He set his bureau ID on the counter. "I'd like to speak to Mrs. Norcross."

She glanced at his badge and immediately got flustered. "She's, uh, not in yet, Agent Sheppard. Ah mean, she was here, but she had to run out to interview a prospective resident. She should be back shortly."

"Could you please call her? It's urgent. And in the meantime, I'd like to speak to William Curry."

"Ah'll have someone take you upstairs." She quickly punched out two numbers on the phone, spoke quietly to the person on the other end. "David's on his way down. He's Dr. Curry's primary caretaker. Ah'll call Mrs. Norcross right away."

"Thanks, I appreciate it."

Within a few minutes, a large, muscular, and very dark black man strode over to Sheppard. "I'm David, Agent Sheppard. Dr. Curry is with his memory-enhancement class right now. I'll take you up there." He had a quiet voice, with a crisp, precise way of speaking. "Have you ever dealt with Alzheimer's patients before?"

Sheppard shook his head.

"They're easily excitable. Some of them go through emotional extremes in the span of just a few minutes or even seconds. I'll introduce you, but Dr. Curry probably won't remember your name. He can be very lucid at times, but most days he can't even remember who he is, much less who anyone else is."

Would Curry remember him as the man who had arrested his son thirteen years ago? He didn't know. But just in case, he asked David to simply introduce him as Wayne. "Tell me about his family," Sheppard said as they waited for the elevator.

"His wife, youngest son, and middle son are dead. His other son, Keith . . . I've only seen him once in three years. I understand he lives outside of the country. His daughter is here regularly."

Sheppard tried not to sound too excited. "His daughter. That would be Allison?"

"Dr. Hart. Yes. She's an ER doc here in Savannah."

"Do you know her address or phone number?"

"I don't know her home address, but her phone numbers are posted on the wall in Dr. Curry's room."

"I'd like to see those phone numbers."

"Sure thing. I'll take you to his room, then I'll get him."

The elevator doors opened and two women, arms linked, got off. The one with wild white hair wore a robe and Bugs Bunny slippers and the other looked as though she were dressed for an evening on the town. "Hi Jane, Lillian," David greeted them.

"Honey," said the woman named Jane. "Is our cab here yet? We're off to dinner in the Village."

"I haven't seen a cab yet, but you'd better ask at the front desk."

Lillian whispered something to Jane and they both giggled. Jane looked Sheppard up and down, then met his eyes. "Lillian says you're about the tallest man she's ever seen. She thinks you're mighty handsome and we're wondering if you'd like to join us for dinner."

Sheppard, somewhat flustered, managed to smile. "Thanks very much for the invitation, but I'm afraid I can't join you tonight. Maybe some other night."

"You two honeys take care," Jane said gaily, wiggling

her fingers in the air, and she and Lillian wandered off into the lobby.

"Two of our more colorful residents," David remarked with a smile. "They're always on their way into downtown New York to go to dinner or the theater."

"I thought these facilities were locked wards."

"We don't take escape risks. From time to time, residents forget where they are, but they can't get out unless the person behind the desk opens the electronic doors."

"Does Dr. Curry get many visitors?" Sheppard asked.

"In the three years I've worked here, I've only seen Dr. Hart, his son, Keith, and a young woman who's a friend of the family. She's only been here twice that I know of."

"Who is she?"

David thought a moment, then shook his head. "I don't recall her name, Agent Sheppard. I assumed she was a friend of Dr. Hart's, but I honestly don't know."

"You said Dr. Curry's youngest son was dead. Tell me about that." *Refresh my memory.*

"I don't know all that much," David replied. "It was a drowning accident in the family pool in Miami, when little Ray was around five."

"Does Dr. Curry talk about it?"

"He cries about it. Sometimes he thinks Ray's alive, sometimes he knows he's dead. I know that Dr. Hart found the boy. I believe she was a resident then. She gave Ray mouth-to-mouth, but he was too far gone. Here we are. Dr. Curry's room."

Room 33 had a large wooden plaque on the door with Curry's name on it and shadow boxes on either side of it with a collage of family photos that spanned the years. In the pictures Sheppard picked out Dean, Keith, little Ray, even Mrs. Curry, but no Allie. Interesting omission, he thought, and followed David into the room.

"Here're the phone numbers, Agent Sheppard." From

a corkboard on the wall, David removed a sheet of paper with a list of names and phone numbers. "I'll be right back with Dr. Curry."

As David left, Sheppard looked down at the sheet, his excitement so palpable now that his fingers left perspiration marks on the sheet of paper. Four numbers were listed for the daughter, who was referred to as Allie: home, cell, two work numbers. She undoubtedly had caller ID both at home and on her cell phone, so Sheppard picked up the receiver on Curry's desk and called the home number. The voice on the answering machine shocked him—soft, pleasant, with a seductive charm. The message ended with: "If this is an emergency, please call Dr. Yarborough, who is filling in for me during my absence. Thanks and have a great day."

He called one of the work numbers next and was told that Dr. Hart—*her professional name, finally, Hart, what a joke*—was on vacation and wouldn't return to work until January 3. When he called the cell number, he got a message that the subscriber had traveled out of range or wasn't available. Next to Keith's name was a cell number with a South Florida area code and a long number that looked to be an overseas exchange. He called the cell first and got a message that the number was no longer in service.

The door opened and David came in with Dr. Curry. He looked greatly changed from the man Sheppard remembered from thirteen years ago. He was completely gray now, with stooped shoulders, a shuffling gait, and vacant blue eyes. "Dr. Curry, this is Wayne."

"My memory's fine, just fine." Curry sounded cranky and sank into a chair by the window. "I've got some new ideas about the drug, is that what you want to talk about. . . . What was your name again?" He looked directly at Sheppard, his rheumy eyes narrowing, squinting.

"Wayne."

"Right. Wayne." Curry fumbled for something in his shirt pocket and brought out a pair of glasses, which he put on. The lenses were dirty and he cleaned them vigorously with the tail of his shirt. "As in John Wayne. Good name. Any relation there?"

"Uh, no, sir. Not that I'm aware of."

"John Wayne owned a silver mine in Colorado that he gave to his friend Ed. Ed and I once went to the Lost City in Colombia. Flew in by chopper. I was looking for pharmaceuticals in the vegetation. I think Ed was looking for adventure." He paused and fitted the glasses onto the bridge of his nose. "Or Ed was looking for John Wayne." He slapped his thigh and exploded with laughter. "So there was John *Wayne* that I knew through Ed; then there was a guy named *Wayne* Sheppard. I knew him because of my son Dean."

"I'll be back in a few minutes," David said, and hurried out, leaving them alone.

"Wayne." Curry nodded. "I like that name. Names are revealing. My sons have one syllable names. Ray. Keith. Dean. But my wife, daughter, and I have two syllable names. Lori. William. Allie. Well, her real name's got three syllables. Al-li-son. She goes by a two-syllable name, though. Much cleaner. Yes, sir. Much cleaner."

Shit. "It's Allie I wanted to ask you about. I understand she's on vacation. Do you have any idea where she went?"

"Vacation? No, no, she works all the time. She was here awhile ago. Yes, sir. We went fishing. Well, I went fishing, she was in the house, doing whatever she does in the house."

"What house is that?"

"Where we live. On Tybee."

"She lives on Tybee Island?"

He narrowed his eyes now. "You look familiar to me. Do I know you? Have we met? What was your name again?"

The door to his room opened again and a slender, prissy-looking woman hurried in, her mouth pursed with disapproval. "Excuse me," she said to Sheppard. "May I speak to you in the hall?"

"Hi," Dr. Curry said, waving at her.

"Hi, Bill." A quick smile for the resident. "We'll be right back."

She and Sheppard stepped into the hall and she quickly shut the door and propped her hands on her hips. "Look here, Agent Sheppard. You can't just barge in here and harass the resi—"

"I didn't barge in and I'm not harassing. I need answers and I need them now. Allison Hart is our primary suspect in a quadruple murder and kidnapping."

Mrs. Norcross looked as if she'd been punched in the stomach—her eyes bulged, her mouth dropped open. "That's . . . that's the most ludicrous thing I've ever heard. Dr. Hart is an emergency-room physician at Savannah Hospi—"

"I don't need a character witness," Sheppard interrupted. "I need information. Her home address, where she went on vacation, who she went with, the last time you saw her, how you're supposed to contact her if anything happens to her father while she's gone. . . ."

"I—I can't just give you confidential information."

"You don't get it," he snapped. "A woman's life is on the line. If she dies, it's on your conscience. Now, what's it going to be, Mrs. Norcross? Are you going to cause me to lose valuable time by forcing me to go through official channels?"

"I . . . well . . . okay. But I believe you're grossly mistaken about this, Agent Sheppard. I've known Allie for ten years. She's treated me in the ER, treated residents of our facility. She's—"

"Like I said before, I don't want a character reference. What's her address on Tybee?"

"One ninety-two Campbell Street." She spat the words, as if to do so would be to exonerate herself. "She's lived there for fifteen years. It used to be the Curry family's summer home. In the event of any crisis with her father, I call her cell number and leave a message. I know she took some time off, but I don't know where she went. She didn't say. But she was here yesterday, visiting her dad and—"

"*Yesterday?*" The old man was right. The old man had remembered. "You saw her?"

"Yes. She'd taken a day out of her vacation to visit him. She took him out for the afternoon, made him a special meal and fed him. She's very attentive to her father, very responsible, which is more than I can say for her brother."

Then she was close enough to drive here and back in a day, he thought, and old man Curry wasn't as far out to lunch as he initially thought. "Does the doctor fish?"

"Yes. Whenever Allie takes him back to the house, he fishes from the dock."

"Tell me about Keith."

She made a disgusted sound. "An irresponsible play-boy who makes it here about once a year. He lives most of the time in Panama."

"Do you have a current phone number for him?"

"Only the number on Bill's list."

"Does he have an address in the States?"

"If he does, I'm not aware of it."

"What do you know about Dean?" he asked.

"That his death was a terrible blow to Allie. When the

prison originally notified her, they called it suicide. She hired an attorney to investigate. They subsequently concluded he had been hung and, uh, skinned alive by several other inmates, but to my knowledge no one was ever caught."

"How often did she see him?"

"At least twice a month."

"Did she ever speak to you about when he escaped from the place he was originally sent to?"

"No. She's a very private woman, Agent Sheppard. I mean, I've known her a long time, but never well."

"When we go back into Bill's room, I'd like you to ask him what he and Allie did yesterday when they left."

"He probably won't remember."

"Ask anyway. And refer to me as Wayne, not Agent Sheppard."

"Why?"

"Because thirteen years ago I was the agent who arrested his son, Dean. I don't want to trigger that memory and upset him."

"Sometimes faces stay with these patients." She opened the door to the room and she and Sheppard went back inside. "Bill," she said. "How was your class?"

"Fine, fine," Curry replied, looking up from a magazine in his lap that was upside down.

"So what'd you and Allie do when she picked you up yesterday?"

"Who's he?" Curry pointed at Sheppard.

"Oh, that's Wayne. A new caretaker." She repeated her question.

"Fished. I fished."

"That's it?" Mrs. Norcross prodded.

"I cried." Then he pressed his fists to his eyes and began to sob.

Mrs. Norcross put her arms around him and patted

him on the back as though he were a small child. "It's all right, Bill."

After a while, his sobs subsided and she motioned toward the door. "I'll have David come right up and challenge you to a game of chess, how's that?"

"Great, that's great."

When they were in the hallway again, Sheppard jotted his cell number on the back of a business card. "Please call me immediately if you hear from Dr. Hart. I can't emphasize enough, Mrs. Norcross, how dangerous it would be if you mentioned that I have been here. It could spell the difference between life and death for Dr. Hart's hostage."

She paled. "Yes, I understand. If I hear from her, I'll call you immediately. But tell me something, Mr. Sheppard. Does that arrest thirteen years ago have anything to do with what's happening now?"

"It has everything to do with it."

"And who is her hostage?"

"My fiancée."

"Dear God," she whispered.

Sheppard had just stepped outside the building when his cell phone rang for the umpteenth time. The caller was listed as *unknown.* "Wayne Sheppard."

"Agent Sheppard, my name is Lia. I'm traveling with Keith Curry."

Lia? "Lia West?"

She hesitated. "Only a few times when I visited Dean." She paused. "Keith and I are in customs, at the Atlanta airport. He just got off the phone with Mira Morales. I have a cell number where you can reach her."

The bottom fell out of Sheppard's stomach and he backed up to the wall, trying to assimilate what this woman had just said. "Slow down, Lia. Now, who are you exactly?"

"Lia Phoenix. Lia Davis. Lia Phoenix Davis Curry. Take your pick. I'm Dean Curry's alibi, Mr. Sheppard, for the night of the accident. But that's for another day. I'm going to hand the phone to Keith. He'll explain."

A chill breeze blew across the porch and Sheppard zipped up his jacket and hurried out to his car, the cell phone still snug against his ear. The man who came on the line spoke quickly, succinctly. He related his conversation with Mira and explained why she had Nick Whitford's phone. He gave Sheppard the address for his place on the Coosa River, a description of his sister's SUV, the trailer she was pulling, and the cell number where Sheppard could reach Mira. Talking to him made Sheppard feel as if he'd plugged himself into some very powerful computer to download badly needed information in one fell swoop.

"I'm putting you on hold, Mr. Curry. I'm going to arrange to have a chopper pick up you and Ms. . . ." Curry had said Lia had married Dean. Sheppard couldn't even begin to speculate what she was doing with Dean's brother. At this moment. Exactly when he needed them. "You and Lia. I'm going to have the two of you flown here to Savannah. I need your expertise on your sister. Leave your phone on. If we get cut off, I'll call you right back."

"Agent Sheppard, Allie left me a phone message to call her. You want me to wait on that?"

"Definitely."

Sheppard put him on hold and called King. Three minutes later, he got back to Curry. "Someone's on the way to your river house and a chopper will pick you up in fifteen minutes. I'll meet you at the FBI building in downtown Savannah. One of our people is calling customs and immigration right now. You'll be escorted to another airfield. If there's a problem, call Kyle King." He reeled off the number.

"Listen, go to Tybee. To her house. She's very organized. Check her computer. Check her closets. You may find written plans or photos. Or a journal. And keep in mind that when things don't go according to plan, she gets rattled. Right now, she's probably extremely edgy and unpredictable."

"Do you have any idea about the place Mira mentioned that was important in your childhood?" Sheppard asked.

"Tybee's the first thing that comes to mind. Allie's house is the old family homestead. But trust me, she wouldn't take Mira there. That's her sanctuary. I've got to give this some thought."

"I appreciate it. We'll be in touch."

Sheppard was in the car now, the engine running. His cell phone battery was low, so he plugged in the car charger, connected it to his phone, and attached headphones so that he would have his hands free. He punched out Nick Whitford's number. *Please answer, please.* . . . Two rings. Three. Four. His anxiety ratcheted upward. Then, on the fifth ring, she answered in a voice so soft, so tremulous, that Sheppard was terrified that if he spoke, the connection would break.

"Shep."

"Mira."

His own voice cracked. He shut his eyes, trying to see her in his mind, to visualize her face, to *connect* with her in some way. For precious moments neither of them spoke. He heard her breathing, choking back a sob, gulping in air.

"Look, we'll find you," he said quietly, quickly. "Right now, I need anything you can tell me about your location, where she may be taking you. . . ."

"I'm in a trailer—"

"Keith told me that. And I know about the family stuff. I need information about *her*, Mira."

"Before I forget. She cut her hair, dyed it reddish." Mira gave him a physical description, then said, " I can't pick up information on her when I touch what she's touched. It has to be direct contact. She makes sure I don't have many opportunities to touch her. There's someplace in Florida, I think northern Florida, that's connected to strong family memories for her. Early memories. Before Ray. That's where she's taking me. It's not the location she had in mind. I think the original spot was Cassadaga. But so many things went wrong in her original plan that she had to shuffle the details around. This place is near water or connected to water in some way. There could be a water reference in the name of the town."

He took notes on everything she said. "What else? How long have you been in the trailer?"

"I don't know. When I took Nick's cell phone out of the glove compartment, the time readout said it was two-thirty. Or three-thirty. I'm not sure. It was hard to read. Then . . . then she knocked me out. I don't know if she drove the whole time I was unconscious."

"Keith told me you have a Swiss Army knife. You need to be prepared to use it." He said this with a full under-standing of how completely Mira abhorred violence.

"I had a chance to shoot her and I—I couldn't do it. That won't happen again. I—I can't kill her, Shep, but I can slow her down."

"We're going to try to triangulate your cell location. It may be tough to do if you're in a rural area and on the move. But I need to know what service his cell phone has."

"Okay. Ho—"

And he lost the signal.

"Fuck."

He slammed his fist against the steering wheel and felt a sweeping, crippling hopelessness sweep through him. *It's just what Hart wants you to feel, hopelessness, despair. If you give in to it, she wins.*

Sheppard pushed the feelings down deep inside himself and sealed it up in a steel box. He called the number again, but got a recorded message that the subscriber had traveled out of the calling area. He started the car and headed out of Savannah toward Tybee and kept speed dialing the number. Each time he got the same message.

He lowered all the windows in the car and let the cool air sweep through. By the time he hit the island expressway, he still hadn't been able to get through and she hadn't called him. He called King and asked him to run cell numbers for both Whitford and Allie Hart through the major cell phone providers in Georgia. Once they knew who their cell service providers were, triangulation would be a matter of comparing signal strengths and time lags for the signals at each of at least three cell stations. *If* Hart was on an interstate, in a populated area, and *if* either of their phones was a newer variety, and *if* the phones were on, then it would be possible to triangulate their position with a degree of accuracy. But if Hart was in a rural area, where cell towers typically were spaced farther apart—or if she was still in the mountains—then triangulation was going to be far more difficult.

Too damn many *ifs*.

And that terrified him.

23

1

A thick, pervasive gloom clamped down over Mira. Sheppard's voice had connected her to the outside world and now his voice had been cut off and she was isolated again. But really, what good was a voice? A voice couldn't help her, not even Sheppard's voice. A voice made her feel less alone, but it couldn't get her out of the trailer. Even if Sheppard could triangulate her position, the bottom line was that at this moment, right now, she couldn't depend on him or anyone else. She had to help herself.

She swung her legs over the side of the bed and tested the parameters of her movement. It wasn't much, not even enough to get as close as she needed to one of the windows so she could get some sense of where they were. A rural area or an interstate? Mountains or flatlands? Georgia or Florida or somewhere else altogether? But she could stretch her left arm out enough to plug the cell phone charger into the wall. Once it was in, she connected it to the phone and stared at the little window, waiting for the confirmation that the phone was charging. But nothing happened.

She reached up and turned the switch on the bedside lamp. The bulb didn't come on.

No power in here.

She jerked the charger out of the wall, wrapped it up,

put it back into the pocket of Nick's jacket. How much juice was left in the phone? She clicked through the settings and checked the battery meter. She had maybe a third of the phone's full capacity. If she left the phone on, the remaining power would leak away and the phone would be dead by nightfall. A judgment call. Until she knew whether she was in a populated area where cell towers were more numerous or in a rural area where they weren't, she decided to keep the phone off to preserve power.

She studied the handcuff. It was connected to a metal loop on the bed frame. It wasn't clear to her what purpose the loop served, but she sure as hell couldn't cut through it with any of the blades on the Swiss Army knife. The cuffs were made of a single piece of metal rather than several pieces held together by screws. Although the cuff was tight, it didn't cut off her circulation. Maybe . . .

A long shot, but what other choice did she have?

Mira pushed back onto the bed until her spine rested against the wall that served as a headboard. She extended her legs straight out in front of her. She shut her eyes and began to breathe as Nadine had taught her when Mira was a child, alternating nostril breathing. When she did this, she could still hear the rattle in her lungs. Thanks to the pneumonia, her breathing wasn't as deep as it usually was. But the motion of the trailer lulled her quickly into a more relaxed state.

It took her much longer than usual to achieve an altered state, and even when she did, she wasn't disassociated enough from her body. But it was the best she could do. She focused her attention on her right wrist and began to shut down sensation to it. *The brain controls the body, but the will controls the brain:* Nadine's mantra.

The first time Nadine had told her this, Mira was seven or eight and had found a frog on the porch of Nadine's home on Tango Key that was dragging its injured foot as it tried to move. Mira, upset that the frog was hurt and that she was powerless to help it, had taken on the injury, her own foot swelling, her toes turning inward, the bones and tendons straining against the skin that covered it. Nadine had found her on the porch, crying, and had said the words to her then.

Mira had no idea what *will* meant, but she'd gotten the gist of it. With Nadine's guidance, she'd put herself in an altered state and had done what she was doing now, shut down the sensation to a particular part of her body. Within half an hour, she had learned one of the most essential lessons in her long and complex apprenticeship with her grandmother.

The will controls the brain.

That same energy can be turned outward. This last truth hadn't come from Nadine. Who had said it?

When she could no longer feel her fingers or joints, when it seemed that her hand no longer existed, she twisted her wrist in a certain way and dislocated it. She felt discomfort but no pain. In seconds she was able to manipulate her hand free of the cuff. She twisted her wrist again and heard the soft *pop* as the joint snapped back into place.

She lay there, completely spent, her body drenched in sweat. Then the pain assaulted her, a screaming banshee that drove hot nails into her bones and nerve endings. Her entire arm felt as though it were consumed in flames. Mira gasped and struggled to maintain her altered state.

Will controls brain, will controls brain, will . . .

Mira visualized her arm encased in ice, killing the fire.

The final vestige of pain left her and she raised her arm and opened her arms and flexed her wrist. The skin around it was bright red, that was all. She sat forward, away from the wall, and got up from the bed. Her legs felt shaky, her thigh ached and burned. She went over to the window and pushed the blinds to the side. Tall, skinny pines. Florida pines? No telling. The land looked hilly, but not flat, the road was narrow, she didn't see any buildings or other cars. The sky was heavily overcast, the color of lead.

Mira raised the blind. The window was an old-fashioned jalousie that had to be cranked open. The lever had been removed. Even if she could get the jalousies open, she wouldn't be able to escape through the glass slats. She looked up at the ceiling, but didn't see an escape hatch.

Two doors. She opened the first. A closet, a few clothes hanging inside. She grabbed a T-shirt and a pair of jeans, shrugged off Nick's jacket and tore off the long T-shirt she'd been wearing for what seemed like years, and put on the new clothes. The jeans fit her in the waist, but were too long. She rolled up the cuffs and eyed the pairs of shoes hooked onto a shoe rack. Sneakers, high tops, scuffed loafers. Wacko's shoes? She crouched and brought her hands to the sneakers. Nothing came to mind, no impression, no nudges. Definitely Wacko's shoes.

Mira sat at the edge of the bed to put them on. Her feet were a mess, scraped and bruised and swollen, and she eased them into the sneakers. They felt tender when she stood, but at least she could run in sneakers. She put Nick's jacket back on, brought out the Swiss Army knife. She selected the longest blade, prayed that she wouldn't have to use it on Wacko, and went over to the bedroom door. She turned the knob and opened it.

A new prison, she thought, and made her way out into the rest of the trailer. The first thing she did was turn the dead bolt in the front door, unlocking it. But it apparently was locked from the outside—with what? A padlock? Well, two could play that game. She put on the chain. If Wacko stopped in the next few minutes, the chained door would give Mira a little time.

Mira used the bathroom, washed her face, and returned to the main part of the trailer. The fridge was on, but appeared to run off a battery or gas rather than electricity. It was well stocked with bottled water, fruit, hard-boiled eggs, juices, small containers of fruit yogurt. She ate standing up, vigilant for any change in the trailer's speed, any turns, rises, or dips in the road. She went over to the dinette table and peered out the blind that covered this window.

She caught sight of a green road sign, but the trailer was moving too fast for her to read it. The land definitely looked like northern Florida, but the area was rural. Not good. Except for Jacksonville on the east coast and Tallahassee to the west, northern Florida was a wasteland. Farther south and inland lay Gainesville, then Orlando, and Ocala, but she sensed they weren't that far south.

Wacko eventually would have to stop for gas or to use the bathroom, right? But maybe she'd stopped hours ago.

If she could get the front door open, she could jump. But at this speed, she might break a leg or her foot or worse. As long as the trailer was moving, she was safe. Even Wacko couldn't be in two places at once.

She brought out the cell phone again, turned it on. *Searching for network.* She turned the cell phone in another direction, but the message in the window didn't change. Mira turned the phone off and unfolded all the blades in the knife, taking inventory of what she had that might be useful. A tiny screwdriver, a pair of scissors, a can opener, three blades of varying lengths and sharpness. She sat at the dinette and raised the blind partway and tried the screwdriver on one of the screws that held the window frame in place. If she could remove the goddamn frame, she could kick out the jalousies, and when the trailer slowed sufficiently, she could jump and run like hell.

The screw was badly corroded and refused to budge. She raised the blind higher and counted the screws that held the frame in place. Fifteen of the little suckers. She went to work on another screw and the trailer hurled on through the wasteland.

2

Tybee Island stood at the mouth of the Savannah River, about twenty feet above sea level. It was connected to the mainland by a series of bridges similar to those that connected the Florida Keys, except these bridges crossed river and marsh instead of ocean. These vast salt marshes fell away on either side of Sheppard, broken up here and there by sagging wooden docks that led to homes hidden in the dense trees that lined the marsh.

Once Sheppard was actually on the island, he turned right at the first light, just as Mrs. Norcross had instructed, and immediately liked the looks of Campbell Street. It angled through the shadows of huge, towering live oaks draped in Spanish moss. The complex richness of the air spoke of ancient Southern traditions, of lives that unfolded with a kind of sweet predictability. It occurred to him that it was the ideal spot for a woman like Allie Hart. *I'm ordinary, I live here among regular people, and you will never see what's really buried in the darkness of my heart.* Old wooden homes on stilts rose on either side of him, the kind of homes where people lived out their entire lives.

At 192 Campbell, he pulled into the curving driveway and stopped in front of the house. It was wooden, forty or fifty years old. A wooden fence enclosed the yard on either side. Two stories. The second level looked much newer than the rest of the place. It had a corrugated metal roof, like many of the newer homes in the Florida Keys, and large front windows. He didn't see any sign advertising a security system. A place this old wouldn't be difficult to break into and he didn't intend to waste time getting a search warrant.

As he got out, he plucked his cell phone from the seat, pressed automatic dial again, but got the same message for Whitford's phone number.

Sheppard hurried over to the wooden gate and let himself into the yard. No lawn, just native plants and several huge trees that kept the place in perpetual shade. He spotted a dock that jutted out about ten feet into the marsh, a fishing pole standing upright in a corner of it. It held two beach chairs with a small wooden table between them.

The gate behind him creaked and he glanced around. An old guy with thick white hair eyed Sheppard with extreme suspicion. A black-and-white cat wound between the old guy's legs.

"Reckon you're trespassing, my friend."

His Southern accent immediately brought to mind grits and hotcakes sizzling on a griddle. "Reckon I'm not. Agent Sheppard, FBI." He held up his badge. "And you are . . . ?"

"Freddie Pringle. Live down the street. I keep an eye on the doc's place, gather her mail, when she's away."

"Any idea where she went, Mr. Pringle?"

"The mountains. On vacation. She was here yesterday. Brought her dad over for a while. He don't fish too good anymore, but he still seems to enjoy it."

"So, does Dr. Hart live here alone?"

"Uh-huh. Fifteen years. One year she was married to

her second husband, then they got divorced and she's been here alone. Shame, her being such a good-lookin' woman and all. She's real good at what she does. People come into ER shot up, drugged up, messed up from the get-go and she fixes 'em up. Hell, one night I'd had too many beers and did a job on my finger. She stitched it up jus' fine." He held out the index finger on his right hand. "Can't see so much as a scar. And she never charged me a dime. She's done that for folks up and down Campbell."

Another glowing character reference, Sheppard thought. But it fit. Take care of the people among whom you lived and they would never speak ill of you. A perfect camouflage.

"She can fix bodies up just fine. But when something here at home breaks down, she calls me up like some helpless young thing and wants to know who she should call even though she can fix anything. Once, the pipes under my sink done broke and I had me one big flood. She happens by and fixed it. Jus' rolled up her sleeves and got to it. Seen her do it with the AC, her car, the dock. . . . Don't know why she hires anyone to fix anything."

"What else do you do besides pick up her mail?"

"If something needs fixin', I take care of it. Just keep an eye on the place, same thing I used to do for Bill and Lori."

"How long has the family owned the place?"

"Well, I've been livin' here for close to thirty years, when Campbell was jus' a dirt road. The Currys used to come up here for holidays, summers, guess goin' back nearly as long as I've been here."

"I guess you knew her brothers."

"Sure did. Ray, the smallest, never really got to know him too well 'fore he drowned. Dean and Keith, knew them both right well. Dean was one real special kid. Never did believe that he killed someone with his car. He was always mowing my lawn for free, picking up stuff at the store for me, washing my car. Keith, well, him I didn't care for so much. Selfish, seemed to me. There was one real pretty girl Dean hung out with for a summer. And doncha know, I'm over here one day last August, I think it was, and there she is, just sitting down on the dock. She remembered me. We had a nice long chat. I caught her up on all the Curry family news."

"You remember her name?"

"Sure thing. Lia Phoenix. Her folks still live on the next street over, third house on the right. She told me she ran away from Tybee when she was fifteen or sixteen and that she lived in central Florida now. Has a kid and all."

I'm Dean Curry's alibi. But that's for another day. Once again, this went so far beyond any synchronicity he'd ever experienced that it might take him the rest of his life to figure it all out.

"Where's she live, do you know?"

He frowned, thinking about it. "Some odd town in Florida I've never heard of. Cassanova? No, that wasn't it."

"Cassadaga?"

He snapped his fingers. "Yeah, that's it."

Interesting, Sheppard thought. Ian West had been from Cassadaga.

Pringle rubbed his unshaven jaw. "Just curious. Why's the FBI poking around here?"

"Dr. Hart may have gotten herself into some trouble."

"Aw, Lord, they've had more than their share of bad luck."

"I was hoping to get inside the house and look for leads on her whereabouts, Mr. Pringle."

He winked an eye shut. "Mind if I see that badge of yours again?"

Sheppard handed him the badge and Pringle examined it with the scrutiny of a bank teller looking for counterfeit twenties. "Reckon it's legit. C'mon, we can go in the back."

Pringle led the way onto a glassed-in porch, a kind of sunroom. Sheppard noticed the rattan furniture, the decorative concrete floor, and the profusion of small, green plants. "She's a gardener?" he asked.

"Them's herbs. She's big into alternative medicines." Pringle unlocked the double French doors.

Sheppard felt strange when he entered the house and stood there, listening to the silence, taking in the smell of the air, the colors and furniture, the texture of Allie Hart's life. A solitary life. But at a glance, there was nothing here that indicated she was at the edge of madness or that she was one of the heirs of the Curry family fortune. The place was simply but expensively furnished in pine and rattan, with two bedrooms and a bathroom downstairs and another bedroom, bath, and computer room upstairs, with a balcony that overlooked the marsh. Comfortable, excessively tidy, everything in its place.

She liked art: The walls were covered with paintings, lithographs, sketches, pen-and-ink drawings. In the bedroom hung two paintings by an artist whose name Sheppard recognized—Edna Hibel, a Florida artist, now well into her eighties, whose mother-and-daughter images were favorites of both Nadine and Mira. In the downstairs bedroom, the walls were covered with framed family photos that included a number of Allie Hart, some of which looked recent.

Pringle, standing in the bedroom doorway, cleared his throat. "You stay as long as you need to, Agent Sheppard. Just lock up when you leave."

"Before you leave, Mr. Pringle, tell me which of these photos looks like Dr. Hart now."

The old man shuffled into the room and lifted one of the large poster-size collages off the wall. "This one right here."

"Great. Thanks. I certainly appreciate all your help, Mr. Pringle."

"Jus' take your time," he said, and let himself out.

Sheppard immediately removed the recent photo of Allie and imagined her with shorter reddish hair. He would fax this photo to King, tell him about the different hairstyle, and within an hour, it would be on the Internet and in the offices of the Florida Highway Patrol.

He pressed speed dial again. No change.

Sheppard climbed the stairs to the second floor. She had a fax, a scanner, the works. Keith Curry had advised him to search his sister's computer. He booted up the Dell PC, set Hart's photo in the scanner, and when the computer was ready, he went into the scanner program. He put Hart's photo into My Pictures, e-mailed them to King, and started scrolling through the dozens of thumbnail photographs. Halfway down the page, he stopped, leaned closer to the screen. "What the hell," he murmured, and double-clicked the picture to enlarge it.

Labeled SHEP517, it showed him and Mira on the Tango boardwalk late last spring, he remembered the day. She had taken off a couple hours from the bookstore and they had gone out to lunch and shopping afterward. He clicked on another labeled MIRA822 that showed Mira sweeping the walkway in front of the bookstore. The shadows against the walk indicated that it was late afternoon. He clicked through dozens of such photos—of him, Mira, Annie, Nadine, his home, Mira's home, outside and inside the bookstore, even the front of the bureau's Tango Key office. The photos dated back at least nine months and the most recent had been taken Christmas Day, when they were packing the car to leave for North Carolina.

Thanks to the Internet and the high-profile cases he had investigated over the years, he undoubtedly had been easy to find. And once she'd found him, she'd documented his life with the precision of a researcher. She had stalked and studied him and the people in his life, establishing his patterns, his affections, his vulnerabilities.

He kept scrolling through the photos and came across another set of thumbnails that looked intriguing. They were labeled BLANK1 through BLANK11. He enlarged each one, printed it out, then copied the entire picture file onto a CD and popped it into his laptop.

While the file was copying, he arranged the photos in the order he'd printed them. Everything in life, from DNA to cloud formations and weather, to crimes and habits and lifestyles, was composed of patterns and he sensed this was one such pattern. But of what? Fields, lakes, hills, roads, trees, ruined buildings. The pictures of the buildings had been taken at too great a distance to tell very much about them. The road didn't include anything as convenient as a sign. And the nature shots—shit, they could have been taken anywhere.

He turned off her computer, removed the hard drive, gathered up all the backups, and stuck everything in his laptop case, except for the eleven pages of fields, trees, lakes, and buildings. The jigsaw. He clipped these pages together and left them on top of the laptop case to study in the car.

Sheppard used Hart's phone and called Whitford's cell number again. Same message. Subscriber out of range. He called King and told him he'd e-mailed Hart's photo and that the art department should touch it up so that she had shorter, lighter hair.

"Curry and the woman should be landing in Savannah

in about thirty minutes, Shep. Hart's cell service is with Cingular. I'm still working on Whitford's."

Sheppard suddenly remembered that Mira's cell phone was missing. "Alert T-Mobile as well and give them Mira's cell number just in case Hart has that phone and uses it."

"Got it. I'll be in touch."

The room began to feel excessively warm. He opened the doors to the balcony and stood in the cool breeze, gazing out over the marsh. The tide was moving in and the muddy flats he'd seen earlier were gradually filling with water. Way on the other side of the marsh, the docks that jutted out like thirsty tongues into the tall weeds seemed to shimmer and shine in the light.

Rhythm, he thought. The life that Allie Hart had created for herself here was all about rhythm—the wild, chaotic beat of ER counterbalanced by this strange and lovely cadence of nature. The water in the marsh rose and fell with the tides, the sun rose and set on Tybee beaches, and everything in her private life was cyclical, predictable, known. She had tried to plan the events of the last several days with the same sort of precision that she brought to her private life. That was what all the research and investigation had been about. Sheppard suspected that she hadn't counted on killing five people and shooting Mira. So, right from the start, he thought, the unpredictable and chaotic had intruded. *And keep in mind that when things don't go according to plan, she gets rattled,* Curry had told him. *Right now, she's probably extremely edgy and unpredictable.*

He turned, eyeing the room slowly, studying it. Closet, he thought, and went over to it and opened the double doors. A walk-in. Not too many clothes, but everything arranged with obsessive neatness. Three black designer dresses hung together at the left end of the closet and at the right end hung half a dozen pairs of designer jeans. In between, clothes were arranged by type—slacks, cotton shirts, silk blouses, T-shirts, sweats, jackets, and coats—and the types were arranged by color, from lightest to darkest. Her shoes, perhaps a dozen pairs, were lined up like toy soldiers. In a closet organizer, three cubbyholes contained wool sweaters arranged in neat piles from light to dark; another cubbyhole held nothing but socks, each pair perfectly matched, and other cubby holes held underwear, bras, slips.

The organizer held a small cupboard, and when he opened the door, he found several photo albums. Sheppard carried them over to the computer desk and wasn't surprised to find they were as meticulously arranged as her clothes. The top two albums held e-mails and letters from and to Dean and about Dean. Much of it was legal material that related to Dean's arrest and defense and the investigation into his death. But there were five or six love letters that Dean had written Lia.

The third album held old family photos that dated back to the 1970s and '80s. Sheppard paged through it, noting that some photos had been captioned and dated. *Tybee 1973. Paris 1979. Farm 1975.*

What farm? Where?

He went through four photo albums in all, but didn't find any more pictures identified as *farm*. And among these several hundred photographs, he found only two that had little Ray in them, a wisp of a kid with huge soulful eyes and a winning smile, flanked on either side by his parents.

Odd. Why only two pictures?

This was where Keith Curry might prove extremely helpful, Sheppard decided, and carried everything downstairs and out to the car. As he slid behind the wheel, his cell phone rang. Mira's cell number came up in the window. It was her. The bitch. He doubted if T-Mobile was on the case yet, but he couldn't very well put her on hold to notify King. He rubbed his hand over his face, anxiety churning through him. How to play it? Was she calling to gloat or was she ready to kill Mira?

What would happen if he didn't answer it? Would she call back? Would he have time to contact King and find out where things stood with Mira's cell service provider?

Suppose it's Mira?

He pressed the answer button and said, "Mira? Mira?"

Breathing. "Oops, wrong woman, Sheppard." Her silken voice flowed through him and around him like some exotic and toxic liquid. "Are you suffering yet?"

"Allie Hart," he said.

"Well, you've figured it out, have you?"

"Is that what it's been about? Making me suffer? Or you playing God?"

"I play God every day in ER, Sheppard. This is about you. Payback. An eye for an eye. Getting even. And I think you're dying inside right now. I think anxiety is whipping through you like a cyclone. Now you know how I felt for thirteen years."

"Dean's arrest and jail time were about *you*, Hart? Your problem is that you tried to control his life and he refused to let you do it. He left you completely out of the loop about his wife and child. He left you out of the loop on a lot of the finer details that—"

"What bullshit." Gone was the silken tone. Her voice had filled with vengeance. "You don't know what you're talking about. You don't know shit about my family, Sheppard."

"I know that little Ray drowned when he was five and that you found the body. I know that Keith had to leave the country to get away from you. I know that Dean hated you, that—"

"Shut up," she hissed. "And listen very closely, Sheppard. Just in case you're operating under the usual cop delusion that you'll find me before I kill her, let me tell you that the odds are definitely not in your favor. I figure you've got about three hours."

With that, she disconnected.

24

1

Panama to Atlanta to Savannah, and now Keith Curry was inside an FBI office, not entirely sure how he'd gotten here. He, Lia, and Sheppard sat at a long conference-room table, where Sheppard spread out maps, pictures printed from a computer, and numerous old photos, some in faded color, others in the sepia tones of advanced age. Curry sipped from a bottle of cold water that a secretary had brought into the room, his eyes skipping over the photos that Sheppard had taken from his sister's place.

He stared at a skinny kid with a shit-eating grin on his face. *Is that me?*

He picked up the photo, studying it. He was wearing swimming trunks. His hair was very short, a summer buzz cut. He stood at the edge of a pond or a small lake, with an inflatable raft on the ground next to him and a paddle upright in his hand. Next to him stood a smaller kid, a toddler with hair that looked white. Dean.

He had absolutely no memory of where or when this photo had been taken.

In another photo Allie stood between him and Dean. She was tall and thin, maybe twelve or thirteen, with budding breasts no larger than pimples. Curry wondered who had snapped the photo. The where and when for this photo were also a blank.

"Do any of these pictures seem familiar to you, Keith?" Sheppard asked.

"No. It's like they're from someone else's life."

Sheppard, pacing now, removed a notepad from his shirt pocket, flipped through it. "Mira pinpointed northern Florida, a place that holds strong childhood memories for your sister. The place is near water or connected to water in some way. There could be a water reference in the name of the town."

"My God," Lia breathed. "That's what it says in the Book of Voices."

"The what?" Sheppard asked.

She quickly explained. Sheppard listened closely. It was obvious to Curry that he listened with a mind far more open than his own, and he wondered about that. He knew that some cops used psychics on their investigation, but most refused to admit it. *I picked up something about a Plan B*, Mira had said, and Curry suddenly thought he understood what she had meant by that.

"Excuse me. How did Mira get such specific information about Allie's plans?" he asked.

"She's psychic."

"Jesus," Curry spat. "That's what we're basing all this on? More psychic input? You have that much faith in her?"

Sheppard nodded. "Absolutely."

Lia sat forward, her eyes strangely bright, excited. "This is verification, Keith. It's right in sync with the Cassadaga predictions. A place near water or with water in the name. A curry, a shepherd, a mirror. *Mirror* and *Mira* are close enough to be the same thing. The information is valid. But your memories are vital to the whole picture. What place in northern Florida holds strong childhood memories for your sister?" She pushed one of the photos toward him. "This picture is labeled *Farm 1975*. Where is it? You're in the photo, so is Dean. Can you remember where this might have been taken?"

Curry pushed back from the table, got up. "Give me a break. I was eleven in 1975. What can you remember of your life at that age?"

She sat back, looking annoyed. "Quite a bit, actually."

"Well, I don't remember shit from my early childhood." His childhood memories had gaping holes. He never had had his sister's obsession about the Family, and where she could cite dates and places and events from thirty years ago, Curry was largely clueless. But Lia and Sheppard expected him to dive into the gaping holes of his memories and come up with information. Fat fucking chance. He paused at the picture window and gazed out into downtown Savannah. The sky had turned dark to the east and south, sagging with clouds that promised rain within the hour.

"Is this you and Dean?" Lia asked, holding up another farm photo.

Curry turned and walked back to the table to look at the photo. In this picture that same skinny kid was holding a toddler sucking on a bottle. The toddler was definitely Dean. "Yeah, that's Dean." He glanced up at Lia. "Did he ever mention a farm to you?"

"I don't think so. But he used to talk about almost drowning in a sinkhole and then learning to swim because of that experience."

Almost drowning? Curry suddenly felt uncomfortable. *But why?*

"A sinkhole?" Sheppard sounded excited. "That's what the body of water could be. Not a pond, but a sinkhole. North and central Florida are covered with sinkholes."

"The area around Cassadaga has a lot of sinkholes," Lia said. "But I don't think your folks ever owned a farm around there, Keith. I would've remembered Dean saying that. In the Book of Voices, some of the earlier predictions pinpointed Cassadaga as the location. But the later predictions are ambivalent about location."

"Because Allie changed her mind," Sheppard said suddenly.

Even though Curry wasn't as skeptical as he'd been twenty-four hours ago, a part of him still balked at this strange world these people inhabited. He shook his head. "Excuse me, but this requires a quantum leap in faith."

Lia raised her eyes from the photo of him and Dean and looked at him in that mysterious and penetrating way she had. "Maybe that's what this journey is about for you, Keith."

"This journey is about closure," Curry said.

"Let me try Whitford's cell number again," Sheppard said. "Then you try your sister's."

They had tried the numbers dozens of times, but always got the same message. The service providers involved were now alerted to the situation, and if either phone was turned on, they would be able to triangulate his sister's position to within nine hundred feet in a populated area or within several square miles in a rural area. Personally, Curry felt that Allie kept the phone off for exactly that reason. She might be nuts, but she was functional.

He studied the maps in front of him, highway and topographical maps of Florida, maps of cities and towns, villages and hamlets. He glanced at several more photos that Lia passed to him and one of them caused something to stir deep inside him.

The photo seemed to have been taken in the same area, near the pond or sinkhole or whatever it was, but sometime later. Dean looked a little older, a little taller, around four years of age. He was facing the camera, his arms thrown out as if to embrace not only the photographer, but the entire world. He was laughing, his beautiful face consumed by sheer pleasure and joy.

Just in front of him was the photographer's shadow, the lines so crisp and clear even now that Curry could see that the photographer was crouching so he or she was eye level with Dean. Off to the photographer's left was another shadow, less distinct, except for triangles at the sides of the person's body. Curry suddenly knew the shadow belonged to Allie, that she was standing with her hands on her hips and the light shone through the triangles made by her arms.

And right then, a memory snapped into place with such shocking clarity that he felt it in the pit of his stomach, in the marrow of his bones.

You're not doing it right, you idiot. The light's all wrong.

Curry winced and ran his fingers over the surface of the photo. Seconds after he'd snapped it, Allie had marched over and snatched the camera out of his hands. *You're so incredibly stupid.*

And then she had run toward the house with the camera, and Curry had torn after her and tackled her. As they rolled around in the grass, biting and punching each other, screams erupted behind them and Curry whipped around and saw Dean flailing in the sinkhole. Dean, who couldn't swim. He wrenched free of his sister, raced to the sinkhole, and dived in.

His sister, of course, blamed the whole episode on him, and his old man beat him to within an inch of his life. But the next day, he took Dean down to the sinkhole and began teaching him how to swim. And the place where this had happened was . . .

There could be a water reference in the name of the town, Mira had said.

"High Springs." His head snapped up. "The farm was

outside of High Springs, north of Gainesville. But it wasn't a farm, it was just an old wooden house with an unused stable out back and five acres of land with a sink-hole on it."

He grabbed the map, located the town, circled it in red marker, and exploded with laughter. "This is it. This is where she's taking Mira." Another detail clicked into place. "It's over two hundred miles from Savannah."

"We're outta here," Sheppard said, and quickly gathered up everything on the table and headed for the stairs that led to the roof where the chopper waited.

2

It had started to rain, a cold, driving rain that blew across the road in great, sweeping gusts and caused the trailer to fishtail, forcing Allie to slow down to sixty. She didn't want to slow down. Speed kept her in the groove, in the pattern. When she wasn't moving fast, her thoughts were flung backward and forward in time or got stuck in her conversation with that pompous prick Sheppard. How the hell had he figured out her identity? How? It had shaken her when he'd said her name, shaken her certainty, her resolve.

Your problem is that you tried to control Dean's life and he refused to let you do it.

He didn't know shit about her relationship with Dean. And the crap about the wife and kid . . . yeah, sure, she wasn't about to fall for that. There had been a time during the trial, though, when the subject had come up—and Dean had denied it, denied all of it.

And why hadn't Keith called her back? She'd left him a message hours ago. He was probably off playing with some sweet young thing and might get back to her next week or next month. Fuck Keith. Fuck all of them. When this was over, she would flee to the Amazon and study herbs. Who would bother her in the Amazon?

She accelerated again, racing south along U.S. 41, a county road that would take her from Lakeland to High Springs. A few cars passed her, but the road was basically deserted. She was getting low on gas, but not that low, not low enough to take time out to stop. She would stop when she got to the old farm. She had been through here last summer, en route to Tango Key, and even though the area had changed vastly since she was a kid, she had managed to find the road that led to her parents' old home.

There wasn't much left of the old place, just an empty house with vegetation pushing up through the rotting floors, and rats and mice scurrying around in the darkness. But the metal garage still stood and the stable with its four stalls had survived the passage of time, and of course, the sinkhole was there.

The sinkhole where the trailer, with Mira inside, would plunge down so deep that it would never be found.

How deep was that sinkhole? A hundred feet? Several hundred? Riddled with underwater caves, deeper than outer space, the trailer would sink and be lost forever.

She had been towing her trailer last summer, too, because a guy in Gainesville was doing the work on it, and had spent two days in here, making preparations just in case Plan B became *the* plan. Which seemed to have happened.

Well, she was okay with that now. She was. She was flexible. She could go with the flow if she had to. Inside that padlocked garage was a Mini Cooper that would get her to Miami. A clean break. A fresh start. A new Allie Hart now named Sandra Bedford. Not such a bad idea, right?

The wipers flicked back and forth across the windshield, smearing dirt in sloppy half-moons across the glass. She was doing seventy again, which would bring her to her turnoff in just a few minutes. As she started to change lanes, she checked her side mirror—and saw a cop pulling up close behind her. No siren yet, no spinning lights.

Her heart slammed up against her ribs, a hot, dry taste coated the inside of her mouth. *Move on, guy, please, I don't want trouble.*

But suddenly the siren screamed and the lights spun and the cop sped up alongside her, signaling that she should pull over. Allie couldn't outrun him, not while she was towing the trailer, and if she pulled over so she could shoot him when he approached the window, she wouldn't have the advantage of darkness. He might see her gun and shoot first or he might approach the car with his weapon drawn. It would depend on whether he was stopping her for speeding or because there was an APB out on her car. The latter seemed damn unlikely; such a description would have to come from Nick and he was dead. If she forced the cop off the road without killing him, he would radio for backup and she would still be as good as dead.

Decide fast. What's it going to be?

She put on her blinker, signaling her intention to pull over, and tapped the brake, slowing down. She pulled her gun from her bag, tucked it under her thigh. *One cop, I can handle one cop. I can even handle two cops.* But she couldn't handle a battalion of cops, and if this guy called for backup, that was what it would be and it would be the end of her. Like the people at the farm, this cop was in her way, and by pulling her over, he was leaving her no choice but to shoot him.

Allie popped a CD into the player so music would cover any sounds that Mira might make, then came to a stop, but without turning off the engine. The cop got out, wearing a yellow rain slicker with a hood. She watched him in the side mirror, her hand on the gun.

3

Mira knew that if she screamed, Allie would kill the cop and his death would be on *her* conscience. So as the Rover slowed to a stop, she popped out the window frame whose screws had taken her hours to work out, carefully lifted away two of the jalousies, and used one of the blades on the knife to cut a large hole in the screen. Then she stepped onto the dinette table and wiggled out through the opening.

She dropped to the ground, the rain and wind masking any sounds she made, and ran, hunkered over, toward the rear of the trailer, her body crying out from all the abrupt movement, pain searing through her thigh.

But the cop already had gone past the point where he could see her. Mira moved quickly to the other end of the trailer. Heart pounding, she cupped her hands at the sides of her mouth and shouted, *"She's armed, get down!"*

Then she spun and hobbled toward the cruiser, a state trooper car, cutting between the two vehicles, making it nearly impossible for Wacko to see her in the driver's side mirror. The rain stung her cheeks, her eyes. Her soggy sneakers slapped the pavement. She yanked open the door of the cruiser, and as she scrambled inside, two shots rang out, echoing across the empty road.

Mira hunkered down against the seat, shivering from the cold; shudders of terror ripped through her and she prayed that the cop had shot Wacko. In the event that it was the other way around, that *she* had shot *him,* she hoped that Wacko would think Mira had shouted from inside the trailer and would take off.

The wind whistled around the cruiser, rain pounded

the windshield. No keys in the ignition. But there was a radio. Mira grabbed the mike, pressed the button on the side, spoke softly, urgently. "Hello, Mayday, Mayday, this is a Mayday, is anyone there?"

Despite her five years with Sheppard, she didn't have any idea what the protocol was on a police radio. Were you supposed to say "Mayday"? And just how the hell did this thing work, anyway?

She dropped the mike and raised up, slowly, carefully, her heart pounding in her throat, and peered over the curve of the steering wheel. And suddenly the cop appeared, running toward the cruiser, and Mira frantically waved her arms and realized he couldn't see her because of the rain. She hurled open the door and scrambled out, rain hammering her face and eyes, and stumbled toward him.

The wind whipped his hat away, he faltered, and then he toppled forward like a little tin soldier that some malicious kid had knocked down. It wasn't until he struck the ground face first that she realized her own need had blinded her, twisted her perceptions. He hadn't stumbled, and he hadn't been running back to the cruiser to call for backup. He'd been shot and was fleeing, and now he was dead.

And when her head snapped up, Wacko struck her in the temple with the gun. Stars burst in Mira's eyes, she felt herself going down—and then shot upward again and rammed Wacko in the chest. Wacko stumbled back, the gun went off, and she tripped over the cop's body and sprawled gracelessly in the road. Mira's only thought was to get away, to escape, to run like hell. And so she ran, but Wacko lunged at her, grabbing onto her bad leg, her injured leg, and Mira fell.

After that, she wasn't sure of the sequence of events.

Everything ran together like warm butter, the sequence didn't matter. She was fucked.

Time blinked off and on. Rain, darkness, pain. Rain, darkness, pain. Then: she was inside the Rover, behind the wheel, Wacko shrieking, *"Drive, Freak, drive."*

The gun was jammed to Mira's temple, pressed so hard into the skin that it seemed she and the gun were one, they had gone into a kind of Spock mind-meld, with the metal coughing up Wacko's secrets. *Shoot her now, do it now, doitdoitdoit. . . .*

Foot to the accelerator. Hands gripping the wheel. Rain streaming down. Thigh on fire. Blood soaking her jeans.

. . . leaning over the little boy's body, whispering . . .

What? What was Wacko whispering?

Off again.

On again. Wacko screaming, "Turn, slow and turn. Jesus, where'd you learn to drive?"

Brake, slow down. Turn wheel to the left. Good, she was doing good, except that she could barely see the road.

The tires kicked up pebbles, dirt, mud. The Rover slammed through potholes. The headlights burned through the darkness, revealing massive trees to either side of her.

"Slow down," Wacko yelled.

"Then take the fucking gun away from my head," Mira shouted.

The pressure of the gun against her temple vanished. But the gun didn't go very far away. It poked into her ribs now, a hard, constant pressure, and Wacko described in graphic detail what a shot at point-blank range would do to Mira. She got it. Even though she wasn't afraid to die, even though she knew death was just another transition, she didn't want to die. Not yet, not here, not like this.

"Follow the road."

"It's not a road, it's a goddamn footpath."

They passed the crumbling ruin of an old house. "It's the summer place," Wacko said. "I didn't want to bring you here, it wasn't in the original pattern. But we're fully into Plan B now. Dean almost drowned here one summer. It was Keith's fault, the whole thing was Keith's fault. And afterward he felt so guilty he taught Dean how to swim." She giggled. "I lost my virginity here, up in the loft of the old barn. It's still standing, see it over there?"

No, Mira didn't see it. She could barely keep her eyes focused on the road. When had it gotten so dark? What day was it? What time? *Who cares? Think, think, we're coming down to the wire here. She's going to hang you, skin you alive.*

Gun in her ribs. Bleeding in her thigh. Stitches torn, ripped out, she was on her own.

"Through here," Wacko said.

"There's no road."

"You can get through. Drive, Freak, just drive."

Mira drove until they ran out of road. Until the Rover stood at the lip of a sinkhole, the beams of the headlights shooting out over the still black waters.

"Get out," Wacko said, her voice strangely calm, even, almost soft. "End of the line."

The Rover idled, the rain fell, and the wind blew, shuddering through the trees. Her thigh screamed, her temple throbbed; she felt the hot, insistent pressure of the gun in her ribs.

"I said, get out, Freak."

Fuck you.

And Mira floored the gas pedal.

25

1

The chopper came down through the pounding rain and the rapidly fading light, and landed in a field just past the abandoned police car. Sheppard leaped out, Curry and Lia close behind him, and loped across the slippery grass. His raincoat flapped at his knees, the blowing rain stung his cheeks like needles.

They had spotted the cruiser from the air, while the pilot had been looking for a place to land because of the inclement weather. The pilot had made one low pass and Sheppard had seen the body sprawled on the ground near the cruiser, a sure sign that Allie Hart had passed this way. Like some rampaging force of nature, she left bodies strewn in her path.

Sheppard reached the body first and turned it over. A young guy, less than thirty. He'd been shot twice, from what Sheppard could tell, once in the shoulder and again in the abdomen. His skin was still faintly warm and the water that streamed around him was pinkish, not red. Sheppard guessed he'd been dead for maybe fifteen minutes.

Sheppard patted him down quickly, found his car keys, took his weapon. "What do you want to do?" Curry asked.

"Get him into the chopper. Then we'll take the cruiser."

Sheppard tossed the car keys to Lia and she hurried

over to the cruiser while Sheppard and Curry picked up the dead cop and carried him over to the chopper. They set him on the floor and Sheppard shouted at the pilot to get the body to the nearest state trooper headquarters as soon as he could take off again. Then he and Curry grabbed their bags and raced back to the cruiser.

Lia was already behind the wheel, revving the engine. Curry got into the front seat with her, Sheppard scrambled into the back with the bags. "The radio's been destroyed," Lia said as she swerved out onto the road.

"It looks like a rabid animal went after it," Curry added. "She's definitely gone over the edge."

"She went over the edge years ago," Lia remarked.

The words filled Sheppard with an elemental dread. At this point backup wouldn't arrive in time to help them. He unzipped his bag, brought out a flashlight, his SIG, Goot's Beretta, and the cop's weapon. "Can you shoot a gun, Keith?"

"Yes."

Sheppard passed him the Beretta. "Lia?"

"I've shot one, but I'm no gun whiz, Shep."

"It's for defense." He passed her the cop's weapon.

"The turnoff's just ahead," Curry said, pointing. "It'll be on the left, Lia."

"How far in is the farm from the turnoff?" Lia asked.

"Maybe half a mile," Curry replied. "But she'll hear the car if we get too close."

"The rain will mask some of the noise," Sheppard said, leaning forward. "Let's play it by ear." He wondered if Mira's future had shrunk to minutes or to mere seconds. "Step on it, Lia."

Moments later, the cruiser whipped into a turn and slammed onto a dirt road. Trees rose on either side of them like thick, wet walls. The cruiser bounced down into a ravine of mud; the tires spun, the engine died.

"We're stuck," Lia muttered, and threw the gearshift into reverse, forward, reverse again, trying to rock it out of the hole. The engine flooded. She turned it off.

"Fuck that," Sheppard said, and hurled open the door and leaped out, flashlight in one hand, gun in the other.

2

The Rover's engine shrieked, the tires spun, and for seconds Allie couldn't believe what her senses told her. The freak was going to take them into the sinkhole. *Them.*

She didn't intend to drown. *It's not in the pattern.*

Then the car suddenly dipped and Allie realized that the combined pressure of the Rover and the trailer was too much for ground already eaten away by the relentless assault of the rain—and the subterranean springs and rivers that fed the sinkhole. Like the little figure in the old-fashioned Pac-Man games, the water had an insatiable appetite and eventually there was nothing left beneath the surface and it caved in.

Allie's brief distraction nearly proved fatal. Mira suddenly whipped sideways and her arms or her hands struck Allie in the side of the head and she fell back into the passenger window. Her finger jerked back on the trigger and the gun went off, blowing out the rear window. In such close quarters, it was as if a bomb had detonated inside Allie's skull. Her ears rang and the reverberation sang through her bones and blood. And then the freak was on her, pummeling her with her fists, biting her, clawing, her wild, primitive fury driving Allie down into the seat.

Allie struggled, one hand grappling for the door lever, the other clawing at Mira's face, her chest, whatever she could grab onto. But she had no leverage, she'd lost her grip on the gun, and now the freak's hands tightened around her throat, tightened until darkness swam in Allie's peripheral vision. She jerked her knees toward her chest and they struck the small of Mira's back. She reared up, gasping, her hands loosening just enough so that Allie could breathe. That single breath revived her and she snapped forward at the waist, the heels of her hands aimed at the freak's windpipe.

But the freak grabbed onto Allie's hands, twisting them, and slammed her forehead into Allie's. She fell back again, pain shuddering through her skull, the shock of it echoing through her teeth and gums, eye sockets and sinuses. She thought she blacked out briefly, because the next thing she knew, the driver's door was open, Mira was gone. More ground gave way under the car and the Rover tilted into a steeper angle.

Allie scooped up her weapon and her flashlight and scrambled out of the car.

3

Mira had rolled under the trailer and huddled against a tire, her body drawn into a tight ball. She struggled to stay conscious, to make herself small, to blend into the deep shadows. The Rover's headlights were still on, and in the ghostly backwash, she could see Wacko's legs, her feet.

Don't look under here, please, don't . . .

She dug into the pocket of Nick's jacket, looking for the knife, but realized she had left it inside the trailer. She knew that Wacko's weapon had fallen to the floor of the Rover and wished she had scooped it up and hurled it into the sinkhole. Then they would have an equal advantage. But she'd been in too big a hurry to escape, to run, to get the hell away from the wacko. Now she struggled not to shiver and kept her mouth clamped shut to keep her teeth from chattering.

Wacko stood about four feet from the trailer, turning slowly in place, the beam of her flashlight moving as she moved. Mira pressed more tightly to the tire, arms wrapped around her knees, her forehead pressed into her bleeding thigh.

The beam passed just in front of her, inches from the tip of her shoes.

No, no, no . . .

And then the light went away, shining off into the trees.

Mira flattened out against the ground, arms sinking into the mud, and crawled toward the opposite tire, propelling herself with the tips of her sneakers, fingers hooked like claws and sinking into the mud, seeking something to grab onto. She crawled out from under the trailer, stood on legs that threatened to collapse any second—and Wacko slammed into her from the side and they crashed through the door of the trailer. They rolled across the floor, locked together, and suddenly the trailer shifted into a thirty-degree angle and they rolled through the galley.

Mira screamed and the Rover shifted again and she managed to free an arm, a leg, and then her other leg. And suddenly she was on her feet, moving against the angle of the trailer as though she were on a treadmill. The temperature in the trailer suddenly plunged, the lights winked on, off, and on again, and then maintained a dim but steady glow.

And then between her and Wacko, a shape seemed to materialize from the cold, as though the cold itself were giving it form, life.

"What the fuck," Wacko said, her voice choked, soft, and terrified.

As the shape drifted toward Mira, it assumed greater

clarity and detail, and Mira heard a quiet, familiar voice in her mind. *May I?* Dean asked.

4

Allie's senses told her that the air in the trailer had turned bitterly cold, that a soft glowing shape that looked vaguely human now drifted toward Mira, and then seemed to cover her or slip inside her with the ease of a lover. Allie's senses recorded it all, but nothing registered. She had no concept that fit or described this impossible strangeness.

Her arm jerked up and she squeezed the trigger—and nothing happened. The gun had jammed. Allie wrenched back. Mira's body twitched, her eyes opened wide, and it seemed that her face began to shift, change, to rearrange itself. One moment she looked like herself, the psychic freak, and the next moment she looked male. "Allie, Allie," Mira said in Dean's voice. "Give it up. First Ray, then four people in the cabin, then the cop . . . It ends here."

Allie's jaw dropped open, her gun fell from her hand, and she started to scream.

5

She and Tom are lying on a thick rug in front of the wood-burning stove, his hands moving over her with such familiarity. . . .

And at the same time, Mira was aware of a presence sharing her physical body, her perceptions, using her senses . . .

. . . and aware of Wacko's screams. . . .

Tom holds her tightly and she begs him not to go, not yet, please. . . .

Images exploded inside her skull, events from Dean's

life, Wacko holding little Ray underwater while his arms flailed, his legs kicked, and she kept holding him, holding him, shaking her head. *No, no, six is one too many. . . .*

And Tom touches his fingers to her mouth. "I'm never far away."

And now Wacko carried Ray's lifeless body out of the pool and set him on the ground. . . .

And the screaming went on.

6

It was a sound so primal that it took Curry a moment or two to realize it was human and that it was coming from someplace very close by. He raced toward it, crashing through underbrush and low-hanging branches, and emerged in a small clearing where the sinkhole was.

A trailer was hitched to his sister's Land Rover, which was tipped at a steep angle, the headlights shining down into the water, the ground beneath it crumbling, the trailer listing to the left.

Curry burst into the trailer like some foul and random wind, clutching the Beretta in front of him, his adrenaline pumping. The air inside was as cold as the Arctic in the dead of winter, so cold he could see his breath in the strange, muted light that seemed to emanate from everywhere and nowhere. His sister was pressed up against the wall, eyes as wide as dinner plates, hands curled into tight fists under her chin. The scream came from her, a scream that alternated between a wail and a weird, staccato burst of air.

"Keith," Mira said.

But the voice was deep, familiar, and when Mira turned, when she looked at him, Curry saw his brother

Dean's eyes, nose, chin, and mouth superimposed over Mira's.

"I never had a chance to thank you," Dean said.

And then Lia and Sheppard came through the door and Mira turned to her and held her arms open and spoke in that voice that was not her own. Lia uttered Dean's name, the word falling from her mouth like a stone; then she was moving toward Mira and Curry simply stood there, unable to take it all in.

Mira's appearance shifted, transformed, seemed to flow endlessly from male to female and back again. In one moment she looked taller, more robust, her hair so blond it was nearly white, and in the next moment she looked like herself again. Curry felt as though he had fallen through Alice's looking glass.

Frost now covered the windows. The air in the trailer grew colder and colder. Allie kept screaming, Lia was in Mira's arms, and Sheppard just stood there in a kind of shock.

Then Allie stopped screaming and the abrupt silence was somehow worse, more ominous, and she lunged toward her fallen gun, swept it up, and aimed it at Mira and Lia.

The ground seemed to heave, like some huge giant expelling his breath, and the trailer shifted violently, throwing them all to one side. Curry hurled himself at Lia, knocking her out of Allie's way, and Sheppard fired. The first shot shattered the windows behind Allie, the second hit her hand and she shrieked and dropped her weapon, and the third shot struck her in the shoulder and she fell back, clutching it, her face seized up in shock.

The Rover struck the water and began to sink. The trailer, subjected to impossible pressure, shrieked and moaned and squealed as joints and screws and metal surrendered to the inevitable. It snapped into a forty-five-degree angle. Cabinet doors swung open, dishes tumbled out and shattered against the floor. Canned goods rolled down the steep slope, following the forward tilt of the trailer. The lights winked off and on, and Curry, still gripping Lia's arm, scrambled toward the door.

7

Sheppard's awareness seemed to have split down the middle. Part of him saw Mira sway like a frail tree in a high wind, and the energy or essence or whatever the hell it was slipped out of her. He saw it, saw the glowing somewhat-human shape leave her, and drift toward Allison Hart. The other part of him was aware that the ground beneath them and around them was collapsing and that the Rover was sinking. Unless the hitch snapped, the trailer would be next.

He grabbed Mira around the waist and shoved her toward the door. The trailer moved and shifted with the violence of a sentient creature in its death throes, and water now poured through the window that his bullet had shattered. The lights went out. The trailer door banged shut. He heard Curry shouting, Lia screaming, heard the rain and the collapsing earth and the wild, frantic hammering of his own heart.

Then he and Mira fell out the door and landed in mud and mush and muck. She lay there, unmoving, the trailer now sliding down over the lip of the sinkhole, surrendering to the force of the vortex created by the sinking Rover, and the ground around them collapsing at an alarming rate.

Allie shrieked, hideous sounds that echoed through the darkness, then were abruptly eclipsed.

Sheppard shot to his feet, jerked Mira up, and ran,

Mira stumbling alongside him, the mud sucking at his feet, his shoes, his ankles, and directly behind them the ground kept caving in as the sinkhole claimed it. He ran like a man possessed, fleeing what felt to him like nature's Armageddon. He didn't stop until he reached the trooper car. He shoved Mira inside, Curry and Lia piled into the back, and Sheppard peeled into reverse, forward, and the tires sprang free.

The cruiser sped down the dirt road, slamming through potholes, rain pelting the windshield, the high beams stripping away the darkness. Just as they came out of the final turn before reaching U.S. 41, the air in front of them glowed, that same eerie glow that had filled the trailer, and there stood Dean, his arms cast open, as if to embrace them all.

The car plunged into the light and Dean vanished, the temperature in the car dropped and the radio came on. Dean's voice moved through the car like music. *Love each other.*

Then they shot out on the other side of that light, the radio crackling with static, and Sheppard swerved the car onto the highway.

Epilogue

April 2004

The slope of the shallow hills, the tall, scrawny pines, the dance of light between the trees, the sweet scent of the air: all of it stirred feelings that Mira knew were not her own. They came into town on the wide main street, and even though she had never stepped foot in Cassadaga before, she recognized landmarks. There, the old meeting hall. Here, the grocery store where Dean and Lia used to buy ice cream cones. And over there, the Cassadaga Hotel.

"Turn right just after the hotel," Mira said.

Sheppard wagged the piece of paper where he'd written the directions that Keith Curry had e-mailed him. "Keith said to turn before the hotel."

"Just turn *somewhere,*" Annie said, exasperated. Beside her, Ricki the dog whined, begging to get out, please, it had been a long trip.

"Spirit Lake is on the road after the hotel," Mira said.

"How do you know that, Mom?" Annie asked. "I thought you'd never been here before."

"I haven't."

"So, this is one of Dean's downloaded memories?" Annie asked.

"Yeah, I guess it is."

Downloaded memories. That was Annie's term for what had happened to Mira when Dean had borrowed her body. She supposed it fit. She now knew a great deal about Dean Curry—maybe more than she wanted to know—and, through him, about the entire Curry clan, locked in their silent, dysfunctional lives. She understood that Wacko's obsession with Dean had risen from her murder of little Ray and that its origins went back to some other life. It was as if she felt compelled to make things balance out.

From time to time, his thoughts or feelings got mixed up with her own. So even though she had recovered from pneumonia and from a second surgery on her thigh to remove bullet fragments that Wacko had missed, she hadn't quite recovered from this strange melding of personalities. But there were some profound compensations.

When she read now for strangers, Dean sometimes came through in the reading. It wasn't his voice that came through—she wasn't channeling him—it wasn't ever as bizarre as what had happened in the trailer. But she could draw on his knowledge, and occasionally she felt Tom's presence as well. As a result, her work had become more complex and yet more liberating and insightful.

She had a difficult time articulating this to Sheppard, but he was certainly more open to her world after the experience in the trailer. After all, he, Curry, and Lia had seen what she had seen, had heard what she had heard, and had experienced much of what she had experienced. Their worldview had been permanently changed because of it, and their fears about death had been stripped away. But none of them knew what it had felt like when Dean had slipped into her, trying on her body for size, and her own soul, her essence, had stepped out of the way.

She couldn't explain that to anyone.

Most of the time, she couldn't even explain it to herself.

Sheppard, in his report to the FBI, hadn't tried to explain what had happened. He simply reiterated the facts, not the weirdness, and Keith, Lia and Mira had backed up his report with reports of their own.

They drove down the narrow road, past strange, crooked little houses painted in a variety of bold, bright colors. She realized she knew some of the names of people who lived in those houses. "Wait, stop here, for a second," she said.

Sheppard stopped. "What?" he asked.

"Jean lives here."

"Okay. Who's Jean?" Annie asked.

"A medium who gave Dean and Lia information they needed."

"Can I drive now?" Sheppard asked.

"Sure. Yes, okay. Drive," Mira murmured, fascinated by all that she saw and felt.

And just ahead was Spirit Lake, a glistening blue eye in the middle of a green marsh. Dean had hiked here during a drought, when the water was low and the ground in the marsh was dry. And there, across the street from the house, that was Ian West's home. Dean had mowed that lawn, Lia had sat on that porch watching him.

And now, just ahead, the Colby House, where Dean and Lia had stolen time together, two kids living borrowed lives. Cars were parked in the driveway, music rolled out the open windows.

"Sounds like the party has started," Annie said eagerly, sticking her head out the window. "So tell me, Mom, is this Natasha kid weird?"

"I've never met her."

"But Dean was her father, you should know this."

"She was just a toddler the last time he saw her. But hey, you're both about the same age. You'll get along fine."

"Yeah, well, we'll see." And Annie and Ricki were the first ones out as soon as the car stopped.

Mira and Sheppard remained in the car a few minutes longer. She gazed at the house, Dean's feelings and memories of this place rolling through her. The front door of the house opened and Lia, Curry, and a tall, thin man she recognized as Ian West stepped out onto the porch, all of them waving. Curry, she noticed, was holding Lia's hand.

"So what do you think?" Sheppard asked.

"That they'll be married by fall," she replied.

"Yeah? And what about us?"

She squeezed his hand. "A double wedding?"

"I suppose anything is possible," he said with a laugh.

Then they got out of the car and walked up to the house to embrace the rest of Dean Curry's world.